Héctor Abad

Aside From My Heart, All Is Well

Translated from the Spanish by Anne McLean

archipelago books

Copyright © Héctor Abad Faciolince, 2022
by arrangement with Literarische Agentur Mertin Inh.
Nicole Witt e.K. Frankfurt am Main, Germany.
English Translation © Anne McLean, 2026

First Archipelago Books Edition, 2026

All rights reserved. No part of this book may be reproduced or transmitted
in any form without the prior written permission of the publisher.

Library of Congress Cataloguing-in-Publication data available on request.
ISBN: 9781962770590

Archipelago Books
232 3rd Street #A111
Brooklyn, NY 11215
www.archipelagobooks.org

The authorized representative in the EU for product safety and compliance
is eucomply OÜ, Pärnu mnt 139b-14, 11317 Tallinn, Estonia,
hello@eucompliancepartner.com, +33 757690241

Cover art: "Portrait of Raymond" by Amedeo Modigliani
Book design: Mark Byk

Published with the assistance of the Reading Columbia program,
which cofinanced this translation and publication.

Archipelago Books gratefully acknowledges the generous support from
the Carl Lesnor Family Foundation, the New York City Department
of Cultural Affairs, and the New York State Council on the Arts with the
support of the Office of the Governor and the New York State Legislature.

PRINTED IN CANADA

Aside From My Heart, All Is Well

For Cecilia Faciolince, with a skeptical son's love for his devout mother

So the heart is the center of life, the sun of the Microcosm, as the sun itself might be called the heart of the world. The blood is moved, invigorated, and kept from decaying by the power and pulse of the heart. It is that intimate shrine whose function is the nourishing and warming of the whole body, the basis and source of all life.

—William Harvey, *Exercitatio Anatomica de Motu Cordis et Sanguinis in Animalibus,* 1628

My loyal heart fares better in the shadows,
It is the miter and the valve ... I would tear it out
to carry it in triumph to meet the day,
the stole of violets on dawn's shoulders,
the purple cincture of the sunsets,
the stars, the jovial outline of women.

—Ramón López Velarde

If a heart could think it would stop.

—Fernando Pessoa

Overture

Even though Luis and I were both priests, very few people called him Father. I called him Córdoba, and almost all his friends called him el Gordo. Now he, Father Luis Córdoba, had been forbidden to return to our home on the corner of Carrera Villa and Calle San Juan. They finally let him leave the ward in the León XIII Clinic, where he'd spent the last weeks, but he couldn't come back home, the home where we had lived together for the last twenty years. For him, it was like a banishment, and for me, his colleague and best friend, like an exile that prevented me from taking care of him, an involuntary divorce we were both forced to accept. My only consolation was that he'd found a good place to take refuge while he waited for someone to die and save him. His life depended on someone else's death, and this was a sacrifice that I, even if I'd wanted to, could not offer him.

The house where Córdoba went to live had four chambers, like a heart. Each room, cast in light from the street, emanated its own shadow and its own pulse. I don't know if everyone sensed the beating, but I could hear it. The first two rooms, on either side of the entrance hall, were the smallest. This was a sort of covered atrium with a pergola full of anthuriums so red and shiny they looked artificial. "A communist red," Luis said. Teresa, the owner of the house, used to water them every three or four days with a fervor that Luis called baptismal. More than talk to them, Teresa prayed to her anthuriums, and they responded by growing, bowing to her, flowering in partisan red, nurse white, and another red so red it turned black, black like the blood that spurts from a vein. The room on the left, the middle door, was a bedroom for Teresa's children, Julia and Alejandro; the one on the right, behind the other wall, the room of games and toys. It was this second room that Teresa emptied completely so Córdoba could occupy it, and when he arrived, it contained only a tall hospital bed, a painting of Saint Anne teaching the Virgin to read, an empty wardrobe that smelled of lavender, and a big armchair for reading with a standard lamp, its shade directed toward an imaginary book, invisible in the air, halfway up, inundated with warm light.

Through the center of the entrance hall, behind a big iron door with circles of wine-colored glass, you entered the living room, which was divided into two symmetrical spaces, almost like two oval lungs. The living room breathed with a cool, intermittent breeze that blew in from the central courtyard. One lung was the sitting room, with a sofa, an old chest of drawers, a coffee table, a big Persian rug with tiny red honeycomb cells, and a couple of armchairs; the other was the dining room, with a round comino crespo table, which seated six people, or even eight if we squeezed in a little. The wood of this table made words vibrate with a deep, frank tone, more baritone than tenor, more contralto than soprano.

Beyond the living room were the other two rooms, face to face. On the right was the master bedroom. Teresa slept there in a bed too wide for one person. She looked at it as one might view an empty casket. Several months earlier, her husband Joaquín, after falling in love with a younger woman with fresh, firm flesh, had abandoned that bedroom, that belly, and that bed. The room on the left was the most spacious of the house, and in a certain sense the most important: the library. This had also been the absent husband's study and workspace, lined from floor to ceiling in books that had been read, underlined, wrestled with, and presided over by a large desk of solid wood, now almost completely taken up by a big bothersome television set, recently arrived from the house at Villa and San Juan, Córdoba's house, which I had come to consider also mine, after so many years of living in it with him.

Behind the small central courtyard, in the back, the guts of the house were hidden, those spaces that are less talked about but where perhaps the most vital things happen: a spacious kitchen with an auxiliary dining room – square, with a white marble counter – where everyone usually had breakfast or snacks; a well-stocked and perfectly ordered pantry; a luminous laundry room with sunshine and water, with its respective drying yard, six taut, parallel clotheslines to air freshly washed garments. Gordo liked to touch these six lines with his hand, like someone strumming a guitar. Behind a spacious room with its own washroom and shower, where Darlis, the housekeeper from the coast, slept with her daughter, Rosa, who everyone apart from her mother called Rosina.

So my dear friend Luis Córdoba went to live in this house in Laureles when he was approaching fifty, a time when most people, if they are not mad, prefer not to have adventures or move house. This happened on January 8, 1996, a Monday, after Córdoba had spent Christmas and New Year's in the cardiology ward of the León XIII Clinic of Medellín, and if I put down the exact dates it's not because I remember them so well, but because I have them noted down in the diary I had at that time, which, who knows why, I never wanted to get rid of.

Two days earlier, Luis had been authorized by a medical committee to leave the hospital, with some conditions: he must keep almost absolutely still and rest, take his medications religiously, not be subjected to stress or strong emotions, and not undergo any physical effort. In particular, he couldn't get agitated or climb stairs, and he must be ready to go back to the cardiovascular clinic at any moment to undergo a heart transplant if a compatible organ became available. Considering the serious deterioration of his heart, only a transplant could keep him alive. Doctor Juan Casanova, Luis's head cardiologist, true to his name, had given his patient one last piece of advice, with a wink: "And, most of all, one final recommendation: don't even think of making love. Not with anybody, not even yourself."

Of these requirements, there was only one that Córdoba could not fulfill: avoiding stairs. To get to our house at Villa and San Juan (at the intersection of two steep Medellín ridges) and to reach his room on the second floor, he would have to climb several flights of stairs – from the sidewalk to the door, for a start, and then from the main floor up to the second. Our house was unsuitable for a patient like him. If he didn't want to stay in the hospital indefinitely, we had to find a single-story residence where he could wait calmly for a heart that he could have transplanted. Luis used to say there is nowhere less hospitable than a hospital, and he racked his brains thinking of who he could ask for lodging without imposing.

He was in luck. The same day he was conditionally discharged, Saturday of the Lord's Epiphany, when Córdoba was in the midst of his prayers, Teresa Albani, the owner of the four-chambered house, arrived out of the blue. She had come to visit him on the cardiology floor of the León XIII and brought him a bouquet of white flowers. Luis's face lit up as if the angel of the annunciation had arrived. Hearing the requirements for his discharge, Teresa immediately offered him a ground-floor room in her house in Laureles. Córdoba and Teresa had been good friends for ten years; she was living through the depression and pain of being abandoned by her husband, Joaquín Restrepo – another of Luis's old friends – and Teresa's spacious and cool, yellow-and-green house possessed the ideal conditions in which to wait, quite patiently, until an appropriate donor appeared.

A heart suitable for him, Dr. Casanova had warned Luis, would not be so easy to find for two reasons: his blood type, B positive, not a very common one, and his enormous size – six foot two and almost 265 pounds. Though it was quite true that in Medellín at that time there were plenty of people killed by acts of violence and therefore plenty of organ donors, almost all of them were young, short, and malnourished kids. For these reasons, Luis needed to find a friendly, serene place where he felt at ease and where he could stay as long as necessary until he won the donor lottery.

The following Monday, an ambulance drove Córdoba from the León XIII Clinic to Teresa's house in Laureles. Following the ambulance was a taxi in which I, Aurelio Sánchez, Lelo, a Cordaliano priest like Luis and his companion since our time at the seminary, carried a suitcase with a few changes of clothes and three big boxes with Luis's stereo and video systems, as well as stacks of records and films. I was also bringing, in the back seat, the enormous television set that Darlis and I set up on the desk. These last things represented, surely, the most important part of Luis's luggage and the reason for his desire to go on living: music and cinema. "My toys," as he used to say.

A

Before he became heartsick as well, Joaquín's memories of Luis would catch him off guard. He told me so himself. A Verdi aria sung by Maria Callas drifting from a distant window; a Mozart quartet or a Bach cantata in a doctor's waiting room; a nude photo of Nastassja Kinski, with her ineffable belly button, dangerously wrapped in a boa constrictor, at the peak of her beauty. Things like that, he told me, took him back to an evening of opera or a movie night at our uncassocked priests' residence at Villa and San Juan. But since he had found out his heart was also now ailing, memories of Luis became continuous and obsessive.

It wasn't like that before. What most made him think of Luis was seeing a film he found moving, like Sorrentino's *Youth* or *The Great Beauty*. When he saw the latter, he would have liked, with all the intensity of impossible things, to have had el Gordo by his side watching it with him. He imagined the emotion Luis would have felt seeing, inundated with light, the Rome he so loved, the Rome of his youth in the mid-sixties, the Via Appia and the Collegium Cordialum, the Rome of Fellini and Mastroianni and *8½*. Although when he saw a movie he didn't like at all, he'd say to himself that Luis wouldn't have liked it either.

This had happened once when Luis was alive. When he came out of *Pulp Fiction*, the famous Tarantino film, Joaquín had a dispute with his friend, Zuluaga, who was crazy with enthusiasm for that garbage, for that stuffing of blood and guts, and Joaquín had told him bitterly that he thought it was a despicable show of the banality of violence, normalized by laughter, and he was sure Luis – the film critic they both most respected – would be appalled as well. Zuluaga accused Joaquín of being an old fuddy-duddy, claiming that Father Córdoba, ever youthful and less soft and moralistic than Joaquín, was going to love that masterpiece, that path to the future of cinema, and he bet him a thousand pesos. Zuluaga lost the bet, though he never paid and Joaquín never asked him to. That very Sunday (Joaquín still has the cutting) Gordo had written the following in his cinema column in *El Colombiano*:

> *For Tarantino, love matters as little as anything else in life, including death. One gets the impression that nothing really matters to this director, that injecting heroin, eating a hamburger from Burger King, or blowing someone's brains out are all the same for him. There is no distinction between humor and drama, and one is expected to laugh at a massacre, at the injection of adrenaline into a heart, at two human beasts sodomizing a Black mafia boss or two gangsters carefully cleaning a car after accidentally blasting a friend's brains all over it.*

Joaquín told me that for years he'd sometimes thought of Luis when he heard classical music – which Luis had taught him to listen to – or when he went to the cinema – where Luis had taught him to see – but he had never remembered him with such intensity as when he began to be aware all the time, night and day, in dreams and upon waking, of having a trembling and treacherous creature in his chest that squeezed like a knot and moved at whatever rhythm it wanted, stabbing him in the ribs, giving him dizzy spells, sometimes leaping and biting him in the sternum or the throat like a rabid cat.

Joaquín told me he never thought of el Gordo with such devotion as when the doctor who was performing his catheterization – a Dr. Escobar – told the nurse that Joaquín's coronaries were clear, but there was something interesting there, on the outskirts of his heart, in the aortic valve, and that he was going to inject it with epinephrine to accelerate the pulsations. And he did, despite the nurse saying he better not, that first they should ask the gentleman's cardiologist, Dr. Ocampo, if she agreed.

"To hell with her consent. I don't work here to ask for permission," Escobar mumbled between clenched teeth.

The nurse then took the hand of the trembling, defenseless patient lying on the examining table and asked: "Don Joaquín, how do you feel?"

He looked at her in alarm, and what he answered sounded more like a plea than a reply: "I'm scared; it hurts . . ."

At that moment Joaquín felt a sensation rising from his groin and invading his entire body, a sudden heat in his thorax, feet, and head; he heard his heart galloping like a runaway horse in his chest, thought he was going to die on the operating table, remembered Luis twenty-five years earlier, and, at that precise moment, the world left him.

It must be said, however, that this story does not begin with Joaquín's death, and probably won't end with his death, or with mine. We have to keep in mind that any tale, any film or novel, if it goes on long enough, will always end in the same way, with the death of its protagonist, and even of its narrator. In that sense, the future is more unchanging and better known than the past. A happy ending, according to Orson Welles's famous epigram, is simply a premature ending. Is the marriage of a bride and groom who finally declare their love in the face of everyone's opposition a happy ending? Marriage, in fact, is the beginning of another kind of vexation that should be told in another film.

Thinking it over more thoroughly, however, I realize the ill-fated end of a life consists of it ending too early, before reaching – for example – the highest achievement we've proposed for ourselves. The end that arrives without us being able to get hold of the most serious aspiration of our existence, be it having a child, planting a garden, winning a battle, or writing a book.

On April 12, 1945, on the brink of achieving the definitive victory of the Allies over the Nazis, having recently arrived at the Yalta Conference after being reelected for a fourth term as president of the United States and posing for a watercolor portrait that his mistress had commissioned from a Russian American painter, Franklin Delano Roosevelt complained of a stabbing pain at the back of his head, under the base of his skull. Two minutes later, he fell forward in his chair, unconscious. The president's personal physician did everything in his power to resuscitate him. He even injected a dose of adrenaline directly into Roosevelt's heart, as John Travolta did to Uma Thurman, but all in vain. FDR was declared dead and could not witness the victory over the Nazis, for which he'd fought for years. This was indeed an unhappy ending and an unfair death, no matter how deserved it might have seemed to his wife Eleanor, as punishment for his prolonged marital infidelity.

In any case, I insist that this story does not begin or end with death, rather, with something that announces it or makes it present: with two serious illnesses. With Córdoba's, three decades ago, and with Joaquín's now – in both cases, heart failure. When two friends have the same illness, even if many years apart, the shared suffering unites them. Joaquín's trouble (aortic stenosis) does not matter too much because he is still alive. Maybe it won't be that valve that kills him, and it is possible that when they do open-heart surgery and replace his obstructed valve with one from a greedy pig or sacred cow, he'll return to life good as new, with the mechanism repaired, as cardiovascular surgeons like to say. Luis's illness, however, is the origin of this story, and though not exactly what killed him, it did trigger the last events of his existence, his passionate attachment to life when it was fading, his desire to turn his diagnosis into a second chance, and the final – let's call it imprudence – that led to his premature death.

B

Córdoba's malady had to do with what he essentially and very visibly was, that is, emotionally and corporeally: with his size, his weight, and his way of being. In the words of a friend of ours, Sara Cohen, el Gordo was a gentle ox, calm, slow, sedentary, and always chewing on something, as if ruminating. When it wasn't food – a cracker, a piece of salami or chocolate – Luis ate paper. Sara remembers, for example, those perforated edges of old-fashioned printer paper. Every time Gordo printed his movie reviews for the newspaper, he would carefully detach those strips of paper and keep them crumpled up in his pocket to put in his mouth at any moment of anxiety. Luis had the stature of a basketball player, at one time weighing 306 pounds, detested physical exercise, and, apart from the last months, never wanted to renounce the pleasures of eating in abundance and drinking wine in good company. "The epicurean curate," as his enemies in the priesthood called him.

I should clarify, however, that Córdoba was undoubtedly fat, but not opulent. He wasn't majestic either, despite how tall he was, much less imposing. They say tall men are more commanding than short men, earn larger salaries, and have better jobs, but he wasn't that kind of tall man. Perhaps he was fat so he wouldn't seem stuck-up, to give simplicity to his large animal bearing. More than respect, he inspired fondness and was much more inclined to laughter than to severity. He was good natured and easygoing, and his own excessive appetite was not offensive because more than voracious, it was constant, leading to a steady grazing. As I said, he was more of a ruminant than a predator.

A pupil in his opera and cinema courses, Fernando Isaza, who was finishing his degree in medicine, had discovered by chance that something wasn't right with Luis's heart. In 1982, as almost every other year, Córdoba had been invited to go as a professional movie critic to the Berlin Film Festival. For this reason, young Isaza, who was a semester away from graduation and had seen the latest technology in stethoscopes, a new generation Littmann, in a journal, asked Luis – giving him the dollars it cost in cash – to buy him one in Germany.

When he returned from the trip, Gordo brought, as he did almost every year, a new pair of black shoes, size 46, that would support his deformed feet and heavy steps for twelve months, several pounds of chocolate-covered marzipan and, this time, a shiny metallic case with the new stethoscope for his friend and pupil. Before handing it over, in the luminous front room of the house on Villa and San Juan, the two friends talked about films for a long while, of course about films, and about the winning picture, *Veronika Voss* (which Luis, having studied theology in Würzburg, pronounced with a very German labial-dental *V*: Feronica Foss). I was coming and going around the house, doing my chores, and overheard almost the whole conversation: "Everything about the trip seemed to be preparing me to see that film, to like it," Córdoba said with a trace of enthusiasm he immediately moderated. "But no, I didn't like it, though I would have liked to like it."

"And why the disappointment?" Isaza asked, tasting a piece of marzipan Gordo had just offered him.

"Look, on the way over, the Lufthansa flight had to make a refueling stop in San Juan because in Bogotá, due to the altitude, it's impossible to take off with the tanks full. They have to be filled at sea level. And when I came out of a bland little room in San Juan, in a corridor filled with depressing neon lights, who should I cross paths with? Can you imagine who smiles at me? Libertad Lamarque! Behind her comes a pack of Puerto Rican girls pointing at her, a bunch of very Caribbean, cheerful chatterboxes: 'Her skin is so smooth. She must be eighty, and she looks thirty.' 'Eighty?' one of the older aunties with them answers: 'A hundred and ten or twenty! When I was little, she already had grandkids!'"

The doctor smiles, looking at the stethoscope case, keen to open it. Luis, without letting go of the case, savors his marzipan, enraptured by the flavor that takes him back to the days of his youth and the long German winters. He munches and looks up at the ceiling, half-closing his eyes like someone looking into the past, and talks with his mouth full, remembering:

"América's sweetheart, the Greta Garbo of our continent, Libertad Lamarque. Cinema, a recently born and already aged art, creates those sphinxes. Seeing her in that waiting room, bent over, hiding her crow's-feet behind huge dark sunglasses, made me feel – I don't know what. And when I arrived in Berlin, who is the chair of the jury? Joan Fontaine, who in the forties was already the shadow of Rebecca. The third day I was going up the steps of the Kino Central and I see a familiar face, also hidden behind big dark glasses with white frames. A few seconds later I realize it's Claudia Cardinale. She's smaller than I had imagined, as if she were just anyone, a neighbor who somehow reminds us of Claudia Cardinale. Getting old is tough, and much more so for actresses. Almost none of them age well."

"But then what? What happened with the Fassbinder film that won the Golden Bear?" Isaza asks impatiently.

"I'm getting to that. I think Fassbinder knew from day one that he was going to win the big prize. He wasn't dressed the way he used to – in jeans and a leather jacket, looking underslept, as if he'd been drinking and smoking all night – but in a three-piece suit and tie. Freshly bathed, smelling good. He had the sure voice and accent of a winner. His films are no longer tormented auteur pieces but cinema entrusted to universal consumption. Fassbinder the sleepless, the drunk, the one who was only going to rest when he died, transformed into official culture."

"Well, that's him. What about the film?"

"It's worthy, with some very beautiful moments, as always with Fassbinder, and it's a melodrama, like some of his others. The worst is that this time the soap opera wins over the analysis of feelings and human relations. *Ferónika Foss* is a typical festival film: elegant, cold, perfect, but one that does not achieve its objective. It sails in the waters of classics like Billy Wilder's *Sunset Boulevard* or

Fedora, but those allusions are not enough to make that decadent actress truly move me. And I'm disappointed, because you know how much I loved the old Fassbinder, the one who never slept."

Finally el Gordo, finishing his analysis, remembers the case with the stethoscope, and he picks it up in his huge, puffy hands. He places it in front of Isaza, with twelve dollars change and another bar of marzipan. The quasi doctor opens it carefully, as if he were receiving a very delicate relic, some antique porcelain. He puts in the earpieces and auscultates his own heart. He closes his eyes. He speaks: "It's fantastic, Gordo. If you could hear the clarity of this sound; it's as if I had each atrium and each ventricle of my heart in my hand, as if the blood were flowing through my ear canals. Look, put them in, listen."

Luis had been the sound engineer for a film by Víctor Gaviria, *The Magnifying Glass at the End of the World*, and everything to do with headphones, music, shouts, and whispers fascinated him. He put the stethoscope on and was listening to Isaza's heartbeats and respiration, his murmurs, enchanted with the mechanism of the body, which always seems so silent to us, but is actually speaking, murmuring, bubbling all the time. For an instant he feels ecstatic, swimming in his friend's guts. I've stopped dusting. At some point they change roles and the student listens to his film teacher's chest.

A couple seconds later the festive expression on his face suddenly changes, turns serious, as if something has surprised and worried him. He asks Córdoba to take his shirt off, he wants to hear better: take a deep breath, hold it, breathe out, breathe in again, cough. He holds the new toy against Córdoba's chest, against his back, his neck. Then he presses his open hand on Luis's left nipple. He moves it and slides it under the armpit on the same side. .

"Put your hand here for me, Gordo. I want you to feel something."

Isaza has unbuttoned his own shirt and asks Luis to put his open hand on his left nipple. Then he asks him to put his hand under his armpit on the same side. And then he tells him to feel the same parts of his own body.

When Luis puts his big right hand under his left armpit, Isaza asks him: "Do you feel that?"

"Of course I do; it's beating. In case you didn't know, priests have hearts too."

"Yes, Luis, I know. But I have learned that we should feel a normal heart more under the nipple than under the armpit. Furthermore, there's something strange in the rhythm. Sometimes there's an extra beat or two, I'm telling you. Don't be alarmed, but sometimes there is an out-of-sync beat to the pulsations. I think there are extra systoles in the left ventricle, though I'm not sure. You have to see a cardiologist, Luis, and I hope it can be this week."

In the face of news like this, people react with incredulity, with sadness, with stupor, and sometimes with rage. Córdoba was neither sad nor stupefied: he was angry. Had he carried that device from Berlin for this? What was this young kid, who wasn't even a doctor yet, thinking? He buttoned his shirt quickly and grumpily, stood up brusquely from the armchair where he'd seemed so comfortable moments before and mentioned some urgent business as an excuse to take his leave. He felt perfectly fine and had no intention of listening to that aspiring doctor just trying out his new German stethoscope, he told me later. When he was saying goodbye, near the door to the street, he let loose: "All hearts sound different, Fernando. Do you know how Sylvia Plath's sounded? *I am, I am, I am*. And do you know what your heart sounds like? I just heard it: *goddamn, goddamn, goddamn*."

"You can be quite offensive when you put your mind to it, Luis," Fernando said, turning his back on him. Then he looked back at him: "It's not my fault you're ill, and, to continue your little joke, your heart says: *smoke, a-smoke, a-smoke*. So, if you're enjoying this life, I recommend you give up tobacco once and for all, for good."

Rather than simply closing the door, Córdoba slammed it. I watched him climb the stairs heavily, red faced with rage, and heard him take refuge in his room and lock the door. After a while I could hear he'd put on a Bach oratorio. It was not the kind of music he often played, and when he did, it was more for therapy than for pleasure. He only listened to it when he felt a very strong emotion and needed to calm down.

Córdoba's coronary heart disease was, in fact, confirmed a few years later, when Luis finally decided to consult a cardiologist after something strange and somewhat disgusting that I witnessed myself. It happened during a bad case of flu that confined him to his bed for several days. One morning, when I was in his bedroom, Córdoba had a violent coughing fit. Half suffocated by phlegm, he stood up, and suddenly something heavy and solid hit the wall. It was a gelatinous blood clot wrapped in bubbly sputum. I wiped off the red stain with toilet paper and pretended as best I could, but that day I resolved to force him to see a doctor, whether he wanted to or not, and he agreed. A short time later they did the first in-depth examinations and found the disease that explained a number of Luis's symptoms: fatigue from walking, shortness of breath, sudden dizziness, occasional confusion.

Before defining it, I should warn you that this might sound like a worn-out metaphor, a cliché from a sentimental movie, a vulgarity. Therefore, instead of fixing it in ordinary words, I prefer to provide a technical description of his ailment.

Hippocrates, in his sixty-ninth aphorism, says that sudden death is more common in the naturally rotund than in the lean. Other doctors of antiquity observed that people of short stature live more years, on average, than tall ones. It's possible that these observations have some physiological explanation. According to Dario Maestrini's *Legge del cuore* (law of the heart), there is a relationship between the blood that enters the left ventricle during diastole (when the cardiac muscle relaxes) and the quantity of blood the heart is able to pump around the whole body during systole, when the left ventricle contracts and expels through the aorta the oxygenated blood we animals live on and are nourished by.

The normal effort of the heart and the most important measure of its functioning is the ejection fraction, in Spanish the FE, which has little to do with *fe*, or the faith of believers, but rather the percentage of blood pumped out in every heartbeat or, equally, the volume of blood that remains in the left ventricle immediately after the systole. This EF or FE, then – and Luis always said, humorously, that he had a problem of faith – is what indicates how healthy our heart is. I remember the appointment when Dr. Casanova explained to Luis and me why that EF was such an accurate indicator of heart failure. I learned the lesson and like to recite it like a good student, but if someone is not interested in how our hearts work, they can skip it.

As long as a heart can pump out even half of the oxygenated blood that enters the left ventricle (from the left atrium and the lungs), a person is fine. A healthy person, in general, pumps two thirds of that volume, more or less, about 66 percent. If the left ventricle receives 100 cubic centimeters of oxygenated blood when it relaxes, when the heart contracts or pumps it should be able to send the body 60 cubic centimeters of that blood, that is, 60 percent of what came into it. A good human heart pumps seventy milliliters in each systole, slightly more than four liters a minute. With sixty heartbeats in sixty seconds, almost all the blood our bodies contain will have passed through the heart and been oxygenated by the lungs.

Perhaps Córdoba's problem had to do with his size or, rather, his weight; maybe with an unresolved hypertension; and very likely with an inherited condition. The fact is, when Isaza listened to his heart by chance, he was not expelling 60 percent of the blood his left ventricle received, but maybe only 45 percent, or something like that. Years later, when he finally decided to consult a doctor after the fright of the clot, his ejection fraction was only reaching about 40 percent. And as time went on, when this story begins and Luis went to live in the house in Laureles, his EF was barely 20 percent.

Since the total volume of blood a body needs to keep going has to be the same, Córdoba's heart compensated by letting more than a normal amount of blood in during the diastole. The problem was that, in order to let more blood in, the heart had to relax its fibers, dilate, and grow. That way, if 150 cubic centimeters fit into his dilated heart instead of 100 cubic centimeters, with an EF of 40 percent he could get the same amount of oxygenated blood pumping through his body as before. If it only expelled 20 percent of what entered, the volume of the left ventricle had to be even larger.

Anything one writes about the heart turns into an image and a metaphor. What I described in medical terms in the previous paragraphs, dilated cardiopathy, can also be put in common words, not so technical and precise as those above and with the aggravating factor of sounding sentimental: Luis had a very big heart. But, contrary to what the expression usually means, a big heart does not augur anything good. Cervantes might have said that "he who has a stout heart is braver than a small-hearted man," but that is not in fact the case. A big heart is the prologue to cardiac failure, for it means that day after day the muscles suffer more (they swell, need to make more effort, harden, lose elasticity) to carry out their function.

C

Some fifty-five pounds before his heart condition was discovered, Córdoba had found a way of living that, without distancing him from the priesthood, kept him linked to the three things he was passionate about. He believed he could fulfill, in his own way, what the Cordaliano community required of its priests, that is, Christian ministry.

This possibility arrived thanks to a gift that came wrapped in sadness, with the death of his mother, Doña Margarita – acute myocardial infarction – when Córdoba was living in Manizales with a parish in his charge. Luis's father declared in a tone as sad as it was irrefutable that he would never again set foot inside the house where he had lived for forty years (and raised three children), which brought him such fond memories of her, and now such sadness in her absence. Dr. Felipe Córdoba had asked his youngest daughter, Emilia, for lodging so he would not have to return to the big house full of courtyards and light, flowers and stairways and reminders, lovely as they were, that now pained him unbearably. He had not even wanted to go pack his clothes or choose any personal objects to take with him.

Emilia, married to a well-to-do advertising executive, Alfonso Arias, had seven children and a large house. Her husband and father were friends, primarily due to their shared political opinions, since both were active members of the Conservative Directorate. And even though Emilia and her husband didn't have a spare room in their big house in El Poblado, there was in fact a space they never used, the fancy room, for important visitors, which was closed up almost year round. They just needed to take out the furniture covered in old sheets, take down the bucolic landscapes in heavy gilded frames, and get rid of the useless porcelain ornaments to turn that space into a bedroom. Emilia reclaimed a single bed (since her father did not want to sleep again in his conjugal bed), as well as other furniture, from the house at Villa and San Juan, where she went without her father, followed by a small truck into which she piled several boxes, a wardrobe, the double chest of drawers, the desk, the chair, and old medical books her father no longer read but continued to display as evidence of a lifetime dedicated to curing the sick.

The big house on the corner of Villa and San Juan was left empty and available to Luis for whatever he might want to do with it. Lina, his older sister, had died years earlier, prematurely, the same week Luis was ordained in Germany and said his first mass. Emilia had no interest in the old, clapped-out house, located in no-longer-fashionable downtown Medellín, which was already beginning to deteriorate. The same truck that had moved the bed and furniture had also taken, as an inheritance from their mother, the bohemian porcelain dinner service, the silver trays and cutlery, and one or two mirrors or obscure knickknacks, proof the family had not suffered hardships for more than a century. The shell of the house with the rest of its furnishings Emilia signed over to her brother the priest, without doing any accounts.

To be able to live his own ministry, to not have to account for all his actions to any reverend father superior, to be able to preserve the scant liberties his ordination and priesthood had left him, Córdoba then resolved to convert his childhood home into a residence where a number of priests, seminarians, and missionaries could live. Not too many, because the house was large but only had a few rooms. He thought it would be best if two priests lived there, me and him, and, for shorter stays, two or three seminarians we could choose between the two of us.

With that idea he requested a meeting with the provincial superior of the Cordaliano order.

Like all of us, Luis had taken vows of obedience to his superiors when he was ordained; also vows of chastity, renouncing the possibility of having a wife and children, and – as far as possible – the libido and carnal relations, as if he were a eunuch. Under those conditions he had been a priest in a rural parish near Munich and in an urban parish in Manizales. The same vows committed him to devote himself to the service of others and his objectives in life must not aspire to lucre or any personal benefits. But after these sacrifices and abdications, and after thinking it through carefully, Córdoba had resolved not to deprive himself of his other three remaining passions, two of them almost spiritual and the third – the one he had most trouble confessing – carnal: classical music (especially opera), cinema, and fine dining. Had not Jesus multiplied loaves and fishes? Had he not turned water into wine? Had he not bid farewell to life with a last supper? Well, exactly.

The founder of our community, the blessed Ángel María Corda, was convinced there were many ways of practicing a Christian ministry, and with some old letters from Corda in hand, Córdoba turned up, neat and tidy and freshly barbered, to see the Cordaliano provincial of Medellín, Father Hoyos, who was accompanied by his secretary, a hypocritical and obsequious little priest whose name I do not care to remember. The arguments Córdoba laid out were ingenious, almost indisputable: for our Father Corda, it was possible to live a religious vocation even while in one's own home. Had he not written a book called *Priests in Their Houses and Instructions and Rules for Young People Who Want to Live Religiously in the World*? Well then, that was how Father Córdoba wanted to live, in the same house in which he'd grown up, as celibate as a maiden, but practicing his ministry, carrying out his own mission in the city and in the world, by teaching the subjects he was passionate about.

To this, the secretary, much more conservative and jealous (in all senses of the word, including that of envy) than Father Hoyos, objected that he did not see in contemporary cinema – which he knew delighted, not to say excited, Luis – edifying content. And he thought the same could be said for operas as obscene and libertine as Mozart's *Don Giovanni*, not to mention other works by the same composer, vomit-inducingly full of disgusting Masonic allusions. The provincial kindly asked the secretary to at least allow Luis to finish explaining his ideas and desires.

Córdoba carried on as if the secretary had not opened his mouth and, instead of asking for less, asked for more. He told them that in those times when young people were deserting the churches, the clergy had to seek them out in the places they frequented: movie theaters and concert halls. He gave the example of one of his teachers in Italy, a Jesuit, Angelo Arpa. He had been a personal friend of Rossellini, Fellini, Blasetti, even Pasolini...

The provincial – Luis insisted – who had studied in Rome and lived on Via Appia, in the Collegium Cordialum, surely remembered the days when clergy could not go to public spectacles, especially to the cinema. Well, Father Arpa was the one who organized the film circle at the Colegio Pío Latino Americano. There he had led them, seminarians from many countries, to Fellini and Pasolini. He had even shown them scenes from *The Gospel According to Saint Matthew* that weren't included in the official version. Father Arpa practiced his ministry through cinema and even founded a production company that served as a bridge between Italian and Latin American producers. That's how Rossellini's *Escape by Night* was made, and also...

Since the provincial seemed to be getting bored with this string of cinematic allusions, Córdoba brusquely returned to the subject of the house, in which he planned to behave not like an abbot in his monastery, but like any other servant of the Cordaliano community. He wanted to request, with all humility, that he be allowed to share the residence with another father who was a close friend, Aurelio Sánchez, professor of bible studies at the university, expert in literature and interpretation of sacred and profane works, who had, most importantly, something Luis lacked:

an organized administrative mind and practical good sense. (This, I'll remind you, was me, Lelo, his best friend, having returned from Rome after graduating from the Pontifical Biblical Institute.) If they allowed him to take me in, the provincial could choose a few other brothers, seminarians or missionaries, to fill up the house, no more than four or five in total.

Córdoba knew that in those days the Cordaliano finances were not thriving, and he also knew that they received more applications for novitiates than there were spaces in the seminary in Envigado, so it would be in the order's interest to be able to count on an additional residence (gratis) where some of those pupils could be lodged. Therefore, the provincial debated between his secretary's envy and the general benefit of the community. Furthermore, the provincial knew very well, and some of our colleagues had told him, that those two friends, Luis and Aurelio (the film buff and the bible-studies professor), were becoming increasingly ungovernable within the rigid standards of a priory. If he refused permission, he ran the risk of their leaving the community and even leaving the priesthood, as had Fray Francisco Antonio Posada, who Father Córdoba was now talking about (a monk who had founded the first cinema in Colombia, the Kinematógrafo or something like that, and who had left). That is why, with a certain benevolent air, he asked for a few days to think about it. Luis knew that this, in the Catholic church, was much closer to a yes than a no, so he began to say thanks and take his leave.

Already standing, he went to add something, one last thing: that one of the servant's quarters could be allotted, at least for a few days a week, to a young communications student, an orphan without means who was already working as his and Aurelio's assistant, secretary, and factotum: Ángela María Chica.

This, to the secretary, seemed to be the last straw, and his face flushed so much that it looked like it might explode like an overinflated tire. Unable to contain himself, he got up and said in a voice that came sharply out of his throat, charged with indignation:

"Just as ecclesiastic celibacy exists, the obligation to set up conditions to respect it also exists! All the synod's statutes forbid clerics to cohabit with women under the age of forty. Tell us, Luis, how old is this little angel called Ángela?"

"Twenty-three, Father, but she is like a niece or a cousin to us, and there should be no room for suspicion on that front."

"Whether there is room for suspicion or not should be defined by the ordinance, and not by you. Your insistence already makes one think of a concubinary relationship with this Angelita!"

The provincial did nothing but smile and wave dismissively with a sufficiently ambiguous phrase:

"I don't think a provincial should have to concern himself with the service arrangements in every residence. I'll leave that to your conscience, Father Córdoba, if I do approve this beguilement of yours of living in your own house."

And he also stood up to shake Luis's hand, turning his back on his secretary, who, red as a tomato and paralyzed with rage, stood still, tense, his butt cheeks clenched and as though a very strong glue had fixed his shoes to the floor.

This was in the mind-opening times of the Second Vatican Council, which Father Hoyos had attended as a provincial. He'd participated actively in the second bishop's conference of the Latin American Episcopal Council (CELAM) in Medellín, in August and September of 1968, famous for defending some theses in which the Catholic Church committed to undertaking much more liberal educational and evangelical methods, open to the cultural and social demonstrations of the contemporary world. Córdoba, who was very familiar with the documents of that conference, backed up his verbal arguments with quotes from them in the papers accompanying his request. Ministry did not always have to be practiced through catechism and Sunday sermons; a Christian life could be lived and taught by showing a film, helping people listen to and understand a Mozart symphony, a Bach oratorio, a Verdi opera, or a Rohmer movie.

Days later, the father provincial summoned Córdoba in to accept the proposal and Luis's conditions. We could try it for a couple of years and see how we got on. We should keep accounts and a strict register of expenses; anything over our salaries would be returned to the provincial community. Furthermore, he advised us to be prudent, modest, and restrained in all that we might do.

"Remember this, Luis, no scandals. The Church forgives and even loves the sinner, but abominates sin and, most of all, detests scandal. Let it be as you wish, but as I said, no scandals."

To which Luis had replied with a childlike smile, open and happy, and a bow so deep it looked like he was taking leave of Paul VI himself, the Pope at the time, whom I'd had the privilege of meeting in Rome and whose hand I'd kissed. Luis had bent so low, he told me later, that the button of his trousers flew through the air and landed at the foot of the chair that belonged to the secretary, who luckily was not present. The provincial, restrained and discreet, pretended not to have seen the small incident, but said goodbye with an indirect prompt.

"I hope in your new house you'll eat a bit less, Luis. Confront gluttony with temperance. It would do you some good to lose some weight."

Gordo, clutching the waistband of his trousers so they wouldn't fall down, promised to make every effort to slim down. Once before, in the middle of Mass, kneeling during the Liturgy, he'd had the same accident: his button had popped off and his trousers had fallen down, fortunately underneath his cassock. But that time he could not move from where he stood and had to finish saying Mass in an uncomfortable stillness, his trousers around his knees. As soon as the ceremony was over, he was able to pull them up, by doing contortions with the smiling help of the sacristan.

In the house at Villa and San Juan, we lived the happiest years of our lives. I got up early to celebrate Mass at the convent of Adorers of the Blood of Christ, who had named us both as chaplains. Later I went to the Universidad Pontificia to teach my bible classes. Córdoba sometimes heard one of the nun's confessions, sometimes married a couple of friends or baptized a newborn, but actually, more than priest's offices, for which he received some alms, he lived off his workshops and more mundane passions: old movies, contemporary cinema, and classical music, especially operas by Mozart and the Italians, Donizetti, Verdi, and Bellini.

We had a cool, bright, and clean house, decorated with everything we liked: books (lots of books); artworks that our painter friends gave us; and a stereo system with the latest model amplifier, speakers, and turntable, which Luis was liable to turn on at any hour of the day or night, not the few moments permitted in a traditional community, and fill the house with the most beautiful music ever composed – Mozart's, again, but also Beethoven, Mahler, and Shostakovich, the songs of Schumann, the sonatas of Brahms or Chopin, the great piano concertos of Schubert, Tchaikovsky, Mendelssohn, Liszt, Luis A. Calvo, and all the rest.

Luis was a very good friend of the directors of the Goethe-Institut and the Centro Colombo Americano, Heinrich Berenberg and Paul Bardwell, and both offered him their classrooms to teach well-paid courses on Mozart's operas or symphonies, Bach's cantatas, the history of German cinema, the best of Hollywood (John Ford, Joseph Mankiewicz, Billy Wilder, Alfred Hitchcock), post-war Italian film, or whatever occurred to him. He eventually had a radio program, as well, on the cultural channel of the chamber of commerce. Many young people of Medellín, who adored him as a teacher, followed him faithfully from one place to the next and in his company were educated in subjects not generally taught in traditional university degrees. In his courses he never introduced himself as a priest, and this information, which he didn't hide either, only came out if the conversation turned to some theological or religious argument. Neither Luis nor I ever wore cassocks, believing that a habit doesn't make a monk, and also because, although we venerated the priesthood, we didn't like its costume. Córdoba wanted as much not to frighten away anticlerical students as not to attract bees seeking only the nectar of the consolation of the hereafter.

Also, shortly after moving back to the city, he began to write a movie page for *El Colombiano* every week, which paid relatively well. On Thursdays, he used to say it was time to "fire up the oven," and from that moment on everything revolved around Luis's movie page, a whole sheet with different articles and columns, which he wrote from top to bottom, and until his task was finished, we all had to observe the silence of a spiritual retreat, including the parrots and dogs, who seemed to respect the hours devoted to creativity. The house was maintained, to a certain extent, by that page, and therefore we all had to help it come out right. I myself, on Friday afternoons, was in charge of submitting the articles Córdoba had whipped up in two days of intense, concentrated work. After the delivery, the whole house was once again filled with laughter and joy: Gordo had brought his page into the world, and we devoted ourselves to normal life until the following Thursday – a life increasingly full of visitors and friends, as a group of movie buffs and music fans grew around Luis, coming over to continue the official classes with conversations, musical recitals, and screenings of rare films.

Luis had gradually turned into the most respected film critic in Medellín, perhaps the most important in Colombia. Fernando Trueba nicknamed him the Colombian André Bazin in his *Dictionary of Cinema*, putting him on a level with the founder of *Cahiers du cinéma*, even before Luis founded his own movie magazine, *Kinetoscopio*, with a group of friends from the Centro Colombo Americano. In any case, if the Sunday edition of the *El Colombiano* sold a lot of copies in those years – not only in Medellín but all over the country – this was due largely to the film reviews he conceived every week and brought into being in two days flat. I confess there were times when Córdoba couldn't manage to see all the movies that were showing, and I would sometimes see one or two more marginal or commercial movies and describe them to him. Then he would write about them and critique them as if he'd seen them himself. (Nobody could understand when he found time to see so many films and take so many notes.) I also helped him by looking up answers in libraries or encyclopedias to detailed questions he gave me on little slips of graph paper.

Besides Luis and myself, the first inhabitants of the house were a housekeeper from Chocó, Conchita (a great cook, who had worked for several years making splendid feasts for the bishop of Quibdó), and our young assistant Ángela María Chica, whom we often called Angelines, only on certain days of the week. As for the seminarians, the provincial preferred, at least in the early years (and maybe to avoid the two of us having a negative influence over them), that only missionaries arriving ill from the Chocó jungle come to stay in our house. He asked that we take them in for the duration of their convalescence, as if we had more of a sanatorium than a house. They would come to rest and calmly recover from dysentery, malaria, dengue, or whatever strange tropical fever they had picked up in the jungle. Luis accepted this arrangement while keeping his principal condition in mind: that I would always be his ecclesiastical administrator and companion, because he did not feel capable of running practical things, such as the shopping; fixing leaks in the roof; dealing with plumbing or electrical problems; paying the household staff, water rates, and hydro; buying our food; and caring for the animals, without my help.

∽

Córdoba and I loved having companion animals. To pet a dog and believe he understands and loves you; to hear a cat purring in your lap; to chat with the echo of a parrot; to hear the courtship song of a bird, even through the bars of her cage; to be hypnotized by the weightless fish behind glass – these were almost sensual acts, daily pleasures. In Teresa's house, however, there were no pets. I reminded Luis, to see if I could make him feel nostalgic for our house, for our chaste clerical connubiality. The only thing there, in the backyard of the house in Laureles, was a mute and inexpressive tortoise with the features of a venerable old lady, who appeared every once in a while, to the delight of the children, who squealed when they saw her and offered lettuce leaves and apple slices that she sometimes ate and sometimes scorned. When she emerged from her underground hiding places, they called Gordo to come see her chessboard breastplate, turned her upside down to show him that she could flip herself over after kicking and squirming for a while. They called her Flash due to her lack of haste. When she didn't appear, they looked for her, shouting, *Flash, Flash, Flash*, but complained she was deaf and only came out when she felt like it. She wasn't a great pet. Flash gave me the creeps and didn't give Córdoba much to talk about. The only thing he could say to the children was that tortoises could live for up to two hundred years, going blind, their heart tiring until it eventually stopped, apparently without the animal suffering. It seemed advisable to have cold blood, live slowly, and have a carapace.

In the house at Villa and San Juan, we always had warm-blooded animals. A lot of time has gone by, and it's possible my memory has distorted some of the details, but Joaquín has asked me, I don't know why, for a list of the animals who lived with me and Gordo. Who could be interested in this list? It only gives me a sort of melancholy for so many attachments that have disappeared, like leaves that rot, like tree trunks laid to rest on the sand by ocean waves.

The cat we loved best was beautiful, jet-black, agile, and very lively, an unforgettable domestic beast whom Córdoba called "a perfectly condensed panther." Whenever Luis stood up from his reading chair, she leapt up and sat in the concave hollow he left behind, as if in search of the remains of his warmth. When we adopted and baptized her, we were both watching, at lunchtime, perhaps the only soap opera we saw in its entirety in our whole lives. It was Brazilian, and I don't really remember why we got so hooked, but the fact was we never missed an episode. It was in black and white, and the heroine was called Zuca. So that's what we named the black cat, though I don't remember where she came from. As far as I remember, the Zuca of the telenovela was the daughter of a Black slave and a white landowner. She was played by a gorgeous actress, Glória Pires, and I think Córdoba was as much in love with her as I was with the young man who courted her, Fábio Júnior. Someone told me that they later married in real life and went on to have little Zucas. We never watched any other soap operas and only turned on the television to watch the news. Our Zuca had lots of black and tortoiseshell kittens. We found good homes for them. We sent each kitten off to its new family with a bow of colored ribbon around its necks, a bag of sand, and a can of tuna.

When Córdoba went on trips, Zuca looked for him for a while, offended, almost indignant, meowing with rage, and then she ran away. Once, when Luis went to try his luck as an employee of Deutsche Welle Radio in Cologne – perhaps the worst, most regrettable mistake of his life – Zuca ran away forever and never came back. When Gordo came back, we kept one of Zuca's kittens, as black as she was, and we called him Recaredo, after the Visigoth king, but he hadn't inherited his mother's mysterious charm. I'm not sure why, maybe because of how predictable males always turn out to be.

We had a German shepherd called Lucas. He used to rummage through and lick half-empty beer bottles because he liked beer, obviously, honoring his origins. Once, due to this unhealthy inclination, he swallowed a bottle cap. The explanation for his persistent dog cough, his pained restlessness day and night, was revealed by X-ray, and he had to have surgery. It was a Pilsen cap. We spent almost a whole month's budget on that operation, but Lucas was never the same. When we took in Lucas, we lost Recaredo; the arrival of the German shepherd puppy made Recaredo uncontrollably jealous, with violent macho arrogance, and since they were the same size, the cat ferociously attacked the detested puppy, almost taking his eye out at one point.

Then we asked the nuns of our chaplaincy, the Adorers, to take in our cat for a few months, at least until Lucas grew and learned how to defend himself. Recaredo adapted so well to the nuns, who grew fond of him, that they asked if we would let him stay there in their convent above the Girardot battalion. The nuns had a big vegetable garden, which was guarded at night by a pack of fierce dogs to keep at bay the recruits from the battalion, who seemed to be vegetarians because they loved to steal beans. The problem in the convent was Recaredo's lust; as is typical with jealous ones, he had an insatiable carnal appetite. The nuns knew when he came back from his nocturnal dalliances with the neighborhood queens because the dogs welcomed him by howling and barking, maddened with fury at the promiscuous, late-night partying cat. One of those dawns, the reception was more riotous than usual, with worse howling, running back and forth, and growling. The next day, the nun in charge of shutting the dogs up in their daytime kennel realized that this time King Recaredo had not managed to escape the morality guard dogs. Of his dissolute life not even his hide was left, just some tufts of fur and a few traces of blood on a cauliflower. Maybe things like this are why it's fashionable these days to castrate pets; it's a terrible custom that even some animal-rights activists practice, but that Córdoba and I always flatly refused.

We had a toucan we called Publio Ovidio Nasón, for the long-nosed Latin poet. We also had three little fish prisoners in an improvised fishbowl, a mortar of thick glass marked with an inventory number from the biology lab at the University of Antioquia. We named the aggressive black fish Sir Francis Drake and the two red cap orandas, eternally pursued by the pirate, Abelard and Heloise.

After Lucas we had a golden Labrador called Judy, for Judy Garland. Before or after, I can't remember anymore, we had a Great Dane we got to guard the backyard (because sometimes thieves would sneak in to steal apples and figs). We named her Gala, like the woman Dalí coaxed away from Paul Éluard (friends are like that), and who was once slapped by the pacifist Buñuel.

There was also a rescued mutt, modest in appearance and name, Pirula. There was a talking parrot, Guillermina, Australian parakeets, canaries . . . I don't remember what else, and I don't think anyone can do anything worthwhile with this list, though I have enjoyed reviving in my imagination all these animals who will die only when I die.

D

When the doctors found his arrhythmia and swollen heart, three treatments were prescribed to Córdoba: a pacemaker, a diet, and exercise. The first was the fastest and most effective. One morning in the cardiovascular clinic in Robledo, Dr. Medina installed the apparatus under Luis's clavicle. It was one of the early ones, not tiny like the ones they have today, but almost as big as a modern cell phone. That was how Luis's left ventricle did not get out of control again but maintained its even and rhythmic pace for several years. He felt a sudden relief from the moment he woke up from the anesthetic, he told us happily.

The day after they discharged him, the whole household at Villa and San Juan began to get the other two treatments started. Very early in the morning, Gordo put on the extra-large tank top and shorts Angelines had found at a Big and Tall shop in El Poblado. I was in my room, still in bed examining my conscience, when I suddenly felt the whole house begin to shake as if it were going to fall down on top of us. I thought it was an earthquake because the wooden beams creaked and the columns seemed to sway from their foundations in the bedrock. Gordo had remembered that the only exercise he'd liked as a boy was skipping rope with the little girls next door, and so he had bought a jump rope. Every jump sounded like a cannonball landing on the floorboards of his room, *boom, boom, boom*, which reverberated around the whole house, *boom, BOOM, boom*. Lucas barked, the parrots swore, and Conchita, the cook, shouted from downstairs: "Don Luiiiis, Don Leeeelo, what is going on?"

It seemed like the end of the world. In Luis's room, a 304-pound elephant was jumping, and the house shook. But it was all soon over, fortunately, because after twenty or thirty skips Córdoba tired himself out and came down for breakfast, sweating, a green towel around his neck, still in shorts with the Doric columns of his legs exposed, as hairy as a black sheep, and, for the first time in many years, barefoot.

When he saw his breakfast, which consisted of a boiled egg (with its yolk amputated); one plain, unsalted soda cracker without butter; a tiny slice of white queso fresco (so thin it was almost transparent); and a black coffee with neither milk nor sugar, Gordo looked at us with the face of a punished dog. He chewed with a mute sadness and notable displeasure. I tried not to let him see my arepa with cheese or my croissant with marmalade, but it was useless because he watched me eat the way poor children watch rich children eat ice cream. I tried to swallow as quickly as I could, carried my empty plate and cup through to the kitchen, took my time washing them, and gave Conchita instructions for lunch, which wouldn't be much better than breakfast: half a portion of chicken breast, grilled without salt; a large salad of lettuce and broccoli with vinegar and a single drop of oil; and one soda cracker. No juice, just water. No dessert: coffee without sugar.

"Can't I even make him a little white rice?" Conchita asked.

"Not worth the risk," I told her. "Doctor's orders, and we need to follow them if we don't want Córdoba to get even sicker."

Luis, in the courtyard, was trying to teach the parrot Guillermina the word *diet*.

"Diet, Guillermina, say diet, *dieta*, *dieta*!" Córdoba repeated over and over, looking at her with melancholy. But the parrot did not understand, cocked her head from side to side with mistrust, and instead repeated something Angelines had taught her when she was young and learning to speak: "*Teta!* Tit, *teta*, tit, tit!"

After two weeks of Córdoba's skipping waking us up every morning with its rhythmic earthquake and shuddering of joists, something happened unprecedented in my long coexistence with Luis, my most beloved classmate and companion since our distant days at the Sonsón seminary. Conchita had made his dinner according to my instructions, a piece of boiled catfish, without salt but with lots of cilantro; two little potatoes, boiled in their skins (to see if that made them look a bit more substantial); and salad of leeks and green tomatoes, with vinegar and two drops of olive oil. But she had made rice pilaf with almonds for me, boiled in a broth of ribs and onion, which smelled exquisite and dangerous, and instead of bringing in one portion on my plate as I had requested, she put the whole serving dish in the middle of the table, halfway between Luis's plate and mine. The dish steamed like temptation, like a naked youth wrapped in the mist and vapors of a Turkish bath.

After trying a bite of his bland fish, Gordo, bold as brass, half closed his eyes and reached out his arm, greedily picked up the serving spoon and, licking his lips, heaped onto his plate not one, not two, but four spoonfuls of rice pilaf with almonds. He gripped his fork with an avarice and eagerness I'd never seen before and began to voraciously shovel heaping forkfuls of that aromatic ambrosia into his mouth. I watched him without a sound, but after seeing his fork rise and descend several times in the rhythm of a Pelton turbine, I dared to say, calmly but firmly, pointing at his plate: "Córdoba, you shouldn't do that. Remember you're not allowed rice."

Gordo let out a long huff, as if deflating from the depths of his being. He rested his fork on the right side and gripped his knife with his left until his knuckles turned white. Very slowly, he opened his right hand and picked up all the rest of the almond rice pilaf on his plate. He pulled his arm back and threw it in my face with all the force he was capable of. I suddenly found myself with grains of rice in my eyes and ears, slivers of almonds under my nose and lip, and warm drops of greasy broth down my neck and shirt collar. Between my tears I managed to see Córdoba brandishing his knife while threatening me: "And the next time you point that at me, I'll cut your finger off!"

Without saying a single word, I wiped my forehead and eyes as best I could with my napkin and left the table and the untouched plate in front of me. I didn't want to look at Córdoba, so I don't know what kind of face he was making, whether it was still that of a Hitchcock murderer or if he was laughing with repentance or the pleasure of revenge. I went to the bathroom and washed away the remains of rice and almonds with soap and water and then left the house and walked around the neighborhood in an attempt to calm down. In a canteen on Torres de Bombóna I ordered a beer, and a second beer, a third, and finally a double shot of aguardiente. The piano was playing Gardel tangos and rancheras by José Alfredo. "You and the clouds drive me crazy, you and the clouds will be the death of me." "Don't threaten me..." It was almost ten at night when I went back to Villa and San Juan and saw the living room light on. Córdoba had put on *La traviata* and was drinking whiskey. I headed straight for my room, without allowing my eyes to meet his.

"Lelo!" he called when he saw me go past. "Lelo, come here. I don't want us to be angry. Forgive me. Come and have a whiskey with me." I went into the room with my head hanging. He poured me a whiskey on the rocks, and I, already pretty tipsy from the beer and aguardiente, sat down opposite him, still without speaking, a bit dizzy not being used to that much alcohol. Gordo, with his eyes closed, leaned his head back on the chair and followed the music with one hand. Watching him, so happy and so calm, I remembered something he had said several times: "Music replaces reality, which is sometimes unbearable." After a while he started humming the aria Maria Callas was singing.

Sempre libera degg'io / folleggiare di gioio in gioia, / vo'che scorra it viver mio / pei sentieri del piacer. / Nasca il giorno, o il giorno muoia, / sempre lieta ne' ritrovi, / a diletti sempre nuovi / dee volare il mio pensier.

Then, when the tenor came in, he sang along with him, happily, as if I weren't even there.

Amor è palpito / dell'universo intero, / misterioso, misterioso, altero, / croce, croce e delizia. / Croce e delizia, delizia al cor.

Next Callas emits some harmonious shrieks: *Gioir, gioir, gioir! Rejoice, rejoice, rejoice!* Yes, Córdoba seemed to be rejoicing, because in the end he said, looking into my eyes when Callas finished her aria on a very sharp *iiiiiiiiiii*:

"Lelo, the diet is over. I am going to eat normally. No more exercise either, before this house collapses from my skipping. If I die of this, I'll die happy. Besides, what happened has never happened before, and it's never going to happen again . . . I mean, what happened today at the table with you. That wasn't me. Forgive me."

Joaquín maintains, and I agree with him, that if there is still any passion for opera and especially for good cinema in Medellín, and even in Colombia, this is to a large extent due to Luis Córdoba and a few other pioneers who in the second half of the twentieth century started film clubs, opened art-house cinemas, founded specialized magazines, and wrote movie reviews for the newspapers.

"In a certain sense," Joaquín tells me, "Luis was cinema for us. He was the movies we watched and, most of all, the movies we hadn't been able to see because 'they didn't bring them over.' It was Gordo who made us doubt our tastes or confirmed them, who explained with wise words why and why not. Even though we sometimes disagreed, that disagreement was not to scorn or impose our opinions over his (nor his over ours), but to confirm the indisputable fact that aesthetic judgment is always precarious and irremediably doubtful and insecure, never definitive and totalitarian like the final judgment of a supreme court judge or an infallible Pope.

Those agreements and those discrepancies were aired from Luis's page, which was, with no room for doubt, the most important in the country. It came out every Sunday and film buffs awaited it anxiously each week. Most of them bought *El Colombiano* only for that page. There were magazines too, of course, Alberto Aguirre's *Cuadro*, or *Ojo al cine*, put together by Andrés Caicedo, Carlos Mayolo, and Patricia Restrepo, even if they didn't last too long, and finally the one Gordo started with his friends: *Kinetoscopio*, which did survive and prevailed.

Before Córdoba started writing for the paper, the only things *El Colombiano* had about movies were ads paid for by the people who showed them, especially the distributor Cine Colombia, and a small inset on one of the inner pages titled: "Moral Classification of Films," which was done, according to sexphobic, retrograde, and fanatical ideas, by Father Jaime Serna Gómez, who signed with the pompous pseudonym Dr. Humberto Bronx. In order not to have trouble with the archdiocese or with the very conservative owners of the newspaper, Luis was warned by Darío Arizmendi, the editor in chief, that the inset would have to stay on the page offered to him. Gordo answered that the classifications seemed as antiquated as censorship, as deplorable as the *Index Librorum Prohibitorum*, which the Council the Church had resolved to stop publishing, and that "moral classification," which included a line of "films forbidden to all audiences" (generally assigned to movies with any sex scenes), struck him as a backward step led by traditional priests opposed to the teachings of Vatican II and obsessed with the sixth commandment. For Córdoba, these orders of Mr. Serna – aka Dr. Bronx – were nothing more than the final belches of Monsignor Builes, master of them all. Arizmendi agreed but said to Gordo, with a wink: "That's right, Father Luis, but if we want them to leave the page be, we have to throw a little flesh to the lions."

Córdoba smiled and nodded but warned him that while the "moral classification" inset contained the line "forbidden to all audiences," it was possible he might praise and recommend that same film as unmissable, or at least as the best movie playing that week – as would indeed happen many times. Arizmendi agreed happily, saying only: "Even better."

Other art-loving priests had played a similar role to the one Córdoba wanted to develop in Medellín. He often recalled his Italian and Spanish mentors with fondness. In Mexico there was

Julián Pablo, a priest who Luis Buñuel had liked a lot, "because he was frivolous and a Dominican." The great Spanish director valued him so much that he named him theological advisor on several of his films, as well as "interpreter of dreams," especially when he dreamt of the Virgin Mary. Apparently, nothing seemed more erotic than those paintings in which she showed nothing but one foot or leaked milk out of a swollen nipple.

Buñuel, in his memoirs, describes "Father Julián, a modern Dominican, an excellent painter and author of two unusual films. He and I often talk about faith and the existence of God, but since he's forever coming up against the stone wall of my atheism, he only says: 'Before I knew you, Luis, my faith wavered sometimes, but now that we've started these conversations, it's become invincible!'"

Julián Pablo had also run a magnificent film club at the Cultural University Center, where many young Mexicans saw their first art-house movies. He also shared with Gordo a great compassion for women who had to show or sell their bodies for a living. Many of them, when they came out of the cabarets after a striptease, looked for Father Julián to hear their confession so he would pardon them, and he always did, no matter how late, even at three in the morning, because they felt a great urgency to unburden themselves of their mortal sins, even if they were so routine and repetitive that in a few hours they would commit them again.

Mexican friends have told me that this Julián Pablo also directed films and television, one of them presented by Carlos

Fuentes, who was a good friend and, after the death of their mutual friend Buñuel, talked about dogma and theology with him. But adding mystery to their friendship, Julián Pablo had been the keeper of Buñuel's ashes (others say also of his heart, preserved in formaldehyde), which he kept hidden in some secret place inside the Dominican monastery. I also found out that Father Pablo had, as I do, a predilection for young men, and that he didn't always abstain from the pleasures of the flesh, even with some of his seminarian students who later went far in the teaching of philosophy and theology in several universities in Mexico and the United States.

Here I should add that Córdoba, with much discretion and permission from the provincial, offered spiritual assistance to prostitutes and women who worked at massage parlors in downtown Medellín. How my friend practiced that ministry, however, I don't really know. The matter, in a city as straitlaced as ours, could easily turn into a scandal of Mother and Our Lady proportions, so he always kept it in the shadows. I only know, from allusions and gossip from Johns, that some men, among them a close friend of Víctor Gaviria, Johnny Ceballos, swore they'd heard Gordo's unmistakable voice behind the walls of a brothel. What those people didn't know, and I did, is that Luis devoted those hours not to lust, but rather to piety. And anyone who doesn't want to believe this doesn't have to believe it, as simple as that.

There is an indirect detail I can attest to (because Córdoba told me and because I knew the protagonist) that gives an indication of his purely evangelical activities during his brothel adventures. From those early mornings in the barrio of Guayaquil, the red-light district at the time, he remembered a child, the son of one of those prostitutes, who had a very particular and lovely job. Since the women had to work every evening and night, and since cinemas here, with the exception of some Sundays, have never shown matinees, the boy (who had a prodigious memory) was tasked with seeing as many movies as he could. And in the mornings or early afternoons he recounted the movies that the hookers hadn't been able to see. He recounted them chapter and verse, describing camera movements, passionate kisses, love affairs and betrayals, cars pursuing robbers at full speed, adventures in the jungle and in the snow, with almost complete dialogues, words learned to perfection. And while the girls washed their hair or painted their nails, dozed their postprandial siestas, the boy described the images in his own words and told them the stories and became known all over Guayaquil as "the boy who told movies." And sometimes, if he wasn't in a cinema at night, he'd go around the neighborhood canteens and offer the tables of drunken men: "Señor, excuse me, would you like me to tell you a movie? Any one you like, name a title and I'll describe it. One hundred a movie, just a hundred."

And that's how he made a few pesos, telling movies in the canteens, going over old films he knew by heart, some classics among them, repeating other details that came into his head while he was describing them, or even inventing some, or bringing in details from other relevant films. Córdoba was so fascinated by that boy he once told Sergio Cabrera about him and suggested the two of them should write a script and get some producer to help them make a film about that story, which Cabrera also found charming. "The Boy Who Told Movies," they called the project, which never got off the ground.

⁕

It was in those first years in our house, when time went by in an atmosphere of study, reading, cinema, and music, that Luis obtained from a German parish the technical and economic resources to direct a medium-length documentary. The subject had to be a religious one, naturally, but Córdoba found a way to make it much more current and interesting. He wanted to make a realistic portrait, or better, to show the parallel lives of two rural parishes: one of them a working-class parish on the outskirts of Vienna, and the other on the outskirts of Medellín.

If I'm not mistaken, the idea occurred to him one evening when we watched, with a small group of friends, an old black-and-white Bresson film, *Diary of a Country Priest*, inspired by the famous novel by Georges Bernanos. I had seen it a long time ago and had forgotten the details, but I vividly remember what Gordo said to us when we finished watching it, projected on a white wall in the courtyard of the house at Villa and San Juan: "I know, here in Medellín, in the barrio of Corazón, up above Robledo, a priest as handsome and saintly as the protagonist of this film. His name is Carlos Alberto Calderón."

From that evening on, the idea of making a film about Father Calderón became an obsession. First we started inviting him over every Friday at midday to eat beans with pork crackling that Conchita made for us. I remember Carlos Alberto arriving on his light-blue Vespa – I can see him now – around half past twelve. He had a bushy black beard, a handsome, virile presence, and a smooth voice that seemed to caress his words, those sonorous caresses going deep into people's ears. He was the brother of another frequent visitor to our house, Luis Fernando, consummate film buff, and of another boy who had been my neighbor for a time in the barrio of Aranjuez, Julio Jaime Jota, the kindest, most helpful man in the world, who would do me any favor and ask only a blessing in return. This Jota admired his brother the priest so much that he didn't call him Carlos, but Idol.

Córdoba had left very good friends in Germany, from his years training in Würzburg, and knew that a former classmate of his was now working in a parish on the outskirts of Vienna. With the idea of presenting the counterposed lives of those two priests, the Austrian and the one from the Corazón barrio, the film began to take shape in Luis's head, and once in a while he'd read me bits of the screenplay he was imagining he'd make and even let me put my oar in when it came to doctrinal matters. The proposal got approval from the German congregation, and he was able to make the film. What Córdoba and I did not know then was that making that modest documentary in honor of a good priest could unleash the envy, rage, and most atrocious persecution on the part of a bad priest. Maybe by doing a good turn for poor Carlos Alberto, we did him great harm.

∽

The most important moments of Córdoba's sacerdotal life were tinged with heartbreak and disappointment rather than joy and celebration. The first sadness began to incubate a month before he left for Rome to study theology as part of his final training before his ordination. To see Rome – the Vatican, the Sistine Chapel, the Castel Sant'Angelo, Bernini's sculptures, Michelangelo's *Moses*, the *Pietà*, the Coliseum, the Galleria Borghese and its gardens, Caravaggio's paintings, the Piazza del Popolo, Trastevere, the Tiber itself, the Trevi Fountain, the hills, the Forum, the Pantheon – had been his dream throughout his adolescence and youth in the seminary. Before leaving for Rome he made long lists of things he wanted to see, and studied every work or place in the old guidebooks and encyclopedias in the Sonsón seminary.

But his father thought that since Luis was going to have to walk so much between his residence and the Lateran University and from one side of the city to the other seeing all the monuments of Rome – up the Via Appia and down the Aurelia, along the Campidoglio and the Palatine – it was important for him to have foot surgery before he traveled to Urbe. He consulted with a colleague, an orthopedic specialist, and between the two of them they decided an operation was in order. Even more so because in Rome, the novitiates had been warned, as well as their theology studies, they would also have to participate in hikes and camping trips with a group of boy scouts.

Since Córdoba had flat feet and at the same time was tall and heavy (perhaps due to lack of exercise, he began to be overweight from a young age), and since he couldn't find shoes to fit him in Colombia, his toes were retracted and deformed. Luis came from Sonsón to Medellín for the operation, and over several hours in the operating room, the specialist straightened his most twisted toes, putting plates between some of the digits to stretch them and return them to something resembling their original shape. The operation was a success, supposedly, and young Luis left for Rome when the scars seemed to be healed.

Two days after arriving in Cordialum, the residence of the community where he would live for the following years, after a day of long walks through the marvels of a city that seemed much more beautiful than his dreams and all the photos and paintings he had seen, Córdoba took off the large, stiff leather shoes made to measure in Rionegro and felt a lacerating pain and smelled a fetid odor much worse than what you'd expect from a day of walking. The red swollen toes, throbbing soles, and sensitivity to touch let him know something wasn't at all right.

At dawn he woke in a sweat, with a high temperature and unbearable pain. He had to be taken to *pronto soccorso* and, after a quick glance by the doctor on duty, was immediately admitted to the hospital. Even with antibiotics streaming into his veins they feared they might have to resort to amputation if the signs of necrosis in his toes worsened. So instead of walking around the dreamt-of Rome, the Rome of the Quevedo sonnet he knew by heart (*Look for Rome in Rome, oh, pilgrim! / and in Rome itself you won't find her*), Córdoba spent the first two weeks in Italy isolated, not speaking a word of Italian, in a depressing hospital room he had to share with an elderly Sicilian who had gangrene in his extremities and whom he had to see undergo two amputations for nothing. After a night of screaming, raving, and pain, the Sicilian ended up dying at his side, as alone, or even more alone, than Córdoba, who was hard-pressed to keep him company with some prayers in Latin and Spanish.

After the old man's death, Luis was subjected to his own amputation, fortunately not as radical as his neighbor's. The second toe of his right foot had completely necrotized and had to be removed. "Throw away what does not work," said Luis, but no one understood him. They operated, cut off his toe, and Luis in his room, his four-toed foot raised, looked at it with the fear the amputations would extend and climb, as had happened to the Sicilian, until the inevitable solitary death would overcome him. Fortunately, the infection yielded and the rest of his toes were spared. Just that void was left, that perennial absence, which for him turned into not a scar, nor a lack, but a demonstration that in spite of everything, he could continue walking around Rome and even, later, in the mountains with his groups of scouts. I, much more pessimistic than Luis, did not understand it that way and suffered as much for him – in the distance – as he enjoyed himself with his missing-toed foot.

"Don't be such a worrywart, Lelo," he wrote to me. "If they'd amputated my big toe, which is what propels our gait, you might have a right to feel sorry for me. But the second toe doesn't do anything, or at least nothing I've ever noticed. I am so well that I've already been able to connect with the group of boy scouts, and next week we're going on a four-day excursion in the Tyrol Mountains. I'm walking better than ever with my four-toed foot."

His ordination, in Germany, which happened on June 20, 1970, when he had lost a bit of weight and was just twenty-four years old, also came tinged with misfortune, at least from my point of view, not so much for Luis, who then and always was much more devout than me and resigned to any calamity. Exactly the same day that Luis celebrated his first Mass, the twenty-eighth of that same month, the news reached him, by telegram, of the death of his older sister, Lina, in Medellín.

Lina's illness and death, seen from the perspective of the present, might have had something to do with the same compulsion Gordo had for food. In those days, neither Luis nor I could have noticed it, for he was more dedicated than ever to spiritual life, not as much of a glutton as he would come to be, and he was more convinced than ever that the path of the priesthood was a choice so right that for him it meant something like permanent happiness, since it helped him reduce and restrain all his desires.

After the years of preparation in Rome and Germany, after many trials and sacrifices he'd satisfactorily overcome, Córdoba was ordained in the luminous month of June. His parents and two sisters had planned to fly to Europe for the occasion. Weeks before the trip, however, Lina's condition worsened and nobody could cross the ocean. The odd thing is that I felt more disappointment and sadness for Luis than he seemed to, for Luis, and I don't understand how, seemed to have taken it all with an ancient stoicism, with Buddhist detachment more than Christian resignation.

Lina was married to a wealthy Medellín businessman, Don Jaime Mora de la Hoz, who was going to pay the whole family's airfares and expenses so they could attend the ordination ceremony. Lina and Don Jaime had a five-year-old daughter, Margarita, whom Córdoba adored because we childless uncles achieve a sort of vicarious paternity through our sister's children, and Margarita had won his affection even more with her sweet personality, her beauty, and her kindness. But, after giving birth, something quite mysterious had happened to Lina: something in her had fallen out of balance. At first they thought it was just the diet women used to put themselves on after childbirth, the forty days of stillness and chicken recommended by some midwives, or the appetite that comes with breastfeeding, but no. It seemed Lina could not stop eating. She had a voracious, insatiable, overwhelming appetite, at all hours. In the five years since the birth of her daughter, she had gone from being a beautiful young mother weighing 130 pounds to an enormous matron who changed dress size every semester and now weighed twice what she had before her pregnancy.

It had been a gradual, uncontrollable obesity. She looked like a balloon inflated incomprehensibly. Her strange corpulence had gone from morbid to extreme and was not stopping. No advice, jokes, warnings, reprimands, willpower, or punishment could curb her desire to eat. Her husband tried everything – doctors, psychologists – but Lina's gorging mania did not stop. They had resolved not to go out anymore to free her of the temptation of restaurants, pastry shops, supermarkets, grocery stores: they had put locks on the pantry and the fridge at home to keep her from eating cheeses, cold cuts, baked goods, juice, snacks, sodas. But no matter what, somehow, calling to have meals delivered, bribing the maids, even stealing from grocery stores or hiding in her friends' kitchens, Lina found ways to get food. Finally, they diagnosed some anomaly, maybe a benign tumor or a deformation of the hypothalamus; however, the doctors never agreed on how to treat it. An operation in that part of the brain was very risky. And meanwhile Lina's gluttony had also affected her heart, her blood pressure, her ability to move, almost a premonition of what many years later would happen to her brother.

And a short time after they had to cancel their trip to Europe, the unexpected happened, or perhaps what they should have expected of a body that had gone so strangely out of control: Lina died suddenly, as if she'd burst from eating so much. The effort of continuing to irrigate that body, which was now two bodies, made her tired heart simply stop beating. The same day and almost at the same time as Córdoba was saying his first Mass, a few days after his ordination. In fact, he celebrated it, finished it, and then received the telegram with the news.

At this point I feel obligated to say that around the time of Lina's death, while I was also studying to be ordained in the seminary in Sonsón, I received a letter from Luis in which he set out serious doubts about free will and, therefore, the concept of sin. After all, if we are not free, we cannot sin. He explained it this way: if the doctors' best diagnosis was that Lina had a benign tumor in her hypothalamus (*craniopharyngioma* was the term the specialists used), that is, in the part of the brain that regulates hunger, the feeling of satiety, the return of appetite, were we truly free if uncontrollable impulses dictated to our minds, bodies, and souls? Sometimes that same benign tumor, instead of affecting sensations of hunger and taste, could affect a person's sight or hearing. There are patients who, as a result of the same kind of craniopharyngioma, become deaf or blind. Telling those patients they aren't seeing due to a lack of willpower or that they can't hear because they're not trying hard enough, was that not the same as telling Lina not to eat even though she always felt hungry?

In an analogous way, in the same letter, Luis asked me if suicides were not completely innocent when they committed their final act, dictated by some strange neuronal connection or an excess or lack of neurotransmitters. Yes, those people for whom we were obliged not to say a requiem Mass and could not bury in hallowed ground. What about sinners of the flesh, could they not be victims of an immoderate sexual appetite they were unable to control because their hormone levels were so high that the strongest will could not manage to oppose it? Was that not precisely why some saints in antiquity castrated themselves? And saints with whole bodies, those who never transgressed the precepts of the sixth or ninth commandments even in their thoughts, might they perhaps not be a bit less worthy, and might their serene chastity not be explained by a simple lack of internal stimuli? We praise their continence, the strength they showed in never having yielded to temptation, but could it not be possible that they never felt any impulse they had to contain? Not to mention, as well, the chance of the concrete circumstances a person lives in. A conclave of high priests puts two twenty-year-old youths to the test to see which is more chaste and more suited to the priesthood. They lock one of them up in a harem of beautiful naked young women; the other (the one favored by the highest of the high priests), in a nursing home full of decrepit old women on the verge of death. The second comes out unbroken and the first is accused of being lascivious and lustful. Is the verdict fair? I am not going to answer these questions, which are obvious for a heterosexual but are a bit more complex and abstruse for me. In any case, I have allowed myself to include them here as I don't consider them completely out of place and because sometimes the religion I profess demands a great deal, perhaps more than we can give, considering these two concepts: free will and willpower.

E

I can still see Teresa, the young Italian señora, her big black eyes wide open, looking out the living room window, anxiously waiting. A white-and-red ambulance has just stopped in front of that window. The big old green taxi I'm arriving in has stopped behind the ambulance, and I can see that anxious look has turned tender as she opens the front door. I see a straight, imposing nose, and beneath it perfect, even teeth, which seem to line up to welcome him with a frank and angelic smile.

I stay inside the taxi to keep from interrupting this encounter. It's not me those eyes are expecting, those very white teeth, that melodious contralto voice with its hint of a foreign accent, especially in the *r*'s, which stretch a little, and in the *s*'s, which buzz if they're between two vowels. When the young Italian woman comes out, they are bringing Luis out of the ambulance. The stretcher-bearers have to make a visible effort to cope with the weight. Even though he insists he can walk, they force him to sit in a wheelchair. It's protocol, they inform him, and it's obligatory they haul him in like that, as far as his bedroom.

Teresa leaves the door open and does not stop smiling as she dries her hands on her apron with a certain nervousness. Then she approaches, stretches out her arms, and bends down to hug Luis as if he were a wounded brother arriving home after a long journey, a gesture that seems (I felt at that moment) a bit more than friendship and a bit less than love, and that's why I thought of siblings. Her arms cannot reach around, and her black-haired head rests on the chest of the gigantic man who wants to stand up from the wheelchair to greet her properly but is prevented by the nurses' firm hands on his shoulders. Córdoba is keen to arrive, to get away from the ambulance and the nurses, to settle into a house without patients, without stairs, a clean house with three children who have just come out and are fluttering around joyfully in the ambulance lights, looking curiously at the wheelchair and the recent arrival's luggage, which I am beginning to bring in with the help of the taxi driver.

Some of the things are quite heavy, especially the enormous television set, and between the two of us we unload and carry them in while Teresa and Luis say affectionate things to each other in Italian – about how he feels, about the children, about how happy they both are to be able to share the same house. We move them as far as the front hall, where a slender, beautiful, mixed-race woman, Darlis, receives them with a smile that looks like a copy of Teresa's. What is quite heavy for me and for the taxi driver seems to weigh nothing for Darlis, who picks up boxes as if they were full of feathers instead of books and records. She takes them – rapidly and efficiently – a little farther inside, to the room Luis will occupy for the next days, weeks, or months, no one knows, as much time as needed to find a heart compatible with his blood type, his genetics and, most of all, his size. Darlis is so agile and flexible, moves with such feline elegance, that I think she is the human version of Zuca,

Córdoba is going to love her, but I don't say anything. From that very day, and every day, at any hour, Luis was told by Dr. Casanova, he must be ready to run, fly, to the cardiovascular clinic, if a suitable heart appears for a transplant.

After putting the television, with Darlis's help, on the desk in the library, I no longer have a pretext to stay. I want to hug Córdoba, who is now sitting in the armchair in his bedroom, but I say goodbye from the doorway, without touching him, with phrases lacking drama or even warmth. Something like "Speak to you soon" or "I'll call you tonight," anything to take away from the importance of a longstanding celibate couple separating, and not for reasons of a trip confined to certain dates, but for a strange adventure. Neither of the two knows how it will end.

I return to the taxi, downcast and calm, thinking that in this cool Laureles house, with two beautiful women and three children, Luis will be comfortable and content to find himself suddenly turned into a sort of father figure, no longer a priest. The old taxi slowly strains its way up the last steep block of San Juan, and the driver leaves me at the door of our old house, full of stairs, junk, and memories, now bigger and quieter than ever without Luis's music, without his booming bass voice, without his films and articles, his barely murmured prayers, his marvelous appetite that awakened mine, so paltry, without the noisy visits from his innumerable friends and his archbishop- and calamity-proof joy. The same big house where he was born, the Córdoba house, his parents' and his sisters', in which we shared two tranquil decades, and which I now occupy alone with Angelines, our assistant, the same one the provincial's secretary, with his twisted mind (think bad thoughts and you'll be right), with the conscience of a thief who judges by his own condition, says has been nothing but our kept woman, the paramour and concubine of that pair of dissolute, perverse, and irreverent priests: Córdoba and Aurelio, Gordo and Lelo, Luis and me.

～⚘～

A few months before Córdoba's arrival at the house in Laureles, in a typical case, straight out of a manual or a soap opera, Joaquín had fallen in love with a twenty-two-year-old woman, quite a few years younger than him. Camila, Camila Ángel, a girl from a "good family," that is a rich family, with enormous breasts, that is, surgically enhanced. She took him on trips to innumerable properties in the mountains, by lakes, or on the ocean, because she'd gotten it into her head that Joaquín was the man of her dreams, a well-dressed, well-spoken young man, an aspiring writer, who had studied in Italy, a country she thought the most *fashion*, as she put it, the warmest, most beautiful, and, especially, the most sensual on earth.

It goes without saying that eleven years earlier, Joaquín had sworn eternal love for Teresa, whom he had brought from her harmonious Tuscan hills to live in this butchery, this tropical din, this snarl. He had even married her in a church wedding (familial demands), a horror for him, and one tragic night, a few months after dividing his love and his sleep between two women, he had to tell Teresa that he was more in love with the other one, with Camila. Even though he was dying of guilt and sorrow, he was going to live with the other woman in her penthouse in El Poblado. But he wasn't going to abandon Teresa. He was going to work really hard so that she, Juli, and Jandrito would never lack anything in this life, he swore.

Teresa, obviously, told him to go eat shit in hell, in Italian, of course, *Ma vai a cagar, sei uno stronzo, figlio de puttana, cosa credi che io sia, la tua serva, vaffanculo, fai subito le valigie, pezzo di merda, fetente*... And then, in Spanish, "Don't do it, what are you doing, nobody can love you more than I do, think of the children, at least, you're throwing your life away at the same time as you're destroying me, Juli, and Jandrito." All in vain, the insults and the pleading: Joaquín had gone out the front door (the same one Córdoba would walk through a few months later) with a suitcase full of underwear and clean shirts, leaving behind his books, his children, his simple and cool house, his sweet Florentine wife, as celestial as Beatrice, in exchange for a crazy, tropical, youthful love that brought back his desires to fuck and to live.

The yellow-and-green house in Laureles had then been engulfed in the shock of abandonment, the uncertainty of the present and the future, in the sadness of a missing voice, a no-longer-present presence, an absent father who uselessly tries to compensate for his absence with weekends of games, praise, and excessive gifts. And this saddened but still bright and cool house is where Córdoba, my best friend and the person most able to turn sadness if not into joy, then at least into tranquility, had gone to live.

For Teresa, Gordo's arrival, with his deep voice and air of a paterfamilias, was a wonder from day one. Now there was at last that masculine presence she'd been missing. She could also unburden herself to him, in Italian, and tell him the gradual and incomprehensible changes she had noticed in the behavior and psychology of her ex-husband. It had taken only a few months and a change of neighborhood (El Poblado was the elegant barrio of Medellín) for Joaquín to suddenly think himself a better class than the wife with whom he had lived for eleven years. He even wanted the children, whom they'd brought up comfortably but austerely, to also rise in status. He bought them brand-name shoes and clothes he'd previously never have allowed, not only because of the prices but because he and Teresa had thought it ridiculous to dress children as if for an advertising billboard. Their normal clothes started to seem shabby to him when he took them to polo matches and tennis games at the Club Campestre.

Joaquín had become unbearable, Teresa rightly complained. He even wanted the children to change schools to one where they spoke English all the time. He took them on vacations and long weekends to lavish places, estates with swimming pools, luxurious houses on Lake Ayapel, ranches with waterfalls and crystalline rivers Teresa didn't even know existed, with horses and playgrounds and nannies in white uniforms and who knows what other luxuries that, for her, were obscene in a country full of poor people. They set terrible examples for the children, showing them a complete distortion of reality. When Joaquín came out with those ridiculous notions of fine clothes, running shoes of a particular brand, vacations in gated units on the sea, Teresa (when the children came home) had to sit them down and remind them where they were, who that Camila was who had driven Joaquín mad with her millions – who she was and who they were, and who deep down their father was. She sometimes didn't recognize him – always as tanned as Julio Iglesias, and he had even adopted a rich kid's way of speaking (we had *too much* fun in the Caribbean, he'd say) that didn't suit him at all.

F

When I called Córdoba to ask how his first night had gone, his first week, his first month in Laureles, he always told me how comfortable and content he was, the good it did his chest to be far from the gloomy atmosphere of the hospital, without the perpetual smell of disinfectant or the rhythmic alarm of the machines, sleeping soundly, almost always, without fear. He always had some amusing anecdote from his new house and his new role as a father figure. "Imagine this morning, after breakfast, while Teresa and I were having one more cup of coffee, she told me that earlier she had been showering with her little son, Jandrito, both of them naked under the water, and at a certain moment the little boy had stared very carefully at her breasts, very attentively, with wide-open eyes, until he asked her, seriously and intrigued: "Ma, do women have two hearts?"

They had laughed a lot at the child's notion, but an instant later Teresa, after another sip of coffee, having regained a bit of seriousness, said, looking into her cup, that if she did have two hearts she'd donate one to Luis. She even said, Luis told me, that it was strange that we had two kidneys, two eyes, two hands, two lungs, but only one heart.

I told him that if he needed a kidney, I'd give him one of mine, but Teresa was right about only having one heart.

"Octopuses, however, have three," Luis told her, having read a lot about hearts while in hospital. "Maybe octopuses can do heart transplants among each other, at least among family members, without killing anybody."

Then he told me that the oldest known drawing of a heart was more than ten thousand years old, and it's painted on the wall of a cave in Asturias, in northern Spain, the Pindal cave, in the center of a mammoth's chest.

"Mammoths were like hairy elephants, with long trunks," he explained. "This one they call the lovelorn elephant due to the heart that seems to still be beating in his chest. The men of ancient times already knew that we mammals have only one heart, in the middle of the thorax, and if they drew the mammoth's in the exact spot, there must have been a reason. Maybe they knew its importance and its fragility."

When we hung up, I went on pondering the idea of the doubles our bodies contain: it's odd that we men have two testicles but only one penis. A single brain, although divided into two hemispheres with different functions, and one single soul, as they teach us, indivisible and immortal. Five fingers on each hand and on each foot, five toes. But we don't have three of anything, that magic number we find so attractive, and in that sense the Christian idea of the Holy Trinity was even stranger and more unique. I talked to Luis about this when I went to visit him a day or two later, and he said he'd been meditating on the matter as well and had even reached the conclusion that – in reality – it could be said that we do have two hearts.

"How so?" I asked.

"I was looking at some slides about how it works and I noticed that the single heart, ultimately, is made of two pumps clearly divided by a wall. That wall does not allow any communication between the two halves. The heart on the right receives dark, deoxygenated blood from two large veins and then expels that dark blood toward the lungs. And from the lungs, the bright-red, fresh, oxygenated blood enters the left heart, first into the atrium, then into the left ventricle through the mitral valve, and from there all around the body. If by chance there is some escape, some communication between the right and left hearts (some babies are born with such deformations), it is a disaster, because the dark blood mixes with the red, and that is not good for the oxygenation of the whole body. What are two cannot be made into one. The right heart cannot be connected to the left in any way."

"So there is duality there as well, Córdoba, good and evil. The depleted that points toward death, and the aerated that points toward life."

"Yes, something like that. Although my observations are more physiological than symbolic, Lelo. Despite how much those often coincide. A German friend of mine used to say: 'Zwei Kammern hat das Herz, drin wohnen die Freude und der Schmerz.'"

I asked him to translate it for me, and he wrote it down on a slip of paper that I still have in my agenda from that year, handwritten in German and Spanish. It says: "Two chambers has the heart, wherein do dwell sorrow and joy apart." Then he went on developing his theory of the two physical hearts.

"In fact, I asked my cardiologist if my idea seemed like nonsense to him, and he said it was not a bad observation, though heart specialists put it differently: there are two circuits in the body, the first managed by the right side, and the second by the left. The blood is oxygenated in the lungs, so it arrives in the left side by way of the left atrium. And, effectively, in the heart there is a partition wall that separates the two circuits. When there is a defect in that partition (intraventricular or interatrial communication) we get a short circuit in the passage of blood from one side to the other."

"OK, Córdoba, those technical words confuse me a little. I understand that there is also a certain Manichaeism inside my body as well, one principle of life and another of death, but without death life doesn't exist, and vice versa."

"Each to his own, Lelo. I'm spending a lot more time thinking about the pump than about good and evil these days. And I'm trying to understand how they can change this pump for me, that's all."

And since Luis's voice was beginning to have – I always noticed; I knew him very well – a certain bad-tempered tone, I chose to go off on a tangent and distract him by reading something I had discovered, something about that pump, but which spoke of it in a more sonorous way, more poetic and less hydraulic. It's by a Spanish poet, Juan Vincente Piqueras, and it goes like this:

The heart, the corazón, is, first of all, a word. Majestic, if you want, beating, but a word in the end. And it has its manias. Since it is sonorous, it begins with a c. Occlusive, sharp, to mark with a beat its fantastic, liquid rhythm, and, if you look closely, the c is like a parenthesis that does not close. The r gives it something like a tremor of arrythmia that resembles fear, terror. It has its a in the very center and announces the hope of a certain balance. The z slides like a black swan returning stained with blood that carries itself. The o's are like wheels, wells full of pleasure, planets where it's nighttime all day. The n is the quiet that awaits us, the mute parenthesis that closes.

Luis, while listening to me read, watched me with concentration, then smiled. Finally, he turned serious and sank into a silence so dense that I stood up and left without even saying goodbye. I think. I might be misremembering.

༄

The children, spontaneous and frank, were the only ones to protest the most noticeable change in their house after Córdoba's arrival. The food, suddenly, since the first lunch, had become bland. Not only did it not have salt, but there were no more desserts. Even the fruit juice that accompanied their meals didn't taste sweet anymore because sugar had been banished from the kitchen. Teresa, as well as giving instructions to Darlis not to use salt or sugar or panela, had taken the bags and jars that still had a few grains left in them and dumped them down the drain where they washed the mops.

"From now on nothing in this house gets salted or sweetened!"

She had said this in the sharpest voice anyone had ever heard her use.

The seat at the head of the round table – the one that looked toward the green of the courtyard plants – was occupied no longer by Joaquín but by another kind of father, a priest, one who didn't wear a cassock or preach sermons and only introduced the novelty of saying softly, before beginning to eat, a brief grace: "Bless us, O Lord, and these thy gifts which we are about to receive from thy hands, through Christ, our Lord," after which the rest of the diners should say "Amen."

Luis told me that Juli, before he had been in the house a week, said one day when they sat down that she was going to say grace. She put her hands together and lowered her eyes, imitating Córdoba's devout gesture, and said very solemnly: "Bless us, O Lord, and these, thy very *bland* gifts, which we are about to receive . . ."

As on many other occasions since Luis had arrived, the dining room filled with the laughter that had been missing since Joaquín had left home. Teresa's face, which in recent months had acquired a certain bitter widow's expression and had thinned to skin and bones, with the gradual slimming of her whole body, had recovered, since Luis's arrival, a certain energy and spark in her eyes and smile. And even though the food was now bland, as Juli said, their mother was seen to eat again with a healthy appetite. Córdoba, one night, a bit to justify himself, told them: "Salt is poison, children, convince yourselves of that. If I hadn't been so salty all my life, I wouldn't now be sitting here like an idiot waiting for a replacement heart."

That's why those children, who complained their food tasted of nothing during the early days, when they noticed the improvement in their mother and also in Luis, who lost a bit of weight and walked and breathed better each day, stopped protesting and only referred to the bland food to tease Gordo and oblige him to give them his sweet sugar-free confectionary, which he kept hidden, like the incurable glutton he was, in his nightstand. After the joke of saying grace, Juli clarified that she had just been making conversation, because now the rice actually tasted of rice, the chicken of chicken, and the fish of fish, and before everything had just tasted like salt.

After a short time in the house, Luis asked a favor of Teresa, in private. More than a favor it was a question: Would it not be possible, didn't she think it would be good, if Darlis and Rosina sat at the table with them? He found the custom of having service people and, worse, their children eat in the kitchen, or in their rooms, or sitting out on the patio, increasingly unkind. Teresa told him that she had already asked Darlis many times, but Darlis wouldn't accept because she said she didn't know how to eat with all that cutlery, and that meat, for example, tasted much better if you held it in your hand while you ate.

Córdoba, however, offered to speak to Darlis again, and a few days later lunches and dinners gathered not four people around the table, but six, and just the fact of eating together brought a special and immediate camaraderie. With a simple gesture there was more equality in their treatment of each other, a more festive and normal atmosphere in the whole house, not limited to mealtimes but all day long.

Alejandro, the little boy, looked up with astonishment from below, way below, at this giant who had taken over what used to be the playroom. All his toys had been banished to different places (the pantry, wicker chests, mamá's dressing room, Darlis and Rosina's room). Jandrito had told his kindergarten friends, as Teresa told us later: "There's a giant living in my house. He tells us stories, shows us movies, sings us songs, and gives us sweeties that aren't bad for you."

The boy somehow believed he was suddenly living inside a fairy tale. He and his sister were impressed by the priest's voice and way of talking. Sometimes they played at imitating his voice by putting a strawberry or a ball of paper in their mouths because they thought Luis was always talking with his mouth full, as if his tongue were so big it didn't fit between his teeth and the roof of his mouth.

The best part, not only for the boy but for everyone who lived in the house in Laureles, was that this giant told stories that made their jaws drop. He sang, whistled, recited poems he knew by heart, played operas at full volume, and at night invited the whole family, starting with Darlis and Rosina, to watch films that were "suitable for all audiences," even though sometimes naked couples making love appeared in them.

What made the biggest impression on Jandrito was the size of Gordo's hands and feet. Each finger, he thought, had the diameter of a cigar, a carrot, and the shoes were so big that the boy found it impossible to walk in them as he used to in Joaquín's shoes. Since Alejandro's right leg was shorter than his left and he too only had four toes on his right foot, Luis watched with infinite tenderness as he limped when he ran or walked barefoot. One day the boy took a dramatic tumble trying to keep up with the two girls, Julia and Rosina. He was crying on the floor, humiliated and unconsolable, until Córdoba picked him up, sat him on his knee, and took off his own shoes. He lifted his right foot and showed it to the boy.

"Look," he said. "From now on you can say there's something you inherited from me."

Jandrito stared in fascination at the giant's foot, strange, worn, but big and strong, and he stopped crying.

⁓⋰

Those children grew up as little pagans, without first communion or sacred history, without anything to imply religious beliefs in their lives. "They're like uncircumcised Jewish boys," our friend

Sara said. Luis, in any case, didn't have the slightest interest in evangelizing. He had only baptized Julia, the oldest, and hadn't asked if Rosina or Alejandro were baptized or not. For him, they were no better or worse than baptized children; you couldn't tell if they were left with any coating of original sin or not. They acted like all children did and asked the same questions. One day, during breakfast, Julia was curious.

"Is it true, Luis, that you believe in God?"

"I do, of course," Córdoba answered. "How about you?"

"Me? I don't know. What is God?"

"Your papá and mamá haven't told you who God is?"

"Well, they told me it's something that some people like priests and my grandma believe in."

"They told you it was a *thing*?"

"I don't know if they said thing. Something."

"Something?"

"Yeah, something that if it wants can create the world or destroy it. That creates animals, for example zebras, like that." And Julia snapped her fingers.

"For me God is that, but many others *things* as well," Luis said.

"Like what things?"

"Like you and this coffee and the delicious toast with marmalade and butter you're eating (especially the marmalade, which I'm not allowed)."

"I'm God?"

"A part of God. I see God in you."

Then Julia stood up and ran happily to tell Jandrito: "Know what? I am God."

"Don't be silly. Papá said God doesn't exist, and neither does the devil; just like unicorns, ghosts, and witches don't exist."

"Ask Luis and you'll see he says I am God."

Alejandro checked, a little later, and found out that according to Gordo, the three children in that house – he, Juli, and Rosina – were "manifestations of the divinity." Jandrito didn't really understand what "manifestations of the divinity" were, and on his father's next visit he talked to him about God. Even though Joaquín knew that Luis had never been one of those priests dedicated to increasing his church's flock as if they were livestock, when he had the opportunity to speak to him in front of the children, he made his position clear, like someone who was not going to allow an invasion on territory he considered his own. Very calmly he told his old friend something like this (which Córdoba told me at the time and Joaquín recently confirmed):

"You know, Luis, I've always been a meek atheist, not very militant. I'm not interested in converting anyone to atheism. Do you know why? Mostly to keep from offending my mother, who is hurt by my atheism. That's why lately, when I'm asked in public whether I believe in God, I've chosen to reply like this: 'I believe that my mother believes in God.' I do that so she won't suffer. But I don't believe in any of that, and I tell the children the same thing if they ask. Instead of God, I'd rather talk to them about the big bang, the origin of the universe, the origin of life on earth, and the evolution of species. I have a scientific, not theological, vision of the world, shall we say. I don't believe in life after death either. I think that we die completely and forever, just like mosquitoes and cows. And not only do I not believe in God, but I'm not sorry about it either and don't need God to explain the things that exist."

"Yes, Doña Natividad has sometimes mentioned this to me," Luis answered. "I told her it's not necessary for people to believe in God to be saved. They just have to be good and behave well. I have known atheists who are much better people than many believers."

"A little while ago I read an observation that seems to me worth keeping in mind," Joaquín continued. "It's a simple indirect question posed by a philosopher: 'I have never understood why there are people who think God prefers those who believe in Him.' There are believers who conceive of God as if he were the head of a political party or as if he were a monarch in whom it was obligatory to believe and who needed to be venerated and given demonstrations of submission. I suppose the God you believe in is less vain, less insecure."

Córdoba was actually not very interested in theological polemics. For him the demonstrations of God's existence were just as intuitive and indirect. Perhaps that's why he said:

"For me, the music of Bach, his cantatas, or some of Mozart's melodies, or the existence of human beings like these children, or the beauty of some paintings, or some verses written by mystics are demonstrations of the existence of God. I don't go much further. Art and beauty are a war declared against brutality and indifference, and therefore a reflection of love, which is the clearest and most palpable manifestation of the existence of God. What's truly mysterious is not illness or evil, but health, goodness, and beauty. As for the big bang and evolution, if they are as the scientists suggest, I could always say that God created the big bang and evolution. Nothing prevents me from thinking this forms part of God's infinite ingenuity or infinite wisdom. I also think that God created the human mind in a way that certain beliefs sprout from it naturally in all cultures: faith, hope, charity. Don't you think it's strange that evolution should have created the very concept (leaving aside the existence), just the concept of God?"

"Of course, Luis, if a person believes in God, they can say and believe what they like about him. They can even think that God injects into certain minds, like mine, the absolute conviction that he doesn't exist. But that's a circular argument since there is no way of proving if it's false or true. A believer could even say, if they wished, that God hides the proof from our limited understanding."

"I repeat, Joaquín," Luis insisted, a little tired now, "that I don't base my beliefs on logical arguments. One believes in God not with the head but with the heart. That's what Pascal says, who had a privileged head, not lacking in exquisite mathematical logic, but he attended to the beating of his heart."

"We all have to listen to our hearts, Luis, or not. And my hunch tells me the same as my reason: there is no God," Joaquín responded.

"I suppose there are hearts better at perceiving God, just as there are radars, antennae, and telescopes that hear and see farther. Mine, for the time being, is bigger than yours."

With this slightly cruel joke, the conversation ended with compassionate laughter from Joaquín and a sad smile from Luis, who knew very well that in his case, and for his health and survival, there was nothing worse than having a heart as big as his.

G

Being a priest and feeling guilty is almost the same thing. None of us are at the level demanded of us, which is, apart from very few cases of true saints, impossible. Joaquín understands us because the only Catholic element that remains in him is guilt, his guilt for having left his wife and children many years ago. But, that said, I think lay people, those living in this century, those who are born, grow up, reproduce, and die, can never fully understand us priests, the clergy, that group who decides to live apart from the world, to be born, grow up, work, and die without reproducing, devoted by heart and by will to a pleasure others do not know: continence. Abstaining from sex is not suicide, as abstaining from water or food would be; renouncing reproduction and the search for a mate, with absolute conviction, produces a serenity that the lascivious cannot know, or know only in old age, when they talk with relief of the peace of the senses. Buñuel himself said that the only good thing about getting old was the disappearance of that anguished, stubborn, insatiable sexual appetite. The animal has died, or almost died, said another.

In my specific case, as in that of many of my colleagues (almost 24 percent of priests, according to secret statistics, including the odd distinguished Pope here and there) who are at the same time homosexuals and priests, the entrance into the religious life represents a remedy for lust. Or for that deviation, as they used to say, in particular. I was born in a time and in a family in which homosexuality was considered a perversion, or at least a serious disorder and an unspeakable sin. For me, choosing the ecclesiastical life and the chastity Catholics demand of their ordained priests represented a way of salvation, of not acting on deviant inclinations, of not sinking into the swamp of the damaged and sinful, wrapping myself instead in the divine grace of sexual abstinence. I entered with the firm desire to be chaste and good, with the aim of forever repressing the desires I discovered in myself with horror from earliest adolescence. Since my desires leaned toward the most forbidden, other males, the best thing for me was to renounce desire completely, bury it beneath my cassock as if that were an impenetrable steel carapace, an asbestos toga that isolated me from the flames of desire and hell. Reading Freud I also found the hope that those desires, more than repressed, would be sublimated through religious, educational, or creative work. For many years, I tried with all my strength, but only now, at the end of my life, the fire weakened, can I practice with less torment that supposed sublimation of sexual desire. Only in recent times have I been able to preach with the word and also by example, although this has come to me too late, after much sinning by word, deed, and omission.

In this book I am not trying to tell the story of my desire, but I am going to do so here, as briefly as possible, because I think it's necessary to be honest in these notes and clear in my perplexities and doubts.

My childhood memories are of a father coming and going. Periods of stable work and abstinence from alcohol, followed by spells of daily drunkenness, beatings for my mother, and terrible physical punishments for me – "Let's see if this effeminate, shy little fairy can learn to be a man." As a boy I lived in a dark hole without finding my path anywhere; apart from my father's abuse, at school they called me a wimp, a dolt, a silly-billy, because I always had my head in the clouds, they said. The first twelve years of my life went by with this intermittent torture, with a sober man who could turn back into a drunk at any moment. Among all the experiences of my childhood, the most traumatic was my father's abuse of my mother. I would intervene, and then I would be the one to get battered. Later he would suddenly repent, get a job somewhere in the country, send for us (I was the eldest of four children), then become a good father again and everything would work for a while. Until he lost his job, started to drink like a Cossack, and left us, disappeared. We had to call one of our aunts in Medellín, and she would somehow manage to bring us back to our grandmother's house. Living there, in Aranjuez, in a house full of people – uncles, cousins, grandma – was awful. My mother had to pay by cooking for everyone from morning to night, her four children, her brothers, scroungers, Grandma, and our auntie, who was the only one bringing any money into the household and the only good person in it.

In Aranjuez there was and still is the Sanctuary of Saint Nicolás de Tolentino, run by a community of Discalced Augustinians. My family and I went to Mass in their parish on Sundays. Every

Monday, Saint Nicolás's day, ladder buses arrived from all over Antioquia, full of pilgrims who came to attend Mass at the church, to collect holy water from the font to take to relatives who were ill, and to buy bags of little round Saint Nicolás de Tolentino bread rolls. It was a good business because the saint's water, they said, was miraculous and the bread delicious. The Discalced Augustinians had, perhaps still have, their seminary near Manizales, in the village of La Linda, and to incentivize new vocations, when the end of term approached, they would visit the kids in the neighborhood who were finishing primary school and about to start high school and invite us to spend a week in La Linda. It wasn't free, you had to pay, and my aunt, as generous as ever, encouraged by the Augustinians, financed my vacation in Manizales, and off I went.

I was so happy on that vacation and felt so free far from my oppressive family, my violent father, my useless uncles, that I was eager to return for secondary school and maybe afterward novitiate as well. I had felt happy in that vocational truce with the Augustinians. The school was large, bright, with soccer fields, basketball and Basque pelota courts, a swimming pool . . . There was everything. That was a luxury for me, and I delighted in a new and orderly world I hadn't ever known. I came home saying I would love to go to school there. Luckily my father had got a job in those months at the Imusa plant, where they made pots and pans, and among the benefits of the job was a scholarship for me to study at the Discalced Augustinian high school in La Linda. It was part of his salary.

My first year was wonderful and happy in the seminary of those fathers. For the first time in my life I felt free and cheerful, despite the strict discipline. The dormitories were enormous spaces where the beds were separated by nightstands, all under very high ceilings. There were hot showers in long open spaces. We all showered together, but in our underwear. The priest who kept an eye on us slept in a room with glass walls overlooking the whole dormitory. There he lay in his white, floor-length nightshirt, like an albino ballerina behind the transparent walls of a fishbowl. Sometimes we got up for Mass, had breakfast, brushed our teeth, and when we went back, found empty beds, the mattress folded, everything packed up. A couple of classmates had been expelled from the seminary. Why? Later we'd find out that when the fathers saw strange behavior, physical closeness between two students, they sent them away immediately, but we didn't know exactly what had happened. We would put two and two together or find out from rumors and whispers during recess.

Already in the first year, following the instructions of some classmates who explained and demonstrated, I learned how to masturbate. I practiced at night and felt like I levitated and rose up to the ceiling, that very high seminary ceiling, and then floated back down. It was a fantastic discovery. But I always did it alone, thinking about boys, but never with anyone else because I knew that would mean a folded mattress, an empty bed, and expulsion from the seminary. I was very content there and was already thinking one day I was going to be ordained.

I was also happy in my second year. Free of my father, I freed myself as well, and I turned out to be one of the best students. I was second in the class with only one boy ahead of me, Jaime García, who eventually became a bishop. I was chosen to captain the soccer team and was the best player of Basque pelota, an exotic sport I loved. I woke up. What I'd needed was liberty and to be far from the fatigue and oppression of my family. I never sensed that homosexual relations were allowed there. They were Spanish and Colombian priests. They were athletic. They had such a good soccer team that they competed with Once Caldas, of the premier division, and trained there. Two young priests were even offered contracts by Once Caldas: Father Mora, who was a forward, and Father Quintero, a goalkeeper. That's how good they were. Father Quintero flew between the goalposts. But they didn't accept the spots on the team; they chose the priesthood over professional soccer, even though they would earn less.

When I was about to start my third year of high school with the same Discalced Augustinians, my father, who had been working for Imusa for three years, decided to die all of a sudden and ruin our lives again. He left us stranded, indigent, and me without my scholarship. I had to return to that full house in Aranjuez, to my lazy uncles, sick grandmother, freeloading cousins, my mother the cook, and my aunt the provider. There was no money to return to La Linda; there was nobody who could pay for the seminary in Manizales. But since my wish and vocation to be a priest had been awoken, and my aunt knew it, she began to look for something.

My mother's family was from Gómez Plata, a municipality in the diocese of Santa Rosa de Osos, which was the largest in Colombia, they used to say back then, since it included Yarumal and many other municipalities. It was enormous thanks to the ambitions of Monsignor Builes. Through relatives, my aunt spoke to some friendly priests who got me a scholarship to continue my studies in the conciliar seminary in Santa Rosa de Osos.

As soon as I arrived, I began to notice very strange things. The seminary in La Linda was an open space with wonderful views of the snow-capped peak of Ruiz. It had wide, clear, bright corridors and lots of windows, through which we could see beautiful Andean landscapes. The one in Santa Rosa, however, was hermetic and dark, as if closed in on itself. Even though I was in the same mountain range, the seminary was buried in the dampness of the high plains, submerged in a gloomy hollow, with no views at all, surrounded by bare bricks eaten away by mildew, mold, and the elements. Just cold and mist, airless spaces with no windows, no ventilation; and when we got out, we still couldn't breathe. It was like a jail, a prison designed by the sordid spirit of Monsignor Builes, who was venerated like a saint, the shadiest saint anyone could imagine.

At the Santa Rosa de Osos school there were no sports anywhere. There were no courtyards or fields, not even a ping-pong table. The body was considered a disgrace, a filthy container only made for punishing. From class to chapel, from chapel to class, to the dormitories with pale and sickly lighting, from sleep sand to nightmares to the torture of cold showers. It was a very enclosed life, very cold; there was something strange in the whole asthmatic atmosphere we breathed. Despite it being an immense seminary, one felt constricted, smothered. All stifling and anguish. In one wing, behind the enormous mass of bricks, was the junior seminary; in the other, across from it, the senior; and in the middle of the two seminaries, the chapel, which was divided into two spaces like an open mouth, like a dark yawn that was going to swallow us. The two buildings were connected by a corridor, which was more like a tunnel. The gloomy passageway led from the small hell to the big hell.

It was the custom, but also obligatory, that all the students should choose a spiritual director, with whom each of us confessed and unburdened our sorrows, doubts, and questions. I was going into my third year, in any case, and had grown up with the Augustinian fathers. Now I was more than just the silly fool: I liked to paint, I liked to read, I liked sports (though in that place there was nowhere to play any), many things had flowered in me. The beds there were all in a row, one beside the next, as in the dormitories at La Linda. One night I was woken in the strangest way; a hand was touching my parts. It was a classmate, who when I saw him, shushed me and returned to his own bed. The nocturnal visitor was a boy from around there, a municipality in the north, and we called him Pechoelata because he was skinny and had a flat, scrawny chest. He was ugly. The next day at recess I went to find Pechoelata and asked him why he had done that to me, although, to be frank, that odd way of waking me up hadn't annoyed me, at least while

I only felt a hand, before seeing the ugly face that hand belonged to. Then he propositioned me and said that night he would give me a signal to go together to the bathroom, and there he'd explain what it was about. It was easy and seemed very natural to go to the farthest bathrooms. I went there, and Pechoelata was waiting for me; I closed my eyes so I wouldn't have to see him; there was some fondling, nothing transcendental, a hug without pants on. But I was aware I had committed a pretty serious sin. So, after thinking about it a lot, I decided to confess, not to my spiritual director but to another father, because I was ashamed. I looked for another priest and began to confess in the confessional. When he heard the subject, he said that something like that had to be dealt with very carefully and in depth. We should stop there and I should go to his cell later and there, on our own and undisturbed, he would hear my confession and advise me slowly and calmly.

When classes finished, I went to his cell. He was sitting on a stool, and I knelt beside him. He gestured that I should kneel in front of him instead and look him in the eye. I began my tale; he gathered up his cassock. Holding my face in his hands, he tilted my head between his legs. Speak, he said, tell me all about it, get it off your chest, you'll feel better, and he stroked my head. I wanted to cut it short, but he began the inquisition. Tell me in more detail how you and the other boy touched each other. Did you take your clothes off? What did you touch? How? Confide in me. Do this without fear. Everything you did with him you can do with me to find out how sinful it is. He asked me to unzip his fly, to touch him just as I'd touched Pechoelata, exactly the same way, so he could understand just what had happened. I was scared and realized this was very strange. I stood up and ran out of there, not understanding what was going on. I couldn't believe it.

My anxiety was huge. I thought: I'm going to find my mattress rolled up. They're going to expel me and my family will find out and I'll be thrown out of the house as well. I was anguished, but I thought about my spiritual director, who was the rector of the junior seminary, a person who seemed much more proper, and resolved to see him and tell him everything.

I spent a long time in the confessional with the rector of the junior seminary. I told him what had happened first with Pechoelata and then with the confessor. My spiritual director was very understanding and kind; he listened to me in silence, granted me absolution, told me not to worry, that these things happened at my age. I can't remember if he assigned me a penance; I'm sure it was a trifling one. However, from that moment on, his behavior changed notably, becoming much more friendly toward me, increasingly close. He sought me out, was even physically affectionate with me. I was grateful for his care, which never went so far as to be ambiguous. When we were on vacation, he came to visit my mother and me, and he invited me to visit his family too. There were many hugs and much kindness from the rector. Since my father had never hugged but only beaten me, I loved it. I felt pleasure. It seemed wonderful to me, something that had always been missing from my life.

But it all took a turn, got out of hand, shall we say. One time the rector came to pick me up at home and told me his family had a spa with thermal baths where there were saunas and masseurs and you could immerse yourself in cold and hot, medicinal, aromatic waters, with products that were good for your health and skin. I wanted to experience them because it was a complete novelty for me; we were there for several hours, me in my swimming shorts the whole time. At the end we went into the changing rooms to get dressed. He stood naked in front of me and gestured that I could do the same. "There are circumstances when we return to the innocence of paradise and nakedness is not a sin," he said. Then he embraced me and started to touch me. I said no; not that it bothered me, but I would never do that with a priest, I clarified. He told me he was ready to leave the priesthood, if necessary, to be able to embrace me. His assertion surprised and even annoyed me. Then I started to realize that in the seminary, in that enclosed and oppressive environment, this was widespread, the most normal thing.

There was constant movement, a flow of minors from the junior seminary to the senior at night. Boys and young men paid furtive visits to the grown-ups. The damp dark passageway led from solitary beds to those of couples, and since there were so many seminarians and priests involved, many turned a blind eye so they wouldn't be seen either. I saw many of my teenage classmates go to the other building night after night. The older students lived in the senior seminary, of course. Some of them were already deacons and might have their own very small, but independent, cells. So that's where my junior classmates went. From a deacon I learned, some time later, that during seminary he had had a lover from the senior school when he was studying for his high school diploma, and they'd spent those years as a couple, as if it were the most normal thing in the world, in their own room. He told me his case had not been rare, that it was a common custom there and more than tolerated because it involved those who obeyed and those who were in charge, because not talking about it was the insurance for the latter.

I was already sure of my inclinations but wasn't prepared to do anything with a priest. It seemed indecent to me, due to the vows they had taken. My final year in the seminary, before I left, I was an indirect witness to the practices of another priest, of Irish ancestry, whose surname was Moon and whose position was just barely below the rector of the junior school. He knew a lot about literature and taught it quite well. He talked to us about Joyce and Beckett and made us memorize poems by Yeats, whose name he could pronounce, unlike most of us. *When you are old and gray and full of sleep, / And nodding by the fire, take down this book ...*

He was lanky, bald, smart, and sensitive. There was a very pretty boy in our class, so handsome we called him Boy Jesus. Chubby, with blond curls and blue eyes, like on holy cards. My classmates said that Father Moon gobbled Boy Jesus. And this didn't seem strange to anyone. The only one who found it strange was me. Everything there was like that. Father Moon was a screaming queen, his cassock spread at the drop of a hat, he wiggled more than Tongolele, had outbursts of rage where even his coffee-colored freckles would turn red, and he dyed the few auburn locks of hair he still had the same blond as the Boy Jesus. For all this, I decided, in fourth year, not to return to the Santa Rosa de Osos seminary, because I wanted to be a priest, but honest and chaste, especially with other priests. It seemed hypocritical that I had to confess, very remorsefully, if I jerked off, but there was no problem with Father Moon shagging Boy Jesus at night and the next morning, of course without time to confess, saying Mass and consecrating the host. It took several years of hard work before I could pay my own way through the seminary of the Cordalianos, who were cleaner, more like the Discalced Augustinians, and that was where I met Luis and where at last I could be ordained with every intention of living my priesthood in perfect chastity. That I haven't achieved it is another story that I don't think I'm going to tell.

But how can you renounce desire, corporeal love, kisses, caresses, and orgasms? Joaquín asked when we got together to talk, as always, about Córdoba. I don't think he even suspected that the desires that have sometimes tormented me are not those that lead to reproduction, or if he knew, he pretended very well, because he said:

"Lelo, don't you realize that we come into life programmed by nature, or by God, if you prefer, to feel the irresistible urge to unite with another body, to caress, kiss, smell, nibble, penetrate, and die briefly in the climax, in the ephemeral overcoming of the individual, in the dissolution of two into one? If that blind programming didn't exist, we wouldn't reproduce and the human species would have gone extinct long ago. As far as I know, there are no celibate animals. Or if there are, it's not by their own choice but through bad luck: males pushed aside because stronger males would kill them if they approached the females. Erich Fromm, who psychoanalyzed several Jesuits in Cuernavaca, once said something like, Desire for fusion between two people is the strongest force that exists, even stronger than hunger. For him, it is the fundamental passion, the impulse that keeps us united, that creates family and society. And not reaching that union, for this expert in matters of the heart, leads one to madness or destruction, whether of oneself or others."

"Yes, I do realize," I replied, "and don't go thinking that priests, with centuries of obligatory celibacy, have not had time, and temptations, to think long and hard about that. The Church has its doctors. Fromm's argument is no news to us, and there have even been illustrious theologians who have said similar things, especially in the Orthodox Church, where they think for much of the clergy it's better to marry than to burn. In fact, celibacy, since Paul the Apostle, is not commanded but advised, a piece of advice that only those who feel they are going to receive the grace of being able to live in virginity should accept. To understand it, you would have to experience the celestial fascination of celibacy, the sublimation of love directed toward an obscure object of desire that turns into an obsessive, total love, toward all things, all people, all of creation, or toward what we call God. Besides, we make a sacrifice that benefits us because, as the scriptures say, we are eunuchs for the realm of heaven, as if the virginal condition anticipated life in paradise, because even though I believe the flesh will resuscitate in the next life, it will be a flesh without appetite, without sexual or reproductive urges of any kind. It will be an angelic body.

"You realize," I continued, "that life in a couple, beyond the satisfaction of the senses, often turns into martyrdom, into a cascade of resentment and mutual recriminations, into a chain of jealousy and betrayals, unforgivable infidelities and partial forgiveness, stinginess over money, over inheritances, because one child is preferred or detested, out of suspicion or truth, sacrifices, adultery, so many troubles, exaggerations, sentimental abysses that we don't know anything about or only hear about in the confessional. Priests, if we were to marry, would spend half our time dealing with marital quarrels, ridiculous heartbreaks, lovesickness, and helping our children through their sorrows and difficulties instead of devoting all our available time, as is our duty, to matters of our Lord and our congregations."

At that moment I remembered a story and went to my desk to get a little mahogany box that Córdoba had left to me. It was a Russian box, with a ballerina painted on the lid. The girl leaps, stretches out her arms in a weightless jump, her tutu flying up to show her thighs. Her right foot, pointed, is about to land on the floor in spongy red slipper. I showed it to Joaquín.

"Before his operation, Córdoba said he wanted to give me this little Russian box, and he told me the story of a friend of his, Katia Sergueevna, a ballet dancer he'd been introduced to in Vienna. She had known a Colombian student in Saint Petersburg, a communist, who was doing a doctorate in medicine, and they had married. I don't remember her husband's name. After a while, they left the Soviet Union and settled in Austria, she as a professional dancer and he as a gynecologist and obstetrician. One day, Katia – Katechka as he called her – went to Córdoba's parish, in a small town near the German border. She was very upset. A friend of hers had arrived from Moscow, an ex-boyfriend, they'd had a one-night fling, and she got pregnant. Her most anguished doubt was whether she should confess it to her husband, the doctor, who, among other things, was rather half-hearted and absent in bed. She was already three months gone, and the Colombian was happy about becoming a father, despite the cold and sporadic intercourse, but she couldn't bear the guilt. Córdoba, after questioning her about her feelings for the ex-boyfriend (she didn't love him; he didn't matter to her) and toward her doctor husband (she adored him), advised her never to say anything, that the child was her husband's, from that very instant and forever. You see? Our job is to give this kind of advice, but not to live and suffer that kind of soap opera, which would take us away from the meaning of our lives, which consists of soothing the souls of our parishioners. This little box, after more than twenty years of conjugal happiness in silence, was sent to Córdoba by Katia as a gesture of her gratitude.

Joaquín smiled, in part satisfied with and in part skeptical of my explanations and examples, but, after a moment of silent reflection, more objections came to mind.

"Now that I think of it, Aurelio, I always felt sorry for Luis, sadness for the things he didn't get to experience. I won't talk about you, to not intrude on your privacy. But I think Gordo didn't ever know any depths, as you priests like to call them, but I say heights, especially the heights of the female orgasm, so far, oh, and so immensely superior to that of men. It is those heights, I believe, that explain Katia's infidelity, and that of many others."

"And how were you or Córdoba supposed to know those depths or those heights when you're both men?" I said to Joaquín.

"Well, you're right, not know them. I meant witness them, know they exist because you brought them into being. Look: Luis never had the joy of knowing (he didn't take advantage of life to find out) that there are women who have orgasms in color, with visual hallucinations they can't really describe and can only sort of half-tell (and only at the very instant following their climax) with imprecise words and a fascinated soul, absorbed in their expanded senses: rivers and lakes of amethyst color dispersing like a moist cloud or a calm current up in the air or by the ceiling of the room."

Joaquín was gesturing, as if trying to show with his hands how the colors of the female orgasm melted above the ceiling of my own little cell. Then he went on: "Or the miraculous and sudden changes in the taste buds. Do you know that some women's saliva turns more fruity and aromatic than ever when they touch the sky?"

"I had no idea," I said.

"No? And what about the surprising rosary of strung together swear words emerging from an eternally immaculate mouth suddenly converted into a serpent of nameless improprieties, during the whole duration of the ecstasy..."

"Nor that," I said almost angrily. "But that strikes me as less physiological, less poetic, and less interesting."

"Then listen to this," Joaquín insisted. "Sometimes an unexpected release of warm, crystalline streams, like a pure waterfall, springing from the most secret source of life, and not from the bladder, an unexpected spring that flows with water as the unmistakable sign of desire absolutely realized and satisfied. A sort of female ejaculation, Lelo, composed of pure water, holy water, what a baptismal font."

"I'm seeing a mess in the sheets there, my lustful friend," I told him with certain revulsion.

"Then here's something just as beautiful, but more ethereal and hygienic," Joaquín told me. "The progressive fragrance of truffles that emanates from her underarms as the penis or tongue works to bring these aromas from the fathomless well in the center of the earth of woman. Or the involuntary tears of joy, of profound shock, that spill, silent and copious, in waves that soak the tremulous breasts and mix with the perfect sweat composed of the blended waters of two people who have loved each other to the edge of death."

I scratched my head at so many aromas, secretions, sensations, visions. Joaquín's verbal excesses almost managed to trouble me, and I would have wanted him to stop there, but no one could stop him.

"Or landscapes never seen by men, but described by women while they appear and disappear before their fantastical view, in that same privileged instant, theirs alone, forbidden to men, who are composed of simple, domestic hallucinations, let's say a courtyard fountain from childhood and colorful fish in the fountain, all seen with absolute clarity while she shouts in almost epileptic convulsions. Those, yes, those and many other manifestations of the immeasurable female orgasm, which always seems like a distant, unfathomable mystery to the clumsy and primitive male body."

"I believe," I answered, slightly bewildered by his female orgasm oratory, "that something similar can only be experienced by us, we of the priestly caste, in the mystic ecstasy that has been described by some of our most verbally gifted nuns, who have tried to put the ineffable into words. You will have seen," I continued, "in Rome, the marvelous Bernini sculpture of the *Ecstasy of Saint Teresa*, which is nothing more than a transcription in marble of the words of our venerable sister of Ávila, a woman as superb as the orgasmic women you've just described to me, and even, forgive me for saying so, much more so."

I thought of standing up and going to the study in search of a book of Saint Teresa's poetry, or Saint John of the Cross's, to read him a bit of mystical love poetry to counteract richly, and with the purest verses in our language, his pagan and sensationalist rhetoric. Then I decided it wasn't necessary. I knew by heart some parts of the Song of Songs, and there too there were aromas, images, and poetic descriptions that surpassed his prosaic paganism with sacred words. As lewd as his own, if read literally, but with a less offensive eroticism.

"Listen to this," I said, "and don't go thinking this is seduction poetry, even if it is full of love. It's mystic poetry and speaks of the union of the soul (the wife), who is speaking with her loved one (or husband), who is God. Maybe one day you'll manage to understand that 'the spirit cannot be sated by the flesh,' as a great mendicant philosopher said. Don't confuse them, and listen to this that I learned by heart when I was at the seminary in Sonsón, with the Cordalianos:

Let him kiss me with the kisses of his mouth:
For thy love is better than wine.
Because of the savor of thy good ointments
Thy name is an ointment poured forth,
Therefore do the virgins love thee,
Draw me, we will run after thee,
The king has brought me into his chamber ...
My spikenard sendeth forth the smell thereof.
A bundle of myrrh is my wellbeloved unto me;
He shall lie all night betwixt my breasts ....

Behold, thou art fair, my love; behold, thou art fair;
Thou hast doves' eyes.

Behold thou art fair, my beloved, yea, pleasant:
Also our bed is green.

I am the rose of Sharon,
And the lily of the valleys.

As the lily among thorns,
So is my love among the daughters.

As the apple tree among the trees of the wood,
So is my beloved among the sons.
I sit down under his shadow with great delight,
And his fruit was sweet to my taste.
He brought me to the banqueting house,
And his banner over me was love.
Stay me with flagons, comfort me with apples:
For I am sick of love.
His left hand is under my head,
And his right hand doth embrace me....

Behold, thou art fair, my love; behold, thou art fair;
Thou hast doves' eyes within thy locks:
Thy hair is as a flock of goats,

That appear from mount Gilead.
Thy teeth are like a flock of sheep that are even shorn,
Which came up from the washing;
Whereof everyone bear twins,
And none is barren among them.
Thy lips are like a thread of scarlet,
And thy speech is comely:
Thy temples are like a piece of pomegranate
Within thy locks.
Thy neck is like the tower of David builded for an armoury,...
Thy two breasts are like two young roes that are twins,
Which feed among the lilies....

Thou art all fair, my love;
There is no spot in thee....

Thou hast ravished my heart, my sister, my spouse;
Thou hast ravished my heart with one of thine eyes,
With one chain of thy neck.
How fair is thy love, my sister, my spouse!
How much better is thy love than wine!
And the smell of thine ointments than all spices!
Thy lips, O my spouse, drop as the honeycomb:
Honey and milk are under thy tongue;
And the smell of thy garments is like the smell of Lebanon.
A garden inclosed is my sister, my spouse;

A spring shut up, a fountain sealed.
Thy plants are an orchard of pomegranates, with pleasant fruits;
Camphire, with spikenard,
Spikenard and saffron;
Calamus and cinnamon, with all trees of frankincense;
Myrrh and aloes, with all the chief spices:
A fountain of gardens,
A well of living waters,
And streams from Lebanon.

Awake, O north wind; and come, thou south:
Blow upon my garden, that the spices thereof may flow out.
Let my beloved come into his garden,
And eat his pleasant fruits.

I am come into my garden, my sister, my spouse:
I have gathered my myrrh with my spice;
I have eaten my honeycomb with my honey;
I have drunk my wine with my milk:
Eat, O friends;
Drink, yea, drink abundantly, O beloved.

I knew that trotting out the "Song of Songs" was an excessive weapon, just as Saint John of the Cross's *Spiritual Canticle* would have been, but I couldn't think of another way to shut Joaquín up or to explain to him that marriage with God, for us, those of the priestly caste, is even more intense than conjugal or adulterous intercourse is for them, the earthly ones, the overly earthy, who did not understand the luminous sacrifices we made now to earn a much greater and more beautiful and profound and lasting paradise.

"You earthly ones are like children, Joaquín," I said to sum up. "Unable not to eat a sweet right now, even if you're promised a hundred if you wait. If only you were patient, able to wait. Besides, God's love is the prize in itself, virtue in itself, which is no different from happiness."

⁓⋒

When Joaquín left, however, I was once again invaded by doubt and guilt. Doubt about whether all this was just a deceit of ours, an illusion for priests, a tall tale that didn't reflect our anxieties and deepest feelings. And guilt for not having spoken more openly to Joaquín of our doubts and our falls, because this celibacy is freely chosen, yes, but it's an uphill struggle, especially for those as weak as me. Weak and deviant, as they used to say. I didn't tell him, wasn't able to, but once I give him these notes, he will perfectly realize what I feel and think. He'll see that I have not been as chaste and inexpert as he imagines; that priests, if we want, or if we can't avoid it, also live as fully as he does. Perhaps much more.

Joaquín, deep down, is quite naive. He says that the holy father and priests should not talk about sexuality because we don't know about it and don't practice it. Leaving aside the confessional, which makes us experts in all varieties, positions, and muddles of the subject, the immense majority of us, once in our lives, have fallen, have abandoned the virginal state, and those occasions never disappear from our memories, no matter how few and brief they might have been, or even perhaps because of that.

H

Teresa and Luis had met at the Chamber of Commerce in Medellín, downtown, where he was giving a course on Italian neorealism. She had recently arrived from Florence with Joaquín, her Paisa boyfriend, and was trying to find a way into the city's tiny cultural world. She hadn't found a job yet, she was just starting to learn Spanish, and she thought it would be nice to attend a course where she could at least understand everything that was said in the films. She'd already seen them all, but she didn't mind watching them again because they were classics. Joaquín, who had known Luis from before he left for Italy, had encouraged her to sign up for the course.

At first, Teresa didn't know that Córdoba was a priest. Joaquín hadn't told her. She only knew that he had studied in Rome, that he spoke Italian very well (since some of the films didn't have subtitles, he translated them simultaneously, out loud), and that he had taken some film courses there and had even been to the Cinecittà studios, where he had met Fellini, Pasolini, and Rossellini in person.

One evening, when the course was almost over, Luis announced that he wanted to finish the neorealism series with a film that was the complete opposite of realism, a very personal, almost theatrical reconstruction of a Greek myth and a tragedy by Euripides: a film written and directed by Pasolini, *Medea*, which had less dialogue than images, almost all of them from the studio. Before beginning he told the class that the star, Maria Callas, had been his platonic love since the age of thirteen, when he had won a racing bike at the San Ignacio school fair and sold it to be able to buy all her records. And so they would know what a voice she had, the best singer of the twentieth century, and what *bel canto* was, he played them a recording of the aria "Casta Diva," seven and a half minutes of profound, unique, unheard-of beauty, in the sense that never before and perhaps never since had such a sublime interpretation been heard.

Córdoba distributed photocopies of the lyrics Callas was singing in Bellini's aria and explained that Norma, the Druid high priestess, was singing to the moon as if it were a goddess, a virgin, whom she asks for light, protection, valor, and peace. On earth, the peace that reigns in the sky.

For Teresa, who was not a particular fan of her country's opera, listening to this brief extract was like removing a veil from her eyes and plugs from her ears. She suddenly recognized the beauty behind what had previously sounded to her like unnatural, meaningless screaming by fat actors and actresses who were always shrieking, even on their death beds.

> *Casta Diva, che inargenti*
> *queste sacre antiche piante,*
> *a noi volgi il bel sembiante*
> *senza nube e senza vel…*

Tempra, o Diva,
tempra tu de' cori ardenti
tempra ancora lo zelo audace,
spargi in terra quella pace
che regnar tu fai nel ciel...

Pure Goddess, whose silver covers
these sacred ancient plants,
we turn to your lovely face
unclouded and without veil...
Temper, oh Goddess,
the hardening of your ardent spirits
temper your bold zeal,
Scatter peace across the earth
Thou make reign in the sky...

After that, almost as an anticlimax, at least for Teresa, he showed Pasolini's film. She found the movie very strange, very slow. Maybe it was, as the teacher had said in his introduction, what Pasolini called "cinema of poetry." If that were the case, she preferred the "cinema in prose" of *Bicycle Thieves*. Besides, she could not identify with the protagonist's jealous fury, since Teresa, so far, had never felt like that in her life. Perhaps that was why it seemed so absurd to her that Medea should sacrifice her sons only to punish the father of those children, the husband who cheats on her.

She had also noticed the rest of the students getting pretty bored during the screening and Gordo's distress at seeing them yawn. But out of the corner of her eye, Teresa had been watching another movie, a private one, as she noticed how moved the teacher was each time the protagonist Medea-Callas was on screen, and when the camera showed the diva in profile, the haughty features of a Greek priestess or sorceress, it was as though the teacher were still melting with love for the soprano, *La Divina*, who had died eight or nine years before.

In any case, as I said, Teresa didn't know Córdoba was a priest.

She found out one day when she came up to the residence at Villa and San Juan and found Córdoba and I celebrating Mass for no one (though we were decked out in full regalia) at the altar we occasionally improvised in the living room. I had arrived a few days earlier from the Chocó missions and was recuperating from a bout of malarial fever. In fact, Luis had wanted to celebrate Mass to pray for my health and speedy recovery, since I could barely stay upright, with waves of fever, shortness of breath, lack of appetite, and chills that recurred in a chaotic rhythm. Malaria, this time, was hitting me harder than ever.

Angelines, our assistant, opened the door, and the Italian was stunned, flabbergasted, to see us in our stoles and embroidered robes, with my lace alb for holy days, co-officiating this strange Mass with no parishioners.

"Lift up our hearts," Córdoba was saying, and I answered from my seat because I was unable to stand, "We lift them up to the Lord." When the Italian poked her head round the corner, we didn't pause at all. Luis just smiled for a second as he was saying, "It is right and just."

Teresa joined the ceremony and stood up and sat down at the appropriate intervals, but she did not intone the psalms or respond to the prayers or kneel during the elevation or come forward to take communion. She didn't actually know the words to the Mass in Spanish and would have had to guess what we were saying to answer appropriately in Italian. When we finally arrived at "Go in peace" and took off our vestments, Teresa apologized for interrupting *all'improvviso*, but she reminded Luis that he had invited her over for eleven to lend her some opera records. Luis, who lived with his head in the clouds and was distracted by this sort of arrangement, had completely forgotten.

That day Córdoba and I dusted off our rusty Italian from our days as seminarians in Rome and Teresa agreed to stay and do penance with us. When we got to dessert, which, I remember, was dulce de natas with raisins and she really liked it, never having tasted it before, she told us she was pregnant, though she wasn't showing yet, and that Joaquín's family, especially his mother, Doña Natividad, was demanding that they get married "so they wouldn't have a heathen baby." Joaquín didn't want to get married because, according to him, matrimony was unnecessary when two people love each other, and their love, in his view, marked the beginning and the duration of their union, just as falling out of love would imply its ending. To marry, ultimately, is just to share a house, and they were already doing that in the house in Laureles, which they'd just bought with help from one of Teresa's Italian grandfathers, Nonno Antonio. Much less did he want a church wedding, since he hated priests and all that smelled of sacristies and cassocks. At the same time, for Doña Natividad, a civil marriage was the same as not being married. Lately Teresa's relationship with her mother-in-law had deteriorated into a tug-of-war in which Teresa tried to convince Joaquín they should get married not because it was important but precisely because it didn't matter to them and would please his elderly mother.

She also told us, to soften and explain what she had just said about her boyfriend, that the archbishop of Medellín, now also the Church's youngest cardinal, had expelled Joaquín from the Pontificia Bolivarian University for publishing a slanderous article against Pope John Paul II. Due to that expulsion he had gone to Italy, and they had met in Florence, where they were both studying, he literature and she pedagogy. This coincidence, she added smiling, made her eternally grateful to that cardinal, and owing to all those comings and goings she now lived in Medellín and was sitting here eating with a couple of priests who didn't resemble most of the priests she had met in Italy or Colombia.

Her story led to us tell her that we had been victims of the same person who had persecuted her boyfriend, that dreadful archbishop, that unmentionable cardinal. The guy, since our youth and seminary years, when he was not yet a monsignor, much less a cardinal, already had a reputation as a jinx. That is, just pronouncing his name, seeing him, shaking his hand, would bring bad luck. That person, what's-his-name, had also tormented us viciously, Luis for his devotion to cinema and opera, those frivolities, according to him, and me for something I was unable to confess to Teresa (for sharing with him a desire for men) and chose to replace with doctrinal disagreements in my Bible classes in the theology faculty at the same university from which Joaquín had been expelled.

Furthermore, I remembered the episode that led to the expulsion of Joaquín and some fellow students. There were three or four, one of them a woman, Emma or something like that. I remembered the incriminating article, which was called "The Meddling Pope," and I told Teresa that on that occasion, for the first time since the founding of the university and the theology faculty, the students of the latter and some professors, including me, went on strike to protest the expulsion of those kids, who, it's true, had written something offensive against the Holy Father, but still had the right to express their disagreement with an epistle of the Pope's that had to do, precisely, with one of the most delicate and polemical subjects within the Church: its position toward sexuality and toward marriage. Were not almost all priests, in the end, a bunch of celibates tormented by desire and the temptations of the flesh? Teresa interrupted me, smiling: "Joaquín always says that his only literary prize is having been expelled from a Catholic university for an article."

The origin of the whole debate, I remembered very clearly, had been the encyclical *Familiaris consortio*, in which the Polish Pope reluctantly accepted that there might be some pleasure in conjugal sex, without this enjoyment being inherently sinful, as long as the couple never lost sight of the fact that this pleasure was just the path conceived by the Creator for a higher goal, procreation. In that sense, the only birth control the Church allowed was the method of periodical abstinence, during the phases when a married couple knew the wife might be most fertile.

Pope John Paul II picked up where a letter from one of his predecessors, Paul VI, left off. The *Humanae vitae*, or the *Encyclical of the Pill*, as it was also known, praised the self-control of men during their wives' fertile stages, in spite of that being, according to Saint Augustine, a "ruffian method" to avoid the true aim of sexuality, which is procreation. Periodical abstinence, for the Pope, turned into a sort of "spiritual exercise" for married couples, so while avoiding sexual contact they drew nearer to each other in less corporeal ways. The pill, however, was an inhuman technique that made the woman "usable" all month and all year long and turned her into a victim of the male's uncontrollable instincts. As for condoms or *coitus interruptus*, Onan's method, they were not even mentioned, and the husband who looked at his wife only as an object of lust was committing a sin in his heart.

Joaquín and the other kids who were expelled half a dozen years earlier had opposed this quite conservative Church's vision with a carnivalesque, almost cynical point of view. They said, more or less: You people, Pope and priests and Catholic wives and husbands, are missing out, but we are going to enjoy sex without restraint, fear, guilt, or censorship. That was, it seemed to me, a very juvenile attitude, but it was not without its playful side and its raison d'être at a time when contraception had just liberated women's behavior. University students no longer felt an obligation to be virgin brides and slept with whomever they wanted – as men used to do, although with prostitutes – without losing any prestige or being labeled easy, loose, or hookers. The Church's disdain for contraceptives had to do with this, and we discussed it in my theology classes. What were we, what were priests, at the end of the day, if not eunuchs for the kingdom of heaven, according to the abstruse formula of our Lord?

It was as a result of this visit, this conversation, and due to the coincidence of having been persecuted by the same hierarch, that we ended up agreeing that Córdoba and I would marry Teresa and Joaquín, overlooking the fact that Joaquín was a declared atheist and Teresa, agnostic, in a ceremony directed toward pleasing Joaquín's mother and most of all to honor what we called, looking at Teresa's belly, "the fruit of her womb." Months later Luis baptized Julia in the same church, to the joy of her grandmother and godmother, Doña Natividad.

◦❧

Córdoba, as was typical in our generation, was raised to be macho. His father was a little worried by his son's interest in opera and his hostility to all sports. Once he had heard some friends at the Union Club say that "opera is football for faggots," and Dr. Córdoba wondered whether his wife's predilection for melodrama, operatic singing, and zarzuelas might not have a disastrous influence on his son's masculinity and on his sexual identity. Even though Dr. Córdoba had spoken personally with the Jesuit fathers at the Colegio San Ignacio, where Gordo went to high school, to ask them to try to sway him to do some sort of sport – table tennis, basketball, even marbles, anything – it had been in vain. Luis was clumsy at games and tired quickly when he ran, due to his flat feet. He preferred to read in the library, talk to other boys who were allergic to competitiveness, and submerge himself in fantasies and daydreams.

His passion for opera, which began in infancy, would remain his whole life, including when he was a seminarist in Antioquia, in Italy, and in Germany. I remember when we were classmates in Father Corda's seminary in Sonsón, Córdoba wrote reviews of the new opera records his mother sent him from Medellín. He signed them with an anagram of his name, Tulio Corrales de Varbozábal, but he stopped, sorrowfully, when all his records disappeared one day. We never found out if it had been a robbery (quite a rare thing, opera-enthusiast thieves, in a school closed to the outside world) or simply a confiscation by our superiors, maybe at the behest of Cordóba's father, who could not bear those musical outpourings his son was so fond of. Luis, in any case, didn't get his dander up about anything and put up with that theft without accepting the suspicions I myself whispered in his ear. Quite the opposite, in a letter to his mother that I read many years later, he said: "It's possible that God might have arranged for my records to disappear to distance me from my passion for music, which was perhaps distracting me from what's most important on the path to the priesthood. Maybe they weren't in my best interest, since God does good in all things."

That beautiful passion, however, never waned and was part of his elusive happiness. A few months later, Córdoba found out that the Teatro Colón in Bogotá was going to present two exclusive performances of Donizetti's *L'elisir d'amore*, starring the tenor Ferruccio Tagliavini. From the moment he heard about it, Luis began saving for the bus fare from Sonsón and the ticket, and he spent more than a month begging our Cordaliano superiors to let him attend. Church rules were so rigid and pitiless back then that opera seemed like a frivolous and mundane pastime to them, not suitable for priests. After many appeals and negotiations, they eventually allowed him to travel to Bogotá, a fourteen-hour drive, to attend the performance. The happiness that resulted from that experience lasted for months. In a letter to his friends, he told of his awe at hearing the tenor Tagliavini, considered by Don Otto de Greiff one of the greatest of the time. When he felt downcast, he would sing one of the most famous arias from *L'elisir d'amore*, "Una furtiva lagrima," and the sadness of the song would console him.

Years later, when he was transferred from Germany to Austria for a time, already an ordained priest, his passion for opera had not diminished. The problem was that, even though by this stage he had a bit more freedom, he did not have enough money to go to the Vienna opera. He found, however, a way to attend: he sold his own blood. In that era, blood donations were not regulated in Austria and were paid for. Córdoba would sometimes make two donations a week in different parts of the city to get enough money together to buy a ticket.

His father had also not liked the fact that his son had grown up alone among women, the only boy (and the youngest) with two sisters and a mother who indulged him more than she should have. That, Dr. Felipe Córdoba thought, was making him weak and sensitive. There was something else, however, which his father approved of ingenuously but which at the same time might have aggravated the boy's "feminine tendencies." Since his sisters were seven and five years older than him, his mother had come up with an idea to allow them to go to the pictures with their boyfriends, once they were teenagers, without raising suspicions or putting their integrity at risk in a dark place, which – this was so obvious it goes without saying – lent itself to temptations put into practice in the shelter of the shadows. So she gave Luis the job of chaperoning his two older sisters when they went to the movies with their boyfriends. He had to sit beside them for every showing. And Luis had explicit instructions to monitor the girls' impeccable behavior. Their father, for his part, sometimes took him to see cowboy movies, or war or adventure pictures, with the aim of "shaping his character." And at the same time Gordo had to go to romantic movies with the girls, love stories and family films. Luis pretended to be bored in those movies about young women, but – he told me years later when we were old friends – he loved them. It was not unusual that he would have to see the same romantic film twice, once with Lina and again with Emilia. He would protest insincerely at having to sit through those melodramas twice; however, that was what allowed him to discover subtleties in the psychology of the characters, in the framing of the stories, which were sometimes well done, with new and effective techniques.

Feminine influence was fundamental to Córdoba's education in opera and in romantic cinema, comedies of tangled love stories, adulterous transgressions, or justifiable disobedience to parents who wanted to impose certain types of weddings and family alliances. On the other hand, his father's efforts to take him to the stadium to watch soccer matches, to turn him into a follower of some team or even just a neutral fan, were all in vain. In fact, the doctor wasn't particularly interested in soccer either, fully dedicated as he was to science and the practice of medicine. And Luis perceived in his father the same profound boredom that he felt at the matches, so he felt forgiven in advance for his yawns and indifference.

I

Maybe the poem Luis recited most, often when asked about the state of his health, was one by Eduardo Carranza, "Sonnet with a Caveat." He had come across it in Andrés Holguín's *Anthology of Colombian Poetry* when he was first diagnosed, and from his first encounter he wanted to memorize it, or rather to *learn it by heart*, as he liked to say in English. Córdoba would recite it straight through with his right hand on his chest, exaggerating the rhymes a bit and moving his eyes so we could see where he was looking in his memory:

> *All is well: the field of green,*
> *the air with its tuneful gleam*
> *in the air the brushstroke of a branch*
> *and the light above the palm leaf's dance.*
>
> *All is well: her forehead awaits,*
> *water with its walking sky vibrates,*
> *the moist red of her mouth anticipates*
> *my return, while the flag flutters like a fern.*
>
> *Well and fine in dreams the child might be,*
> *fine the year's first blue month and me.*
> *Fine the rose on its fair palfrey.*

It's fine that one rises and then reclines.
The Sun, the Moon, all of life divine,
All, aside from my heart, is well and fine.

After having heard it several times, Darlis, who was always very careful, finally dared to ask him: "And what does *palfrey* mean, Don Luis?"

Gordo was silent for a moment, and then he had to admit: "I have absolutely no idea, Darlis. It must be something like a vase, because of the rose, but I'm going to look it up in the dictionary."

Another time when he recited it, Darlis came out with this question: "Doesn't it seem very selfish, Don Luis, to think that all is well except for his heart? My back hurts when I sweep, for example, and that's not fine, or that there's no aqueduct in my village and no safe drinking water."

"When one falls in love like that, Darlis, love turns into the center of the universe."

"That must be why people in love always seem like such idiots," Darlis said.

"But maybe when the poet says his heart is not fine, what he's saying is that everything is bad, for if one is heartsick, nothing can be fine, or at least there's no way to enjoy what is fine."

"Well, I think that nobody should let themselves be enslaved by their heart," Darlis contradicted him.

"The heart does not only pump blood, Dar. One accepts the dictatorship of love with much pleasure."

"It's a muddle, all this hot air about the heart. First it beats, then it's love, then it's memory, and I don't know what else. But anyway. Did you find out what *palfrey* means yet?"

"Oh, Darlis, I'm sorry. I looked it up, but I can't remember exactly. It said something very odd, something about a docile horse, which in the context of the poem didn't make any sense. What happens is that people in love can go so far as to use words they don't know the meaning of. Maybe Carranza was just looking for a rhyme. It was the last thing he needed to complete his sonnet."

"And it couldn't be a white horse adorned with roses?" Darlis asked.

"Well, it could also have been," Córdoba admitted. Startled by the woman's simple logic.

~◆~

Luis would occasionally see the children's paternal grandmother when she visited the house in Laureles. She'd come to see her grandchildren but would also sit down and talk with him and ask about his health and about shopping and household expenses. She worried that Joaquín wasn't fulfilling his obligations as a responsible father and made sure there was never anything lacking in her grandchildren's home.

Joaquín's mother, Doña Natividad, would show up at any time of the day or night and you could tell it was her because she rang the bell with impatience and unrelentingly. When the door was opened, she said hello warmly and marched straight to the kitchen, leaning on a shopping cart where she'd leave the bags with her contributions to the household provisions. She was so wrinkled that her wrinkles had wrinkles, and for Gordo her appearance revealed an indefinable age somewhere between seventy and ninety, though at the same time she had noticeable stores of energy, a natural authority, and the industriousness of a much younger person.

Doña Natividad would arrive in an old, shiny, dark-blue Mercedes W180, which had been elegant and distinguished in its day, driven by a young chauffeur with a literary name. Víctor Hugo, always in a suit and tie, would open the back door attentively for his employer and then run to the trunk to get the shopping cart out in time for the señora, after standing up slowly and dramatically, to place her purse in the wire basket alongside two or three bags of groceries marked with the name Joaquín (despite the fact that Joaquín hadn't been living there for months), a collapsible metal cane, and an extremely fat agenda where she noted everything she had to do in long black lists, crossing out the tasks with a red pen once she finished them.

Whenever she was there in the evening, slightly before or after dinnertime, she'd ask Darlis to bring her something to eat, usually something simple such as "a plate of white rice with a sunny-side up fried egg on top" (and she'd order it like that, with the triple rhyme: *un huevito frito blandito*) and always the same drink, which was quite unusual for a woman of her age, "whiskey on the rocks, but without soda." It had to be without soda, which Darlis – who would look askance at her because she thought her very forward – always answered the same way.

"Well, it'll be without water, Doña Natividad, because we have no soda."

"But at least the whiskey hasn't run out, or has it?" Teresa's mother-in-law asked, raising her eyebrows.

And Darlis had to admit there were three bottles in the cupboard, all the same brand (Macallan twelve-year-old single malt), two unopened and one half-full, which Doña Natividad herself had brought two weeks ago, "so you never run out, girl, because in a decent house you can run out of everything, sugar or salt or butter, that's what neighbors are for, but you must always have a bottle of whiskey, and not the cheapest brand, because that's only good for unblocking the drains." And she'd never even finish her little glass of whiskey without soda; she had it served with the sole intention of moistening her wrinkled, red-painted lips three or four times, to make sure there was enough and that it hadn't lost its aroma, since there must always be whiskey in a decent house, "since you never knew who might drop by, perhaps the president of the republic, or García Márquez, or the head of Caracol Television, and they, like the Pontiff and Father Luis, always enjoy whiskey."

If Luis didn't happen to be visible, Doña Natividad would sit in the living room with her drink in hand, very straight, very composed, and send Darlis to please call Father Córdoba, and when he arrived with his heavy step to greet her, she immediately started talking to him about the Holy Spirit and the strange disguised ways it liked to manifest itself, such as, for example, in the form of a priest without a cassock who had come to take the place of her son in this house. The place of Juaco, as she called Joaquín, almost at the very moment that he, who knows why, had resolved to abandon the house of his wife and children.

"Do you not think, Father, that this is the work of the Holy Spirit?"

She talked incessantly, preoccupied, as if searching for reasons to excuse her son for the incomprehensible fact that he had separated from Teresa out of the blue, or as if she were trying to defend or understand his decision, not with arguments but by bringing up the strange pathways, the long prevarications, with which the Holy Spirit manifests on earth, sometimes with the appearance of evil, sometimes with the appearance of good, but one, she used to say, must never judge by appearances, which are so deceitful, and the father himself well knew that Jesus could appear dressed as a king or as a beggar, one never knew, and that's why we must welcome beggars as though they were kings and kings as though they were beggars, although I don't know if you've noticed, Father, that today's beggars are not like they were in the old days. Now they're lacking a certain dignity that they never used to lose.

"What a state the country must be in when the beggars are poorer than ever, or frankly, more miserable than ever, when in my day they were merely poor."

And while she was talking about beggars and the Holy Spirit, she would light up and call over to Víctor Hugo, emphasizing the words as she wrote them down in her agenda: "Víctor Hugo, don't let me forget that I promised a clean shirt to that man who asked for alms outside the church of Santa Teresita, the one with the white beard and the clear gaze, who asked for a coin with so much dignity and grace: 'Please give me the first instalment for a coffee with milk.' What do you think of that, Father? I thought of leaving him part of my legacy in my will, but I haven't had time to go to the notary and add another clause to that document, which is already quite long."

Once the subject of beggars was dispatched and annotated, Doña Natividad returned to her true obsession: the Holy Spirit.

"Don't you, Father Luis, see the hand of the Holy Spirit in the fact that Joaquín has left this house almost at the exact moment that you arrived because you needed a house without stairs and a with bright studio to write your movie reviews in? I believe the Holy Spirit intervened, and it pains me to say, so that these beautiful grandchildren of mine wouldn't grow up without a father, but with an exemplary father like you, don't you think? Because my son is a very good son, but he's not a very good father."

Córdoba looked at her dumbfounded and didn't know how to answer, although it did seem a bit egotistical of the lady to consider that such a serious heart condition could be convenient just because it was convenient for her grandchildren. So he looked at her with an absent smile, answering her evasively: "It seems to me that you know a lot more about the Holy Spirit than I do, Doña Natividad."

"What would I know, Father? I don't know what you mean. It's just that it seems very good to me that my grandchildren have a male role model, something I lacked as a child, because my father died when I was very young. Don't you think it's a beautiful thing for the Holy Spirit to do? He realized that what this country is missing most are fathers."

"Well, if all this has happened due to His intervention," Luis answered, "tell Him to please protect me on the day of the transplant so I can come back and keep your daughter-in-law and grandchildren company."

"Of course I'll ask Him, Father Luis. But tell me something: what is the Holy Spirit for you?"

And Córdoba, cornered, felt obliged to answer her with something a bit more philosophical or theological:

"It seems to me, Doña Natividad, that the Holy Spirit, in the hermetic space of the Trinity, is in charge of consoling us. I also think it's the feminine figure, or the most feminine part of the Trinity. That at least was the idea of a very special monk, Abelard, who, alongside a nun he loved very much, Heloise, founded a religious community to which they gave the name Paraclito, or Paraclete, back in the year one thousand and something. And this Abelard, one of the most illustrious names in medieval philosophy, in his *Historia Calamitatum: The Story of My Misfortunes*, considered that the Holy Spirit, through music, was the creator of great consolation. So for me, Doña Natividad, music is the material manifestation of Holy Spirit, which provides my life, and many lives, great solace. And based on this I, following Abelard, call him Paraclete or Consoler."

To which Joaquín's mother simply nodded, open mouthed, bewitched by the wisdom of her interlocutor. I know it was for answers like this that she liked to sit and converse with him, who knew much more than almost anyone about everything.

⁓☙

Since he couldn't move a lot, much less run, Gordo suggested quiet games to the children.

"Let's play hide-and-seek in our heads," he'd say, full of enthusiasm.

The children had learned by then what the game consisted of, which involved them all gathering around the sickbed in his room. To play it, Gordo told them, they had to be very honest, not be a sore loser, and not tell lies. One by one, each thought of a hiding place somewhere in the house, and the rest, taking turns, said where they were looking: "under the dining-room table," "in the pantry," "behind the floral sofa in the living room," "in the hollow under Daddy's desk," "between dirty sheets in the laundry basket," and so on. The last one found was the winner, just as if they'd played it for real.

They also played memory games, with lists of words – "a boat is coming from Havana loaded with . . . fruit" – and they went around the circle taking turns naming different kinds of fruit, until someone couldn't think of one in less than ten seconds and was eliminated. Then they had to list all those fruits in the same order they'd said them in, and Gordo always won with a mnemonic technique he had, visualizing places, which he once explained. Speaking of tricks, Luis also knew magic acts, and the most frightening of all was stopping his heart. For this one they had to take his pulse and meanwhile he made them (including Teresa and Darlis) believe that he, with just the power of thought, could stop his heart from beating. And that's what it seemed like. While someone was feeling his pulse in his wrist, Gordo asked them to tell him when it stopped, and when he made a signal with his face, his heartbeat stopped in his wrist. This amused the children greatly but upset Darlis and Teresa, who begged him not to do that, not to play that game. One day, finally, Gordo showed them his trick: he put a raw potato under the arm where they were checking his pulse, and he simply squeezed the potato, which pressed against some artery, he didn't know which one, and his heart seemed to stop beating.

He also bent spoons with the heat of one finger, like Uri Geller, guessed cards, made coins disappear and managed to make a mandarin rot with a green patch in the shape of South America. He didn't give away how he did most of these tricks.

Luis told me that one afternoon, after he did several card tricks for the children, which they had enjoyed wildly, and was left alone with Teresa, she thanked him for the wonderful cheer that his presence had returned to the house in Laureles, which had been so gloomy and downcast after Joaquín's desertion.

"You have nothing to thank me for, Teresa. Since I came to live here, I have stopped thinking of my death incessantly, concentrating more on the new and vibrant life of these children. You don't know how much life these three kids give me. I had forgotten how lovely family life can be, living with children, well, living with you two mothers who I so admire."

"I had also forgotten that joy," Teresa said. "But for another reason: for my bitterness over Joaquín's leaving, that he had refused this life that seemed beautiful to me, and still does. It's as if he had contaminated me with his conviction that family life is boring, monotonous, asphyxiating. And I didn't used to think that. Since you've arrived, I have remembered how great it can be."

"Teresa, let me ask you something very personal. After this sad experience you've been through, do you still think marriage is a good thing? Maybe now you feel it just leads to abandonment and sorrow."

"Look, Gordo, the best deal a man can get is to marry a woman. We are the only ones capable of an almost mystical sacrifice for love. What you have sacrificed for God, many of us have sacrificed for our husbands. Maybe it won't happen in the future; just as priestly vocations are in crisis, I think the vocation of wife, the kind of wife I was, is going into crisis, or at least it ought to be. I think something like Joaquín leaving should not happen again, not to me or to any woman. And nevertheless, sometimes I realize that, if I fall in love, it's not impossible that I'll fall into the same devotion I had for Joaquín. If you like family life and the company of a woman and children, you should make the most of it now. I think that in the next century this will end."

⁓

From very early on, and not only due to the tricks or questions about strange words in poems, Darlis and Córdoba developed a special relationship. Luis recited, for example, *Tabardo astroso cuelga de mis hombros claudicantes / y yo le creo clámide augusta.* Darlis laughed and shouted:

"Don Luis, all I understood was something's hanging from your shoulders."

"Those lines are almost a *jitanjáfora*, Dar."

"A what?"

"A *jitanjáfora*. A word for nonsense poems invented by the Cuban poet Mariano Brull, but a wise man called Alfonso Reyes made it all the rage, and then lots more *jitanjáforas* were made up. Some are famous, like those of Julio Cortázar, who called them Gliglish: *Each time that he tried to relamate the haircincops, he became entangled in a whining grimate and had to face up to envulsioning the novalisk, felling how little by little the arnees would spejune, were becoming peltronated, redoblated . . .*

Darlis laughed a lot without understanding any of it, just guessing at things in her head, some naughty things, without saying them, and blushed.

When he played one of the most hackneyed (but his favorite) arias from *The Marriage of Figaro* for Darlis, sung by a famous Swiss soprano who he had heard personally in Vienna, Edith Mathis, he would translate the words from Italian, so she wouldn't think they were also *jitanjáforas*, but rather, in this case, a real language, the most beautiful and musical in existence, and with a very clear meaning. For him it was important to play the part about the amorous doubts sung by Cherubino, which he used as insinuation:

Voi che sapete che cosa è amor,
donne, vedete s'io l'ho nel cor,
donne, vedete s'io l'ho nel cor.

Of course this has to be heard in order to feel it, because the words are the least of it, but in any case Córdoba translated them for Darlis:

You who know what love is,
Women, see whether it's in my heart,
Women, tell me if it's in my heart.
What I am experiencing I will tell you,
It is new to me and I do not understand it.
I have a feeling full of desire,

that now is both pleasure and suffering.
At first frost, then I feel the soul burning,
And in a moment I'm freezing again.
Seek a blessing outside myself,
I do not know how to hold it, I do not know what it is.
I sigh and moan without meaning to,
Throb and tremble without knowing.
I find no peace, night or day,
But even still, I like to languish.
You who know what love is,
Women, see if it's in my heart,
Women, tell me if it's in my heart.

Gordo translated each verse with his eyes rolled back, and as he finished a line, he focused on Darlis to see if the words had any effect on her, looking intensely into her eyes until he noticed she was also feeling disturbed and almost wrenched by the same feelings as Cherubino and, maybe, Luis himself, as improbable as a priest falling in love might seem, and much less with her, who felt herself to be poor, simple, and uneducated.

During my visits, Córdoba consulted me, with pangs of conscience, doubts of all kinds, about whether I thought it was okay, if he wasn't abusing his position of power flirting with Darlis so openly, and at first I told him he was, and then no, definitely not, not to worry, for I started to think of the sword hanging by a thread, pointing directly at his heart. What power could a dying man have?

And who was I to judge him and bother him for what that ailing heart was feeling?

What happened to Córdoba with Darlis was something very private, but I don't think I'm wrong to tell it, after all these years. It's something that happens to everybody, if they're lucky, and to priests too: falling in love. I must reveal his innermost secrets because without those depths the story cannot be understood. If I had been Córdoba's confessor, I could not tell this, but since I never was, I know, and I guarantee, that Luis (at least until he met Darlis) always respected his vow of chastity. If I'm not mistaken, and apart from a few episodes with Spanish handmaidens in the cinemas of Rome, Córdoba had not known a woman. Luis aspired, as Saint Jerome said, for his heart to be, truly, a temple to God. He was not like me. I have fallen and gotten up again so many times I've lost count. Maybe it wasn't as hard for him to keep this vow as it was for me. But after half a century of abstinence and control, Córdoba's erotic awakening or rebirth was explosive and tumultuous. A priest like me is not allowed to write like that. Fuck, as they say in Spain, they keep us priests muzzled, and we have our hands tied all the time. Fuck them, as we say here, I don't plan to renounce the chance to be the explicit ventriloquist of this story, and Luis's healthy ventricle.

꿎

After hearing the above, Joaquín wonders who those Spanish handmaidens in the Roman cinemas were. I laugh over the phone when he asks, and then I explain: they were women of a certain age, and apparently Spanish, because of their accent, who went around certain cinemas in Rome and, when they saw a man on his own, would approach, sit next to him, and whisper in his ear: "Vuole una sega?" This means: "Do you want a handy?" And if the man accepted, in exchange for a thousand lira or something like that, they would proceed to undo his fly, take hold of his privates with utmost devotion, and perform the offered service with great dexterity and speed. They carried paper napkins to conceal at least a little of the spasmodic emissions of human seed.

In our college some of the novices used to say, obviously in secret, that there were even more devout handmaidens, whom they called holy handmaidens since their work was done in a more libidinous and sacred way. Somehow (I don't know about this firsthand and I can't really explain it) they place the client's member under their hairy armpit and squeeze the member in the underarm by making the sign of the cross repeatedly, gradually increasing the speed until the client ejaculates in holy gushes. These were the wanks preferred by the most devout members of the Cordialum, because they considered sin and forgiveness to come from the same hand. What was happening there was, as we say here, he who prays and sins evens the score.

J

On that first visit when Teresa came to our house at Villa and San Juan (or even later, when we married her to Joaquín), I did not yet have enough trust in her to confide the gravest problem I've ever had with the institution of the Church. It was something tempestuous, annoying, and sad that has consequences even in my current life.

It happened back in the year... I don't really know. I have to tell it in a very precise order. The first thing I need to say is that from the time I returned from Rome I became a professor of biblical studies at the Universidad Pontifica, which belongs to the diocese of Medellín. My degree was from the Jesuit Fathers' Pontifical Biblical Institute. This institute was, and still is, in the Piazza della Pilotta, across from the Gregorian University, three blocks from the Trevi Fountain. There I learned all that I could about the history and interpretation of the Old and New Testaments. The primary studies consisted of learning Latin, Greek, and Hebrew, as well as some older languages, such as archaic Sumerian, Aramaic (Jesus's mother tongue), or Coptic, to be admitted to the most advanced hermeneutics classes.

Modesty aside – modesty, please step aside – I was a good student, and I returned full of enthusiasm, with firm intentions to be a good teacher and also to sublimate, through biblical science, my baser instincts. They assigned me an important professorship, that of Holy Scriptures, which spanned all four years of basic theology. I was about thirty years old, psychologically healthy, living peacefully with Córdoba at Villa and San Juan, enjoying all my physical and mental vigor; we lacked for nothing, and I prepared my lectures carefully. I'll confess something: sometimes my courses ended with a big round of applause. Not once or twice, but many times. By secret ballot, I was chosen as the best professor in the faculty. The students sincerely liked and respected me, even though I was strict when marking their exams and was not an indulgent professor. Not everyone passed my courses; some had to retake them. The least you can expect of a theologian is that they read the Holy Scriptures attentively. I say this with sincerity, not pride. The deacon himself once told me I had a talent, a gift (and gifts are gifts): the gift of knowing how to teach, how to be clear, how to make my students passionate about biblical studies.

One year there was quite a mediocre student in my class. He was several years older than his classmates, almost my age, or even older, because he had already graduated from law school. He was not a seminarian but a lay cleric; he aspired to be a priest due to a belated calling; I can tell you now that he never was ordained. I've already said that I did not give good marks for nothing. I had my ideals and dreamed that my students would be educated and well prepared. If they wanted to be priests, at least they wouldn't be ignorant ones. Anyway, this lawyer failed my course; he wanted to be a priest but not to study; he wanted the prestige of the priesthood without the difficulties of the training. Since he failed, he had to retake the exam. I won't tell you his real name; let's say he was called Arturo Gil.

To make things easier, at his request, we did the retake in the house at Villa and San Juan, with unlimited time to answer. This Gil arrived one morning, fawning and humble, bringing me a gift of lotion. I told him it was unethical, that I could not accept anything from him. That made him more nervous. The only thing I can do – I told him – is hand you the exam, give you time to answer the questions calmly, mark it fairly, and then we'll see whether you pass or not. I provided him with a normal Bible, without commentaries, so he wouldn't have the footnotes to help. Arturo was sweating, scratching himself, writing things that had nothing to do with the questions he was being asked, pure drivel and clichés. In short: he failed the exam a second time.

A few days later the Cordaliano provincial arrived at our house out of the blue. He said he'd received a call from Monsignor Restrepo Uribe, a Paisa prince, the magnificent rector of the Pontifical University. There was a very serious accusation against Aurelio Velásquez. In the faculty of theology there was another priest, a colleague of ours, named Ómar Velásquez; I am Aurelio Sánchez. To gain time, the provincial had latched on to that inconsistency; he told the rector that there was no Aurelio Velásquez among the Cordalianos.

The accusation had come from a student, a certain Arturo Gil, who said he had seen Professor Aurelio Velásquez, a few months earlier, entering a motel in downtown Medellín in the company of a theology student. Gil claimed to have waited behind a lamppost in front of the motel. After half an hour or so, he had seen the professor leave and take a taxi heading north. A few minutes later, the young student had come out and left on foot. Arturo had told this to the deacon, the deacon to the rector, the rector to the archbishop, and the archbishop had ordered the rector to investigate. Hence the provincial's visit.

I did not hesitate to confess to José Fernando, the provincial, that I was the guilty one, that it was me who had gone into the motel. He told me things like that could not happen. He even used a slightly Jesuitical phrase I learned: "If you can't be chaste, be careful. Since you were neither one nor the other, let's see what we can do." The provincial and the whole community treated me very well; they were compassionate, let's put it that way. It was an offense, without doubt, but the student was not underage, nor was he taking my class that semester, and if we had done something behind those walls, it had not been in exchange for anything. Whatever had happened had been by mutual consent between two adults. The provincial advised me to request unpaid leave, and I went away for a few weeks, for health reasons, to the Acandí Mission. We thought that would give the archbishop time to forget about me, let the matter drop. There were bigger problems in the archdiocese. But that didn't happen. Although he set it aside for some time, one day he returned to the fray.

In any case, before leaving for Acandí, with anguish and remorse gnawing at my conscience, I asked for an appointment with the priest Córdoba and I most confided in: Carlos Alberto Calderón. As well as a priest, he was a psychologist and had an office on Calle Girardot. He told me to come see him the same day I called for an appointment, and he was entirely understanding. While I opened my heart to him, I begged him to listen to me as a priest, as well as hearing me as a psychologist. "I'm asking that you hear everything I tell you here as a confession as well and, in the end, if you see fit, give me absolution," I said. He did so, with all the generosity he was always capable of.

⁓

A few weeks later, shortly after I returned from the missions in Acandí, Angelines said to me, sounding worried, that I had received a call summoning me to an appointment with the archbishop. I had to go to the top floor of Villanueva at such and such time on a certain day, to the headquarters of the archdiocese. On that morning, I entrusted myself to all the saints and headed over there. The prelate kept me in the chapel a long time, more than an hour. The same old trick for making an inferior nervous, making him wait. First, they left me standing in a hall with no chairs. Then they sent me into an outer office where I could sit, but it was a stifling atmosphere, without any windows, so silent and sterile it seemed like a prison cell rather than the waiting room of an office, the last antechamber for someone on death row. Finally, they directed me down a narrow corridor and let me into the archbishop's office by a secret door, disguised as a bookshelf. The archbishop was seated at his desk and had what looked like a dagger in his hand. When I approached, I saw it was a letter opener with a marble handle and a gleaming blade that looked like gold and glittered under the light of the chandelier in the middle of the ceiling. For a while he didn't speak or ask me to sit down, as if engrossed in the slow, meticulous opening of numerous envelopes. He opened each one slowly, as if to be sure of never tearing one. He glanced at each piece of paper, raised an eyebrow, sighed. I didn't dare even clear my throat to remind him of my presence. I stood there waiting with my hands behind my back. Finally, he deigned to look up, regarded me from head to toe, and said condescendingly, as if speaking to a child:

"What do you do, Lelito? I can call you that, right?"

"I teach Bible studies at the university, your excellency."

"Yes, I knew that. You also know that the presidency of the university's governing board pertains to the archbishop of Medellín, don't you?"

"I do know that, your excellency."

The archbishop carried on brandishing his letter opener and slowly opening his correspondence. The most humiliating thing was having to endure in silence his studied disdain and the repellant haughtiness that emanated from each and every one of his gestures. He pressed a button with his index finger with its shiny manicured nail, and a cassocked and submissive assistant instantly appeared and was asked to bring in one of his auxiliary bishops, the vicar of religious matters or something like that. A moment later another bishop arrived, bowing, and informed him that Monsignor Escudero had had to step out for an urgent matter. The archbishop looked at me, without dismissing his auxiliary, and said: "You will present yourself in Monsignor Abraham Escudero's office as soon as you are summoned."

Then he looked at the bishop and gave him these instructions: "Accompany Lelito to the exit. We wouldn't want to lose him in some dark room. I've learned he likes dark rooms, and he's not even a photographer. Monsignor Escudero already knows what he has to do with him."

"Your excellency," I said, and left behind the auxiliary bishop.

A couple days later I received the appointment with Monsignor Escudero. I arrived early, and the monsignor, who'd known me for years, came out of his office and whispered in my ear: "It's very serious, Aurelio. The archbishop is breathing down my neck. He's not going to be there, but his episcopal vicar and a notary are."

Shortly afterward, they invited me in, and indeed there were four people: the episcopal vicar, as stiff as a broom; the bad student who had accused me, Arturo Gil; Monsignor Escudero; and another priest to take notes. He was seated at a desk where they'd set up a very old typewriter. The notary was quite a bit older than the typewriter. They had me sit next to the episcopal bishop and gave the floor to my accuser.

This Gil began by saying I was an excellent professor, but he had had the misfortune to witness, by pure chance, in front of a motel on Calle Bolívar, the Unicornio Motel, to be precise, his wise professor of Sacred Scripture entering that establishment accompanied by a student he had seen in the same theology department where he studied. He didn't recall the name of the young man. Intrigued by something so unusual—

The notary, who was typing nonstop, asked him to speak a little more slowly. Arturo went on: "Intrigued, I decided to wait for a while, to see if I could figure out such strange behavior for a priest, and half an hour later I saw my professor come out, hail a taxi, and head north. A short time later, the young man who had gone inside with said professor also came out. I mentioned these events to my confessor, and he advised I tell my spiritual director, who in turn suggested I tell the deacon of theology, and the deacon told the rector, and the rector the archbishop. That is all I have to declare."

The episcopal vicar, as if staring into a void and without turning to face me, asked: "What do you have to say to this, Father Aurelio?"

"What Arturo has just said is true. I did emerge from a motel on Calle Bolívar, where I had been with another person, but I don't have a reason to say what I did in there. My going in that place could have been for good or for ill. I do feel obliged to say, however, that Señor Gil, who is present here, failed my class at the university last semester and also failed the make-up exam, which at his own request he took at my home."

At that moment, so-called Arturo interrupted and said that wasn't true, that he had passed all his exams. I pointed out that this was very easy to check in the university records. The notary was typing noisily. Gil, at my suggestion that we verify his grades, broke down. He said that he might have had a problem with me over the evaluation of his exam, but that had nothing to do with the testimony he was providing. I thought of also reminding him of the lotion but abstained.

Gil, increasingly flustered, started to make inferences about what I might or might not have done in the motel. He took a deep breath and blurted out in the tone of a public prosecutor: "I saw you enter and exit a sordid locale of the sort that tend to be used in this city to commit, in the shelter of its filthy walls, nefarious acts. Adultery, premarital relations, congress with prostitutes. But the worst of them, the most unnatural, is committed between two members of the same sex, which in this case, has the aggravating factor of being with a pupil."

I asked if that was vengeance or a trial and said that if it was a legal canonical interrogation, I had a right to have someone assisting me. Monsignor Escudero explained that it was only a procedure the archbishop had requested they carry out in the presence of witnesses, that if a trial was set up I could have legal assistance, but for that day he declared the hearing over. Later they would let me know whether there would be another hearing or not. As I was leaving, Monsignor whispered to me: "Don't worry. This will soon be just a bad memory."

⁂

In Medellín it was common knowledge that the nameless archbishop, who at that stage, if I'm not mistaken, was not even a cardinal yet, had clear inclinations toward baby-faced lads just coming into the flower of youth. I knew about these secret preferences of his, which some seminarists complained about, but for me they constituted the least perverse and harmful facet of the archbishop, maybe the only one that made him more human and less unscrupulous, more fragile and less calculating. Curiously, as often happens in the ecclesiastical hierarchy, the fact of being gay didn't make him any less homophobic, just the opposite. If there was anything the archbishop abhorred, it was homosexuality. Knowing that, of course, I expected the worst.

Monsignor Escudero had already told the archbishop about the hearing. His only comment, I've been told, was the following: "Perhaps Lelito and his friend went into the motel just for a siesta, in an irrepressible attack of drowsiness? You are always so benevolent in your thoughts, Monsignor. Did you not make him clarify what went on? You really disappoint me. I'll have to do something myself, in view of your incompetence."

And what occurred to him was Machiavellian and clumsy at the same time, because the archbishop wanted to put our best friend to the test. Carlos Alberto Calderón, whom I had visited to ask for advice and confessed to, was an almost saintly parish priest. The prelate must have known I spoke to him, as he had spies and snitches throughout the city.

The archbishop, who both detested and envied Calderón because he considered him a proponent of liberation theology, wanted to take advantage of the situation to get rid of him, who at the time was also a professor at the Pontificia, although not in the faculty of theology but rather in medicine, bioethics. There, apparently, he had defended something the archbishop condemned: test-tube babies, which for him were a manipulation of embryos, and doctrine declared that every embryo was a fully fledged human being, and all the rest that connects with Catholic doctrine against abortion. That was the least of it. The main thing was that Father Calderón was very popular, poor people loved him, and he was always being invited to give lectures and courses all over the world. That pushed the archbishop over the edge. That a mere parish priest from his diocese was invited more often than he was to talk about Medellín was unacceptable and unheard of.

You could say that this had nothing to do with my case, and that's a fact, but that twisted man found a way to kill two birds with one stone. He summoned Carlos Alberto to the same office of the curia to talk about the subject of test-tube babies and some accusation of misappropriation of funds (a slur) in the neighborhood of Corazón, where he was a parish priest venerated by the community. What follows is what Carlos Alberto told Córdoba and me the same day as his hearing with the archbishop.

The archbishop, he told us, was brandishing a gilded letter opener as if it were a sword cutting through the dense air in the office or as if he were conducting a violent and silent symphony. He had not spoken for a long while, pretending to look at papers with an expression more scornful than enraged. After a few minutes, he sighed, picked up a piece of paper from his desk, and spent a while contemplating it. Carlos Alberto stood there not knowing what to do, but with the profound serenity of a good person with nothing to hide. The archbishop, finally, stood up and began to speak as he handed the piece of paper to him.

"You will understand that, after your duly reported opinions about in vitro fertilization, your position as professor of bioethics at the Universidad Pontificia is in question. What I mean is that, as of this moment, it is definitively null and void. The letter I have just handed you, which I have yet to sign, is addressed to the rector, and in it I'm ordering him to declare you expelled from faculty the very moment he receives it. There is just cause for your dismissal, and it will be immediate and without any compensation."

There was a pause here while Carlos Alberto read, stunned, the letter addressed to Monsignor Restrepo Uribe, the rector. In it, Carlos Alberto discovered that, as well as defending in vitro fertilization, he had also attempted to seduce some female medical students and, as if that were not enough, asked them to go out for a meal, improperly appropriating funds from the scant resources of the Corazón parish for such purposes. Satisfied by seeing Calderón growing pale, the archbishop turned his back on him, picked up another piece of paper from his desk, and spent a while contemplating and caressing this one as well. He sighed once more before turning back toward Calderón and speaking again.

"This other letter is also unsigned, but at the bottom you'll find your name typed. If you will agree to sign it this moment, Carlos Alberto, I would be prepared to lock the letter you are holding, your dismissal from the university, in my drawer, with no intention of taking it out again in the future. In this other letter a matter is exposed that you know all about, being the confidante of the accused and also a friend of that fatso, his companion, who seems to be trying to flatter your vanity with a film, they tell me, that depicts you as a saint."

The archbishop extended his right hand to take the letter firing Carlos Alberto from his professorship out of his hands. At the same time he was handing him the second letter.

"Ingenuous as I am," Carlos Alberto told us, "I thought it was going to be a letter asking forgiveness and retracting my opinions on in vitro fertilization and test-tube babies, but no. What I held in my hands was so filthy and disgusting that I could not have even imagined it."

The second letter was a very detailed denunciation against another priest, against me, against Aurelio Sánchez, professor of Bible studies and Calderón's colleague at the same university.

"In this letter I myself accused you, Lelo (for my name and title, Associate Professor of Bioethics, were written at the end of the letter), of a series of disgusting and repeated acts with a drove of theology students, all male, with whom you would have sexual relations in different motels in the city in exchange for good marks on their biblical exegesis exams. Only a very twisted mind could have written that letter full of slanderous and sordid details. The letter maintained that I had been a direct witness to your repeated acts of seduction and relentless pursuit of your students or had serious and reliable information with respect to these acts, since you were my patient, and I was also the spiritual adviser and confidante to several of the implicated students. The complaint against you, which the archbishop intended me to sign there in front of him, was addressed: Excelentísimo Señor Archbishop of Medellín, with his name and titles and all the rest."

The unexpected thing happened at that moment. After reading the letter, after rubbing his eyes and rereading it because he couldn't believe so many lies could be linked together, right under the archbishop's nose, without his hands shaking and without saying a single word, Carlos Alberto tore the missive into hundreds of pieces. A blanket of tiny white bits of paper fell onto the archbishop's purple carpet like snow, and Father Calderón had turned his back on him and left without a word, coming straight to our house on his Vespa to tell us, without boasting, I should say, of his bravery in facing one of the most powerful leaders of the universal Church. He told us as though he had simply taught a lesson to a dishonest teenager disguised as a bishop.

Córdoba turned pale as Calderón told us the end of the story of his interview with the archbishop. When Carlos Alberto stopped, smiling and satisfied, as if he'd told us of a childish prank, Gordo stood up. Very slowly, very emphatically, as if he were spelling out each word so its importance and urgency would be understood, he surprised both of us and made us tremble in our chairs: "This very minute, Carlos Alberto, without waiting a moment longer, you are going to hide in the most obscure corner of this world. That man is capable of anything, and he has friends and accomplices in such filthy caves that no one can even imagine. I am going to ask one of the novices to take that Vespa from here to your parish, right now, and leave it there. It cannot be outside the door of this house a minute longer. You've got something like twenty brothers, don't you? So tell me, which of their houses are you going to hide in – not tomorrow or tonight, but right now. And you're not leaving here through the front door but by the backyard. You're going to go good and far away from Medellín, I hope, out of Antioquia, out of Colombia, as far away as you can."

Only at that moment did Carlos Alberto and I realize the dimensions of what he'd done in the archbishop's office. It seemed like the insolence of an old-fashioned romantic hero, but, according to Córdoba, it had been suicide. We immediately began to conceive, trembling, an escape plan, which was finalized later that night: an apartment in Cartagena at dawn and then months of exile in Switzerland. But that was the least of it; that wasn't the worst part. The worst was that on his way to the Corazón parsonage, that very afternoon, just as the sun was setting, Amaranto – the novice Córdoba had sent to take the Vespa back to Carlos's neighborhood, driving up the road to the sea above Robledo – was attacked by people trying to steal the motorbike, and in the struggle, the police told us, was shot twice in the chest, once in the gut, and once in the head. The bullet pierced Carlos Alberto's blue helmet. The fact that the thieves rode off on the blue Vespa at top speed through the narrow streets of the Corazón barrio –that beloved barrio Carlos Alberto could never go back to – proved the motive was robbery.

The first news that came over the radio was that the much-loved Father Calderón, so respected by his community, had been murdered and his well-known blue Italian Vespa stolen. The next day people found out the victim had not been him but a novice missionary, a tall, handsome, level-headed young man from Carepa, Amaranto Mosquera, whom, without a second thought, Córdoba had given the most dangerous mission of his life.

K

The corporeal, prior to the spiritual, union between Córdoba and Darlis began almost by chance, and I know all the details by heart. I know them by heart, I should clarify, because I've imagined them so many times, starting from several loose threads I have been able to tie together over the years. The first thing I learned was that in that house in Laureles there was a luxury – or something unheard of here in those days, a sensuous luxury, if you will, although nothing excessive or grotesque, as you'll see – that came from a custom Teresa had imported from Italy or Thailand or some other part of the world. It consisted of a high sunbed or folding chair that would be rolled out into the courtyard on Tuesday afternoons, if the weather was fine, for a pleasurable ceremony that priests like Luis and me would never have allowed ourselves.

Since long before Joaquín left Teresa and the children, every Tuesday at dusk came a certain Mohán, who called himself a physiotherapist and disguised himself as one, always in white from head to toe, though he was just an uncertified masseur who gave a full-body massage to the lady and gentleman of the house. The man was skilled and muscular, with dragons tattooed on his biceps, and he knew how to use his hands, although to Joaquín's sensitive skin he seemed a bit exaggerated and brusque in his puffing and pressing, which he claimed helped unknot the nerves beneath the epidermis. The main problem, to tell the truth, was that he was quite pricey, at least considering the tight budget of the home, and this became obvious when it came time to pay, since the householders had to get together all the money they could find, even the change from the money jar, to make up his fee, and sometimes they had to owe him a portion the following Tuesday. Maybe that was why one afternoon when the man didn't show up or call to apologize – and Teresa and Joaquín showed their disappointment and bewilderment by looking at the ticking clock and empty sunbed – Darlis offered to do the same thing, or something very similar, for half the cost.

"Two for the price of one," she said.

"You mean you're also a masseuse, Darlis?" Teresa asked.

To which the girl replied that "what you call massage, in Cereté we call kneading, and I know how to knead. Not people though, rather bread dough and arepas."

As Darlis told them when she'd already started to knead Teresa, who had stretched out face down on the sunbed without a moment's hesitation, her father had been the town's masseur, and she had learned the skill from him, by watching, and she was perfectly prepared to massage them both, as long as she didn't have to do it out in the sunshine and rain in the courtyard, as they were accustomed to with that physiotherafaker, but rather in the semi-darkness of a room, with old songs from her village, which is how her father had always done his cures. If they proceeded with care and left it in her hands, the lady and gentleman would see if she knew how to do it or not. And it turned out that Darlis was a much better masseuse than the masseur, who was dismissed.

When Córdoba went to live in the house, the Tuesday ritual was still alive and well. And not just Tuesdays, but any day that Teresa was tense or simply felt like a little backrub, as Darlis called her extra task, and as it was extra, she was paid separately for it, and for her it was a welcome bonus that brightened up her biweekly paycheck.

One of Luis's problems with his cardiac insufficiency was that his feet and legs swelled up, so sometimes, while listening to an opera or watching a film, he would prop his feet on a stool that he tried to make higher with an additional cushion. And one of those Tuesdays, when she finished with Teresa, who then went out, very relaxed, for a beer with some girlfriends, Darlis offered, as she put it, to knead Don Luis's feet to get the swelling down.

"Look, my papá was an expert at this, Father, and many swollen people would come looking for him in Cereté and other towns around the coast because he had a hand that seemed blessed to reduce inflammation in any part of the body, and even the soul. I believe that my papa, if he were here, would be able to even massage your heart and relieve it, I do say so."

Córdoba looked at Darlis with a mixture of astonishment and embarrassment, almost with fear, thinking especially of the deformity of his feet, his missing toe, which he didn't like to let anyone see. He tried to play for time, without following his first impulse to say no, because deep down he was dying to say yes.

"Thank you, Darlis, but I don't know if I can. I'm going to ask the cardiologist in the coming days and see what he thinks."

The young woman stared at him for a long time with her angelic, understanding smile and took out of her apron pocket a piece of folded paper: "I have your doctor's phone number right here, Father, look: Dr. Casanova. Teresa gave it to me in case there was any emergency with you. I'll dial it right now and pass you the phone."

Without waiting for a reply, Darlis turned around and slipped into the kitchen like a sea breeze. Gordo, surprised, walked slowly behind the girl to the phone. She had already dialed the number and asked for Dr. Juan Casanova. When he came on the line, she said: "Father Córdoba wants to ask you something. I'll just pass him the phone."

And she handed Luis the receiver, and he had no choice but to check to see if foot rubbing was advisable. Dr. Casanova answered that he didn't think it was a bad idea, and in the trade it was recommended by a very pompous name – a lymphatic massage – and it could help to move the fluids that accumulate in the extremities due to cardiac weakness and lack of circulation. That if it didn't do him any good, it certainly wouldn't do him any harm. That he should not worry and try it. At the end the doctor allowed himself a joke that made Córdoba blush up to his ears: "One thing, though, Don Luis, you mustn't have a massage with a happy ending, because that's a very high voltage and your left ventricle wouldn't be able to handle it."

Córdoba was left speechless. When he told me about it, he said that he didn't like his doctor's double entendres. But he'd only been able to mumble his thanks into the phone and hang up.

When the call was over, he looked at Darlis's expectant face and nodded, elaborating a mental excuse (which he would later try to reconcile with me, feeling scruples with his conscience) that a massage was not voluptuousness or lust or debauchery but part of his treatment. Luis then walked, still red faced and reluctant, toward Darlis's room, where Teresa also had her massages lately. While the girl lit aromatic candles and opened the bottles of oils she used, he sat on the edge of the bed and took off, with much difficulty, his enormous size 46 German shoes and his depressing, faded Carmelite socks and, like someone peering over an abyss, fearfully approached the sunbed where Darlis had spread a striped blue-and-white towel.

"Will this thing hold me?" said Gordo, looking incredulously at the skinny metal legs of the cot. "Remember that I weigh more than two hundred pounds, Darlis."

"I'm not sure, Father. You know what we're going to do? You better lie down on my bed, that'll hold you," and Darlis took the towel off the sunbed and spread it on top of her bed.

"On your bed? Are you sure? Does it not disgust you?"

"Why would it disgust me, Father? I know full well that you wash every morning. No clean body disgusts me. Did they not teach you that all God's children are the same?"

"You believe, Darlis?"

"It's not that I believe, Don Luis. I'm sure. Lie down there, close your eyes, and stop making such a fuss. Ah, and unbuckle your belt, I have to take off your trousers."

"No, Darlis, that's going too far. No way."

"The problem with you people from this part of the country, Don Luis, begins with a very simple thing: you Paisas are afraid of the body. You're ashamed to be naked. You should see the struggle I had to get Don Joaquín out of his clothes; Doña Teresa, however, stripped off from day one, because she says that in Italy the sea is nearby everywhere. Up by the coast we aren't like you. It must be the heat, but we live almost naked from the day we're born, and it's normal for us to see our families go in and out of the shower. So do me a favor, take your clothes off without shame, and close your eyes, I'm not going to be looking at you. I've seen many things better and worse in this life. Also I'm going to cover up what most embarrasses you, your unmentionables, as you people say, with this clean cloth that looks like a shroud." And when she said the word *shroud* she laughed out loud.

Gordo obeyed her every instruction, except for closing his eyes. He didn't take his underwear off either. Then Darlis opened a drawer and took out a black blindfold made of a very soft material and placed it across his face so he would be more comfortable in the dark. Then she put on a cassette tape of accordion and drum music, rhythmic and sad at the same time, music that Córdoba had never heard, and which was sung with syllables more than words, with very long vowels, simple melodies repeated over and over, a sort of mantra.

Aiiiiauuauyenta aiiiiauuauyenta maluuujusuuuculenta ayyyyauuuuauyenta maluuujusuuuculenta . . .

Luis's deformed and long-suffering feet, with their trigger toes, stuck out over the edge of the bed, and Darlis sat in front of them on a computer stool she'd brought in from the living room where it was used as a footrest. Her soft, clear voice accompanied, quietly, the melody that was playing. She smeared her hands with an oil that smelled of eucalyptus mixed with citrus and rubbed them together. The scent reached Gordo's nostrils, and he was grateful not to see anything as Darlis began, very slowly, to stroke one toe, another toe, and another, until reaching the big toe, then the flat and mistreated sole, his swollen instep, the heels never touched by the hands of a woman, the ankles heavy with blocked fluids. The liquid accumulated in the calves finally seemed to drain toward his thighs, his belly, his kidneys. Thus, feeling in his feet and legs an ease he had not felt since the forgotten days of his childhood, not knowing how or when, he fell asleep. He fell into a deep, serene sleep, a sleep so profound and pleasant that, when at last he woke, more than an hour later, he could only compare it to that uterine serenity before memory and before light. Even before life, he told me; a sleep such as we only experience before being born. He got up from the bed as if revived.

When he took off the blindfold, he saw Darlis's smiling face, with her white, even teeth, very close to his, and her fleshy lips, which murmured, closing and exploding on the consonants, and in an almost mocking tone of voice: "Go in peace."
And the only thing Córdoba managed to say, he told me himself, came out in Latin: "Deo gratias."

Córdoba loved seeing the children running around the courtyard, up and down the hallways, all around the house, with all the breath in the world, never tiring, as if their bodies weighed nothing. He also liked watching Darlis sweep, mop, clean, wash clothes, make the beds, cook, all as if done at the same time, and without complaint, without sighing, without huffing with exhaustion. He liked that sometimes Teresa danced with the children and taught them flamenco steps, stomping her heels and fluttering her hands, the clacking of castanets, and later difficult yoga and pilates positions and stretches that made her seem to be made of rubber, with a flexibility almost of a circus performer that not even the children could imitate.

He had often thought, and had even said in the odd interview, that for him the hardest sacrifice of the priesthood was not in renouncing the libido, the pleasures of the flesh, but in giving up the chance of fatherhood. Luis, like Truffaut and so many other directors he liked, loved children and got along with them really well. In fact, when we lived together at Villa and San Juan, his greatest joy was the annual visit of my nieces from Bogotá, the muses, he called them, for when they came to spend the holidays with us, Córdoba would show movies, teach them how to listen to music, and go downtown with them to buy candy. And now that he lived in Laureles with three children, the greatest happiness for him in that house, what most distracted him from thinking about his transplant was the presence of those crazy little kids who played, ran, asked him things, and watched every movie and listened to every opera with an innocence and wonder that were at once curiosity and happiness.

With Rosina, Darlis's daughter, Luis developed an even closer relationship than with the other two children. Teresa's children, after all, had a father. They had Joaquín, who came to see them or took them out a couple days every week, while Rosina's father was just a distant reference, a guy without even a name who lived in Guayaquil, to whom this daughter meant nothing. Neither Darlis nor Rosina ever spoke of him, so it seemed almost natural for Córdoba to gradually take on the role of putative father.

Darlis did not speak much about her personal life, but Luis had managed, with patience and care, to get the most important details out of her. Although she seemed as though she'd been educated in Switzerland, he said, tidy and discreet as she was, Darlis was born into a family of campesinos and raised on a farm on the outskirts of Cereté. Her father, Justo Garrido, had a small farm where he grew yuca, eggplants, patillas (this is what Darlis called watermelons), other melons, and mangoes. His specialty was fruit, and the whole family went to the Cereté Saturday market to sell what they'd harvested. The most important person in the family was her paternal grandmother, who had reached the rank of nurse's aide but had died when Darlis was just twelve. She was the one who had taught her son how to give massages for certain ailments. That grandmother was from Antioquia and the only one in the family who had gone to school; everyone else was from the coast and had no formal education. Darlis's father, tall and strong, but gentle and calm, had married her mother, his second wife, Emelina, who was an enormous woman with jet-black skin and a strong character. She was the one in charge of the household, especially after the death of her mother-in-law. Emelina, as a young woman, had a beautiful body, before gaining weight with the years, and her two daughters had inherited that body, María Antonia, the eldest, and Darlis. The eldest especially, said Córdoba, who had seen her once, was disturbingly beautiful, so much so that she worked as a model in Medellín and looked like an African princess. Darlis was also pretty, but not as tall, less curvy; you could say she had a more discreet beauty, not as noticeable when she was dressed.

Her character was more like her father's than her mother's. She was conciliatory, cheerful, avoided fights and even arguments, and knew how to make herself invisible when the situation demanded it. Joaquín told me that when she started working for him and Teresa, recently returned from Italy, Darlis was very young, barely nineteen, and extremely shy. Gradually she began to realize she had nothing to fear in that house, but at first she was silent, almost gruff, prudent, barely opened her mouth. Although timid, she was always kind and sweet. Before Julia was born, around the time her bosses got married, she was determined to live with her sister the model rather than sleeping in the Laureles house, but she still went to the house every day, including Saturdays, to work. That was when she met the Ecuadorean English teacher, got involved with him, and her belly began to swell. The man took her on vacation to Machu Picchu, the first time Darlis had been outside the country, and there he did her wrong (as she put it), in the place he considered the navel of the world and, therefore, a privileged spot to make love without taking precautions. When the guy more or less fled to his native Guayaquil, Darlis told her employers what had happened. Teresa asked her to move in, to have her baby in the Laureles house, and they would all figure things out together. So Rosina was born, and she was just a few months younger than Julia. The two girls grew up together, almost like sisters. Darlis did not feel bitter about being a single mother, just the opposite. Teresa said that, with her baby, Darlis's good humor was accentuated even more, her smile, her serenity, and she even exercised a sort of maternity for two. Sometimes the women would breastfeed together, and even interchanged babies so they would be milk sisters, as they said in Cereté.

Teresa told us one night that when Darlis arrived at the house she didn't know how to cook so she mainly took care of the cleaning. Then she was the nanny. She had finished high school in Cereté but didn't have money to do any further education. She had to help out at home and make her own way. Teresa taught Darlis everything she knew about cooking, and the student turned out to have more talent than the teacher. Córdoba could spend hours talking about Darlis's dishes, her seasoning. I sometimes even think that Darlis won his heart more at the dinner table than on the mattress with the massages. According to Gordo, who knew a lot about eating, what Darlis cooked best were garbanzo beans and lentils. He was surprised to see her shelling the garbanzo beans as well as the lentils, one by one. She cooked the garbanzo beans with lots of tomatoes and spinach leaves, and they were apparently incomparable. I never tasted them. She curried the lentils with coconut and a spice mixture she invented herself. On Sundays she made magnificent egg arepas with a tiny bit of ground beef and sautéed onion and tomato – according to Córdoba, the best he'd eaten in his whole life, although he was only allowed half of one. Eggplant parmesan, Teresa's recipe, came out better when Darlis made it, and from the moment he started to smell what was in the oven, Gordo would get nervous and drool like an animal. He could not resist that aroma. And stuffed chicken, and kaftas and kibbehs, which she'd learned on a later visit to Cereté, when she had become interested in cooking and asked some Turkish friends in her hometown for the recipe. I remember Córdoba told me once: "Do you know something, Lelo? It's not true that love catches your eye; love comes in through the palate."

That very special combination – Rosina, who made Luis dream of fatherhood; a single mother who took care of him with love, who touched and caressed him with pleasure, who spoke to all of his senses, and with whom he could converse as with a close friend; and a cuisine that rekindled in el Gordo his oldest source of bodily pleasure – were, I think, the reasons my friend went mad with love and a desire to live again. All very physical, very palpable, and very real reasons, which blended into a spiritual obsession. Although, thinking it through, there was also something psychological. Since Córdoba felt like a burden, a cripple, handicapped, he found it easier to trust a relationship, shall we say, with a person who came from a poorer background, a humbler class. He thought at least that way, if things worked out, he could offer her a certain level of wellbeing and safety she hadn't known. These things, as I know well, do not tend to be spoken in love, because they seem like stingy calculations, but they count and exist and everyone knows it.

L

If I have ever known a saintly, good priest, it was Carlos Alberto Calderón. The only thing that was actually true in the libelous accusations in the cardinal's letter of dismissal was that Carlos was a young and very handsome man, with a thick beard and long hair, like a rock star, who he didn't wear his cassock to classes, but blue jeans, and rode his Vespa, and many girls sighed to hear such a good-looking man speak with such delicate manners, as well as sincerity and an involuntarily seductive smile. But only a few twisted minds, like the archbishop's, supposed Carlos Alberto would take advantage of his good looks to seduce students. At least Córdoba and I knew perfectly well that it was false. Even if it's true that not all priests, starting with me, are cut out for celibacy, I think Carlos Alberto was one of the few who were fully prepared to practice it without much effort or sacrifice. He was committed to serving others and was not only careful with the paltry resources of his parish, but he helped his parishioners and the most needy out of his own pocket, from what little he had.

The true motive of the unnameable one's animosity, and of his nonstop persecution, was envy, an envy that had led to hatred and even something more. The reason for his vengeful and mendacious hatred was not even political, for Carlos Alberto was not a fanatic or a militant of any ideology apart from a profound and sincere Christian feeling, but rather it all came down to the jealousy that an elevated and disliked bishop felt toward a simple priest beloved by his parishioners and invited by clergy all over the continent, among them the famous Hélder Câmara, to speak of his pastoral experiences working in the poor barrios where he practiced his priesthood. The archbishop could not understand why Brazilian, Mexican, and Nicaraguan colleagues would invite this young, inexperienced priest, and not him, who had a PhD from the Gregorian University and who could reflect with authority and knowledge on the complex diocese with which he had been entrusted by the Polish Pope: Medellín.

In the ideological terrain, the cardinal had had a much more direct nemesis. His life had run curiously and mysteriously parallel with that of a much more famous priest: Camilo Torres. The cardinal and Camilo were contemporaries and had both studied in the Conciliar Seminary of Bogotá. When Camilo went to the University of Leuven, where he eventually received a doctorate, the future archbishop went to Rome, where he also did a PhD. And while Camilo, upon his return, founded the faculty of sociology at the National University in Bogotá, the future cardinal became a professor of theology in the seminary where they had both studied. What was at first a simple rivalry began to grow (gradually, on the part of the future prelate) into hatred and envy and a general aversion toward Camilo. One of them went along the path of hierarchy and ascent through the Roman Curia, while the other grew closer and closer to the common people, until reaching the extreme limit of joining the guerrillas and dying in the first armed combat he faced, in which he didn't even manage to fire a single shot, so they say. One in the seminary, the other in the jungle; one in the offices and palaces of the Curia of Rome, the other in the prisons where the rebel priests and union organizers were held.

This rivalry, after Camilo's death – the archbishop of Medellín always needed to have an enemy in mind, a demonic incarnation to combat – had been transferred to Carlos Alberto. As much as Calderón was quite a bit more peaceful than Camilo (he had never taken up arms against anybody), the cardinal kept him in his sights, did what he could to humiliate him. But Carlos Alberto was impossible to humiliate, for to him being with the most humble and humiliated was a vocation, even a longing. And (something that made him even more invulnerable) his preference for the poor, which he thought and spoke about many times, was not manifested through political militancy, much less guerrilla warfare, never by means of violence, but always by trying to follow the peaceful example of the life of Christ. "I have never been able to imagine Jesus wielding a sword or any weapon against the Romans, against the Philistines, against anybody. I truly cannot imagine it." Faced with declarations like this, the archbishop was left with few paths of attack. All he was left with was his blind rage. And not having reasons to expel Carlos Alberto, he invented them, or at least consoled himself thinking (expecting Carlos Alberto to sign the letter accusing me) that his enemy could be as narrow-minded, calculating, and treacherous as he had always been and as he would continue to be until the end of his life.

◦&

One thing the archbishop did know, when all this happened, was that Córdoba had just finished the documentary that had obsessed him – the protagonist of which was none other than Carlos Alberto Calderón himself. That very fact, that one of the priests he most abhorred in his diocese should now be the hero of a European film, I believe, motivated the successive steps ripening in the perverse mind of the archbishop.

The money donated by German Catholics, combined with the support from the Cordaliano community in Austria, had allowed the documentary to be filmed in Vienna and Medellín. Luis hired a prestigious German cinematographer, Michael Ballhaus, who had shot films with Fassbinder (*The Marriage of Maria Braun* and *Lili Marleen*, for example) and who would later work with von Trotta, Coppola, Scorsese, and others. When he came to Medellín, as well as doing the photography and operating the camera for the documentary, Ballhaus gave a workshop at the Goethe-Institut, which Luis attended as a student, but also as interpreter. For young people anxious to become movie directors or photographers, this brief experience gave them the confidence that anything was possible, even shooting films in Medellín with one of the best photographers in the world.

In that documentary, Luis and Carlos Alberto were filmed riding horses along bridle paths in the hamlet of El Llano in the barrio of Corazón, between mountains and along ravines, where the local parish priest went to visit people who were ill, letting them take communion. The misery in the outskirts of Medellín was not comparable to the dignified austerity on the edges of Vienna, but Father Calderón carried out his functions with as much determination and dignity as his Austrian colleague, perhaps more.

The latter went to visit sick people and bring them the sacraments in his private car, a BMW, and arrived at very decent small apartments, which in Colombia would be considered upper middle class. The former walked, or rode his Vespa or a horse, to reach the farthest hamlets with consoling communion wafers. His parishioners lived in shacks, with no medical attention, without even running water. The Austrian was supported by the hierarchs of his region, while the Colombian was persecuted – supposedly for being leftist and a supporter of liberation theology – by the archbishop of his city, the hard man who had offered him salvation in exchange for betraying and destroying one of his best friends.

The deacon of the faculty of theology, in any case, received orders from the rector, who in turn had received them from the archbishop, to get rid of me. Since the deacon and I had a long-standing and solid friendship, he begged me to resign before he had to carry out the order he'd received. It was better to have "resigned for personal reasons" on my CV than "dismissed with just cause." I took his advice and resigned. Córdoba thought it better too and began to make inquiries to friends in other places to find me a teaching position.

The strange thing is that this punishment, in some way, consoled me. It was a deserved punishment, not for the episode in the motel as such – a rash, libidinous act, maybe, but also pure, because it was dictated by love for another body that consented to be touched and to touch mine – but for my inability to be faithful to the vows I had sworn freely to obey. I should have fought, perhaps, from my academic position, to defend my convictions and urge a reform to that vow that is impossible to fulfill for almost all priests, which led us to commit adultery in our hearts, if not in our bodies, because of the physical and mental inability to follow a rule that is against our natures. My duty consisted of undertaking an almost impossible task: convincing the Church hierarchy that the rule of absolute virginity was much more against nature than my own desires, which couldn't be against nature since they occurred naturally in human beings within and outside the religion.

Celibacy should have been an option that some priests could choose, if they so desired, but not all. The Archbishop of Canterbury, for example, leader of the Anglican Church (in which celibacy is not obligatory), launched an initiative that women and gay people could be priests and bishops.

In any case, as long as the legal statutes of our Church do not change, I must submit, then and now, to what I swore to uphold. And if I have fallen sometimes, due to my incapacity to control myself even with all my willpower, I must be prudent, cautious if not chaste, and never scandalous. Hypocritical, yes, that's the word, for hypocrisy, as a French aphorist put it, is an homage paid if not to virtue, at least to the letter of ecclesiastical law.

The bishop (who was known to be as unchaste as the rest of us) with his demonic spirit had performed an act of justice to me without trying to, and justice is always in one's best interest. The cardinal achieved the same thing as the devil in a Juan Villoro novel I read recently: "I am that force that always tries to do evil and ends up provoking good." Our Father Corda said it with a more agricultural simile: "Evil is the manure of good."

I cannot affirm whether the punishment, that is, the horrendous injustice committed against Carlos Alberto, made him indignant or unhappy. The tragedy of evil people is that when they do us wrong, that wrong, sooner or later, turns into our own redemption; malevolent people, no matter how much evil they do, achieve good (at least that's the only reason for evil I see in the world), and that's why evil ends up immersed, as in the case of that man who went as far as being a candidate for the papacy in Rome, in the most absolute abjection. As Jota Jota, one of Carlos Alberto's fourteen brothers, wrote: "The archbishop put his power at the service of envy, threats, and blackmail, using his cunning to disguise what turned out to be a wholesale South American inquisition, with which he could torment to martyrdom one of the most valuable priests of his diocese. Once ascended to cardinal, the only thing he could do in Rome was try to continue harming others while suffering the ravages of the disease that killed him, and with which he contaminated his docile and lascivious apprentices in the seminary of Medellín."

People always talk about the damage Pablo Escobar and drug trafficking in general did to Medellín. They always say that the mixture of mafiosi, guerrilla fighters, paramilitaries, and common criminals turned eighties and nineties Medellín into the most violent city in the world. Those factors are indeed fundamental. What they don't talk about is how the Catholic archbishop of the most Catholic city in the country, during those same years, destroyed the religious fabric of the poorest neighborhoods, withdrawing the parish priests most committed to their own communities, priests who knew the families, the sorrows, the anguish of poverty. Who knew what led some desperate people to join groups and gangs of delinquents, to work as mules for the narcos or as hit men for the mafia. They understood and, in many cases, could have prevented it, if they'd been left in their places, shepherds of their flocks, in those places they loved and were loved, by the sides of the poor. But out of fanaticism or envy, the cardinal had banished them. The Catholic Church, due to the intransigence of that unscrupulous archbishop, abandoned the people of God and left them with nothing, without God and without law, as the people say. One more tragedy among many.

∽

I cannot leave out the fate of this unforgettable friend, Carlos Alberto Calderón, after his exile in Switzerland. I have already said that

Calderón incarnated the kind of dedication to Christian and evangelical life that neither Luis nor I could ever achieve. That almost no priest can achieve. He was, for us, the image of a saint, a true disciple of Jesus, who followed the Bible's teachings not only in theory, but lived them. His desire was to live from below, not for the poor, but with the poor. Perhaps that was why in Switzerland, so clean, so prosperous, so orderly and perfect, he'd never felt comfortable, and had tolerated the comfort there, the tepidness of the easy life, not as a consolation but as yet another sacrifice. Weary of this sacrifice, he decided to return, whatever might happen. His consistency despite any test was a slap in the face for Colombia's highest-ranking Catholic, who, seeing him live a truly ideal Christian life, continued to hate him, no longer from Medellín, but now from Rome.

"I don't want any problems with the cardinal. On the other hand, I feel the necessity to live among the lowest and anonymously," he once declared.

Since it was impossible to return to his beloved Corazón barrio (the cardinal had categorically forbidden it), beside his neighbors, Carlos Alberto turned to a friend upon his return, the bishop of Sincelejo, and asked to be sent to the most isolated and miserable parish he had, one no other priest wanted to go to. This coincided with the parish priest of Morroa being kicked out, almost violently, for having impregnated a teenage girl in that far-flung village. Carlos Alberto arrived there to rescue the reputation of all the priests in the world, behaving like a true representative and follower of Jesus Christ.

A few weeks later, the parishioners had dispelled all doubts and began to love him and rely on him and on his teachings, which he expressed much more through his actions, his affection, his generosity, than through his sermons. Calderón did not preach so much with the word as with deeds, taking ill people to distant hospitals, looking after the needs of the most helpless, marching beside the unjustly persecuted, declaring everyone equal, the poor and the rich, the landowners and the landless farmworkers, the smugglers and the thieves, the venerable matrons and the whores.

The most important economic activity in Morroa was in fabrics and handwoven cotton hammocks. It was an inland village, very poor, separate from the world, where nobody went because it was so far away. It had an unpaved, badly maintained road that was practically impassable in winter, which isolated it further until the end of the rainy season. Its inhabitants were famous for weaving the best hammocks. I still have a woven and embroidered stole, made with the same technique they used for the hammocks, that Carlos Alberto sent to Luis as a gift. It's very brightly colored, dazzling, and still hasn't faded thirty years later. Those cotton fabrics and those hammocks, the most beautiful things they produced in the village, were nevertheless what brought the good Calderón's happy experience in that torrid place near the coast to an end.

Gradually, he noticed that all the hammocks and embroidered fabrics produced by the hundreds of artisans in Morroa – men, women, and children – were sold through the same intermediary, one of the region's largest landowners. This bigwig had contacts with tourist shops in Cartagena, had friends at Artesanías de Colombia, and had developed a commercial network that monopolized all the handcraft production in Morroa. Doing very simple sums, and knowing that his parishioners, no matter how hard they worked, could rarely make ends meet, Carlos Alberto realized that the greater part of the profits was remaining in the hands of one person, the local intermediary, who was also the cacique who appointed the mayor and the town councillors. The one who bought votes for the national and regional elections.

Father Carlos Alberto thought that using the parish jeep it would be possible to take at least some of the village's handicrafts and sell them directly in Cartagena and Santa Marta. He had been in touch with several tourist shops, and, skipping the middleman, those shops could buy the articles more cheaply, but the producers received much more. Omitting one link in the chain, the artisans benefitted greatly and were so happy that they got together to buy a truck to begin to send their fabrics directly to Medellín and Bogotá.

Carlos Alberto received a warning letter that basically said the following: "Father, you are not a peddler. Don't stick your nose into things that have nothing to do with the spirit or religion. Stick to your own business, the hereafter, if you don't want trouble down here." A short time later, the truck taking its second shipment of fabrics to Medellín was set on fire about twenty kilometers outside of town, and all the merchandise, as well as the truck, was lost to the flames. No other shipping company would agree to transport the hammocks made in the village. Carlos Alberto was indignant and denounced the events in his Sunday sermon to the packed church. The following Monday, he got a message at the rectory. A parishioner sent word that he had to confess very urgently. Reluctantly, Father Calderón settled into the confessional and heard someone say: "Father, I'm not here to confess, but I am here to tell you something so it won't weigh on my conscience later. You have to leave. My husband" (and here the woman gave the name of the cacique and boss of the exclusive distribution of handicrafts from the village) "has already hired two guys to come kill you this very night. I don't know how, but they have keys to the rectory; you must leave."

And Carlos Alberto had no choice but to pack his three changes of clothes and escape that very afternoon in the parish jeep. He took refuge in Cartagena in the house of his brother, Jota Jota, enclosed once more in a comfortable shelter he did not seek, and for two months, hidden, he had maybe his only vacation from clerical life. As he told me in a letter I still have, in all that time he did not officiate, nor pray, nor baptize, nor make plans to improve anyone's life. He had to present his resignation to the bishop of Sincelejo who had helped him. And once more his life was up in the air, without a parish or people to help. That was when he received, as if from Providence, an invitation to lead some workshops in Yarumal, at a seminary for missionaries, and he took refuge there for some time. He realized there that the best way he could continue practicing his understanding of the Bible and the message of Jesus was to descend further, to flee onward to places even poorer and more desolate than Morroa or Corazón.

On one of the seminary's bulletin boards, he saw by chance an announcement of a new mission they were opening in Africa, deep in Kenya, run by the same missionary fathers of Yarumal where they did the courses. To be a fully fledged missionary he had to take a special course, and that was how Father Calderón, after being a professor for so many years, turned into a student. He was an outstanding and diligent student during the whole course, and after a year his destination was decided: he would go to the Samburu desert to be with the Maasai people.

The last time he visited us in the house at Villa and San Juan, he told us: "I'm going to Africa because I think life makes sense when one can fulfill a duty to the least protected people on the planet. The situation in Colombia is very tough, but in Africa it's even worse, and I'm happy to be able to spend, to invest (in the best sense of the word) all my energies and faith, my experience of faith, with them. Now I want to live alongside the poor of Africa."

Without the slightest desire for prominence, having just turned forty, he went to Africa with practically nothing but the languages he'd learned: Italian, French, German, English . . . His aim was not to repeat in Africa the kind of evangelism conducted five hundred years earlier in the Americas; there was no colonialism in him, for he said over and over again that he was not going in order to teach the Africans anything or convert them, but to learn from them and help them in whatever way they asked.

By very infrequent letters to us or his family or mutual friends, we heard news of him and his experiences. He gave the impression of feeling happier in each letter. He celebrated his good fortune, for the very night he arrived at the remote village where he settled, it had rained after many months of drought, so the people of that place began to call him "he who brings the rain," no matter how many times he told them it had been luck and nothing more. Since he wanted to dress like them (or in other words, *not* dress), they soon changed his name to Loiborecheke, or "white-bellied man," in Samburu. All he wanted was for his behavior to reveal the love he felt for those around him. He lived with them, ate what they ate, learned a bit of their language each day. If he did the odd ritual or said a Christian prayer, it was just for himself, because his aim was not to evangelize. If he didn't know what to do, he struggled not to be a hindrance. "He who does not hinder does much," he said. But if he was able to imitate some of their labors, what the men did, what the women did, what the children did, he carried them out thoroughly.

Living with the Maasai, he fell ill with the same illnesses they suffered from. He had a small notebook where he kept a sort of diary of what he did each day. Going for water, collecting firewood, planting and tending crops, sewing, playing with children, practicing the language with them, sharing something he knew how to do, a knot, a soup, some weaving. When someone fell ill, he would take them (if there was gasoline and the jeep was working) to a city ten hours away, Wamba, where there was a hospital. And he would bring back whatever the village had asked him to get.

One year, in the middle of March, he contracted malaria. At first, it seemed he would be able to overcome the disease by keeping still, drinking water, resting in his Morroa hammock, one of his few belongings, but bit by bit he deteriorated. The pages of his diary became more difficult to read due to his high fever. But the day of his death he seemed to recover all his lucidity and, on the last page of the last of his little notebooks, with a trembling hand he wrote the following, a brief mystical text, a simple will:

Full moon in the Samburu desert.
The Ilakir of Enkai (which in the Samburu language means
    the stars are the eyes of God) have gone into hiding.
Welcome, sister death!
My fever rises intensely; there is no way to get to the
    hospital in Wamba. As usual, our Toyota is broken down.
I feel a great intensity, joyful before death.
I have lived with passion my love for humanity, for the
    project of Jesus Christ.
I am dying in complete happiness...
I committed errors, I made people suffer... I hope for their
    forgiveness!
How wonderful to die as the poorest most marginalized
    people die... with no possibility of reaching a hospital...

How wonderful if people no longer had to die like this;
I hope you will all commit to this!
An intense embrace of love for you all!
Carlos Alberto

For Luis and I it was always a mystery how a person could submit like that and die with such serenity. Few, very few, priests were like him. We were not capable of being like that.

M

Joaquín told me that he arrived at the house one Sunday evening to bring the children home. It was dark and the house seemed immersed in silence, as if uninhabited. There was no light shining through any of the windows; even the outside light above the door was off. He rang the bell once, then twice, then a third time. He banged on the door with the palm of his hand, but there was no answer. It was strange because they didn't usually leave the house empty, at first to prevent robberies and, since Luis's arrival, so he was never without company. One of the conditions the cardiologist had imposed was that there should always be someone with him, close to a telephone, in case he had a crisis or fainted (something that happened quite frequently to patients in his state) or if a suitable heart became available to transplant.

Had they rushed to the clinic? Joaquín wondered without alarming the children, but then he thought maybe they were walking around the block to stretch their legs and enjoy the fresh evening air. Gordo often went for late-afternoon walks with a violinist friend, Gonzalo Ospina, with whom he enjoyed interminable conversations about Mozart's music. Gonzalo always said he'd learned more about Mozart with Luis than from any of his music teachers.

So the children wouldn't get bored or impatient, Joaquín had suggested they sing the simple round they'd been learning lately. A musician friend, Andrés Posada, had written it:

The night the moon fell down
We did not see it,
We were
All sitting in the living room
Watching television,
Television,
Television . . .

They were getting into the third or fourth round, the two children perfectly in tune, Joaquín conducting with both hands, surrounding the moon with his fingers, turning them into the frame of the television, pointing at his eyes for the verb *watching*, when from the back of the house, he saw a series of lights coming on and gradually brightening the window that looked out at the street.

Finally, the doorstep light came on as well and they heard the sound of the three locks turning and the wooden bar being lifted from across the door. When it opened, in the rectangle of light appeared Darlis's luminous smile, her long, expressive hands, her apologies: "Forgive me, we were on the back patio and didn't hear the bell."

Behind her, with slow and heavy steps, Luis approached, in slippers, his face puffy, as if out of breath from the effort he was making to get to the door with the brief, laborious strides that were his top speed. The children ran in to greet them and then scurried away behind one of the bedroom doors.

Teresa was not home, and Luis, somewhat solemn, invited Joaquín to share a malt whiskey from the bottles Doña Natividad accumulated in the pantry. In some way, Joaquín, although he was tired, understood that he could not turn down an invitation like this at that moment.

Although Luis insisted they drink it neat, to better taste the slight smokiness of the Scottish wood and exceptional waters, Joaquín asked Darlis for two of the largest ice cubes. Thus they raised their glasses, Gordo a little shot glass and Joaquín a short glass with two rocks of municipal water, which, as they said, in Medellín was as good as in the British Isles. They could hear the children playing their favorite game in their room – *orfanotrofio*, they called it in Italian – with a row of dolls very badly treated by the governess of the orphanage, Doña Julia, and her submissive assistant, Don Simón, who was Jandrito's imaginary friend.

Since Luis knew that this game made Joaquín (who felt responsible for his children's supposed status of orphans) nervous, he masked their voices by putting on a record of Mozart's flute pieces. The second was just starting when he set aside the banal warming-up words and went to the point: "Look, I've been wanting to ask you a favor for days, but I haven't dared, out of fear of misinterpretation."

"I'm never going to misinterpret you, Luis. What's this about?"

"I've been imagining the subject for a fictional feature-length film I've been wanting to write for a long time, but with this mess of the transplant, I don't feel up to it. I can't concentrate. I want to ask you if you could write the first draft of a script for me."

"I've never written a screenplay, Luis, but I could try."

I imagine Córdoba would have taken a sip of his whiskey here and savored it before replying: "Good. The subject might sound sordid or scandalous, but I don't want it to be either. It should be a very calm and natural story, like something that goes along without being forced at all, the way a river flows. It has to do with a priest who, for some reason, begins to frequent massage parlors. At first it is just out of the desire for someone to touch him, caress him, an experience he has not had for many years, decades. But then he grows fond, shall we say, of one masseuse, one in particular. And this girl sings to him, caresses him, but she also starts to tell him her life story, her difficulties, her regrets, almost as if in confession, and the priest, even in those very mistaken circumstances, cannot stop being a priest."

"When you say he cannot stop being a priest, what do you mean exactly?" Joaquín asked. "Does that mean he can't not be celibate in any way, that his body does not react?"

"No, no, it's not that. The priest's body does react the way any man's would, and in that sense the priest feels very good. When I say he can't stop being a priest, I mean that although he doesn't want to get involved with his masseuse, at the same time he wants to help her. A matter of charity, you see?"

"I suppose so. But how does he help her?"

"First of all, he takes a genuine interest. He asks for details and gives her advice. He also gives her alms that greatly exceed a normal tip. And he and the girl begin to see each other outside;

he gets involved in trying to find her a decent place where she, his masseuse, or if you wish, his prostitute (though he never sleeps with her), can live with her daughter. He establishes a relationship of helping her. Or I don't know, it maybe more of mutual convenience."

"Okay, and where is the conflict? What's wrong with a priest helping his masseuse?"

"That's the paradox. The priest goes in there like someone falling into temptation, like someone sinning and transgressing an important rule of his perpetual vows. But at the same time, he begins to do good for this young woman. And the conflict occurs when a theology student who lives near the massage parlor begins to spy on the priest, and seeing him go in and out of that place, the best thing he can think of doing is to denounce him to the archbishop. He denounces him as a lustful, prostitute-frequenting priest. And the archbishop opens a disciplinary hearing, which means the priest not only has to stop getting massages but also has to stop helping the girl."

"And what else?"

"Well, she starts to look for him, because she needs him and because she says she's in love with him. Something like that. I don't know whether the priest is in love with her as well . . . He may be, but for the moment I don't know more than this, Joaquín. It's just the seed of a story; we have to make it grow into a tree; you have to water it with your imagination. That's why I want you to help me. It's about showing that in this punishment there is an injustice, not necessarily to the priest, but to the girl he has started to help, and whom he is now strictly forbidden from seeing under any circumstances, even outside the massage parlor."

"I can try to write a few opening scenes, Luis, or maybe what you filmmakers call a 'treatment,' to see what comes out and what you think. Give me a couple weeks."

They clink glasses and enjoy their last sips of whiskey before saying goodnight.

⁓☙

A couple weeks later, Joaquín brought over the first pages of what would become the screenplay of the priest and his masseuse. Córdoba took the neat pages, scrupulously typed with good spelling (though with many punctuation errors, Luis told me), in which a fat priest received massages from the hands of a pretty Black masseuse who was actually more than a masseuse. While she was massaging, a little boy – the young woman's son – was there the whole time telling them the story of the film *Paris, Texas*, by Wim Wenders. While the masseuse caressed the priest, the boy told them that the husband discovered that his wife and the mother of his child – played by Nastassja Kinski – was working as a prostitute and stripper in a special place with polarized glass.

After reading the outline of the first scenes of the screenplay, Córdoba sighed heavily, cleared his throat, and looked at Joaquín with a mixture of sadness, disappointment, and commiseration.

"I'm sorry, Joaquín, but this not a film. This is pure literature. Words, words, words. Just a wordy novel. It's true that the first movies were inspired by nineteenth-century English realist novels, Dickens, maybe Hardy. But the language of the cinema is images and dialogue. Images, not this wordiness, this rhetoric where everything is explained and nothing is left to the eyes or the imagination. I'm going to give you some advice, and don't take it the wrong way, because I'm giving it with all my affection: don't write screenplays. Never let anyone suggest you work in cinema ever again. You're not meant for this. Carry on with your words, with your attempts at novels, with your articles, your advertising, but leave the movies to those who know how to think in images and dialogues that necessitate movement. Also, you're too explicit, you lack subtlety; these words of yours translated onto the screen would be pure pornography, and I, good priest that I am, detest pornography."

Córdoba, I can confirm because I heard him say so many times, did not like pornography (we had even seen some together once) because for him watching people have sex without being in love was like watching couples dance but without music. Dancing without music and sex without love seemed crude and ridiculous to him. He thought that love was to sex what music was to dance, but that music came from within and could not be shown on the screen. The two who love each other carry the music within, which could perhaps be transmitted by words, but it was very difficult to do just with images and sounds, he said. Maybe literature, getting inside the heads of the lovers, could achieve it, but if those words were used on screen, the film would turn into hot air, an illustration of words. Because of their realism, movies ring false if they try to transmit the words the soul carries within and almost always in silence. The great directors achieve it with looks and gestures, with situations, even with moments of carnal union, but not with the long, weighty, and complex time that sex between two people who really love each other can last.

Joaquín felt quite disappointed – he confessed to me now, many years later – but Gordo's words had been so sincere, sounded so convincing, even so full of compassion, that ever since then he has fled from cinema work, as if from the plague.

༄

Sometimes I wonder why and for whom I am writing these notes, if they are for Joaquín or for me. If I'm writing this for myself or just for the pleasure of pleasing him. The more I write, the more I grow fond of the exercise of remembering or reconstructing everything I know about my friend Córdoba, all that he told me. I'm supposed to be doing it so Joaquín can discover details about Córdoba's life. But he's not very clear, and his idea has changed over time. At first, he was talking about a novel, and then he began to say it would be better to write a well-documented biography of Luis Córdoba, an intellectual biography. I don't know what to believe anymore. The last thing he told me was that his only real interest was to establish a contrast that would serve as a parable of Colombian life. We lived in a place where violence, cruelty, and outrage reigned; we had become accustomed to living in a slaughterhouse of hit men, thieves, mafiosi, guerrilla fighters, paramilitaries, corrupt politicians, soldiers, and police without guts or scruples. The only truly astonishing thing in this city and in this country, truly surprising, was goodness, and Gordo was an unusual and exemplary case, a good man in the midst of horror and evil.

Though I am the one writing these notes, these memories of a life and an illness, on occasions Joaquín brings me papers covered in scribbles from the investigations he's undertaken for me to use in my notes. It occurs to me, when I'm in bed about to fall asleep, that he's not going to write anything and that he is secretly urging me to write the whole thing. Maybe he knows that the only person who knew Córdoba to the depths of his soul was me, his companion for more than twenty years. Or maybe what he has is laziness, or fear of not being able to write a good book with this subject so unsuited to our times: a good priest. Joaquín suspects that without being a priest, a person can't understand priests; that without being a doctor, a person can't understand illness, even though they experience it. There is nothing as distant from Joaquín's life as religious matters and the afterlife. There is no one as terrestrial and less metaphysical than Joaquín. I think that's why it's always up to me to carry on. He tells me he doesn't understand, that he's not capable, that priests are the strangest and most absurd creatures in the world, but it's precisely that absurdity that he's most interested in reading about.

Yesterday he brought me, in very disorganized, rough notes, all he had talked about for hours with Sara Cohen, Córdoba's old friend (also mine, but mostly his) who went to live in Israel at the end of the last century. I don't know how Joaquín managed to dig her up and, according to him, spend a whole afternoon speaking with her over the internet. There are pages and pages of scrawled notes in his unsteady handwriting, occasionally so impenetrable I have to invent what it says with my own memories.

I remember Sara very well when she arrived at our house at Villa and San Juan. She was eighteen and had all the originality and intelligence of Ashkenazi Jews born and raised in a Christian country that they know and recognize (without really knowing or recognizing it) as their own country. When she arrived at our house, accompanied by Víctor Gaviria, fledgling filmmaker, and with Esthercita Levi, another young Jewish woman, serious and sweet without contradiction, Córdoba and I were happy to meet two girls of the same religion as Jesus and the Virgin Mary. One of them, I can't remember which, said: "Jesus is the Jew with the biggest clientele of all time. His heresy became much more popular than the original religion."

Córdoba smiled for a moment and then answered: "That clientele business would appeal to the Jesuits much more than us. As for success, I think that was down to Rome's fault, the Empire..."

The two young women, especially Sara, were a bit intimidated to approach our Christian world, in which most of the country had been born and raised, but which they didn't entirely understand or know. Víctor had been appointed professor of literature at Theodoro Hertzl, the city's Hebrew school, and he had wanted to bring his most outstanding and interesting students over to meet his maestro.

"I'm going to take you to meet a priest, a charming priest. I'm not taking you so he'll convert you; he's no good at that. But he knows more about cinema and classical music than anyone in town. His name is Luis Córdoba."

The two girls with long curly hair and freckles came into the house timid and smiling. Their nervousness led them to make that initial joke, I think. But after that their attitude became very respectful, almost reverential. I don't know why at that time our house was full of seminarians from Chocó. So they were not only meeting the rabbis of the Catholic Colombians, who never married and were as celibate as Buddhist monks, but also a whole bunch of seminarians from another distant part of Colombia that they hardly knew: the Black and Indigenous sides. It seemed like he was giving a course in ethnography, Sara Cohen said to Joaquín.

When they appeared, we were talking about Cordoba's aunt, his Aunt Genoveva, because we'd had a problem with her, a problem of neighbors. His aunt lived in the house next door, because she was married to a brother of Dr. Felipe, Luis's father, and she had come over that morning to ask what was going on in her nephew's house, which was now full of Indians and Blacks. Are we going crazy, or what? That blackening (she had said it like that, in a flap) was going to end up devaluing the neighborhood, especially the two-family houses, which were already going down in price. She felt what her nephew was allowing was the last straw.

Luis had very kindly invited his Aunt Genoveva to sit down in the living room, served her a coffee, and talked to her about true Christianity. To begin with he had picked up a Bible, leafed through the pages for a moment, looking for something, and then, pointing with his finger, asked her to read aloud. Aunt Genoveva read:

> *For ye are all the children of God by faith in Christ Jesus. For as many of you as have been baptized into Christ have put on Christ. There is no Jew nor Greek, there is neither bond nor free, there is neither male nor female: for ye are all one in Christ Jesus. And if ye be Christ's, then are ye Abraham's seed, and heirs according to the promise.*

When she finished reading, she shrugged her shoulders and stuck out her bottom lip. Luis explained that what Christ had done by coming to the world was bury the former divisions between master and servant, slaves and free men, women and men, Blacks and whites, Jews and Gentiles, and all the rest. That was exactly what Paul said in his Epistle to the Galatians, which she'd just read. After Christ's coming and Christian baptism, all people were the chosen people, including, obviously, Indigenous, Black, mestizos, and other mixed-race people, and whatever other way it might occur to us to divide people. From that moment on all are equal, equal brothers before the eyes of God.

Then he told her about another novice, Hernando Cortés, who Aunt Genoveva loved because his skin was very white, his eyes very blue; he was handsome and brought her gifts when he traveled to other parts of the world. This Hernando was the community's pilot. He took supplies into our missions in Urabá and Chocó and brought ill people out. For a while he lived with us. Well anyway, that blue-eyed boy she so appreciated for his costly gifts and for the color of his skin had not behaved well.

Córdoba's aunt didn't know this, but as well as his commitments to the community, Hernando began to make longer flights, up to Florida, with stops in Nicaragua and Cuba, in the Cordaliano airplane. Suddenly he had Sandinista and Communist friends. Sometimes, returning from those trips, he would talk to us enthusiastically about socialism, about his friends in the armies of those two countries. He told us he was an expert in flying just above the waves, where radar didn't detect him. He had learned this when flying just above the jungle canopy in Chocó without ever touching a tree. He knew of clandestine runways in Urabá, in La Guajira, and other zones in the north of Colombia. He never told us what he carried on those flights, but other people confirmed what was obvious: he carried cocaine in plastic bags and brought back dollars in burlap sacks. We stopped accepting his gifts, even the cigars and bottles of Cuban rum he begged us to take, sometimes on bended knee.

"No, Hernando, no. You mustn't do these things. They always end badly."

We had to expel him from the community. The last we heard of him made us very sad: the light aircraft he was flying was brought down by two US Air Force fighter planes in the waters of the Gulf of Mexico, near Florida. His last stopover had been in Managua. Hernando's body was never recovered. All that was left were pieces of the small plane floating in the gulfweed of the Caribbean. Luis and I sorrowfully celebrated a Mass for his soul and prayed for his salvation.

Aunt Genoveva couldn't believe it, such a well-mannered, attentive boy with such a nice complexion.

As if that wasn't enough to convince her, Luis brought out some much more explicit letters from Father Corda, our founder, for whom it was not a sin that white men married their Black slaves in Brazil, but something desirable and beautiful in the eyes of God. The brothers who lived in our house came from the poorest parts of Colombia, the Darién and the Chocó, and were taking courses in Medellín to become deacons or perhaps priests and maybe one day would become the first Black or Indigenous bishops in Colombia. Finally, Auntie, at last! Then she, if she were a true Christian, would have to understand and celebrate. Aunt Genoveva, in spite of everything, looked at Córdoba with great skepticism. As she was leaving we realized she was still not convinced.

"That all sounds very pretty, nephew, but I don't understand why all these people have to come and live here with you. It's very kind of you, but I don't think all this mixing is going to bring you any good. See you later, then."

We were talking about that reaction when the two Jewish girls made their entrance, timid and curious. We explained to them what was going on, to start with, and Sara confessed, at once ingenuous and frank, that it was a great novelty for her to meet priests up close, but even more to meet young Black and Indigenous men, for they lived in the bubble of Theodoro Hertzl College. They were grateful to Víctor for finally taking them out to see this other world of Medellín, unknown and fascinating to them, and thankful to us also, for receiving them with such affection.

Later we learned that Sara's father had forced the girl to spend a couple of years in Israel, from the age of fifteen, after she had committed the impertinence, the error, the impurity, of falling in love with a goy. It turned out that the goy she had been in love with was the brother of her current literature teacher. She was not entirely cured, actually, and wanted to see him again, and when she did, discovered that real love was much less interesting than the love she'd been idealizing in Israel for twenty-four months. Upon her return, it all fizzled into nothing. Sara had come back on leave from the army, where she was fulfilling her obligatory military service, which in Israel is long and serious. But she didn't want to return to the promised land. She met Luis, and soon after she deserted, not wanting to carry on learning how to fire the famous mini-Uzis of the army of her second homeland.

Thus, little by little, a friendship blossomed between Sara and Luis that was the deepest he'd ever had with a woman. They were fascinated by each other; she with Luis's culture, his goodness, his serenity in the face of anything, his calm gifts as a teacher, with the very fact that he was male, castrated and inoffensive, in a way, someone who was never going to try to kiss her or get her into bed and from whom she would only receive, with her insatiable thirst for learning, valuable insights about cinema, tips on what to read next, unforgettable music listening sessions, including great Jewish composers, such as Mendelssohn and Mahler, and sublime interpreters such as Itzhak Perlman. Córdoba, for his part, developed a fraternal affection for young Sara. He loved her way of learning, of drinking in what he said, her impertinent and frank way of asking the most private and difficult questions, about celibacy and Mary's virginity, for example, or her incomprehension of the Holy Trinity, which to her smacked of pure polytheism, or at the very least, tritheism, in disguise. Luis had replied with a quote from Jorge Luis Borges's father, the atheist psychologist Jorge Guillermo: "This world is so strange that anything is possible, even the Holy Trinity."

Sara gradually became a constant presence in our house of priests. She came over two or three times a week, at dusk, and she would also come by on the weekends. The only thing she didn't do was sleep over, but she spent so much time living with us that she even went to the Mass on Sundays that Luis said was for the nuns of the Adoration. One of those Sundays, at the moment of communion, Sara joined the line behind the nuns and approached the altar to receive the consecrated host, in a very devoted attitude. When she arrived, she closed her eyes, opened her mouth, and stuck out her tongue as the nuns did. She stayed that way for a few seconds, her tongue out like Zuca, but Luis, instead of giving her communion, placed his enormous hand on her head, held it there for a few seconds, and then sent her along with an accommodating smile.

Sara was fascinated by the modest but very clean, very neat and orderly environment in the house. The silence, when there was no music or film playing, the gleam on the impeccable tiles, the slight scent of lavender in the toilets, the tightly made beds that could be glimpsed behind the doors of the bedrooms, the flowers blooming in the courtyard, the singing canaries with their sticks of seeds, some holy pictures with women in ecstasy or of the sorrowful descent from the cross, the heart of Jesus with his viscera exposed to the stunned gazes of those who cannot put into images the abstract and unnameable idea of God. Since she often suggested religious subjects, the body-soul dualism, and the part of the Bible we shared, we agreed I would give a course to explain what Christianity was, our vision of the world. I prepared it well, with notes from my university class, and as well as the two girls, some of Luis's other pupils came to hear me, among whom I remember Gómez, an orphan whose parents were still alive; Upegui, who made me slightly nervous with his haughty handsomeness and partisan's red scarf; as always, Angelines; sometimes Víctor Gaviria and Juan Hoyos, who always fell asleep because he suffered insomnia at night and made up for it during the day; Luis Fernando Calderón; Fernando Isaza; Maraquero Arango; and people like that . . .

After the Christianity course, we turned to a seminar much more mundane and (I must confess) much more to the taste of Córdoba, who yawned a bit during my classes, envious of Hoyos's snores, but never stuck his oar in. We decided to organize a Saturday gastronomy club, in which everyone, except Gordo, had to prepare a whole lunch, cooking in front of the rest, describing the ingredients and explaining how to cook each dish. The club came into being after we watched one of Luis's favorite films, *Babette's Feast*, and read the story it was based on, by Isak Dinesen, which helped us understand the exuberance of Roman Catholicism compared to the sober austerity of Nordic Reformed Christianity. Sara, in some way, felt that the Jewish people were closer to Rome than to Copenhagen, and prepared delicious recipes she had learned from her Galician and Ukrainian grandmothers: stuffed pasta with caramelized onion sauce, Paschal Lamb, unleavened bread like they had at the Last Supper, red wine imported from Lebanon . . . On one of those Saturdays, near the end of November in the middle of Hanukkah, she and Esthercita brought a menorah to the house, and kippahs for all the men, in different colors and textures, and they blessed the table and shared out the braided challah and wine with Hebrew words. Angelines, for her part, concentrated on typical fare, beans and extremely slow-cooked sancocho chicken stew, and the seminarians from Chocó made us casseroles of fresh fish flown in from the missions in Urabá, accompanied by green plantain patacones, coconut rice, and pureed peach palms.

When we finished the feast, Córdoba – and this was also part of the ritual – asked if anyone wanted seconds of any of the dishes, and when everyone at last declared they were full, he devoted himself to finishing off everything that was left, savory and sweet, soup and starters, meat and fish. There was no way Gordo would leave anything for the next day. At night I'd pay for his excesses listening to his snores, which rattled the windowpanes and unsettled the geese his aunt Genoveva kept in the backyard, who could make more noise than a kennel full of guard dogs.

After the gastronomy club came other excesses, also Córdoba's idea, not of food but of film. We called them cinematic marathons. This consisted of seeing as many movies as possible in a single weekend. Luis was just as happy there as eating, maybe more, and in his element. He prepared the weekend's films and the program, in which he alternated between projecting them and breaking to comment. He rationed out dramas with comedies, classics with contemporary films, Italian films with Russian, Gringo, German, Mexican, even Iranian. Hollywood with *Nouvelle Vague*. Not all the participants, a dozen students, men and women, were able to handle all the films, which might be seven or more every weekend. Only Sara and Córdoba watched them all right to the end and talked about them, got heated when they weren't in complete agreement on the quality.

I liked to spy, from a corner, when disagreements arose between them. The discussions indicated, to my satisfaction, that Sara was able to have critical independence and oppose her teacher's solid arguments. They did not get into fights over matters of cinema, but on other subjects I did come to witness actual logical and rhetorical combat, on the edge of shouting and tears. Sara, almost always, laughed her head off at Luis's points, but there was one subject that exasperated her to the point of breaking. Córdoba knew that she had decided not to have children, that she scorned and hated maternity, not other people's but her own, and especially the imposition of patriarchy of all world religions, the monotheists as much as the animists and polytheists, all of them. Luis begged her to have a child, since that was the greatest blessing there could be, the most obvious proof of women's superiority over men, and said that she shouldn't worry about raising the child, he would help take care of that.

"Oh yeah, you'll help me raise it until it starts to scream. When the little angel starts to cry, you'll hand it right back to me. I've heard that fairy tale of sharing breastfeeding with men, why not, with your prodigious tits. Pure good intentions, pure bullshit. Men do two things: impregnate and leave, that's what magnificent masculinity is about: seduction or rape, escape or abandonment, and that's all there is."

Luis would tell her things about the meaning of life being completed by children. He reminded her that Saint Joseph himself had shown us the infinite love of raising someone else's son. Sara would get worked up, answer that sure, for him it was easy, huddled behind the barrier of the priesthood, protected by his eternal bachelorhood, his celibacy, and exclusive devotion of our

Lord God. She suspected, as I did, that Luis had very contradictory feelings: that he would have liked to get married and have children, but that he hadn't out of fear of women. That's what she shouted at him one day.

"That's your biggest problem, Luis, your panicked, terrified, primitive fear of women. You love them but have a profound terror of approaching them, that the power of a woman would destroy you, make you suffer like a sacrificial lamb. You are afraid of suffering, of your own weakness, of a serrated vagina devouring you whole, and thus your carapace of priestly celibacy. Coward!"

Córdoba, at this psychoanalytical broadside, had turned pale – I don't know whether out of rage or for some secret chord that had touched his heart, like when the dentist's drill bores into the most painful nerve in our gums. In what Sara shouted, with all the crudeness and cruelty, there was some truth. The priesthood, for me as much as for Luis, was at the same time our protection and our punishment, our perdition and our salvation, our arena and safety barrier, a mask and our true face.

In 1991, the most violent year in the history of Medellín, in obscure and incomprehensible circumstances, Sara's father was murdered. Don Salomón Cohen was almost always punctual, coming home at five or six at the latest. When Sara's mother phoned her at our house one night at seven thirty to say he hadn't come home yet and hadn't called, Sara went straight home to wait and try to help. At about nine, she told Córdoba and me, she began to feel a dreadful, overwhelming chill.

"My papá is cold, very cold," she started to say to her mother, trembling. "I don't know why I feel it, but it's atrocious. He's freezing to death, shaking with fright, I'm sure he's cold."

At dawn they received a call from the Caldas police. Not to worry them, but they should go to that town's morgue to see if they recognized a body. It was not Señor Cohen's, they could rest assured, but maybe it bore some relation to his disappearance, which the family had reported before midnight; perhaps it was an acquaintance of Don Salomón's. It was Thursday, and Sara went with her mother to Caldas before noon. From afar, as they entered the morgue, she recognized him by his hair – there was no doubt it was him – and then she went mad, she started to howl, they dragged her out, she fainted, she came to and grew hysterical again. Desperate, unconsolable, unceasing in her rage and screams.

It was Friday when they handed over the body, but Jewish people cannot be buried on the Sabbath. They had to lay him out of the floor of his house, his body in contact with the tiles, barely covered by sacred cloaks, after they had washed and prepared him. In the distance Sara saw Luis, who had gone to accompany her and was watching in silence from a corner. Córdoba told me he had liked the ceremony very much, heartfelt, simple, and deep. He said that a sad and bald rabbi, with a redundant surname, Tulio Rabinovich, had said something like: "Jews are polished by suffering and shined by storms, like pebbles on a beach. Jews are distinguished only when they die, as pebbles are distinguished from the rest of the stones; when a strong hand hurls them, and they skip two or three times over the surface of the water before sinking."

Finally, on the Sunday, they could bury him. Mother and daughter, sick with fear at confusing threats and strange rumors, left Medellín for Bogotá to plan their aliyah, a possible definitive return to the promised land, an escape from hell and a return to Jerusalem. When her mother refused to emigrate to Israel, they returned to Medellín, and from then on the friendship between Sara and Luis grew more intense, but, for his part, more paternal. She started calling him Father then, and Gordo called her Daughter. Sara told Joaquín that she was able to overcome her grief and madness thanks to Luis, to his affection, his advice, his imperturbable maturity, his music and films, his chaste, loving, and unconditional friendship. She said she'd never had such a close and complete friend, as understanding and wise as he was, and she never would again.

When my friend Córdoba was beguiled into going to work for Deutsche Welle, in Cologne, where he had been offered a position, the trip to Europe turned into an obsession, and there was no way of talking him out of it. He was disillusioned with our community; he'd had a disappointment that has no bearing on our story here, and I think he wanted to put an ocean between himself and the Cordalianos of Medellín. His best friends, Sara and I among them, did not agree with this trip, with this radical shift. It felt like he was abandoning the assiduous group of followers he had in the cultural world of the city, and abandoning us as well, abandoning me.

The months he devoted to the trip's preparation caused great upheaval in our house. I was very busy, I'm sad to say, and the established rules changed a lot; not all the routines and schedules were maintained, and I was not able, as I used to be, to keep an eye on everything that was going on. Córdoba was even less level-headed. To begin with, he had decided to sell the house to have additional funds in Germany, and, therefore, all of us who lived there had to rush to find another Cordaliano residence in Medellín or some other part of the country that would take us in. I'm going to say something that it hurts me to recall: in those months Luis was very egotistical, thinking only of himself, of his future in Germany, and very little of us. I don't like to complain, but I'll say it this time: he didn't think of me, who had accompanied him always, through good times and bad. He thought only of the container that was going to collect his things, his books, his films, his stereo equipment and projector, his records, and everything else. One day, at last, a truck with a container pulled up in front of the house, which we all (Black and Indigenous seminarians, Conchita, Angelines, Sara Cohen, and yours truly) filled with books, films, Luis's desk, bed, and other stuff. Córdoba couldn't help us as he was busy with spiritual tasks; in other words, he was writing his weekly movie column.

But let's return to the moment of the error, or what I saw, perhaps influenced by my sadness, as an error. Since we had nowhere to go, the Cordaliano provincial finally offered those of us left homeless – five novices and me – an apartment on Calle Argentina that had been donated to the community. Meanwhile, Córdoba washed his hands of the troubles and chaos provoked by this untimely move. He had his sights set on Cologne, on the majestic Rhine River, on his new radio job, on his contacts with Cordalianos over there, with whom he would live at first, on the colorful container (HAMBURG SÜD, it said on one side) that was taking the most beautiful and valuable things from the house, and nothing more. Luis had farewell dinners, lunches, and breakfasts every single day, with his musician friends, his filmmaker friends, his religious friends, his literary friends, his opera friends, his gourmand friends. Everyone, bar none, wanted to say farewell to him. When at last Córdoba left, saying goodbye to his housemates with a certain indifference that hurt my feelings, and still hurts, we had not yet had time to vacate the house at Villa and San Juan, since the apartment on Calle Argentina had to be refurbished so we'd all fit.

Right after he left, something happened that mortified me and that Córdoba, when I wrote to him about it, completely ignored, not even mentioning it when he wrote back. One of the housekeepers, Esperanza, who came to help us several times a week with the laundry or cleaning, got pregnant. Esperanza was about thirty-five years old and from Donmatías. She was fair, blue eyed, lively, cheerful, and fond of singing. She would do her work singing, whistling, half dancing, as if she never tired, always in a good mood, and everyone liked her. Until one afternoon shortly after Luis left, Angelines came to tell me: "Lelo, it seems that Esperanza is pregnant; all she does is cry in the laundry tubs, look up to heaven and say she doesn't know what to do and she can't tell us who it was. Conchita told me she thinks the father is one of the novices."

That last part upset me most. Córdoba wasn't here anymore to ask for advice, and he didn't reply to my letter, as if the situation had nothing to do with him, even though it had happened amid the disorder and carelessness caused by the preparations for his trip to Germany. So it fell to me, me alone, to take the bull by the horns and confront the woman: "Esperanza, tell me what happened so we can help you. First of all, tell me who the baby's father is."

After much refusal, after many tears and wringing out the soft red coverlet she had in her hands, after several days of going back and forth, after blaming a messenger and a Coca-Cola delivery man, the only thing she gave away was this incomplete confession: "Look, Father, what I can tell you is that the father is one of the novices who lives here. I wasn't forced; we started to play with fire and we got burnt. The thing is I swore that I would never tell, so I'm not going to tell you who it was, because priests aren't the only ones who keep their word. In any case, don't worry, I'll look after the child on my own. Neither you nor the father is going to have to come and take charge of the baby."

No matter how I explained the importance of knowing who was responsible, no matter how simple or elaborate the arguments I used to try to convince her to tell me, I was not able to get that information. Novice after novice shielded himself with complicit silence. I realized that the father, whichever one he was, and the rest knew very well who was responsible, but they'd made a pact not to reveal the truth, and each of them roundly denied paternity and also denied knowing which of them was guilty of getting the maid pregnant. The only thing I was sure of was that in those circumstances I could not dismiss Esperanza but must support her in whatever way she needed. The provincial agreed with this, and as a community we helped the young woman get her own little house in Hogares Corda, a neighborhood the Cordalianos were building up by El Picacho.

While her belly was becoming more and more noticeable, a surprise reached us from Germany: Córdoba had absolutely not adapted to his new job at Deutsche Welle and was planning to come back as suddenly as he'd left. He had even given instructions that as soon as the container arrived in Hamburg, it should be sent back to Cartagena on the first available ship. It was no longer necessary to proceed with the sale of the house at Villa and San Juan, and we could all stay there. The Cordalianos did not have to give us the residence on Calle Argentina and could put it to other uses. The news gave me an ambiguous sensation, halfway between happiness and getting even, as when you recriminate someone to their face: "I told you so." I tried to show only the happiness. I thought it would be best to wait for Córdoba's return to try to solve the enigma of Esperanza's child's paternity. Meanwhile, our cohabitation had deteriorated substantially, in part due to Luis's absence, but most of all due to the secret guilt of one of the novices and the complicit silence of the rest. All trust had turned to suspicion.

Of the five novices from Chocó (or more generally from Darién), three were Indigenous and two were Black. Two of the Indigenous boys were from the Kuna people and had been sent to us for their education, with very good recommendations, by some Spanish missionaries from a Panamanian archipelago on the border of Colombia. Both, oddly, had the same name, Alarico, so we called them Alarico I and Alarico II. I don't remember their surnames. Their mother tongue was not Spanish, and when talking together they almost always spoke their own language, which nobody else understood. The third Indigenous seminarian was Emberá Katío and came from Riosucio; his name was Pancracio Cassama. The three of them were, to me, quite indecipherable. Obedient, submissive, silent, but very much themselves, if I can put it like that. They did not express their feelings; one never knew if they were content or not, if they were satisfied with the religious life or not. They submitted to the rules, the schedule, they got on more or less well in their studies, but it was very difficult to know if they really had a religious vocation or if they were just taking advantage of the order to get an education. To put it simply: I didn't really understand them; they never opened up, and that hermeticism put me in a bad mood.

One of the novices, Ambrosio Palacio, was tall, with very smooth and shiny skin, and since I thought him the most handsome and fun-loving of all the novices, for me he was the first suspect who might have seduced Esperanza. The other, Patricio Pedernera, was more modest in his appearance, less festive, almost as reserved and gruff as the Indigenous ones. He had a marked racial consciousness, so at any observation of ours, at the slightest complaint no matter how gently expressed, he would accuse us of racism. Despite all my efforts, I did not manage to discover the truth. What I can say for certain is that these five novices were all a dozen years younger than Esperanza.

Almost a year later, after Esperanza had the baby, a little boy whom she hadn't let us meet, she asked me to help her translate some documents she'd received from the US consulate. Her parents were living up north, in Massachusetts, and had acquired citizenship and were now applying to bring her there as well. With great pleasure I helped her amass the documents required, and at last she got a visa to go with the baby. Around the time Córdoba returned from Germany (the container had yet to arrive), Esperanza invited us both, along with Angelines, to go to a farewell party at her little house in Hogares Corda. It was a lovely celebration; she wanted to thank us for all we'd done for her. She refused to show us the baby boy, though. He remained behind a closed door. She said we shouldn't wake him, that he had a fever and was sleeping.

We were eating a piece of Maria Luisa cake when the baby suddenly, from the darkness of his room, let out a howl. Angelines, who was always much quicker and more resourceful than us, didn't hesitate for a second: she jumped up from her chair, opened the door, lifted up the baby, and came out to the living room with him in her arms. He immediately stopped crying and stared at us with a very pretty smile. I didn't feel like I was seeing him for the first time but rather recognizing him. Without a thought, I exclaimed what emerged from my soul: "Alarico the Third!"

Yes, the baby was the spitting image of Alarico II – his features, his hair, his smile – you could almost say he was a perfect clone, as if he had nothing of Esperanza, except perhaps a slightly lighter skin tone than the Panamanian. The evidence was so great, my shout had come from so deep within, that Esperanza could not go on denying it. Maybe the fact that she was leaving Colombia forever in a few days also allowed her to confirm, blushing up to her earlobes, that she had indeed had an indiscretion with Alarico II, but she had promised not to say anything in order not to damage his chances of taking his first vows as deacon, which he was about to profess. She was not planning to demand anything of him, and now she had resolved to bring up her son in the United States, where things, she thought, would not be as difficult as here.

"Finally it's not a white man getting an Indigenous woman pregnant," Angelines muttered, almost to herself, "but an Indian who gets a white woman pregnant. About time."

When she left for her new life in a puritan town near Boston, I had no choice but to inform the provincial and the Spanish missionaries in Darién what had happened. It was resolved that the best thing would be for Alarico II to return to the archipelago where he was born, and there those who had recommended him as a pupil apt to reach the priesthood could resolve how to reorient or confirm his vocation. I have to say that none of these novices under our tutelage ended up being ordained. One of them, however, became a senator. Another received a PhD from the University of Antioquia and is now a professor in some city in the south of the country. We heard that Alarico II set up a pharmacy and has a big family on his native archipelago. Esperanza didn't do badly; she married a gringo truck driver who, as she told us in her letters, has generously helped her raise the Colombian fruit of her womb, as well as a daughter they had together. Both Esperanza's children, last I heard, graduated from university with honors.

N

Joaquín has told me that at night, especially when he lies on his side, his heartbeat, or, as he puts it, "the metronome of the music of my life," keeps him awake. Sometimes, during spells of insomnia, he tries to get to sleep by repeating the same lines of poetry over and over again: *All are asleep, my heart, / all are asleep you're not. / All are asleep, my heart, / everyone sleeps and you don't.* It seems, however, that counting sheep does not help him. He sleeps, or, rather, he does not sleep, with his eyes open, searching for a sign in the dark air, his senses alert, ears perked, taste and smell in continuous alarm, touching a palpitating artery on his neck or wrist. A pillow, he says, is like an amplifier of pulses, and sometimes, every fifth or sixth *tun-tun, tun-tun, tun-tun*, he notices a dissonance, like an anomaly, a mechanical click, a *tracka-tracka* that seems like the first alarm signal of a motor beginning to fail. An additional blow, more of a groan than a beat, which he attempts to catch and decipher with all the concentration of that ear sunk in the soft fabric, as if the very act of hearing could protect him from his heart's harmful effects. "If I concentrate on hearing it, it cannot stop," he tells me. "At least that's my superstition."

The cardiologist showed him, when the valve problem was barely beginning, on a flexible rubber heart he kept in a drawer, the correct function of a normal heart: "The unoxygenated blood, dark blue, arrives through the large veins into the right auricle;

from this auricle, through the tricuspid valve, the blackish blood passes into the right ventricle." The doctor stuck his index finger in the large veins, the one that comes up from the lower body and the one that reaches down from above, from the neck and the brain, a big consumer of calories and oxygen. He opened the rubber heart and showed him the internal cavities, the first ones, the atria.

On his pillow, Joaquín does not know how to differentiate the systole from the diastole, in which moment there is relaxation or contraction. Which causes him anguish and perhaps even accelerates the pulsations of the anomalous, excess heartbeat he awaits with fear, like when a person listens for the sounds of a thief on the roof, a murderer's footsteps in the hallway, a skeleton key in the lock. If he puts a hand under his sternum and rests it on the ribs on his left side, sometimes his fingers feel a jolt, a blow. On one of the anomalous jolts a dog in next yard barked and, as they say, his heart did a flip, believing he himself had barked like that.

"Then the right ventricle during the systole (or contraction) sends the dark blood through the pulmonary artery, which bifurcates, one branch to the right lung and one to the left; the blood is oxygenated in the cells of the lungs and returns through the pulmonary veins – bright and red and fresh – to the left auricle; during the diastole (relaxed heart), the blood passes from the left auricle to the left ventricle through the mitral valve; when the heart contracts again, the oxygenated blood flows out of the left ventricle, through the aortic valve, and from the aorta, the luminous blood flows the length of many arteries, taking the body, including the heart itself, through the coronary arteries, all the oxygen and nutrients necessary to move, to think, and to live. It's in that last contraction, the one that expels the luminous, oxygenated blood toward the aorta, that we measure your EF, your ejection fraction."

Joaquín has become so obsessed with his cardiac problem that he reads specialized articles about the heart day and night. When we get together to talk about my memories of Luis, instead of concentrating on Córdoba, he rambles on about the things he's discovered about his internal organ, which, he clarifies, resembles Luis's heart, useless, and another they're going to replace his with, and all of ours.

"The heart, Lelo, was always an untouchable organ par excellence," he instructs me. "Traditional medicine had an axiom that no doctor doubted: just touching the heart, opening the tiniest hole with a finger or a pin, is enough to stop it, and, if it stops, you are dead. The Egyptians, when they embalmed their pharaohs, removed all the guts from the thoracic cavity (liver, intestines, lungs, spleen, gallbladder, kidneys) except the heart, which was left in place, the untouchable sun in the middle of the chest. Almost until the dawn of the twentieth century, no doctor dared to cross that frontier; they operated on the colon, the testicles, liver, uterus, but never the heart. They trepanned brains, extracted the stone of madness, but no one touched the heart, unless to kill. Aristotle said that the heart could not bear even to be grazed with the tip of a knife. Later Galen noted that all wounds to the hearts of gladiators were fatal; he realized that if one of the cardiac chambers was perforated, the gladiator died on the spot from loss of blood, most rapidly if the lesion was in the left ventricle. For centuries it was considered impossible to sew up a beating heart.

"All this changed one day in the summer of 1893, in Chicago, when a Black surgeon received a wounded twenty-four-year-old who'd been stabbed in the chest during a barroom brawl. The blade had entered from the left of the sternum, and the surgeon, unable to see through the gushing and coagulating blood, opened the wound further to explore. The doctor was Daniel Hale Williams, and perhaps he was not aware that he was about to try something nobody had ever dared before. The knife had cut the right ventricle; the blood was dark and veiny. The young man was slipping away. His blood pressure was very low and he was deathly pale. Without a second thought, or thinking with his hands more than his mind, Doctor Williams asked for catgut thread and a needle and sutured the perforated pericardium. He sewed up the muscle at the same rhythm the young man's heart was beating, as if dancing with it, poking the needle in and pulling it through during the diastole. There was another stab wound, another perforation, but this one had a good scab blocking the hole, and he chose not to touch it. The wonder of it was that the patient, a man named Cornish, survived the sutures, his heart kept beating, and he did not die of sepsis, which was common in those days. Two months later he walked out of the hospital. Thus, the heart, thanks to the hands of a Black surgeon in a still very racist era, was no longer untouchable, and since then it has been possible to sew up a heart. Up until that day, people were assured that operating on a heart was as effective as prayer; since then, suturing a heart has been much more productive than praying. No offense, Lelo."

∽

If we rest our head against the chest of a beloved person (and this must be one of the oldest human acts), as well as the agreeable sensation of skin and warmth and the singular scent of our loved one, we suddenly hear those rhythmic beats – that small motor that is proof that we're alive. Nobody remembers, but undoubtedly the first auditory experience of all viviparous creatures is that same serious, obscure, double, cavernous palpitation. In the warm pool of amniotic fluid, that constant drumbeat of flesh must be soothing.

In a state of rest, and if I'm not nervous about wanting to write about my friend Córdoba or about Joaquín's ailing heart, my heart beats at an even rate of sixty beats a minute. They say the minute is divided into sixty seconds because the base of sixty is comfortable. It's the first number divisible by the first five digits: by one, by two, by three, by four, and by five. And furthermore by six, ten, twelve, fifteen, twenty, and thirty. But I think that when we started measuring time in seconds (and that's only when there were very precise clocks), the choice of the number of seconds per minute could have been influenced by the natural rhythm of the heart, without tachycardia or bradycardia or arrhythmia. Sixty beats a minute is a good median point, at least if you measure the cardiac frequency upon awakening without any shock.

I think we priests have always been against abortion because very early, if we hold a stethoscope to a pregnant woman's belly, we can hear the baby's heartbeat. Rather than thinking of this as a fully formed human being, we defend the taboo against killing a heart, stopping it by force.

"The heart of a fetus," Joaquín also taught me, "beats as rapidly as a hummingbird's, which goes at a thousand beats a minute. However, the heart of a great cyclist, let's say Nairo's or Egan's, is as slow as an elephant's, which with thirty beats a minute irrigates her whole body from the tip of her trunk to her tail. Once I saw the heart of a beached whale carved up on the sands of the Pacific coast. It was the size of a Fiat Topolino, able to pump three hundred and fifty liters of blood a minute.

"And the most incredible thing, Lelo: just as the Earth is sustained by the air and seen from the moon seems weightless, light, and blue, the heart is also like that in water, light and red, as if in its own amniotic fluid, always floating, without any contacts or restraints, enveloped in gift wrap, the pericardium, like a star that requires no supports or tethers, like a free spirit."

꙳

I think Córdoba also knew that lesson by heart, and listening to the movements of his heart he could almost picture it, caress it, or at least that's what he told me. Lying down in the darkness of his room, he placed his open hand in his armpit, as Fernando had shown him, and seemed to be touching his overgrown heart. He was going to accept Darlis's offer, yes, it occurred to him, he was going to ask the woman to give him the massage she'd offered, there, on his chest, as her father did in her hometown and which could supposedly heal people. A long massage there, only there. Surely that, he thought, almost asleep, sinking into sleep, that would be a balm for his heart, for his whole body.

~&~

Teresa told me that one afternoon, at dusk, walking home from the school for children with special needs, she saw, from the corner, a big white van. An ambulance, she thought, and began to run. She thought Luis had had a heart attack or died and that they were about to bring him out on a gurney, covered by a sheet. When she got closer, she saw that it wasn't an ambulance but a Caracol TV van. Inside the house they were interviewing Gordo. They'd moved all the furniture, and he was in the middle of the room, calm, sitting in the flowery armchair, answering questions with all the serenity in the world. He was surrounded by lights and technicians making hand signals and putting a finger to their lips to indicate that no one should talk.

I remember seeing that interview of Córdoba in the house in Laureles. It was with the same journalist who had hired him many years earlier to write a movie column in *El Colombiano*, Darío Arizmendi, who now had a program of televised interviews. Joaquín got a copy of the old program and gave it to me to watch again. It was Luis's last interview before his operation. El Gordo, for a start, was not so fat anymore, so much so that in the conversation, near the beginning, he said: "The less I weigh, the better it is for my heart. I reached a weight of 306 pounds at one stage; now I'm down to 198, and I feel much better. I think I am a new man; now I'm the person who was inside me. Of course, I still very much enjoy eating with my friends, conversing with them over a meal. It's like watching a film together, which I also enjoy a lot. That animal that's inside me, the heart that lives inside my heart, which we priests call the soul..."

The interviewer interrupts him here to ask about death and about the transplant he's going to undergo. Luis sighs and responds: "A person thinks they're invulnerable, that they'll never get sick. My heart problem has been with me for many years. We try to play the fool and make plans without keeping death in mind. But it's advisable to keep it in mind and to plan for it. Three or four months ago they offered me the transplant: it's a gift and an opportunity of life that science and my medical team have made possible. Awaiting that heart, in this house, I have felt particularly tranquil. I have felt the love, friendship, and help of others. I am not concentrating on myself or on my illness. It's better to carry on enjoying life: listening to music, watching films, talking to people. I am a lover of friendship and conversation. I am moved by the closeness of my friends, male and female, their solidarity, their constant company, their tenderness. This has been a great discovery, to feel so beloved and surrounded by affection. Lately I've felt much better, compensated. My heart works like an old car, which breaks down occasionally, but you take care of it as well as possible until you're able to get another one. I sleep perfectly well, and I wait."

Arizmedi asks him about the donor. About the fact that someone must die for him to live.

"Of course it's distressing to think that someone has to die so that I can live. On the other hand, it's like a cycle of life that renews itself. Still, it's no less distressing to me that in this city it's not hard to find a donor due to its biggest disgrace, that Medellín is such a violent city. It's a terrible thing, but that's the way it is; it's a fact. In Europe and the United States most donors come from traffic accidents; here, it's from violence. In China they are more practical. Those on death row have their hearts removed in the Aztec style, with the patient still alive. The death penalty and the transplant take place in adjoining operating rooms. In any case, mine has been slow to arrive because the donor and I need to coincide in blood type and size; as I am quite tall, it has to be a relatively large person. It could even be a woman's heart. I'd like that; I hope I get the heart of a woman."

The interviewer insists on the metaphors of the heart and the possibility that later, once transplanted, Luis might decide to change, to have a new life, to no longer be a priest. A little exasperated, Córdoba returns to basics: "The heart is a muscle, a pump that gives life to a person. I shall feel very close to the person who gives me that gift. I shall keep them in mind, but I won't know who they were. The details of the donor remain hidden, anonymous. It's an act of solidarity, although the one who does this for me cannot be aware of their gift. I shall not become another. I do not believe in reincarnation. I think that life goes on eternally somehow in the most beautiful aspects. I have greatly enjoyed life, and I don't think I have any complaints. I have always liked beauty, kindness, art, spirit, thought. In that sense, I would like to continue searching for the same things. My past is here, including my past as a priest. It is who I am, and this cannot be corrected or erased. I would like to have the same life, but to enjoy it to the end. Life is the possibility of being near others, with love. Love is the fundamental basis of existence. Someone's lack means that someone else can have a full, meaningful life. If there were no illness, there would be no doctors. If children were not fragile and small, there would be no motherhood or fatherhood. If we were all perfect, nobody would need anybody else."

Arizmendi asks him about spiritual things, since the gentleman is a priest.

"I am not a dualist. I don't believe in a spirit separate from the body. I don't believe a body is the spirit's prison. Real Christianity is always integral, soul and body united. The Jewish people have kept the fact of the soul and the fact of the body united; perhaps this is why among the Jews there are no monks, those who, theoretically, dedicate themselves entirely to the spirit; rather it was the Greeks who sent us down this other path, that of separation of body and spirit. I believe that part of the greatness of Christianity is the acceptance of life, the acceptance of pleasure, of existence. Saint Francis of Assisi enjoyed his existence and was not complaining that his spirit was imprisoned. I have evangelized on behalf of the things I like best: music and film. This was allowed to me by the Second Vatican Council and the fact that the founder of the Cordaliano order, Ángel María Corda, always defended the possibility of evangelizing by all means. This gave me a nice margin of liberty for what I aimed to do, and I was able to lead a life and practice the priesthood outside the normal blueprint. I have been able to share and communicate what I most appreciate in film and music, which is basically their beauty, their indubitable beauty."

The interviewer continues to ask if he's going to change his life after the operation, if he's going to continue to be a Cordaliano or not, if he regrets becoming a priest. Luis answers: "Come off it with reincarnation. You keep insisting on this idea of reincarnation. It's a mistaken idea. It's not possible that we're allowed to correct our lives, change them. Life cannot be corrected. If it could, I'd tell my niece not to board that plane in which she was killed. Knowing the future, it's very easy to fix a life, but life is beautiful because it's always a rough draft, and being a priest has allowed me experiences fundamental to my education. A priest never stops being a priest, even if he leaves his order. Thanks to the priesthood I got to know the country of my dreams, which is Italy. There I discovered cinema in a more reflective way, and it was wonderful. My essential passion also turned into reflection. I watched film shoots there, heard great directors speak, attended the premiere of Pasolini's *Teorema*, which two days later was banned for all audiences. A famous Jesuit (not long ago I saw that he was an advisor for the film *The Name of the Rose*), Angelo Arpa, introduced us to a couple of his close friends: Rossellini and Fellini. Father Arpa had a film forum in the Pio Latino Americano where seminarians from all over the world would go. (We weren't allowed in commercial cinemas.) Arpa was passionate about cinema; he produced films. He would bring in directors after projecting their films, and we got to talk with them. Thanks to his friendship with Cardinal Siri of Genoa, he prevented the Vatican from censuring Fellini's *Nights of Cabiria*; he made the film be seen as something positive, not as indecency, not as a mockery, but as a celebration of life. I have no great wishes or ambitions; the only thing I aspire to is to have a calm heart. It doesn't sound like much, but it's enough. Those who have one don't realize the treasure they harbor in their chests."

Watching the interview again, however, and noticing how uncomfortable he got responding to the interviewer's insistence about becoming someone else, I read something in Luis's face that no one who didn't know him well could have noticed. He could not be completely sincere in front of the television cameras, and there was something in him that had changed radically in those last months while he waited for the second chance that receiving a new heart would mean. Really it was that Luis hated exhibitionism in front of the camera, sentimental pornography. Anything that he was thinking of changing he kept to himself.

Ñ

There is an old French proverb that describes what was happening in the house in Laureles: "Marriage is like a besieged fortress. Those who are outside want to get in and those who are inside want to get out." Joaquín had said over and over again that he was bored with Teresa, that fatherhood overwhelmed him, and that in his house he felt as imprisoned as a heart behind the bars of the ribcage. "Is that not what marriage is, a prison for the heart?" he wondered.

I don't know if this depends on the chasteness, the goodness, or the nature of the man with whom I lived for so many years, but I did not get bored for a single day of my life with Córdoba. We priests can have marriages as strange as that, as perfect. Sometimes I think that sex is what diminishes everything and complicates it. Sex, for example, is a great generator of jealousy. Almost all men's jealousy is sexual. There is another type, of course, but it is more tenuous, does not produce madness, but rather, at most, a certain manageable annoyance, a discomfort that never grows into hatred for the person we love.

Joaquín, however, has told me several times that Teresa offered him a golden cage with silk bars, certainly, with weightless irons and permission to leave frequently ("parole," he called it), but in any case, marriage and family was an atmosphere that, by its very softness and its warm and monotonous serenity, smothered him. Paradise, he insisted, can only be temporary, intermittent, because if not it turns into perpetual dessert or an eternal Sunday. A pleasant life always threatens to turn cloying or tedious. He felt guilty thinking it, but felt harassed by serenity and sweetness. He admitted that Teresa was little short of a saint, but then concluded: "Saints sanctify."

Córdoba's case was very different. Since his distant childhood and early adolescence, he had not felt the tranquil delights of domestic life. As he had almost forgotten his parents' conjugal harmony and the sweet disputes of childhood games with his sisters, he saw only advantages to his new life. At fifteen he had entered Corda's seminary; in Sonsón, where he finished the baccalaureate, he'd started with the Jesuits with honors and somehow became accustomed to the hard mattress of austerity and the hair shirt of the religious life. Now he loved the hot meals Darlis and Teresa cooked; he found it fascinating to listen to music and watch films with the two women and their children; the children's surprised joy when he taught them anything made him ecstatic, as did their infinite capacity to believe and create and play and dream. Of all that he was experiencing, now it was this that most captivated and exalted him: fatherhood. He saw two girls and a boy growing up and learning to sing, to look, to draw, to act in small domestic dramas, and he noticed their insatiable appetite to know more and more, their tireless capacity to laugh and enjoy themselves. Even their fights amused him, their whims, Juli's bad habit of dominating Jandrito with threats and slaps, or Rosina's whimpering and sulking when she didn't like a meal. He felt as though he'd won the lottery with the three transparent, lively, insatiable children, who spoke frankly and without prejudices on any subject, even about his probable death and his heart.

Rosina, Darlis's daughter, had surprised him one day with that direct, curious question, which she'd asked looking him straight in the eye: "Are you really going to die if they don't change your heart?"

"Yes, so it seems, Rosina. That's what the doctors say," Luis replied.

"And they're waiting for a bad guy to get killed to take out his heart and put it in you?"

Córdoba looked at her, trying to guess where the little girl had got that information. Maybe she had heard Darlis talking to someone, telling some friend about the guest they had in the house where she worked. He tried to modify the information: "Sometimes there are accidents. Someone who crashes their motorcycle, for example, and bangs their head, and won't be able to go on living because their brain is damaged, but their heart still works, and their eyes, and they use those eyes so another person can see."

"Eyes, too? Both eyes? One eye for one blind person and the other eye for another blind person?"

"I don't really know how it works with eyes, but I can find out for you. I guess it would be fairer to give one each to two blind people, wouldn't it?"

He liked the children's merciless and compassionate logic. So they could understand how he was waiting for his replacement heart, he compared his situation to that of those sterile couples who were waiting for a child to adopt. They've made up their minds, they've been declared suitable to be parents, and now they just have to wait for a phone call telling them a baby has been born that could become theirs. Luis put it like that, they were waiting for a child to adopt, like the son Saint Joseph had raised as his own. "That's what the heart is for me: a child they're going to give me." I had told him, as well, that reading the Book of Ezekiel, in chapter 36, I'd found that the Bible also spoke of transplants: "A new heart also will I give you, and a new spirit will I put within you: and I will take away the stony heart out of your flesh and give you a heart of flesh." Luis listened happily to these discoveries of an impenitent reader of the sacred book.

Maybe one distant day, Córdoba thought, the dilemma might be whether to transplant a priest's brain into an injured hit man or the hit man's heart into a priest. That is, if it were equally easy. Luckily, Rosina's mind had moved on to something else – or the same thing, but in a different way – and was concentrating on exchanging the arms and legs of a Black doll, hers, with the arms and legs of a white doll, Julia's.

Córdoba, trying to guess what the little girl was thinking while she played, if she was actually thinking of something and not simply playing at transplanting arms and heads without really knowing why, returned to a thought that began obsessing him once he'd been in the Laureles house for a month: that he had spent almost three decades in his half-century of existence depriving himself of the sweetest sensations of life. That he had chosen to sacrifice many joys and for years that sacrifice had not weighed on him, perhaps hiding behind the dreams of so many films, behind his serene, platonic love for actresses, and behind the authentic (although vicarious) emotion of the opera and other music. But there, in that cool house full of laughter, waiting for a young heart, the heart of a murderer or the luminous heart of a maiden, the suspicion began to spool through his brain that maybe he didn't want someone else's heart, no matter whose, just to go on living as he had before, but also to begin a second different life, lived in a different way, a second opportunity more like this, a normal everyday life with the small annoyances and quarrels and laughter of domestic life, which resembled so many other lives in any part of the world, in ports, mountains, frozen plains, cities, and jungles.

༺

One day, talking with mutual friends, I realized that Córdoba was telling us separately something quite similar. In secret, in private, asking us for silence and begging for prudence, he revealed his intimate thoughts to all his closest friends, pretending to each that they were his sole confidante, when there were several of us all at once. This repeated secret, rehearsed, exposed to the judgment of a witness, was that if he survived the transplant of the heart that must arrive sooner or later, he would hang up his cassock; he would request Rome grant a dispensation through his superiors, and he would marry a woman who (depending on which friend he was telling) was called Bárbara, Beatriz, Laura, Darlis, Lía, Teresa, or Angelina.

He also said that if finally – after thirty years of false or fruitless diets – he really was losing weight, this good lifestyle was not out of fear of death, nor was he doing it so much for his ailing heart or the health of his body, but for the tranquility of his head. He was doing it so that the woman he was thinking of marrying would not be overawed with the excessive, blubbery, imposing vista of his naked mass, which he had spent his whole life ashamed to allow to be seen.

Córdoba also knew that the children, especially the youngest, Jandrito, were still very attached to their father. So much so that sometimes the boy refused to speak for days on end, and when he emerged from his silence, he explained that he just wanted to talk to his daddy and no one else, because only his papá could understand his words. To prove it, when they begged him to speak, he spoke baby talk with invented words. In fact, those episodes of prolonged silence or incoherent babble only ended when his father arrived and the boy received him with shouts and long strings of words, stories, and complex but impeccable sentences, all very clear and joined up with perfect pronunciation and syntax.

After a few hours, or when his father left him in the house after a weekend in the country, at the moment Joaquín began to say goodbye, the child would grab his legs or climb up his neck or invent new games and sudden, urgent questions to prolong the visit. Gordo watched these scenes perplexed and could not understand how the child's insistent pleas – a perfect representation of need and adoration – did not move the steely heart of that father, who a short time earlier had forcibly detached himself from that child and said goodbye with a cold smile, as if his heart were made of stone, and walked away.

Luis could not have seen, however, what Jandrito's father told me years later. That when Joaquín said goodbye, he fled the house as quickly as possible, taking giant steps, tears filling his eyes, and as soon as he reached the corner of the Avenida Jardín, half a block from the house, he fell into a convulsive crying fit and howled in pain, startling passersby and making people come to their balconies and windows to see what sort of madman was shouting like that without having been injured or run over by a car or stabbed by a delinquent. And thus, howling in the street like a wounded deer, he would reach Avenida Bolivariana, hail a taxi to go to the borrowed house of his millionaire lover, and finally, on the way, he would push away the pain and disguise his guilt and his sadness behind a shell of apparent indifference.

There is undoubtedly sweetness and softness when one is accepted into a family; leaving one, however, is always a wrenching experience, especially when there are children and when there is no real reason to distance oneself. One needs enthusiasm to enter one, but a great amount of bravery – sometimes masked as indolence or cynicism – to leave.

∽

Every three or four days, during the week, I would go see Córdoba after saying Mass at the convent of the Adoratrices, which was at six, or after my Bible class at the university, at eight or ten. I preferred to go in the mornings, when Teresa was at the school for children with special needs, teaching them to sing sad songs, when Darlis was busy with tidying and cleaning the house or at the market buying something she needed for lunch, and when the three children were at school, so the house was silent, almost empty, and Luis and I could talk. Even so, we would shut ourselves up in the library so Darlis couldn't hear us, if she hadn't gone out, and there he would tell me in whispers what was happening to him. It wasn't a confession; I never confessed to him, nor he to me – I have always considered it an excess of intimacy to invalidate the sacrament – but what we talked about was almost always a confession, and sometimes more sincere than the frankest and most thought-through confessions.

I can't forget the morning when I found him much more anguished than usual. He was red faced, as if he had a fever, and talked in a way so different from usual that I wonder if he wasn't suffering an episode of delirium or something like that. Maybe his heart wasn't taking enough oxygen to his brain, or maybe it was taking too much.

He began by recounting a dream, as if I, rather than a friend or confidant, were a psychoanalyst. It was a very strange dream in which he was having a party with all his female friends. He told me all their names: Martha Ligia Parra, Sonia Camargo, and Laura Cannas, three Christians; Sara Cohen, Esthercita Levi, and Raquel Lerner, the Jerusalem trio; Ana Acosta, Bárbara Lombana, and Mónica Lombana, the atheist tercet. He told me that in the dream the friends were divided like that, by religion, and all of them were showing him private parts of their bodies that were like testimony of their belonging to Christianity, Judaism, or atheism. The Christians were characterized (don't laugh, he warned me) by having a very bushy mons Venus. It seemed quite natural to him in the dream that they should show him that focal point of attraction, and he said his eyes were drawn toward it. The Jewish women were all bald, and the three of them took off their silk wigs of different colors to show their shaven heads. And the atheists had asymmetrical nipples, as if their breasts were cockeyed: one had one pink nipple and the other coffee-colored; the one beside her had an inverted nipple, like a little hole, the other erect; and the third had one large breast and the other small. He had to inspect and verify the variations. The color of the Christians' pubic hair suddenly changed: one of them turned blond, and another auburn, a coppery red. In the dream he didn't feel sexual attraction but a great curiosity to explore deeply what he really did not know, what he had never seen in person, only in dreams, and in the dream of cinema. He was investigating the women's bodies as if in an anatomy lesson. He studied the atheists' irregular breasts, the Christians' varicolored vulvas, the bald heads of the Jewish women.

He knew, in the dream, that the Jewish women also had a hidden treasure between their legs, consisting of shaved lips as bald as their heads. Their religion didn't allow them to have tattoos, they explained in the dream, and since tattoos weren't permitted, they couldn't show their cucas calvas or their buttocks, where they each had a Star of David tattooed on the left buttock and a menorah, with its nine arms, on the right.

After telling me his erotic dream, he told me of something less symptomatic but much more serious. In recent weeks he was realizing that he was in love with both the women of the house. He was in love with Teresa's soul and Darlis's body, and what he would like most would be to combine the two of them into a single woman. Darlis did not know many things, but since she was very intelligent, that shortcoming could be easily made up. He felt he could educate her and convert her to the religion of opera and film. At the same time, behind the innocent veil, she inspired an irresistible carnal desire.

What made him love Teresa, however, was her classic Pre-Raphaelite beauty, her Greek profile, with the line of the forehead seeming to continue along her nose, her way of being, her integrity facing any test, the sharpness and balance with which she analyzed every film they watched, her capacity to penetrate the deepest emotions and the complex psychology of each character, her precision in seeing technical details of the camera angles or the composition of a frame that even he might miss. Nevertheless Teresa, although extremely beautiful, like a Virgin painted by

Titian, did not inspire physical desire, as no painting or statue of the Virgin Mary ever has. He felt a spiritual love for Teresa, a mystical elevation, respect for her intelligence and her orderly way of living and thinking. He explained that he loved her quiet smile (that way of replacing words with teeth) and the arias she sang, the most spiritual part of her: the sounds that emanated from her lungs, her throat, her mouth. Maybe that's why, he told me, often when she arrived he'd greet her with a few lines from the poet of the Llanos he was most fond of quoting, Eduardo Carranza:

> *Teresa, on whose forehead heaven begins...*
>
> *Child for whom the day rises,*
> *for whom the night awakes and sings...*
>
> *Teresa, for whom I live daydreaming,*
> *for whom with loving hand I write,*
> *for whom the heart exists again.*

Or, hearing her sing, with this variation: *Teresa, in whose mouth the song begins.*

He also liked very much the way she was raising her children, again with few words, in Italian, but all very clear and essential, more concentrated on stimulating what was good than on censuring what she didn't like. He was intrigued by her intense and concentrated way of listening to opera or watching the films he suggested, as well as her brief, apt comments at the end, as laconic as they were precise. She never lacked for words or said too much to note the essential, so he sometimes asked for permission to quote some phrase of hers, unattributed, in his Sunday movie review. She had studied pedagogy in Florence, and this was evident in her every gesture and activity with the children, who were always learning from her without ever stopping their games. Luis felt envious of their childhood and longed to know what would become of them. He imagined Jandrito as a painter or an architect, due to his passion for drawing everything and thinking in images and spaces; he imagined Julia, perhaps, as an actress or director due to her love of playacting and her passion for melodrama. That education also extended to Rosina, who now answered Teresa in Italian as well, and in whom he saw a more rational future as a heart surgeon or engineer.

Darlis, on the other hand, was like Mary Magdalene, pure flesh, and had also been rubbing his feet, and lately his whole body as well. Her scent, especially the smell of her hair, skin, of her perspiration when she massaged him with her strong slender hands, her full lips, the way the skin of her neck and legs shone, it all drove him crazy. He spent his hours anxious, as randy as a teenager whenever she was near; and when he was near Teresa, he was entranced by her beauty, her sensibility, and her intelligence, but at the same time immersed in a sense of peace. Did I remember Plato? Did I remember vulgar, earthly love and sublime love, the two types of human love? Well Darlis was Pandemian and Teresa was Celestial. Maybe it was something that corresponded to the two cerebral hemispheres: with the left he was in love with Darlis, and with the right, Teresa. Or, if love resides in the heart, he loved Teresa with his tranquil auricles and Darlis with his rash ventricles, something like that.

Since he was incapable of containing the current of his thoughts, without even looking at me, he talked unceasingly, going round in circles about the same thing or adding details to his perceptions. Darlis, he explained, had a wild aroma, of a tropical rainforest, full of rare orchids, mosses, and black flowers and woodland plants that were phosphorescent in the night and velvety in sunlight. Her sweat was dew, he said under his breath, sea waves, coral depths, already at the limits of frippery, and the sheen on her breasts was the luminous light of summertime.

Córdoba carried on: "Teresa understands me when I talk of Plato, of the memories with which our souls come into the world. But she also understands me if I say I am not a dualist, that the body and the mind are one and the same, and that whoever loves with just the mind is left halfway down the road, just as one who loves only with the body is condemned to a love that does not last into old age."

Now, however, a problem was arising and intensifying, a problem he'd paid no attention to at first but which was worrying him in those days. The two women were competing for his attention and for his love. After having been close friends and accomplices, more than employer and housekeeper, they began to regard each other with mistrust, with enmity, almost with hatred. They were showing their fangs, growling between clenched teeth, constantly hurling darts at each other and in recent days they'd almost stopped speaking, to avoid quarrels, and exchanged only necessary words. They watched and kept a jealous eye on each other, criticized, without mentioning names, the other's cooking or tidiness in public: a thin sauce in the kitchen, the cleanliness of Luis's bathroom, a plague of aphids on a plant, a dry leaf, a book out of place, a speck of dust, a pair of socks in the wrong drawer. Anything was a good excuse to stab at the other, throw a bucket of cold water, a badly hidden sputter.

Teresa had even hinted that she wanted to fire Darlis, who was very stubborn and only did what she felt like, and Darlis was talking about quitting because she could not abide the absurd whims of her boss, who expected her to juggle and perform miracles. Córdoba was sandwiched into a tight spot trying to calm them both down, to prevent them from doing one crazy thing after another. In recent days, the harmonious home of his first weeks was turning into snarl. "Do you realize," he asked me, "they're fighting over a fat and dying priest who doesn't even sleep with them. Rather than sin with them, I am feeling that my sin is the discord I'm unwillingly sowing between the two of them."

This combat, however, also amused and flattered him. He had always had a certain power of seduction with his students, even with his opera or film friends, but none of those had ever reached the proportions he was experiencing in his new house.

He told me about the conflict with a discreet, worried expression, but when he gave an example, he couldn't help but laugh. He had even forced them to reconcile a couple of times ("I want you two girls to hug each other right now") and praised and reassured each of them privately.

His conclusion took me by surprise: If he survived the operation, he told me, lowering his voice, he wanted to leave the priesthood and marry one of them, first one then the other, or, if possible, both at the same time, to continue living as he was, in the fullness of those two halves who, joined together, represented complete love.

"Now, it turns out that not only do you want to get married, Córdoba," I said to him, "not only do you want to have a family home, be a father to the children of two women, but you want to be a bigamist from the get-go. At this rate, since the heart has four chambers, you'll want four wives, like the Mahometanos."

Córdoba laughed. He said that was almost true, his way of making up for lost time. That he wanted to keep living there, the way he was living, married to both women, one white and one dark, and have white and Black children. He was silent for another moment, and then he looked me in the eye and said: "If Saint Augustine could say to the Lord: 'Make me chaste, but not yet,' allow me to say: 'Jesus, my Lord, I've already been chaste half a century for you. Allow me not to be for what's left of my life.'"

Sometimes his eyes grew moist, and sometimes he laughed strangely, neither cheerfully nor ironically, a deep, operatic laughter as if from another planet, Mephistophelian without being diabolical, with his mouth agape, almost revealing his innards, for I did catch a glimpse, beyond the amalgams of his filled molars, of his palate and, behind his tongue, the uvula, tonsils and, if I'm not mistaken, even his vocal cords vibrating tensely like the strings of a well-tuned guitar.

"I'm not asking you to forgive me, Lelo," he insisted. "I'm not telling you all this in search of absolution, or even agreement or advice. I'm just asking you to listen to me and, if you can, to understand, and if you understand, can you explain to me what is going on?"

"Nothing less than what you ask of me; nothing more . . . hogwash," I answered.

I saw in the gleam in Luis's gaze, in his anxiety tinged with joy, that now, as well as cinema and opera and food, he had discovered two women, that is, two more reasons to go on living. He had started to live his own romantic movie. All this for me, and I think for any human being with the least experience of life, was very clear: he was happy because he had fallen madly in love with two women at the same time, but these things cannot be explained, so I simply recited Lope de Vega's famous poem defining love:

To faint, to dare, to be furious,
rough, tender, generous, elusive,
bold, mortal, dead, alive,
loyal, treacherous, cowardly and spirited:

not to find a heart or rest outside of goodness,
to act bright, sad, humble, haughty,
angry, courageous, fugitive,
sated, offended, suspicious:

turn your face at clear disappointment,
drink poison as if it were soothing liqueur,
forget benefit, love harm:

believe a heaven fits inside of hell,
give your life and soul to disillusionment,
this is what love is; he who has tasted it knows.

O

"I never imagined what looking after someone expecting a heart transplant might be like," Joaquín told me one afternoon. "I know that the night before a transesophageal echocardiograph or a stress test with electrodes or, finally, a catheterization, the feeling is the same as the one you get right before you take your final exams."

And he went on talking, remembering and thinking at the same time: "Without anything actually trembling, it feels like your whole body is trembling, like an internal motor that won't let you rest. You seem to be switched on, plugged in, and you purr like a cat, not with the serene pleasure of cats but with a nervous, electric buzz, like a fridge in the middle of the night. It must be something like the Roman gladiators felt the night before they were to go out into the arena to confront the lions. It's not a sensation of fear, but something above and below fear, something for which I'm not finding the word."

He went on, after a pause: "Except that in this case the beast is your own heart, and the emperor and dignitaries who observe you attentively from the tribune (*Ave, Caesar, morituri te salutant!*) are the cardiologist and the nurses, who watch you and watch machines, sensors, and needles that decide who wins, the beasts or you. You have a lousy night, and at dawn your head aches. You're convinced your blood pressure will be through the roof, and that will do nothing but worsen the prognosis of those tests where they'll tell you whether you can keep holding the reins of your own life or if, from now on, what life you have left will be in the hands of others. Others will decide what you can do, what you can eat and drink, how you must sleep, if you'll stay up late or get up early, which pills you're going to take when you get up, when you go to bed, or at midday. And all because of that damned pump that has almost lost its whole halo of mystery, of nobility. They used to declare you dead as soon as your heart stopped; now, a person can be dead with their heart still beating, or a person can be alive and not have a pulse or breathe, which is what happens when they change a valve in your heart, with your lungs collapsed and your blood circulating around your body in a continuous flow, without beating. The body's most illustrious guest, the most venerated and quoted and heard, the sun for William Harvey and for the pre-Columbian Indigenous people, who knew how to remove it from the chest, still beating, after cutting a slash in the thorax of a young maiden with an obsidian knife, stopped being the sublime organ that brought warmth to the whole body and turned into a simple beast of burden that worked without rest, without complaint, night and day, for more than eighty years, until completing its secret number of beats (because your heartbeats are numbered, Lelo), which in you and me and anyone are approximately two billion, more or less, if it's a long life, or a bit less than half that if it's short, like so many with heart disease. A little while ago I read of eighty-three-year-old identical twins who died on exactly the same day, an hour's distance from each other, both of heart attacks."

I noticed he wanted to explain everything clearly to me, to encourage me to write about how Córdoba was waiting for his transplant, how he had lived through those weeks and months of expectation. He carried on talking, almost without punctuation: "After your final baccalaureate exams, they tell you what careers you can aspire to and which ones you cannot, if you might have what it takes to be a doctor or a physicist, a bricklayer or an electrician. But in heart exams, what is at stake is your whole future, the life you have left. Just as your finals tell you if you've studied hard or not, or if you've wasted your time, in cardiac exams they tell you, halfway through life, if you have lived well or have eaten too much salt or too much fat or too much sugar, if you've exercised enough, how much you've smoked, if you have allowed yourself to be overcome by stress, if your conscience has let you sleep calmly over the last half century or if it has all been a mistake, if you had bad luck in the lottery of viruses or genes, and all this is reflected in your heartbeats. There they are, looking inside and outside your heart, reading the mysterious irregular mountain range of the electrocardiogram, measuring the flimsiness or thickness of your heart's walls, calibrating each of its electrical impulses, its diastoles and contractions and gradients, its capacity to carry blood as far as the farthest neuron in your head and the last nail on your little toe. And it's as if that machine, that tireless mule that is the first to begin to work in your body and the last to stop, reveals the secrets of all that you are, of what you've suffered and savored, of what you've cared for or been careless of, your excess of ambition or lack of goals, if you're willful or timid, the sorrows that upset you and the joys that fill you with energy and hope. The judges can see, on the screen, how it beats, how it regurgitates, how blood flows calmly or turbulently, how it goes to the lungs for oxygen and how it leaves from the left ventricle discharged by the aorta to distribute the oxygen as far as the last corner of the brain, to the penis so it gets erect, to the liver so it secretes bile and nourishes, to the intestines so they move, to the kidneys so they filter, to the heart itself so it never stops pumping, to the neurons so they give us a solid illusion that we have a soul, choice, the sensation of being what we are, the chimera of free will, a vague memory of what we were, an intense anxiety about not knowing what we are or what we are not, and senseless yearnings."

When Luis was still in the Leon XIII Clinic, he shared a room with a young campesino from Carmen de Viboral who had an even more serious cardiac problem than he did and was also waiting for a heart transplant. They gradually became friends because the young man was fascinated with the strange mixture he saw in his roommate. This priest did not resemble any priest he had ever met in his life. He prayed a little, he didn't give sermons, laughed a lot, told nonstop jokes, and almost every day received visits from beautiful women who brought him food, fruit, and ice cream, spoiled him, stroked his hair, rubbed lotion on his neck, declared their admiration and affection, and were always telling him they were sure he was going to get better soon.

"Where do you get so many pretty friends, Father?" he asked him over and over again.

Córdoba simply laughed and explained that they were students from his courses on cinema and opera. Then the young fellow, who was called Albeiro Henao, asked Luis to teach him to understand the appeal of opera, those guys and girls who shrieked with their drawn-out *aaaa*s, *iiii*s, *uuuuu*s . . . When he returned to his village, he said, he would get a lot of girlfriends if he could teach them the wonders of those Italian singers. Luis gradually gave Albeiro a course on the history of opera and played the most famous arias for him, told him the plots, told him the names of the most important composers and librettists, the tenors and sopranos who sang the best notes, and every day the kid enjoyed it more.

They both had to go for short and slow walks in the clinic corridors, holding on to their equipment, which followed along like hanging shadows of parapets on wheels. People made fun of the unlikely pair, the tall, fat man in his fifties, the scrawny boy, as thin as a noodle, with legs so skinny he seemed to be walking on his arteries. And while Gordo exhibited his two swollen birch tree trunks, limping a bit on his flat feet, Albeiro moved his little legs like a pair of trembling and insecure vines.

Due to the ugly legs they both had, their other roommates, also cardiac patients waiting for new hearts, laughed at the inseparable friends and said they weren't waiting for heart transplants, but leg transplants, and they were waiting for the cardiologist from the coast, Alexis Candela, to die so they could aspire to hers. Dr. Candela visited them daily dressed in miniskirts, which they would see on the ceiling in bouts of insomnia and which showed a pair of marvelously toned (Doric? Ionic?) columns that swayed coquettishly as she walked, a stethoscope swinging like a lure between her XL breasts.

Albeiro had been very much impressed, as well, one evening when there was a great commotion in the hallways of the hospital, and the governor of Antioquia, Álvaro Uribe Vélez, surrounded by lackies and bodyguards, arrived in their room. He was short and rigid, like a strict and embittered priest, and the national education minister accompanied him, an elegant, smiling woman, María Emma Mejía. Gordo must have suspected something, though he hadn't been told, because that afternoon, instead of staying in his striped pajamas as usual, he had had a careful shave and put on trousers, shoes, and a clean, freshly pressed shirt that Angelines had brought him from the house at Villa and San Juan.

The governor received from a secretary a small, red, velvet-lined case, took a medal out of it, and pinned it to Córdoba's breast pocket, reading a short speech about the reverend father's virtues and his intrepid efforts in promoting culture in the department. After that, minister Mejía, with more sincere words and shining eyes, presented Córdoba with the doctorate *honoris causa* in communication sciences awarded by the University of Antioquia, recorded on a lustrous parchment in a calligraphy so dense no one was able to decipher it. When both dignitaries had left, a group of friends (mostly women) arrived to celebrate, including me, with two bottles of Catalonian cava. I recall the only commentary Luis made, regarding the abstruse diploma and opaque medal with certain melancholy: "Now I really do think I'm going to die. These attentions only go to those of us who are almost in the grave."

"Then it's better not to have received that prize, Father," Albeiro said with a certain lucid naivete.

And Luis answered: "The thing with honors is there's no way around them. You look bad if you receive them, and much worse if you turn them down. And I would rather look silly than arrogant."

Córdoba had grown very fond of Albeiro, of his daily chats with him, and when they finally let the priest go to Teresa's house, when he said goodbye, he left his roommate five opera records: a Verdi, a Mozart, two Donizettis, and a selection of Spanish zarzuelas. To the surprise of the other patients, they said farewell with a long hug and even, from Luis, a big paternal kiss, an absolute anomaly among Antioqueño men. Albeiro, to top it off, was left weeping and saying that he would never again have a father like Father Luis.

When Córdoba had been in the Laureles house for a few weeks, he heard from Angelines that an organ suitable for Albeiro's slight body had turned up, and he had successfully survived his heart transplant. Ángela herself had visited him when they transferred him to a room after several days in intensive care, and from the joy of his new heart, full of hopes for a renewed life, Albeiro handwrote this letter to his former roommate and teacher:

> *March 27, '96*
> *Hello! Luis: I don't have to ask how you are for I know you are very well.*
>
> *Friend, I have missed you. The operation was a bit tough, why deny it, but we must go forward with this great opportunity. Knowing that you will soon be in the same situation encourages me even more and makes me happy. It would be nice, I hope, for your heart to arrive while I'm still here recovering, and we could see each other, both transplanted, once again back in the same room.*
>
> *I can tell you that this heart I'm trying out is from a young country girl, though they won't tell me from which village. They just told me that it's in the southwest. A poor girl who fell backward down a staircase and lost her brain due to a hemorrhage and was declared brain dead. I feel fine, and I'm breathing better than ever with this new heart to which I know I owe my life from here on out. And do you know what? I feel good, as I'm sure that girl was a very good person.*
>
> *I trust that your heart will also arrive soon so we can have a glass of wine together and listen to the music we like to hear. I'm not going to tell you to come visit me because it's not the time for you to be out and about. But when I can stand up and walk well, I'm going to come see you in your new house,*

which Ángela tells me is very pretty and full of children.
From one who awaits and appreciates and loves you,
Albeiro

Luis found the letter very moving, and he took it out of his pocket to show me when I went to Laureles to visit him that week. That day we talked about a subject we rarely touched on because it concerned us both intimately. Even though he was talking about Albeiro and not me, it was also about us, for it was about the love that exists in friendship, in the camaraderie that develops when two men share a space, a house, a room, an illness, a belief, an adventure.

He said that his shared path with Albeiro, the heart failure, united them as we had been united by religion and our destiny in the priesthood. Albeiro was a simple young man, who had barely a basic education in his village and had many limitations due to his congenital heart problem. Although the lad believed he had learned many lessons from the priest, it was really Córdoba who had learned from the young man, for Albeiro maintained a cheerful and optimistic attitude despite any suffering. Albeiro had inspired in Luis a confidence in the future that he hadn't possessed and made him see how privileged he was to have so many young, bright friends. No one had visited Albeiro, but he was capable of greater happiness than Luis was.

Two days after he showed me the letter, Córdoba found out that there had been a complication with Albeiro's transplant and that the heart of the campesina they had given him had stopped beating. He called me in shock, as if his roommate's death was actually the death of a brother, and he asked me to come over to see him, because in a moment like that, all that occurred to him was to pray.

And I went straight over, and, although the two of us almost never talked about religion – I don't really know how – the conversation drifted into Catholic mysticism. He reminded me that, in his childhood home, there had been an enormous painting of the Sacred Heart of Jesus. It was not a beautiful painting, he said: "More than that, it was a painting like the one Gonzalo Arango described in his chronicle about Cochise Rodríguez, the cyclist. Do you remember? The founder of Nadaism said the ugliest Heart of Jesus was in the living room of Martín Emilio, Colombia's first world champion. That the flash on the chest threatened to burn the whole house down and singe our Lord's hair. But no, Lelo, I swear the bleeding heart in our house was uglier and scarier even than Cochise's. Do you know why?"

I told him I did not, that he'd never told me. Then he said that the painting in his house was a strange image specifically because the heart was not painted; rather it seemed like a real heart. Embossed, in relief, of a material somewhere between cloth and rubber, a dazzling red. Doña Margarita, his mother, who was a very pious woman, kept a pincushion below the painting full of pins with different-colored, round heads. And whenever Gordo committed a misdeed, like telling a little lie or eating a cookie without permission or answering his father or one of his sisters disrespectfully, his mother would take him by the hand to the holy image and oblige him to stick one of those pins into the Sacred Heart of Jesus while she said to him: "Imagine how that sin of yours hurts our Lord's heart. Each time you do something bad, it hurts him, you make him bleed. Stick it in, stick it good and deep so you can feel the pain that He feels." Then the pin would stay there for several days, until finally, after much pleading and penitence, his mother would forgive him and agree to remove the pin.

Albeiro's death had given Luis a stabbing pain in his heart, and he had remembered that small torture from his childhood. Besides, now so much of his memory revolved around stories of hearts that he had read in sacred and profane books.

He reminded me of Saint Teresa of Ávila's vision, which he had reread in *The Life*, which was there in Joaquín's library. He stood up to get it and quickly found what he wanted, which was the episode when she goes into ecstasy and has visions. He read it to me out loud:

> *The Lord chose to give me the following vision. I saw an angel in bodily form standing quite close to me on my left side. Although angels have appeared to me many times, I have rarely seen them in bodily form. Usually I see them without my eyes, like in those visions I was telling you about before.*
>
> *This time, however, God wanted me to see the vision like this. The angel was not large; he was quite small and very beautiful. His face was so lit up by a brilliantly lit flame*

that I thought he must belong to that highest order of angels who are made entirely of fire. He didn't tell me his name, but I know there is a big difference between various angelic realms. I wouldn't know how to explain such things.

I saw that he held a golden spear. The end of the iron tip seemed to be on fire. Then the angel plunged the flaming spear through my heart again and again until it penetrated my innermost core. When he withdrew it, it felt like he was carrying the deepest part of me away with him. He left me utterly consumed with love of God. The pain was so intense that it made me moan. The sweetness this anguish carries with it is so beautiful that I could never wish for it to cease. The soul will not be content with anything less than God.

The pain is spiritual, not physical. Still the body does not fail to share some of it, maybe even a lot of it. The love exchanged between the soul and her God is so sweet that I beg him in his goodness to give a taste of it to anyone who thinks I might be lying.

On the days the vision appeared to me, I wandered around in a kind of stupor for many hours. I didn't want to look at anything or say anything. All I wanted was to embrace my pain and hold it close. This was greater glory than any created thing could ever offer me.

"That's the famous transverberation of mystics," I told Luis, "one of the most glorious experiences of our beloved Catholic religion, which is reserved for only a few, almost always women, who feel their heart or their body pierced by a supernatural fire."

There I recalled that saint I'd been told so much about in La Linda seminary, Saint Catherine of Siena, who had devoted herself to curing the sick during the most contagious plague, when no one dared to help them except her. I told Luis two episodes, first the one a sister in the monastery, Sor Andrea, who had a gangrenous and festering sore on her breast, and no other nun would get near her out of fear of contagion and the unbearable stench that emanated from the wound. Only Catherine would take care of her, and there came a day when the stigmata swelled up with so much pus that Saint Catherine, to punish herself for the disgust she felt while draining the abscess, collected all the pus in a ladle and, after crossing herself, drank it down to the last drop, and – as she herself told Fray Tommaso Caffarini – never in her life had she tasted such a sweet and delicious drink.

Here Córdoba grimaced with disgust and said a German word that I did not understand: *Liebfraumilch*. Then he seemed to reconsider, turned serious, and said something paradoxical: "It's strange the beauty they could find in revulsion, ugliness, and sacrifice in medieval times. It's no longer like that, though it sometimes occurs in movies that I don't like."

I didn't want to say anything for or against a particular era, so I immediately moved on to another episode, which, given the circumstances, I thought might involve Luis in a way that was closer to his current experience.

This was a vision Saint Catherine had in the Santo Domingo church of her own convent, when, leaning on one of the octagonal pillars, she went into ecstasy and saw Jesus approaching her wrapped in a golden cloud. He opened up her left side, extracted her heart with his hand, and kept it for several days until, when she was leaning on the same octagonal pillar, Jesus returned surrounded by light, again opened her chest, and put inside not her own heart, but rather his, while telling her, in perfect Latin: "Here you are, my dearest daughter, and since the other day I extracted your heart, I now donate my own to you. From now on you'll always live for it."

"No more nor less than a mystical transplant," smiled Córdoba, not without a bit of skepticism that I did not want to contradict. Then, as if remembering why we were together, slightly ashamed of his memories and mine, he said, "Let's pray to Saint Catherine and Saint Teresa of Ávila and the Sacred Heart of Jesus for Albeiro's soul, which is pure and deserves the reward of eternal life." And we repeated a thousand and one times, "Sacred Heart of Jesus, I trust in thee, Sacred Heart of Jesus, I trust in thee, Sacred Heart of Jesus, I trust in thee," until we lost our voices and felt dizzy with that monotonous, sedating mantra.

Once in the dead of night, when everyone in the house was sleeping soundly, everyone except Córdoba, who was tossing and turning and trying to sleep on his right side, the telephone began to ring.

Luis didn't know whether to get out of bed, because he was very aware of how long it would take him to sit up, put on his slippers, and walk to the phone. When he was just about sitting on the edge of the bed, the ringing stopped. The house went back into silence before any lights had been switched on, but a few seconds later the telephone began to ring again. Luis heard Teresa's door open, noticed a strip of light beneath his, and heard footsteps rushing into the living room and the harmonious and sleepy voice of his friend, perhaps confused by her dreams, answering in Italian: "Pronto," but she immediately corrected herself: "Hello, hello."

Luis walked slowly toward the door, opened it, and saw Teresa nodding emphatically and assuring the caller, more than once, that everything was ready. When she hung up, Gordo was in front of her and looking at her anxiously. Teresa looked at him with wide eyes and then with a hopeful and apprehensive smile: "It seems there is a donor in Santa Rosa de Osos. He's five foot eight, has your blood type, and at this moment an ambulance is bringing him to Medellín. They say he's almost the same size as you and probably brain dead. We have to pack your bag. You have to fast and have everything ready by dawn. As soon as it's confirmed they'll let us know, in two or three hours, and we'll have to get a taxi to the cardiovascular clinic at five or six. They'll operate today."

Córdoba was stunned, mute. He felt like a silver coin was spinning in the air. He heard his own heart inside his chest, that old friend, that placid ox that had worked for half a century in his body, which in a few hours would be thrown in the garbage wrapped in gauze and disposable gloves. He knew there was not much to think about because the decision had been made months before. He felt like praying right there, out loud, but he restrained himself. Instead, he said: "Will you help me? I have the suitcase ready and very little to pack."

At that moment Darlis appeared in her nightgown. She looked like a Black fairy dressed in white. She offered to help Don Luis so Doña Teresa could go back to sleep.

"Apart from the children, nobody's going to be able to sleep here," said Teresa. "Let's all three go."

Luis wondered if he should have a quick shower and get dressed. The women thought it a good idea, then Teresa immediately changed her mind.

"I don't think we're going to have to leave before four or five. I think it would be better if you get back into bed and stay still. Relax. We'll pack in the meantime. Your shower can wait. Also, you have to remember that it's no ordinary shower; it's the special shower they explained to us, with the antiseptic soap they prescribed at the clinic that's in the drawer."

They did what Teresa said. They went into Luis's room, and he got back into bed, under the covers, with his arms behind his neck. Darlis turned a crank to raise the head of the bed. She smiled as she turned the handle while whispering a sort of mantra: "Inside a house, a room; inside a room, a bed; inside a bed, a body; inside a body, a heart; inside a heart, a hunch. Inside the hunch . . . only Don Luis knows."

Luis looked at the ceiling and listened to Darlis. Teresa, at the same time, was going back and forth and enumerating things: one pair of pajamas, a bathrobe, slippers, medications, toothpaste, toothbrush, electric razor, deodorant, lotion, a couple of clean shirts, a pair of trousers, two pairs of socks, the black shoes. One sweater and a blanket in case it's cold. She couldn't think what else to pack. Was she missing something? Maybe a book? What would Luis like to read? Córdoba said any good long novel would be enough to distract him or keep him company if he couldn't sleep. Darlis went to the library where Joaquín's books were and picked three thick tomes at random, murmuring, "Inside the book, a story." The books turned out to be *War and Peace*, *The Magic Mountain*, and *Les Misérables*. Gordo asked that they pack *The Magic Mountain* since it had to do with illness and a sanatorium. Teresa and Darlis brought two stools in from the kitchen and sat beside Luis's bed, one on each side. The watched him staring at the ceiling and waited for him to speak.

"It's strange, I feel quite peaceful," he said without looking at either of them. "I am very grateful to both of you. I have spent just nine and a half weeks in this house, a little over two months, but to me it feels like much longer. They've been very happy weeks, good and calm ones. So serene that I was starting to think my heart was getting better, that there was no longer a need for a transplant or anything, that all I needed was your kindness and this heart would fix itself. Now it turns out they still need to take it out, exchange it for another. It's very strange, now that I feel healthy."

The two women looked at him, their smiles almost devout. Darlis leaned over to take his hand. Córdoba kept talking.

"Sometimes I feel like crying and saying I don't want to be transplanted anymore, I'd rather die with my own heart. But I don't know. It's not sensible." He paused for a long while and then changed the subject. "In any case, before I leave, I'd like to wake the children to say goodbye. I don't want them waking up tomorrow and asking where I am and knowing I left without saying goodbye."

"But you'll be coming back, Luis; or we'll bring them to the clinic in a few days, when you're feeling better," Teresa said.

"One never knows . . . I want to say goodbye. If you prefer me not to wake them, I'll give them each a little kiss and that'll be that. Rosina as well, of course. You two can tell them I said goodbye without waking them."

"Whatever you want, Luis," Teresa said.

The dog next door began to bark nonstop, as if he heard a strange noise or as if he could sense the tension in the air. Darlis carried the suitcase to the front door so everything would be ready. She asked who would accompany Don Luis to the clinic; she offered to go, but Teresa said it would be better if she looked after the children and got them off to school. Darlis nodded obediently, but didn't look convinced and sought support with a glance toward Luis, but he was still staring at the ceiling. Only half an hour had passed since the phone call. It was an impatient, uncomfortable waiting, in which none of the three knew what to do with the time. Darlis offered to give him one last foot and leg massage so he would arrive at the hospital relaxed and not swollen. Without awaiting a reply she ran to her room for the oils and to the laundry room for a clean towel. She came back in her uniform with her face washed. Teresa said she was going to lie down in her room, though she wouldn't be able to sleep until they called back from the hospital with the exact time of the operation. She reminded Luis that he couldn't eat or drink anything, not even water, and that he had to wash thoroughly, with the special soap they'd prescribed.

Darlis turned off the light in the room and left the bathroom door ajar so just the faint light reflected from the mirror shone in. Luis would actually have preferred to pray or talk than receive a massage, but he didn't say anything, and when Darlis began to rub his first little toe with her long, soft fingers, he thought it was Darlis who'd been right, not him. It was better not to speak, not to think, but just to receive. Feel contact. Fingers spoke better than mouths. Everything in the room had something unreal about it, the light, the air, the walls, Darlis's fingers.

He quietly prayed the Magnificat, over and over again, his mother's favorite prayer: *Magnificat anima mea Dominum, et excultavit spiritus meus in Deo salutari meo, quia respexit humilitatem ancillae suae. Ecce enim ex hoc beatam me dicent omnes generationes, quia fecit mihi magna qui potens est, et sanctum nomen ejus, et misericordia ejus a progenie in progenies...*

When he had repeated it several times, Darlis said: "I don't understand any of what you're saying, Don Luis, but it sounds pretty."

"It's a prayer in Latin, Darlis. I'll tell you how my mamá used to say it: *My soul proclaims the greatness of the Lord, my spirit rejoices in God my Savior, for he has looked with favor on his lowly servant. From this day all generations shall call me blessed: the Almighty has done great things for me, and holy is his Name. He has mercy on those who fear him in every generation. He has shown the strength of his arm, he has scattered the proud of their conceit. He has cast down the mighty from their thrones and has lifted up the lowly. He has filled the hungry with good things, and the rich he has sent away empty. He has come to the help of his servant Israel, for he has remembered his promise of mercy, the promise he made to our fathers, to Abraham and all his children forever. Glory to the Father and to the Son and to the Holy Spirit, as it was in the beginning, is now, and will be forever. Amen.* If you want, I can teach it to you. It's called the Magnificat, and it's what María said to her cousin Saint Isabel when she discovered just by hearing her voice that the Virgin was pregnant."

"Yes, please, teach it to me, Don Luis."

And while Darlis was massaging his feet and legs, they repeated the Magnificat line by line many times. Luis didn't have to think to say the lines, so as he spoke, his mind went elsewhere. He was thinking of his open chest, from which they would remove his heart and install someone else's. What would they do with the wreck of his? He would have to ask if they simply threw it in the garbage. Like a cancer, like a recently extirpated malignant tumor. When Darlis could almost repeat the Magnificat on her own, complete and by heart, they were startled by the sound of the telephone ringing and Teresa's barefoot steps running to the living room from her bedroom.

"Oh well, that's okay," he heard Teresa say. "I'll tell Luis. Yes, of course, these things happen."

Then she hung up and walked over to Luis's room, where Gordo and Darlis looked at her expectantly. The expression on Teresa's face was not encouraging.

"It seems the donor had a crisis in the ambulance, just after they left Santa Rosa. 'The dead man died,' they told me. The nurses did what they could to revive him, but they couldn't. When they reached the cardiovascular unit, too much time had passed; they had to rule him out, it was too late; hearts degrade very quickly. It doesn't work anymore and can't be transplanted. They said they're very sorry. False alarm, wishful thinking."

Teresa came over to the bed and embraced Luis. After a moment's hesitation, she leaned one ear against his chest, sadly, but lifted it almost immediately when she heard some rapid beating she hadn't wanted to hear. Luis sighed heavily. He went back to staring at the ceiling. After a while, he said: "Maybe it's better this way. I won the lottery and then they took it away. It means I'm not meant to be rich."

The women went back to their rooms and tried to sleep. Córdoba closed his eyes in the half darkness. At dawn, with the first light of day, the three of them met in the kitchen and shared some hot coffee. Almost in unison they all admitted they hadn't been able to sleep. From the yard came the sound of birds singing and their song gave all three the bit of spirit they were lacking.

P

I, Lelo-Cura, as my closest friends call me, learned to distrust happiness from a series of tragic coincidences that happened to my friend Córdoba. To distrust luck, which seems designed to betray us at the moment we most need it. He was not like me. Impervious to misfortune and tragedies, he continued to have Panglossian optimism, always trusting in the future, in spite of everything. I think his hope and his faith were stronger than mine; his was a faith like Job's, immune to the deepest sorrows and hardships, to the trials God sends us.

I'll never forget the homily he gave at his sister Emilia's funeral. She was his youngest sister, the second to die, the only one he had left. It was at El Poblado church, and his message consisted, basically, in saying that life was a gift, and gifts should be enjoyed intensely. He came to say something more drastic, which almost scandalized me, being a more traditional priest in those days, because it was something very different from what we'd learned in the seminary. He said, emphatically, and raising his voice, that "the only mortal sin we could commit," and he stressed it twice, "the only one, is unhappiness."

And all this in spite of the fact that the best moments of his life, the happiest, most significant, and most exciting, had always come in tandem with the opposite: bad luck, loss, and pain. It was as if God wanted to send him a message, it seemed to me, always the same message: Don't trust a happy life, don't think you're on this earth to enjoy it, because things are constantly happening to remind you that this is no longer the Garden of Eden but rather a vale of tears, a godforsaken planet, a purgatory, a place where joy, when it arrives, is always tinged with sadness and horror. As one of his favorite arias in *The Magic Flute* put it, "Weil Rosen stets bei Dornen sein," in other words, "Roses always come with thorns." Nevertheless, Luis always, always, seemed to see and feel only the petals and forget or ignore the thorns, even if he noticed his fingers bleeding.

What I want to say, in any case, has to do with my mistrust of happiness and not Córdoba's stubborn hope for it. People pay lip service to that word, but it seems to me happiness is a sensation that, perhaps for all my experiences in a long life, and even more for my friend Luis's tragic experiences, I have come to consider overvalued.

There was a moment (before the last, final one that gave me the most unhappiness) when Luis's happiness was suddenly stained with sorrow. It happened due to a series of unjust, unfortunate, and almost inevitable events. And it coincided almost exactly with the days in which the second and final film he directed, *El niño invisible*, was about to premiere, with much excitement and some hope of success.

The film was going to be shown to the public on the Friday, in El Subterráneo, the art cinema in the plaza of El Poblado, and we had hired Pacho, a waiter, bought a case of champagne, and rented tall glasses to toast with at the end of the projection. What follows is what happened on the Tuesday, Wednesday, and Thursday before the premiere.

Luis's favorite niece, Margarita, Lina's daughter, even more favored after losing her mother, was obviously invited to the premiere, first on the list, and had confirmed her attendance for Friday at the Subterráneo. The previous year Margarita had married Carlos Esteban Botero, a classmate of hers at EAFIT University, and everything promised a happy and fruitful marriage. In fact, the day Gordo called to invite her, she told her uncle that they'd just had a positive pregnancy test that week and that she and her husband were expecting their first child. They were leaving for the Cocha lagoon in the south to celebrate but were going to make sure they'd be back Friday morning to accompany him at the premiere that evening.

Margarita's father-in-law, that is, Carlos Esteban's father, was the owner of a cargo transport company, Raúl Botero Rodríguez. The Boteros had inherited a fleet of trucks, which still exists, Botero Soto, specialists in distributing goods all over Colombia. As well as his thriving transport company, Raúl Botero, along with other Antioqueño nature lovers, had colonized a lost paradise in the north of the country, the Ayapel swamp. That swamp, near the Caribbean Sea, was fed by the waters of the deltas of several rivers, among them the Nechí and the Cauca, which formed the Caño Barro, and a little farther down flowed into the Magdalena. It was a wonderful place to practice the sports he and his friends were passionate about: hunting, fishing, and bird-watching. At that time Ayapel was a hidden and inaccessible area, where before the arrival of the Paisa settlers there was just a small community of descendants of runaway slaves who had blended with the last remnants of a native tribe. There were no roads into Ayapel, and the swamp was accessible only by water, along the rivers and a labyrinth of channels, or a short time later, by air, when they built some sandstone runways on a few islands where the settlers had built their cottages.

Raúl Botero had his cottage and airstrip up there. He got his pilot's license and bought a Cessna 185, the Jeep of light aircraft. On the tail of the Cessna he had painted an image of the Chilean cartoon character Condorito, since Raúl was tall and skinny, with a large nose and Condorito was his nickname. His plane was also nicknamed Condorito. Sometimes Raúl, tired of working in the office, would take a day off in the middle of the week and head to Olaya Herrera Airport, in the middle of the Medellín valley, to fly up to his Ayapel cottage first thing in the morning. His Cessna flew over the peaks of the central range of the Andes and in two hours reached the flatlands of the north coast; he landed on his runway in Ayapel, shot ducks, fished for beardfish, took a siesta in a hammock in the shade of some horse chestnuts, and returned to Medellín with the day's last light, before they closed the airport at six, loaded with fresh fish and game for dinner.

The Monday before the premiere, under a starry sky, Raúl Botero called Artemio, his assistant at the airport, to get Condorito ready at dawn. Artemio was a magician at preparing small planes to perfection, filling their gas tanks, checking the oil levels, and adjusting whatever had to be adjusted; he was one of the most seasoned and reliable mechanics around. On Tuesday, Raúl arrived very early at the airport and was pleased to see his Cessna gleaming in the first rays of sun, made ready by Artemio, barefoot, wearing his grease-stained khaki overalls. When Raúl was about to climb aboard the light aircraft, Artemio said to his boss, pointing at a man sitting on a toolbox near the hangar: "Don Raúl, there's a man over there, a friend of Don Payo Mejía, who's going up north. He asked me if you might be able to take him. You can drop him off in Ayapel, and then he'll figure out how to get to where he's going."

Margarita's father-in-law did not hesitate to invite the man aboard. The trip was uneventful, but when they were approaching Ayapel, above the coastal plains of Córdoba, the guest proposed that they fly a loop over an area near the swamp where, he said, they were building a lot of airstrips, barely hidden in the forest. The pilot agreed, and the only thing that seemed strange was that, while they flew over those runways he'd never seen, the man pulled out a camera and took photos of the tiny airports. His only comment was that they were secret, clandestine runways. The illustration of Condorito on the tail of Raúl Botero's Cessna was quite visible from land; it was almost like he shouting his own name and displaying his own portrait.

A short time later they landed on the Botero family runway, and the man hired a canoe with a motor to get to terra firma and carry on to Montería. At least that's what he said. Don Raúl had a good day's fishing, but not much hunting, because there weren't many ducks around at that time of year, took a deep and restorative siesta, and landed back in Medellín by half past five. As soon as he reached the hangar where he kept the Cessna, and even before he'd switched off Condorito's single engine, Artemio approached the window and told him there were a couple guys asking after him who had been hanging around since three in the afternoon. He added that he didn't like the faces or attitudes of these men at all, that Raúl should be careful. "He who has nothing to hide has nothing to fear," Raúl answered, and walked off to see what the two men needed.

They interrogated him. First of all they wanted to know who exactly he had traveled with to Ayapel. Don Raúl answered with the truth, that he didn't know precisely, and all he remembered was that, when he introduced himself, the man had identified himself as Quique, which meant he was probably called Enrique. That was all he knew about him. Then they asked why he and his companion had not flown directly to Ayapel but instead had been flying over a hacienda belonging to a friend of theirs, or specifically, their boss. That worried Don Raúl a bit more, and he replied they'd simply flown a circle over the plains to admire the scenery, since that Quique had told him it was his first time in the area and he wanted to see a bit more. That information did not convince the two guys, who told him, raising their voices now, not to play dumb – did he think they looked like idiots? At this point Don Raúl, who couldn't stand rudeness, excused himself, saying he wasn't going to keep talking because his fish would go bad. He picked up his cooler and left, climbing somewhat nervously into his BMW 323, in which he drove away, according to Artemio, at such a speed it looked like a plane about to take off. The two guys left on the same motorcycle they'd arrived on, sparks flying from their eyes and curse words from their mouths.

That night, Raúl's wife Victoria made delicious baked fish. She followed a recipe Raúl loved, the Prince Alberto, which had a sauce of raisins, tomatoes, onions, and capers. Despite the fresh fish and the fact that the dish had come out better than ever, Don Raúl did not even want to taste it. He had long telephone conversations with his best friends in Ayapel, the Escobars of the Escobar Foundation, the Londoños or Eduardoño, Bernardo and Augusto Ochoa, the Ángels of Caribú . . . They told him that the airstrips he'd overflown were clandestine and used by the mafia to send drugs up to the United States. They told him the names of the owners, who had the same surnames as the rich families of Medellín: Escobar, Londoño, Ángel, Ochoa. But they immediately clarified that those were other Escobars, other Ochoas, Londoños, and Ángels. It was not a good thing at all what had happened, they thought, and he should be careful. It would be best not to go up to the place in Ayapel for a while, to allow those people to come to their senses and wait for the waters to calm.

Early on Wednesday, before eight, after having his usual breakfast of black coffee with arepas and cream cheese, Raúl Botero drove his car out of the garage and set off for work, taking his usual route. He left his house near the country club, took Avenida El Poblado, turned left toward the Aguacatala roundabout, after which he would take the northern highway almost as far as Calle Barranquilla, near Antioquia University, where the head office of his family's transport business was located. But when he reached the Aguacatala roundabout, a Toyota pickup truck blocked his way, and two motorcycles pulled up on either side, with two men on each. The four men got off the motorbikes, with high caliber weapons, and shot him in the driver's seat. He was hit by more than fifteen bullets all over, and before they left, they made sure that at least one bullet lodged in his brain and another in his heart. When a taxi driver took pity on him and stopped next to his BMW, the windshield and windows destroyed by bullets, it took no more than a couple seconds to see that there was no sense in taking the body to any hospital. Margarita's father-in-law was dead.

Córdoba and I heard the news of the murder over the radio, and the misfortune left us feeling miserable. Luis tried to get in touch with Margarita, but it was impossible. What he already knew was confirmed: she was in the south of Colombia, near Pasto, at the Cocha Lagoon, with Carlos Esteban, her husband, son of Don Raúl. Raúl's brothers, through the company, had contacts all over the country, but there was no way to communicate with Carlos Esteban to give him the bad news. Carlos and Margarita were with some friends from university, the Vásquez Lunas, who were coffee growers in Nariño, and with Juancho Maya and others, but they had gone to an isolated farm near the border with Ecuador where there was no phone. All of Wednesday passed without anyone being able to give them the bad news, which Carlos Esteban and Margarita only came to hear on Thursday morning, not from a friendly voice, but from a brief crime story at the end of the television news. Finally Carlos was able to speak with his mother and his Botero uncles, find out more details, and also learn, between tears and wails, that the funeral Mass and burial were scheduled for that very afternoon at five in the chapel of San Ignacio College, where Raúl had gone to high school.

Since Carlos Esteban knew his father was a member of the Colombian Air Patrol, he called one of his dad's pilot friends, who, out of solidarity and their own grief over the news about Don Raúl, organized a light aircraft to fly from Bogotá to Pasto to pick him up and get him to Medellín in time for the Mass and burial. The Pasto airport is one of the most dangerous in the world because planes not only have to land on a narrow high plain surrounded by mountain peaks, but must also confront a treacherous tailwind as they land, the precise opposite of what's recommended. The plane that was sent to take them to Medellín made two failed attempts to land but finally managed it.

The conversations during that trip were recorded on a black box that, some months later, Luis got access to listen to, in an incomparable outburst of masochism, at least I thought so. The most serious error happened at the beginning, and the worst advice came from the haste and anxiety to arrive. First there was a discussion about weight, since the pilot hadn't known that Don

Raúl's son was also with his wife. The pilot told Carlos that the plane could really only carry two people. After talking about it for a while, the pilot agreed to take Margarita, on the condition that all the couple's luggage stayed on the ground. Once in the air, a short time after taking off, the pilot told Carlos Esteban that he would need to make a pit stop, whether in Popayán, Cali, or Pereira, to fill up with gasoline, as they had just barely enough, especially now that the weight was greater than expected. Here there was a second discussion. Margarita insisted they should stop and fill the tank; Carlos Esteban said that if they made that stopover, they'd be late for the funeral; the pilot insisted it was advisable, but he washed his hands of the matter and said that if he carried on, he did so because it was Don Raúl's son, but Carlos was running a risk and would be held responsible for the decision. Córdoba told me they didn't speak again for almost an hour, that the pilot simply reported in to all the airports they flew over and sometimes mentioned in a murmur how many liters of fuel they had left. Carlos Esteban, who had piloted the Condorito many times, also knew how to fly.

After flying over Alto de Minas and beginning the descent toward Caldas, the pilot lowered the speed to save gasoline and muttered that he thought they'd be able to make it. Margarita dared to speak a few times to encourage her two heroic pilots. Shortly after that, the aircraft reported to the Olaya Herrera Airport and said they were flying over the town of Caldas. They requested absolute priority to land as they were flying with very little reserve fuel. Priority was assigned. It was almost half past four.

At that time, Luis and I had just arrived at the San Ignacio College chapel. Although there was more than half an hour until the service began, the church was already crammed with people. A short time later, the hearse arrived from the Betancur Funeral Home and parked in front of the atrium. Córdoba greeted Don Jaime Mora, Margarita's father, who had come sorrowfully to say farewell to his son-in-law's father. Don Jaime told Luis that Margarita was coming from Pasto and about to arrive. Twenty minutes later we were surprised by murmurs and strange movements among the mourners. Evidently something very serious had just happened, although we didn't know what.

Shortly after passing over Sabaneta, the plane coughed. Amateur pilots know the old adage: "When a plane coughs, look for a place to fall." The propeller kept spinning for another half a minute or so, perhaps on the scent of gasoline. It coughed again, the engine cut out, the pilot swore, Margarita invoked the Virgin, and her husband told the pilot they had no choice but to coast and find a clearing in the valley to attempt an emergency landing. The light aircraft coasted well, with stability. Carlos Esteban and the pilot maintained an admirable level of calm, and only Margarita's voice can be heard once in a while, murmuring an Ave Maria. The pilot said to tighten their seat belts.

Carlos Esteban pointed to a clearing and some soccer fields near the river, before Envigado. The pilot steered the plane, which was still gliding well, toward the spot. They were descending slowly, aiming for the clearing, which looked flat and empty. Suddenly

Carlos Esteban shouted: "Look out! Hydro cables!" "Fucking wires!" the pilot managed to say. "Blessed be the fruit of thy . . ." Margarita's voice can be heard muttering. At that moment, those who saw it from land say the pilot must have pulled up the wheel, because the plane's nose lifted and was about to clear the electricity cables. And it did, but the tail did not. The blow against the back of the aircraft made it swing around backward like a bell and then do a nosedive at the foot of cables that carried extremely high-voltage power from the hydroelectric plant at Guatapé. All three died instantly from the crash, though the plane didn't catch fire since it didn't have a single drop of fuel. That same day, just before midnight, Córdoba had to collect his niece's body from the Envigado morgue. She had bruises and fractures all over her body, he said, but her beautiful face was intact. Her linked hands covered her womb, as if she were trying to protect it. The funeral at San Ignacio College had been interrupted. The next day, instead of a hearse, three long black vans arrived not at the chapel but at the college's arena. Before three coffins, Mass was said for the three deceased people. Father, son, daughter-in-law, and a plan for another life that was never mentioned.

That's how I learned to distrust happiness, from the evidence God sent to my friend Córdoba. He has sent me some clues as well, but I'm not going to talk about those.

Luis's second film, *El niño invisible*, the only fictional one he made, did not premiere that Friday or ever. A few of his friends saw it on small screens, but Córdoba said it didn't matter, that after all, the movie wasn't that good and he'd just made it to amuse himself. He never told me, but I think he always associated it with his niece's death and lost affection for it – even forgot about it.

Joaquín, in this respect, does not agree with me. For him Luis's film is a splendid piece on friendship and loss, as it happens in the mind of a child. The game of invisibility turns into something perfectly tangible when the child protagonist's friend is killed in an accident. Maybe Joaquín's right; Córdoba, I have sometimes thought, has been nothing other than my secret invisible friend.

※

Making those ten minutes of *The Invisible Child*, in any case, affected Luis deeply: It turned him into a more compassionate critic. Five days of filming with a small crew, working with a limited budget, equipment, and a finite quantity of film stock, gave him an understanding of the vast difference between the dreamt-of film and the concrete realities of directing movies.

The result was not what he had wanted, but rather what he could manage to do, and all in spite of the fact that two friends, Víctor Gaviria and Sergio Cabrera, who went on to become more-than-competent filmmakers, had guided him through the whole process of filming and editing, Cabrera as a cameraman and Víctor as an assistant director. Weeks and months of sleepless nights, difficulties in finding funding, limitations and errors of actors and crew – all this made him humbler and more compassionate toward those who made films.

Q

After the twarted heart donation, one afternoon when Darlis had persuaded Luis to let her give him a massage, she interrupted her humming and began to recite the Magnificat. *My soul proclaims the greatness of the Lord, my spirit rejoices in God my Saver, for he has looked with favor on his lowly servant. From this day all generations shall call me blessed...* Luis, who had his head facing the wall because he felt embarrassed looking in her direction while she was touching him, began to turn his head to congratulate her.

"Very good, Darlis! I see you haven't forgotten the Magnificat. I think it's 'savior' instead of 'saver,' even though in the original Latin..."

And since Darlis was repeating the prayer like a mantra while she rubbed Gordo's swollen legs, he – almost without realizing – started to fall asleep and have visions. As he slept, he could still hear Darlis's mellifluous voice. He heard, or dreamt that he heard, her say: "I thought that all priests smelled bad, but you smell good, Luis."

When he heard that, he woke up, or thought he woke up. He half-opened his eyes, and they saw what he had never expected to see. First he saw Darlis's warm face, as if in a close-up on screen. But when he looked down from her expressive eyes to her clear, open smile, down her long aristocratic neck, her straight, prominent collar bone, he saw that the woman's skin and nudity carried on down her body, and before his thoughts could catch up with him, a pair of harmonious breasts appeared, like twin gazelles, with their dark nipples erect, and a smooth and glossy midriff, a perfectly elliptical belly button, a pubis obscured by dark curls, and firm thighs so well toned they seemed painted. Córdoba's eyes did not blink, the firm camera of his fantasy did not tremble, but his respiration and heartbeat grew suddenly agitated, and his throat could only emit a long sigh that sounded almost like a moan of pain: "Aaaahhhh!" His own fantasy had jolted him awake. Had he really seen what he had seen? Córdoba, when he told me, did not clearly define whether it had been a vision or reality.

Darlis carried on with her back rub, a little harder now, and continued repeating the same words she'd now said hundreds of times: *My soul proclaims the greatness of the Lord, my spirit rejoices in God my Savior, for he has looked with favor on his lowly servant. From this day all generations shall call me blessed . . .* Then she repeated a single part: *for he has looked with favor on his lowly servant, for he has looked with favor on his lowly servant, for he has looked with favor on his lowly servant.*

Córdoba told me that he'd fallen back into a sort of doze or stupor. He closed his eyes, and he could see Darlis completely naked. In his dream or in this material world, he swore again he did not know which, he whispered: "I . . . cannot . . . believe . . . it." The four words were separated by air that went in and out of his mouth, each more tremulous than the last. He sighed again and managed to add, slowly: "The most beautiful sight my eyes have seen in my whole life."

Darlis stopped praying and stroked his head with infinite tenderness as she said: "The other day you said, Don Luis, when you were going to go to the hospital for the transplant, that you thought your heart was improving. I think the same. I think you're better every day. And I think the only thing you need to get completely better is a little happiness."

"Happiness? If that's all I need, I am happy just looking at you, Darlis. I don't think I've ever, even when I was ordained in Germany, been so happy." All this he said with his eyes shut, tightly shut and with the blindfold on that Darlis put over his face to calm him.

"Do you know what we call it in Cereté when a man gets excited, when you can see from the center of a man's body that he is excited? We say that he's happy. And I want you to be happy in that way too."

Córdoba opened his eyes for a moment under the blindfold and tried to be aware of all the sensations and reactions of his body. Then he closed them again and said: "Yes, Darlis, in that sense I am happy as well. I even think I'm very happy."

Luis felt an indomitable sleepiness. It was as if he'd been given a sedative, as if he were falling into that pit that announces the beginning of a general anesthetic. The girl, in that intermediate state between wakefulness and sleep, took Gordo's hand, his big, thick fingers, and without letting go of it, turned slowly and put in front of Córdoba's eyes a round buttocks, of a perfection and firmness that he neither expected nor had ever seen, even in the most beautiful films that lived in his memory. *For he has looked with favor on his lowly servant, for he has looked with favor on his lowly servant.* And Darlis's slender, long hand, her agile and smooth fingers, made Gordo's hand rest on her waist and slip down toward that pair of big, ripe, perfect fruits. Córdoba touched them very gently and again said, in his dream, he thought, "I cannot believe it. This I can believe even less than what I just saw."

His whole body, he told me, began to tremble as if he were having a feverish attack. Darlis, seeing him like that, like a fragile branch, asked: "Are you afraid?"

Córdoba was awake again when he answered: "Maybe I am," and he took a breath and sighed. "I'm afraid of what the present, when it is the past, will do to me in the future."

Darlis told him: "The past does not exist, and the future is now. All is present."

Córdoba stopped trembling and began to sit up in the bed, behind Darlis, who was still standing with her back to him, and both his hands began to caress slowly, very slowly, as if afraid of breaking a spell or a fragile glass object, Darlis's back, the nape of her neck, her shoulders, buttocks, and her legs, up and down, again and again, enraptured by the softness and wonder of that sleek, healthy skin, by the firmness of that flesh, by the perfection of the shapes of that instrument whose music he longed for. While he caressed her, without really knowing why, he began to say the names of all the women who came into his mind and with whom, perhaps, he had slept many times in his imagination: Romy, Brigitte, Shirley, Marilyn, María, Ingrid,

Nina, Greta, Zuca, Nastassja . . . all the divas of his musical and cinematographic life.

Darlis then turned around to face him. *For he has looked with favor on his lowly servant, for he has looked with favor on his lowly servant,* and Córdoba stretched out a hand to touch her left breast, but at that same moment, he felt a stabbing pain in his heart, then a sort of cold sweat that burst from his forehead, pain in both arms, in his shoulder, and he had to drop back onto the bed. The frame or the springs or the legs, everything shook as if about to collapse.

Not knowing whether he had lost consciousness or woken up, Córdoba took off the blindfold, looked in terror at Darlis's white uniform, her hands smeared with oil, her smile, heard her mantra again, which she had not stopped saying, *for he has looked with favor on his lowly servant, for he has looked with favor on his lowly servant.*

"You want to kill me, don't you, Darlis? I'm going to die during one of these. My heart is racing a thousand beats a minute. I think it's too much for me." He smiled for an instant and added: "Well, I'd die happy, that's for sure."

Darlis paid him no mind. She laughed merrily and then dared to say, changing her smile into a sudden serious expression, "Don Luis, forgive me for asking you such a personal question, but are you a virgin?"

There was a strange, deep, unfathomable silence. The sound of an empty church at dawn, Córdoba told me. A bird trilled on the patio, perhaps calling for its mate, an unanswered song. Luis's baritone voice came sincere and thick from his chest. It seemed like the recitative from a sacred opera. "More virginal than the Virgin Mary, Dar," he answered at last, and he did not say it with a long sigh, more like with his last breath. What had been a strain, or a sadness, had turned into a simple sentence.

Darlis again smiled tenderly, almost joyfully. She told the priest to stay like that, face up, to breathe deeply, slowly. Then she smeared lots of oil on her hands and began to rub his chest with all the energy she had, up and down, up and down; then in concentric circles; and even, at the end, with loud pats, holding her hands open and concave so they made a sort of rhythmic, profound, serene drumbeat.

"Don Luis, I am not only not going to let you die. I'm going to cure you. Close your eyes. Close your eyes and leave it to me. Take a deep breath, inhale ... exhale. Inhale ... exhale. Breathe at exactly the rhythm I tell you."

And at the same time as she tapped a drumbeat on his chest, above the place that for Darlis was the body's sun, and guided his breath to her chosen rhythm, she told him to think only about breathing, not to think about her or her hands or his body, much less about his heart beating disorderedly in his chest, to simply think about the air entering and leaving his body.

Then she started whispering things for him to think about, or rather to picture in his mind: a lake hidden in the mountains with steep crags behind it; an old, worn wooden table; an empty hut in the tropical lowlands, with a palm-thatch roof and dirt floor and a stool in the middle as the only piece of furniture; a blaze in the town square, set with dry ferns, in which a whole pig is roasting; a river so wide you can't see the other bank; a flock of pelicans flying in formation; the pink of flamingos in a lagoon; a perfect spiderweb against the light at daybreak; a pair of old black shoes, like in the Tuerto López poem he recited for them; an invention that nobody has invented yet to cure hearts, made from the hearts of sacred cows in India...

And so, little by little, Córdoba's heart began to recover its normal rhythm, its jogging out of step, its large-hearted heavy beats, without him opening his eyes or remembering more than vaguely the wonders he had just seen and touched in his half-dream, and the woman noticed that the man's happiness was no longer so notorious, that his body recovered its languid and exhausted normal shape, and Luis went back again from being a man to being the priest he had been for almost his whole life, since he'd entered the seminary at fifteen years old, until he came, almost dying, into Teresa and Joaquín and Darlis and the children's yellow-and-green house in Laureles.

R

While it lasted, I enjoyed the routine of visiting Luis in his new neighborhood. On the one hand, I witnessed the transformations of my friend on the threshold of a probable death. On the other, Laureles, the neighborhood, was pretty, full of trees, circular avenues, and nice houses, which were spacious without being enormous. Midweek mornings, the house would be empty apart from Darlis, who worked in the kitchen singing and came in occasionally to offer us fruit or coffee or some kind of juice we liked, lulo or guanabana, mango or sapote. As the weeks went by, especially toward the end, I noticed that Córdoba treated her with more affection and familiarity. He was totally entranced by her, he said so himself, and Darlis noticed. She was sure of her charm and her power over him.

I admit that I was almost jealous when I saw how cheerful Córdoba was in that house. We, I thought, had also lived in harmony together, in our peculiar celibate marriage of companionable priests. At year's end and Easter, I brought my nieces so he could practice what he always said was the biggest sacrifice the priesthood imposed on us: the renunciation of fatherhood. He loved children; he related to them perfectly; he treated them as if they were grown-ups, and children were grateful for that without having to say it. He showed them wonderful films, played music he knew they'd like, taught them to draw, to write rhyming verses, to solve riddles, read them stories, told them silly jokes, always the same ones. "Some oranges fell to the ground around the trunk of an orange tree during a windstorm. And the oranges that stayed on the branches started to make fun of and laugh at the fallen oranges. Then the fallen ones shouted up from the ground at those on the tree: 'You're so immature!'" He always laughed the hardest at his corny jokes.

At Laureles, he suggested plays they could perform and filmed them with a video camera Teresa had. Then they'd watch the results and he'd give them acting tips. He had always done that with my nieces, who he also gave music theory classes, but Córdoba seemed more at home in his new house than he had in ours at Villa and San Juan. I complained: "You seem so well here that I think you're never going to want to come back to live with me, with us."

He concealed his agreement.

"Not at all. When they get that house without stairs we've been looking for in Conquistadores, I'll be back with you guys. This is just a temporary solution."

"You look happier here. And I don't think it's just because of the kids. Now there are two women in your life."

Córdoba smiled and chided me. He told me not to be jealous.

"One day you'll have to try a massage, Lelo," he said. "The Church has forced us to give up something necessary, fundamental. Remember when Mary Magdalene washed our Lord's feet and anointed them with perfume? There is no condemnation of this kindness in the Gospel, this show of affection, this courtesy. Remember she wet them with her tears, and she dried them with her hair, and then she perfumed them, right?"

"Well, it's not certain it was Mary Magdalene. The Gospel of Luke says it was a sinful woman but does not give her name. And then John speaks of another woman who anointed Jesus with perfume, but not on his feet, on his head. The fact is there are no condemnations. Jesus thanks her and forgives her sins. And in the Apocrypha, Saint Thomas, if I'm remembering correctly, goes further because he said Jesus slept leaning on Mary Magdelene's chest, and they kissed, and the apostles got as jealous as you now say I am."

"You know much more about the Gospels than I do, Lel. But it was something like that. If I'm not mistaken, she receives our Lord very well in her own house. Was it not Lazarus's, before he resuscitated him? And Mary of Bethany sat at his feet, entranced, and listened to him preach. Well, Darlis treats me like that in this house. She sits at my feet and anoints them with perfumed oils. Once, you won't believe it, she leaned over me for a long time, her nose millimeters from mine, and she was breathing my breath and I hers. We were swallowing each other's air, and you can't imagine how beautiful that can be. We didn't kiss, no, we simply breathed for a long time, without stopping, as if I were her air and she my inspiration. Darlis had a daughter out of wedlock, it's true, the lovely Rosina, but for me she is not a sinner. She's a victim of men, of the millions of men on this continent who abandon their children. And in spite of everything, she anoints my feet and washes them and dries them, not with her hair, because hers is short, but with a towel. Do you think she's doing wrong, or that I'm doing wrong? She tells me I don't smell like a priest. That priests in general smell rancid. You don't know how good I felt when she told me that, and how good it feels when she anoints and rubs and dries me. I feel good because I feel loved."

"No, I don't think there's anything wrong with that," I told him. "As long as it doesn't go much further."

"Ay, Lelo. And what would be further? Don't you see that I'm dying and I want to extract a little bit of pleasure from the time left to me?"

"We're all dying every day, Córdoba. Maybe we should all be devoting ourselves to pleasure due to the simple fact that we're going to die. And that is not what we've been taught. And what have we been taught, then? That we should suffer. It's a dilemma that neither you nor I can resolve. You yourself must have noticed that whenever you've taken great pleasure, when you're on the point of being happy, you have always paid for it with suffering, with a fall."

"It might have been like that, but it doesn't have to be. I'm tired of suffering, Lelo. And do you know what? If I manage to survive the transplant, if I am saved, I'm going to leave the priesthood and get married. I think I already told you, but now that we're on the subject, I'll reiterate and confirm it. I've decided."

"Get married? And to whom, if one might know?" I asked after a moment of feigned stupor, because I knew his answer.

"To Darlis, to Teresa, whoever. To the first woman who walks past my door and says yes. Don't think a fat sick man with no money has a lot to choose from. But you don't know how marvelous this life is. I never noticed that true happiness is a family, living in a family. The Church forbids us from experiencing a family precisely because they know there's nothing as wonderful as this, nothing as strong, nothing that creates such close bonds, such firm habits, such solid attachments. It's not like this for rabbis; Jewish people don't even have monks; the Orthodox Church doesn't force these sacrifices on their priests; protestant pastors can marry if they like, never mind the ayatollahs, with several wives. Meals together, games, bedtime, the sounds of waking up, warm breakfasts, saying goodbye for a few hours, the daily returns. You don't know. The only one I don't understand is the one who left, Joaquín. Who could think of giving this life up? That guy is mad, stark raving mad. But I'm grateful to him for unintentionally ceding his place as father and husband to me. It was something very important that I needed to experience."

S

My nieces from Bogotá came for Easter that year, and Córdoba invented a "Festival of Children's Cinema," for them as much for the children he was now living with. He had put on one before, years ago, with the people who ran Subterráneo, the only art-house cinema in Medellín. Despite its success, it was the first and last children's film festival in our city. And without Luis, and with the perpetual platforms nowadays, I don't think anyone is going to do anything like that again, because they're no longer creating and educating an audience for the future of movies in cinemas. It's one of those pleasures that seem to be on its way to extinction: darkness, silence, the wonderful expectation in a room full of people seeing the same story at the same time and reacting to it in different ways.

Luis spoke to Pocholo and other friends and got the reels and permissions he wanted. Every day during Holy Week in the courtyard of the Laureles house, on a big screen I brought over and with Córdoba's old projector, twelve children were able to watch the ten films that Luis had chosen for them. He showed two movies a day with a half-hour break for a drink and snack. He gave an introduction, and each child received a handout with the film's credits. Teresa made a little marquee to invite her children's friends and the neighbors. I still have a list of the movies Córdoba showed them:

Au revoir les enfants, by Louis Malle, with Gaspard Manesse
The Jungle Book, by Disney
L'enfant sauvage, by François Truffaut, with the director himself in the leading role
Paper Moon, by Peter Bogdanovich, with Ryan O'Neal and Tatum O'Neal
The Crimson Pirate, by Robert Siodmak, with Burt Lancaster
The Princess Bride, by Rob Reiner, with Mandy Patinkin
The Navigator, by Buster Keaton
O meu pé de laranga lima, by Aurélio Teixeira
La guerre des boutons, by Yves Robert
Modern Times, by Charles Chaplin

As a bonus, on Easter Sunday, he played an opera for them: *The Magic Flute*, in Ingmar Bergman's cinematic version. Also in this case, Luis translated the script from German, and the children watched what was happening with fascination, without really knowing whether the Queen of the Night was good or bad, because after all, if she was bad, she was also the one who sang the most impressive arias.

Julia was terrified by the aria when the Queen of the Night enters her daughter's room and hands her a dagger with which she orders her to kill her father, Sarastro. She thought if her mother told her she had to kill Joaquín, she would not be able to obey her. Luis translated the most important bits, and there was a slightly sadistic gleam in his eye watching the terror on the face of a nine-year-old girl. The most beautiful aria, musically, but the most terrible in its death command, sung by the Queen of the Night, goes like this:

Der Hölle Rache kocht in meinem Herzen,
Tod und Verzweiflung flammet um mich her!
Fühlt nicht durch dich Sarastro Todesschmerzen,
So bist du meine Tochter nimmermehr!
Verstoßen sei auf ewig, verlassen sei auf ewig,
Zertrümmert sei'n auf ewig alle Bande der Natur.
Wenn nicht durch dich Sarastro wird erblassen!
Hört! Hört! Hört! Rachegötter, hört der Mutter Schwur!

And Luis, in his baritone voice, translated:

Hell's vengeance boils in my heart,
Death and despair blaze about me!
If Sarastro doesn't feel the pain of death through you,
Then you will not be my daughter anymore:

Disowned be you forever,
Abandoned be you forever,
Destroyed be forever

All the bonds of nature.
If not through you Sarastro will turn pale!
Hear, gods of revenge, hear the mother's oath!

⁓⋆

At the end of that week, inundated with children, perhaps the most cheerful and crowded ever in Laureles, with no Easter processions but lots of movies and music, Darlis dared to say something to Luis for which she had to overcome her twenty-nine years of shyness and ancestral sayings à la "man proposes, woman disposes."

"You love being a father . . . in a family," she said. "If you want, I can offer you Rosina so you can help me raise and educate her. I am very simple and barely finished high school, but with you we could both learn many beautiful things. Lots of things like we learned this week. Would you accept us? Adopt her; or better yet, adopt us both. Say yes, don't be scared. Didn't you tell us that the heart you're waiting for is like when a couple is waiting for a baby to adopt? Make the most of it and adopt three things at once: a heart, Rosina, and me."

T

The man was born in Minas Gerais, Brazil, but he had specialized in several centers for thoracic surgery around the world (Toronto, Cleveland), and he seemed to have all the titles and diplomas of a great cardiovascular surgeon. He was forty-eight years old, two years younger than Luis. Gradually, since he also had the knack for selling himself, he had become a sort of worldwide celebrity. He had appeared on lists of important personalities in *Life* magazine and was considered one of the great Latin American heart surgeons. He'd done internships and residencies in universities and clinics in the United States, Canada, England, and France. When he invited his colleague and friend, Dr. Villegas, founder of the Medellín cardiovascular clinic and Colombian transplant pioneer, to watch him operate in Curitiba, Dr. Villegas did not hesitate. In Curitiba they firmed up a visit from the Brazilian doctor to the Medellín clinic so the doctors there could watch him operate and learn from him, since our city had a long list of patients with dilated cardiomyopathy awaiting transplants. There was plenty of raw material for his experiment.

They were anxious to receive an eminent surgeon who could perhaps teach them something new. The doctor had visited Harvard, no less, a few months earlier, where he had demonstrated his new surgical technique. Handsome and charismatic, he liked to appear at his press conferences with a piece of myocardium floating in formaldehyde in a glass jar. It was a wedge from a left ventricle wall that he had cut out of one of his patients. The piece of muscle looked like a tiny shield. His name, Randas Batista, sometimes appeared alongside that of the other great Latin American surgeon, the Argentine René Favaloro, a true medical humanist who had revolutionized the procedures of the coronary bypass.

The "Batista procedure" was quite risky and audacious but was based on physiology and physics. According to Leplace's law, "the greater the radius of a vessel, the greater the tension on the wall to withstand the internal fluid pressure." Following this law, Batista proposed reducing the stress on the left ventricle walls (which is what provokes the heart to dilate), simply by reducing the radius of the ventricle itself. His procedure to achieve this appeared simple: he cut out a section of the ventricle to normalize the ejection fraction, that is, the relation between the volume of the ventricle and the quantity of blood expelled. At the same time, he returned the heart to its most efficient shape, less spherical and more elliptical, which by the elemental laws of physics also diminished the effort of the cardiac muscle.

The surgeon's imperturbable physical and rhetorical self-assurance, his competence in outlining the laws of physics he based his theories on, added to his capacity for seduction, meant his operation became fashionable in the mid-nineties. Since the Medellín cardiovascular clinic was one of the most prestigious in Hispanic America, one of the places that performed the most heart transplants in the whole continent, Dr. Batista was flattered to do a public demonstration of his procedure there, before his most notable Colombian colleagues. From here he would return to his native Brazil, where there was an abundance of patients who had dilated cardiopathy after having suffered Chagas disease without any treatment. One of the most common side effects of that illness endemic among the Black and Indigenous populations of Brazil was the dilation of the heart, and it was among them that he had practiced and perfected his procedure, many of them surviving for some time. How many and for how long? That information was not available to the public. Batista said that, after two years, 60 percent of those he'd operated on survived. Other sources said only 15 percent, but Batista was unfazed and maintained those numbers were slanders invented by his detractors.

For the Medellín demonstration they chose seven patients who were on the waiting list for a heart transplant. Of course, they did not force them to submit to this trial, but they suggested it gently and cautiously, well wrapped in hopeful and encouraging words. Dr. Casanova called Luis one morning, May 13, Our Lady of Fatima's feast day, and told him he had some very good news.

"One of the world's most famous surgeons, Dr. Randas Batista, who has been doing demonstrations in Harvard and Cleveland, is coming to Medellín. Since we have not had success in finding a heart compatible with your size and blood type, Father, this procedure seems to us to be your best option, given the gravity of your heart failure. Dr. Batista informs us that a relatively young person with dilated cardiomyopathy is the ideal type of patient for his surgery, PLV, and therefore we want to enthusiastically recommend it to you. You would be in the hands of one of the best surgeons in the world."

Córdoba, obviously, did not know what lay behind those letters, and even if he'd wanted to ask, he couldn't bring himself to, for he wasn't quite sure whether Dr. Casanova had said BLB, PLB, PLP, or what exactly. Even if it had been clarified, however, the words partial left ventriculectomy would not have been much use to him. Luis repeated to himself, in silence, that old aphorism of Jardiel Poncela's that goes: "Medicine is the art of accompanying Greek and Latin words to the grave." Not knowing what to say, he asked for a couple days to think about it. Dr. Casanova told him not to worry, that he had a whole week to think it over, since the celebrated Dr. Batista would not arrive in Medellín until the nineteenth. In any case, he told him before hanging up, if he had been chosen as one of the few who could benefit from this surgery, he should see this as a privilege and an opportunity.

Luis, I can see him now, did not drag his slippered feet, but moved with some agility, something unusual for him, and went to the kitchen, where he found Darlis sitting at the white marble table, drinking a milky coffee.

"That coffee smells delicious, Darlis."

"Shall I make you one, Father?"

"If it's not too much trouble... but black, please. And don't call me Father, please call me Luis."

"OK, I'll do that right now, then, Luis."

In less than five minutes the coffee was bubbling above the blue flames of the gas stove. Face to face, in silence, they gazed at each other with serene smiles while sipping their coffee. Finally, Gordo told the young woman about the conversation he'd just had with Dr. Casanova. Darlis shook her head from side to side, skeptically, and she measured her words carefully as she replied.

"I think it's better if they do those experiments on sheep or goats or pigs, but not on you. I can see you are now much better than when you arrived. If there was something you were missing, it was affection, and we are curing you here with love."

"That might be true, Darlis, but it's not scientific. We tend to think the heart is like the soul, which can be cured with peace, caresses, and words, but the heart is not the soul; it's a pump, or rather a mechanism. It's the workhorse of the body and does not stop night or day, beginning to beat inside the mother's womb, when a person is the size of a baby finger or smaller. The first part of us to live and the last to stop living."

"It might not be scientific, but I can see it, I can touch it: your body is better, and if you could touch it, you would say your heart is much better too. You're thinner, you walk better, breathe better. You don't even remember the fat, slow gentleman who came into this house five months ago smelling of hospital and sacristy, but I do. You're a new man, Luis. And the heart is not a machine, don't say that. Your noble heart has responded with love since you arrived here. Listen to your heart, Luis, and believe it. There's something we say a lot in Cereté: 'The brain is a beguiler. The heart is true.'"

"I admit I feel better, Darlis. You're right about that. Better in spirit, in mind, and in what many of us say is the heart. More than that, I feel content in ways I haven't felt for many years. And I'm going to tell you something very important..."

At that moment, as if to give more solemnity to what he was about to say, Luis stood up and leaned his hands on the edge of the table before pronouncing, very slowly and looking Darlis in the eye: "If the operation goes well, I'm going to leave the priesthood, adopt Rosina, and adopt you too. Or rather, I'll marry you. If you'll have me, of course." He finished, looking at the floor, surprised and embarrassed by what he'd just said.

Darlis was not expecting this abrupt and untimely finale. Córdoba had not planned it beforehand; it was just something that came out at that moment, he told me a few hours later. "It came out of there," he said, "that part I'm not going to mention now because it would be ridiculous. Maybe my fear of the operation dictated it." As for Darlis, Luis told me that he could see her blushing up to her earlobes. After a moment of exalted happiness and a wide smile, a doubt struck her, and she asked brusquely and with an uncertain voice: "And are you going to say the same thing to Doña Teresa, that if you don't die, you'll marry her?"

Luis smiled and stood pensively for a moment. Then he said, speaking slowly as if underlining every word: "If I could, I would, Darlis. If marriage to two people were allowed, I'd marry both of you, the same day, one on either side, in the same church. But that is not permissible, nor practical, nor practicable. I have thought a lot about it, and if I have to choose, or rather, since I have to choose, I choose you. I choose you. And Rosina. I'm even going to ask Teresa to be matron of honor at our wedding, after the operation."

Córdoba stopped. He felt like he was living in a movie script, more like a soap opera with a happy ending in which the tall white man marries the dark-skinned, poor maid. He suddenly felt sad and ridiculous. If his life were a movie, he thought, it was a very bad one, and he hated bad films. If this were a script, at that very moment he would tell the screenwriter it was absolutely necessary for the priest to die on the operating table. He then abruptly told Darlis: "But let's not make these melodramatic scenes. First I'm going to accept the operation with that trailblazing Brazilian doctor, and then, when I get out of the clinic, we'll tell Teresa and everyone what we plan to do, without any fuss. Whatever the case, the first step is this operation with that Dr. Batista. It's decided. He'll operate on me."

"Well, I think, Luis, if you have that operation, we won't ever get married. You told me they're going to take out a piece of your heart... Well, know and understand that I believe the piece of your heart they're going to remove is precisely the part where you have me. I don't know why I think that, and it's silly, but I do. If at least it was a transplant, a whole heart, maybe I could accept, but taking a slice of it as if it were a mango, I don't like that. A heart shouldn't be divided or shared. We better get married before they take that piece out, and then at least I'll stay in your conscience. Let's swear here, before God, with these walls as witnesses, and then later we'll see if we can get married more seriously when you come out of the operation. Surely Don Lelo will marry us, with or without the bishop's permission."

At that moment, Córdoba remembers the scene in the second act of *Lucia di Lammermoor* in which Lucia and Edgardo marry, without a wedding, and swear eternal love to each other. He says yes to Darlis, they'll do that, but he'd like to bring some music to celebrate the marriage with her. In that opera, a couple marries in the same way she has suggested because the man has to undertake a risky voyage out of the country to wage a life-or-death battle. If Darlis approves, they could play a segment of that opera in her room, and he could marry her there.

Córdoba told me that he went to the library for the tape recorder and returned to Darlis's room with her after finding the part of the opera on the cassette that he wanted them to listen to together, to marry before God. There was nobody else in the house. Teresa was at school, the children in school, the birds in the yard, and the tortoise Flash buried in some corner. They didn't close the door; they lay down on Darlis's bed. Darlis began to scratch Luis's back from top to bottom with her nails, and from the speakers came the voice of a man, Edgardo, who said, according to Luis's translation: *M'odi, e trema,* hear me and tremble, *sulla tomba che rinserra il tradito genitore,* over the tomb where my betrayed father lies, *al tuo sangre eterna guerra io giurai nel mio furore,* in my rage

I swore to wage eternal war on your kin. And Lucia can only manage to say *Ah!* Edgardo goes on: *Ma ti vidi... e in cor mi nacque altro affetto, e l'ira tacque.* But I saw you, and another emotion stirred my heart, and anger fled. *Pur quel voto non è infrancto... io potrei, si potrei compirlo ancor!* But that vow is not broken. I could well fulfill it yet! Lucia tries to calm him: Come, calm your anger. Control yourself. Is my suffering not enough? Do you want me to die of fright? Banish all other feelings except love from your heart; a nobler, holier vow than any other is pure love, ah, only love. Yield, yield to me, yield to love. But Edgardo insists: But that vow is not broken, and I could well fulfill it yet! He says it over and over again: *Io potrei compirlo ancor!* Suddenly, before he leaves, he asks her to marry him: *Qui di sposa eterna fede, qui mi giura al Cielo innante. Dio ci ascolta, Dio ci vede... tempio ed ara è un core amante.* That is, he sings: Here, pledge yourself eternally, before heaven, to be my bride. God hears us, God sees us. Church and altar is a loving heart. And he puts a ring on Lucia's finger, saying: *al tuo fato unisco il mio, son tuo sposo.* In other words: To your destiny I link mine, I am your betrothed. Then Lucia takes off one of her rings and places it on Edgardo's finger, saying: *E tuo son io.* And I yours. Then they both sing: *Ah! Soltanto il nostro foco spegnerà di morte il gel!* Ah! Only icy death can quench our passion. Then he says they must part and Lucia exclaims: *Oh, parola a me funesta! Il mio cor con te ne viene,* which means: Oh, how I dread those words! My heart goes with you. And Edgardo tells her: *Il mio cor con te qui resta.* My heart stays here with you. And then comes the aria of farewell, which is what I want you to listen to most carefully, Darlis, but don't stop rubbing my back, go on, go on. First Lucia sings, and she says:

Varranno a te sull'aure	*On the breeze will come to you*
i miei sospiri ardente,	*my ardent sighs,*
udrai nel mar che mormona	*you will hear in the murmuring sea*
l'eco de' miei lamenti ...	*the echo of my laments.*
Pensando ch'io di gemiti	*When you think of me*
Mi pasco e di dolor.	*living on tears and grief*
Spargi un'amara lagrima	*then shed a bitter tear*
su questo pegno allor,	*on this ring!*
ah, su questo pegno allor!	*Ah, on this ring!*

And then Eduardo repeats exactly what she sang, like an echo: *Varranno a te sull'aure* ... And, at the end, they sing it together before saying their final farewell. Against Lucia's wishes, Edgardo leaves on a ship, sails away from Scotland for France. Lucia does not know if he'll return. Nor does he. I'm not going to tell you, Darlis, if he comes back or not. That will be discovered later. In any case, our destiny, whatever destiny we might have, we must face with valor, with love and with valor, because that is how life is. Maybe opera is an exaggeration of life, a dramatic hyperbole, but it's not a lie. The human heart and our understanding can be slow on the uptake. That's why we need to exaggerate to understand. That's why the hyperbole that is opera exists.

⁓☙

Joaquín went to visit him on Monday, three days before the operation, at dusk. From outside, he could hear music playing in the house. He recognized its beauty, but didn't like what it seemed to be announcing: They were listening to Mozart's Requiem. When Darlis opened the door, he saw Teresa and the three children crowded around Luis, looking at a book with portraits and notes about Mozart while the music came solemnly and ritually from the speakers of the living room stereo.

Luis was telling them that this absolute musical genius was only four foot nine, and in spite of having only lived thirty-five years, ten months, and nine days, he had left such marvelous works as *The Magic Flute*, which they'd seen at the film festival, and the one they were listening to, the Requiem, which Mozart wrote in the last year of his life and left unfinished. He told them that Mozart had rehearsed parts of the Requiem with his friends when he was weak and bedridden, barely able to sit up. He was singing the contralto part, but when he reached a segment called "Lacrimosa," which they would hear, he had begun to cry so much they had to interrupt the rehearsal. Mozart had told them then that he could not bear the sadness anymore, for he had the taste of death on his tongue, and even though weeping was always singing in his mouth, he no longer felt able to continue singing as he used to, and he would soon fall silent forever, for he knew he was dying.

The boy, Jandrito, seeing Joaquín, walked away from Córdoba's sad talk and went over to hug his father, then began to repeat the composer's endless name, which after hearing for the first time he'd learned by heart: Johannes Chrysostomus Wolfgagnus Theophilus Mozart. Johannes Chrysostomus for his saint day; Wolfgangus for his grandfather; Theophilus, which means "loved by the gods" in Greek; and his surname, Mozart.

Julia also approached her father at that point to inform Joaquín that Mozart had changed the last part of his name, translating it into Latin, because it sounded more musical: instead of Theophilus, Amadeus. "Both names mean the same thing, Papi, in case you didn't know: he who loves God." But she said that in their house they didn't call him by that pretty name, but called him *Wolfgangerl*. And both children laughed and repeated the name over and over again: *Wolfgangerl, Wolfgangerl, Wolfgangerl.*

Córdoba called everyone's attention to ask them to listen to the part where a very ill Mozart had started to cry: "Listen, children, here comes the Lacrimosa. It's sad, but very beautiful. Let's listen in silence. One, two, three—"

They all fell silent. Teresa and Luis even closed their eyes. Darlis and Rosina were standing a little apart. None of the children moved, but they watched the adults with a mixture of fear and surprise, which made them giggle nervously. When the piece was over, Luis read them something a Mexican poet had written about the musical genius they'd been listening to:

> *Mozart's current had the full measure of the sea and, like it, justifies the world. Against collapse and against the chaos that we are, he opens the way in concentric waves for the pleasure of perfection, the absolute enjoyment of incomparable beauty that requires no languages or spaces. His delicate effort speaks of everything to everyone. He enters the world and makes it resonate light. Music speaks through Mozart and in Mozart: our only way to listen to the flow and sound of time.*

When Luis finished reading, Darlis wanted to know why the composer had died so young.

"What did he have? Was he also heart sick?"

"Some think he was poisoned," Luis answered. "But I don't believe it. No matter how much Salieri and some Masons hated him, their wrath did not go that far. Besides, he had many afflictions since his childhood: chicken pox, dental abscesses, various pains, fevers, and infections. Medicine at that time was not exactly scientific: he was treated with filthy concoctions made of toads' eyes and ground worms, or with leeches. In those days the best idea was to not consult doctors and let nature take its course."

"Medicine in Mozart's day was as effective as prayers," Joaquín said.

Luis, as if he hadn't heard this, went on to say that according to the consensus of the most serious doctors he had read, Mozart's final illness was neither cardiac nor pulmonary, but an infection or kidney failure. Some say, however, that since he had rheumatic fevers, his death might have been caused by heart failure originated in the throat infections and tonsillitis he suffered so many times in his life. In any case, as he saw it, Mozart died of his times, for having been born in 1756. A century and a half later, almost certainly, he would have lived to write many more sonatas, concerti, and symphonies, which is what one regrets, those years he did not have. Whatever the case, in his short life, he had produced the most beautiful, joyful music in existence, according to Córdoba. Full of depth, but also of humor and levity, of the joy of living. Without avoiding the serious moments either, he conjures a sadness so full of beauty it overcomes the suffering with a depth impossible to define in words.

At that moment, the children came running back in from the yard, shouting and chasing each other, saying that the tortoise had won a race against the plush bunny rabbit. Luis knew how to win their attention back again.

"Do you know what Mozart said to go to sleep every night?"
"No idea," said Julia.

"A prayer," said Rosina.

"What?" asked Jandrito, always the most direct.

"He said this, which doesn't mean anything, but made him laugh and calmed him down: *oraña figata fa, marina gamina fa*. Let's see if you can repeat it with me: *oraña figata fa, marina gamina fa, oraña figata fa, marina gamina fa*."

And the children repeated the phrase over and over again, laughing with Luis, before returning to the courtyard and their games.

Watching all of that, Joaquín thought that Luis was a much better father than he himself was. He taught them things both funny and interesting; he knew how to reach them with a blend of games and teaching, and children had fun with him, without getting bored or fed up. The spirit of Mozart seduced Luis, fascinated him, because they were similar: they were cheerful, hard working, creative, in love with life as an invaluable gift that had to be harnessed with action and joy, delighting in every minute as if it were the first or the last, with as much enthusiasm as possible, even if approaching the last difficulty or the last medical bet on life. On his deathbed, Mozart's light grace still produced beauty, without heaviness or drama.

What Córdoba did not know at that moment, maybe, was that, just as eighteenth-century medicine had contributed more to Mozart's death than to his health, the ultra-scientific medicine of the twentieth century also led more often to defeat than to victory. Mozart and Luis trusted medicine and science too much and walked calmly and optimistically to their own abattoir.

U

I am in a ramshackle and noisy bus on my way to Marinilla. The driver is playing reggaeton at full volume and driving like a madman. If I survive, in an hour I should reach the town. A few times Córdoba and I, with his friends Esthercita and Sara, visited this town during Semana Santa for a festival of sacred music. We stayed in a modest but clean hotel and went to eat rabbit with fines herbes and mussels in white wine at a hole-in-the-wall restaurant run by a Belgian. Luis scraped our plates, but the bread and dessert we left unfinished. We were in good spirits. He told us about the music we were going to hear, and at some point we realized that the whole restaurant was hushed, listening to his every word with more devotion than they would a sermon in Sunday Mass.

Now I'm going to Marinilla for a less joyful, culinary, or musical reason. Joaquín says he needs to discover, by whatever means necessary, Luis's clinical history. At the clinic they told him the only person authorized by Father Córdoba to access that history was me. I didn't know, or else I'd forgotten. What did Luis's medical details or the evolution of his illness matter? Why is it important to know how exactly he died, so long ago, when I've been carrying around his absence for years? Well, I'm doing it for Joaquín. I'm doing it for the sake of these notes, which I've grown fond of.

The cardiovascular clinic is in Robledo, in Medellín. It has a melancholy entrance, a beautiful bamboo tunnel, a passageway like those who have been brought back from death say they've seen, the same tunnel I saw with Córdoba when I accompanied him there the eve of his operation, on May 22, 1996, the day of Julia's tenth birthday. When he said goodbye to her, the little girl told him: "Luis, we're not going to celebrate my birthday today. My mamá says it'll be better to have a party when you come back from the clinic with your new heart. I'll be waiting for you here so we can celebrate both things."

Luis answered happily that he would bring a pint of vanilla ice cream so they could eat it together. Then he gave her a big kiss on the forehead and got into the car with me. His eyes were shining, and he couldn't speak. From the door, the two women, the Italian and the Colombian, waved goodbye. They couldn't speak either and were trying to hide their emotions. Rosina and Jandrito hid behind their mother's legs and moved the fingers of one hand, playing piano in the air.

When I got to the clinic's archive in Marinilla, a charmless shed with metal shelves that rose to the roof, full of file folders – a perfect fire hazard. Endless papers about people with heart disease, many of them dead, some already transplanted, some saved, operated on, declared terminally ill, maybe one or two still alive. The private dramas of thousands and thousands of people who struggled against death and won the battle or lost the war. In this clinic they performed the first heart transplant in Colombia, in 1985, the third in Latin America. First they had to change the legislation. Before, a person was only declared dead when their heart stopped; they had to change that concept and decide that there were deaths, cerebral deaths, in which the heart kept beating. Without that change, organ transplants would be impossible. In Japan, heart transplants were forbidden until the end of the last century for that very reason. In their concept of life, death only arrives with the heart's hush. There was even a joke among Japanese cardiologists, that went: Don't worry about your heart, it'll last your whole life. The Chinese, on the other hand, have always been practical when it came to transplants. They take death row prisoners to the operating room and remove their functioning organs, among them the heart. In this they resemble a little the ancient Romans, who, when staging a play where a person is assassinated, would take a prisoner who has been condemned to death onto the stage and kill him in front of the audience.

I take out my ID card and request the clinical history of the patient Luis Córdoba Uribe. I have his ID in my hand, on top of mine, as I've always kept it in the darkness of my nightstand drawer. Number 3,267,090, issued in Sonsón, Antioquia, in 1966, when he turned twenty-one while studying at the higher seminary there. Profession: priest, says the document, six foot two, olive-skinned, born in Medellín on June 21, 1945, just before the end of the Second World War. That last bit is not on the ID card, but I tell the young lady, who looks at me a little stunned and asks me to wait. She doesn't take long. She checks that I am the person authorized to withdraw the clinical history, then hands me a cardboard folder. The pages are not as yellow as I'd expected. The handwriting is by different doctors, some more legible than others. There are also typed pages and computer printouts.

I photocopy the documents nearby and go back to the storehouse to return the originals to the archive. I walk to the station and wait for the next bus back to Medellín. Sitting by a counter I begin to read the file. It's not the whole story, as it only begins in 1995, on August 8. "Admitted to second floor. Patient, fifty years old. Priest. 1) Idiopathic dilated cardiomyopathy for seven years." I wonder what *idiopathic* means. It sounds familiar. I look it up on my phone: *1. adj. med. Relating to or denoting any disease or condition for which the cause is unknown.*

I continue: "Seven years of evolution. Ex-smoker, seventeen years ago." I remember when we first moved into the house at Villa and San Juan, Córdoba was still smoking two packs of Marlboros a day. When he finally quit, thanks to Fernando Isaza's jibes, his lungs improved significantly, but he gained even more weight. He doused his nicotine cravings with food. I look for the EF, the FE in Spanish, *faith*, the body's faith, not the soul's, the fraction of ejection. In August of 1995 his was 30 percent, about half of what's normal. "The patient reports dizziness when standing for the past month. Palpitations without perspiration, no fainting. Examined by Dr. Casanova, who orders Holter monitor, which shows TV. Admitted to EEF." I feel dizzy too, whether due to reading this page or the curves of the highway. I don't know what TV is, or EEF. I suppose TV is not television. EEF sounds to me like an acronym of religious fanatics. Every profession has its secret language, its jargon for initiates. Let Joaquín decipher those if he's so interested. I stop reading and close my eyes. I doze off and am surprised when we are already in Medellín.

Joaquín comes over and we read the clinical history together. He explains that TV stands for ventricular tachycardia, and that's what's shown by the Holter monitor, that exam where one is connected for twenty-four hours to an apparatus that monitors your blood pressure and the electrical activity of your heart. The EEF means that they referred him to an electrophysiology specialist. We continue reading. In September Luis was declared "depressed." He fainted. I remember it very well. Luckily he was sitting down, at home, and it didn't last long. At that point they changed his old pacemaker for a much smaller modern one. A month later, Córdoba was declared asymptomatic and calm. In November and December, however, they note "malign ventricular arrythmias." That's when he was admitted to another clinic, the social security one, for a "pre-transplant study." At the León XIII Clinic, the records say he "tolerates daily perambulations without fatigue." They discharged him at the beginning of the following year, and on January 8 he was allowed to leave the hospital. That was when he moved to Teresa's house in Laureles. His blood pressure, when he left the clinic was perfect: 110/70.

We see more monitoring in February. They report that he's lost weight and that there is no edema in his legs. The history does not say that this is due to his new diet in Teresa's house or the regular lymphatic massages from Darlis. In March they register that he continues to lose weight, but they do not notice an improvement in his cardiac symptoms. The supraventricular arrythmias persist. They adjust his pacemaker, and he improves considerably. They do register, however, episodes of symptomatic hypertension.

At the beginning of April they say his general conditions are acceptable, although he's hydrated. He's without breathing difficulties and stable. However, they observe "multiple extrasystoles, racing ventricular rhythm, diminished vesicular murmur." Again, they mention his extremities not being swollen. The plan is to "monitor the left weakness."

Joaquín wants us to stop reading the file. His heart is hurting a lot. The more we read, the more it aches, and he feels dizzy. He has been fainting and suffers from angina due to the stenosis of his aorta. We stop there, and I give him the papers to take with him; he's pale and upset.

"Sorry, Lelo," Joaquín says, "but when I read Luis's medical history it seems like I'm reading mine as well. It's unsettling. It seems like I'm about to reach the part where I die. There are so many things I need to do before my time runs out. I'd better leave right now."

⁓♦

For Joaquín religion is nothing more than a sophisticated superstition, a superstition based on sacred books, or so-called sacred books. It is constructed by people who see signs from the hereafter in the simple things of earth, in each coincidence, in happenstance, in the falling of blossoms, and in the color of ripe fruit. "A little more complex," he says, "but along the same lines as when my sister Inés drops a tomato and says, 'Someone's thinking of me. Is it Tomás, Tiberio, or Tito?'"

Then he equates our religion with mythology. "What are myths if not forgotten, defeated religions? I feel a great sympathy for the defeated, for those who lose the battle, for Hector, who dies before Achilles, a demigod he opposed with fear but without doubt. Now Catholicism is collapsing before our eyes, being buried alive in pederasty scandals, becoming a fable. All that you and Luis believe in an unadulterated way, day by day moves closer to mythology: the myth of the cross, of the Trinity, of celibacy, the monotonous God of monotheists, the creation of the world in seven days, the tablets with the Ten Commandments, the myth of Adam, the Judaic heresy of the New Testament, the platonic heresy of Paul's letters. A mythology that for a few centuries received the pompous name of theology but today is returning to clay and its true dimensions: myth, myth, myth. As Nanni Moretti puts it: *La messa è finite*. Mass is over, Lelo."

He thought about it a moment longer and then continued, with thinly veiled condescension: "What makes no sense at this stage, Lelo, is to disparage priests. They're already fallen, fucked, and have no way of defending themselves. Fell the fallen? Never. Even an atheist like me can feel compassion and nostalgia for faith and for priests. I respect you, Lelo, and I respect faith, thanks to my mother, who venerated priests and had a strong faith without being stupid. These days priests, and even the Pope, do nothing but apologize humbly for all the Church's errors throughout history, and the more they apologize, the more they are attacked and scorned. Journalists write Pope with a lowercase *p*, as if he were a potato. Now it seems that all of you, all without exception, are child abusers, perverts; lustful, smelly, and dirty beings. And that's not true. At least you and Luis were never like that. I allowed my own children to live with Córdoba, and I'm sure he never did anything bad to them. Quite the opposite, both Julia and Alejandro still dream of that sort of temporary father they lost. They dream, literally, very beautiful dreams, which they've told me about. Now priests, as well as fallen, hated, and defeated, are asked to bury themselves with their own hands. For you and Luis I feel only affection and compassion, solidarity and bit of sadness for such a hard and absurd life that was imposed on you in such a brutal way."

Joaquín looks me in the eye and concludes: "I see you, Lelo, so kind to me, such a good person, even able to write the book that I wanted to write. Now I don't dare judge priests. Thanks to you and Luis, I feel a certain respect and affection for Catholicism, though I still don't believe in it. Now that I see how your religion is collapsing, Lelo, I'm starting to feel nostalgic. When it's finally reforming, modernizing, now that the Pope, with a capital *p*, says he is no one to judge homosexuals, who asks forgiveness for burning heretics, for the judgment against Galileo, for the savage indoctrination of

Indigenous Peoples, now that they are finally opening their eyes, it's dying. You walk into a church, and there's never more than six devout women and a couple elderly men. Every once in a while, a weepy lover praying for a miracle. There are no more faithful ones. Because the faithful want not light but darkness, want to feel not compassion but fear, want to be not understood but threatened, chastised, and punished. If not, explain to me how the devout ones who slip away from you end up in the claws of the evangelicals. Look, Lelo, I hear what the evangelical Christians say, and I miss the old Catholic priests, you Cordalianos, the cultured and questioning Jesuits, the Benedictines, who don't do anyone any harm with their psalms and Gregorian chants. Now I get furious with myself for being so ridiculously anticlerical. The lot of you, at this stage of your decadence or fall, the only thing you inspire in me is infinite, tender, Christian compassion."

V

I don't think it rains anywhere else the way it rains here. Tropical mountain rain in the Andes is at once hard, placid, and constant, extremely pure water that falls in curtains like parallel showers wanting to wash the whole earth. One of those rains fell for the two nights before Luis's operation. Sara had gone to pick up Córdoba from the yellow-and-green house in Laureles as evening fell and had taken him to eat something he hadn't had in the five months of his strict regimen: pizza. They went to Angelo's, the restaurant of the Sicilian who made better pizzas than anybody else in Medellín, on a hill in El Poblado. And after the pizza and beer, he allowed himself a generous helping of tiramisu, his favorite dessert. Sara had twisted his arm, telling him that he'd return to his diet when he got out of the clinic.

The downpour let loose as they left the pizzeria. Sara and Córdoba got to the little fortress, a mustard-colored Renault 4 that belonged to Sara's family, just in time. Luis had just sat down, just spilled into the passenger seat, very agitated, exhausted just from quickening his pace a little to seek refuge from the first curtains of water.

"Don't start the engine yet, Sara. I want to tell you something," Córdoba had said.

The rain intensified, producing a soft percussion on the roof and windshield of the car, I imagine. Inside the glass began to fog up. Rain, darkness, silence. That car, closed shut like a confessional, seemed predisposed to sincere words and confidences. Sara did not open her mouth, and for several minutes, she didn't know how many, Luis spoke: "Many lovely things have happened to me in these months, Sara. I've been living in a real family. Don't take this the wrong way, but Teresa and Darlis have been like my wives, and their children, my children. Forgive me for bringing up this same old story of children. I'm not saying it for you. If you don't want them, don't have them, but I can tell you that their company was a good part of my recovery, at least my wellbeing in these months. The children's games, Teresa's gentleness, her way of existing so prudently that she's almost invisible, the joyful, uninhibited beauty of Darlis, *la costeña*. All this, Sara, all these simple things, have changed me inside. Years ago, you told me I was afraid of women. And you were right; you hit on a true and deep key to my way of being. But these women are impossible to be afraid of because of their tenderness, their spontaneous and natural goodness, because of the love they've treated me with all this time. They're not intellectuals like you; they're not calculating or farsighted or astute like you, but they are profoundly good, good and natural and sincere, frank and transparent. There is no duplicity or deviousness in these women. I don't have to doubt when they talk to me; no suspicions arise. They are as they are, and that's that. I immediately felt myself to be among women who reminded me of my two sisters, and even my mother, the three women I grew up with. As the days, weeks, and months have gone by, I've become convinced of something growing inside me like a vine climbing within my body: I must allow myself a new life. Yes, something like a new chance on earth, the opposite of what that great book says at the end. Our life, the priesthood as it has been conceived by the Church for centuries, is a horrendous and unnatural sacrifice. I think those who want to should be able to be priests and be celibate; those who decide to be, those who feel able to be like that and can be happy being like that. But it's an injustice and an absurd rule that all priests must be celibate. That should be left only to those who have the vocation, psychology, and maturity to be monks. Because it's not good for most of us; it's a damaging rule, an obligation that breaks us down psychologically if we fulfill it and destroys us with guilt if we don't. Some even, desperate for caresses, seeking a little tenderness and warmth, do horrendous, disgusting things, like taking advantage of those they can most easily take advantage of, boys and girls, a monstrosity. I have not been one of those. All my life I have adored women, actresses, singers, students, cousins, colleagues; but all my life, as you rightly pointed out, I feared them. The priesthood was my refuge to not face up to those mysterious and distinct beings, as natural as trees or rocks. It has been years and years of containing myself, repressing, hiding an impulse that was a torture to feel without being able to satisfy it. I hid behind my other passions, food most of all, which in part is what has made me ill, and this madness for cinema, which has been like another marriage for me, and music, which has always served as my hiding place and sublimation, consoling me and, like water, putting out so much interior fire. Married to cinema, with opera as my mistress, that's how I've lived. My illness itself I believe has transformed me; the obvious nearness of death has made me consider my half century of life as a celibate virgin, and then, maybe, hope has been born in me, perhaps, for a new life. I believe that the day after tomorrow, when they operate on me, I am going to survive. I am almost sure I won't die. I have a premonition. The very name of the Brazilian surgeon, Batista, announces a second baptism for me, a second opportunity, the possibility of living a different life, a fuller life, a life that includes my body, flesh, sexuality, but without the torment of fear, guilt, or sin. I can tell you this, openly. Only Lelo, apart from you, knows about this. And one woman also knows, Darlis. Don't open your eyes like that, yes, Darlis. When I wake up with my heart mended, when I can run in the rain again, I am going to request a release from Rome and I will leave. One is a priest until death, and I won't stop being one, because I love and profoundly believe in my religion, but I'm not going to live by pitiless rules ancient councils have imposed on me, which I can no longer stand. It's strange that something so traditional, a family, should be revolutionary for me, and a liberation, not a bond or a knot. In fact, I have already formed an atypical family with Aurelio, a family of celibates who lived together in harmony for twenty years. But now that's not what I want. I want a family like others have, a family like you and Guillermo might have one day. I'll have an adopted daughter for a start, Rosina, and I might even have a daughter or son of my own. It's strange that I, a repressed, virgin priest, long to procreate. But I do. I want to with my whole soul, my whole body, and my whole heart. The heart, I believe, is the place where the body and soul flow together. And it's ironic, but only my heart prevents me at this moment, although, if they manage to fix it, if they baptize me again when they open me up, I will also open myself to this different life, to being a husband and father. That's what I wanted to tell you, Sara, because I feel close to you. I'm not asking for support or permission. I simply wanted to tell you, and now, if you want, we can go, as I still have a lot of things to prepare for the day after tomorrow, the appointed day for my new life, my transformation, my second chance."

Sara is sure that at that moment, as abruptly as it had started, the rain suddenly stopped, and she drove slowly and in silence back to the yellow-and-green house in Laureles, where Teresa and Darlis were waiting, full of worry, for their beloved imaginary husband, their dear priest, Luis.

W

After informing Dr. Casanova that he would go ahead with the operation by the Brazilian surgeon, Luis decided to consult with his friends, to ask them to help him make a decision he had actually already made. I don't know if he was looking for a winding path by which he could back out of a mistake in time. Maybe he was expecting to hear some well-founded argument to change his mind. He asked me for advice as well when I went to visit him, and I encouraged him to have the operation, assuring him it would go really well.

"Don't be so predictable, Lelo," Córdoba said. "Everybody's telling me the same thing, that it's going to go well, but none of you has the slightest idea how it will go. Not even the doctor knows. I don't know, nobody knows. Maybe the only one who is telling me the truth is Fernando Isaza; he says it's like flipping a coin."

"Mine was a way of encouraging you and telling you not to be afraid, Luis," I answered. "I don't know anything about medicine and prefer to trust those who do."

"I'm not afraid. We're all going to die sooner or later, and I am not afraid of death. Another matter is that I don't want to die. Not yet, at least. At the moment I would rather keep living and take more pleasure from life. Most of all from loving and being loved."

After this brief conversation, I rushed off to phone our doctor friend, Fernando Isaza, to ask what he thought. He was an anesthesiologist and knew much more than we did. I told him Luis had told me about the coin toss. Was that the case, a fifty-fifty chance? His frankness, I still remember it vividly, was almost cruel: "I told Luis it was a flip of a coin to encourage him. It's less than that; it's more like a one in ten chance of winning. It's almost a sure thing that he'll die on the operating table or in the following days. If it goes really well, a year later. That's the truth."

"So why are you advising him to have the operation?"

"Because a heart that would serve him for a transplant is very difficult to find. There's nothing more to do. If he keeps waiting, he'll die at any moment, today, tomorrow, in two weeks, or six months. He is on the brink of an abyss they call sudden death."

I remember I never hung up a phone feeling as disconsolate as that. Hanging up a phone like cutting off a life, like quieting a voice, like resigning oneself to death. Our friend Isaza said it coldly, but also with the sincerity of affection and friendship. And I, fatalist that I am, listened to his words in resigned silence; I never had the strength for rage or indignation.

Maybe what Luis liked best about the operation they were offering him, the so-called Batista procedure, a revolutionary method, was that nobody had to die for him to live. "Risk my life, change my life, anyway I've already lost it," he used to repeat. In the last weeks, waiting for a heart, he told me he was tormented by imagining parents who had to accept the death of a son or daughter who, though appearing alive, though still warm with lungs still inflating, though with a heart beating firmly and steadily in their chest (that strong and healthy heartbeat was precisely what made them more valuable as a cadaver), was declared dead, brain dead.

For the Church, life was not in the brain, nor in the heart. Life was something intangible and very difficult to define because it wasn't corporeal but spiritual. Life is a spirit fed with every inhalation of air, which blows where it wants and keeps life alive. Life is what animates inert material and supplies it with movement, will, pain, even with a mind and thought. But in our time, incapable of demonstrating the existence of the spirit, or the soul, which cannot be seen or perceived with any apparatus, religion no longer has the monopoly over defining life or death. Life and death are now decided by those who cure; doctors and scientists are the new high priests who determine who keeps living and who dies. Nevertheless, in the older, more primitive mind of Luis, the scruples of his conscience continued. How dead was the dead man they were going to cut up? At what point had the soul – if we still believe in the soul and the spirit – left that body? Was the dead man who was going to give him life really dead?

It's fine that they kill cows, pigs, and horses to remove tendons, membranes, and pericardia with which to fabricate valves and biological prosthetics. Animals' guts are used to save human beings. That he could understand and forgive, he who was a guilt-free carnivore without much compassion for the creatures he ate. But using human bodies as if they were an organ depository keeping spare parts for others, that was something else. He remembered one of his friends, Pilar, whom the doctors asked, part by part, for her son's organs. His skin? Yes. Eyes? Yes. Kidneys? Yes. Lungs? Yes. Heart? Yes, yes, yes, his heart too. But that donation, organ by organ, ended up breaking her forever, without it being much consolation that others now lived with remnants of her young son. She would like to know who now walked and loved with her son's heart, yes, but she doubted it would really console her, no matter how much head and how little heart she put into it.

X

Joaquín told me he'd seen the names of the surgeons who were present in the cardiovascular clinic when they operated on Córdoba. The surgery was on a Thursday, May 23, 1996, and I know they went into the operating room early because I was with him in his room until the last moment. At dawn, in the yard adjacent to the hospital, where there was a seniors' residence, a procession of little goats passed in a perfect line. When one of them bleated, Luis closed his eyes, sighed like them, and said: "They might be a little off key, but they've come to wish me luck." The nurses came with the gurney at seven on the dot. I remember having looked at the clock on the wall, at my watch, and also at Luis's clock on his bedside table. Even the nurses looked at their watches. Our farewell was optimistic, smiling and without any hugs. No tears or poignancy. A brave goodbye. We never fell out of our habit of not touching each other. A friendship without contact, I used to say. The night before, some of Luis's friends had come to visit him. Darlis had not come, but she had phoned; she was at home looking after the three children. When she called, I left the room, so I don't know what they talked about.

Between Monday and Wednesday, Batista had already operated on four patients with the same condition as Luis, dilated cardiomyopathy. All four had survived the operations and been transferred to the intensive care unit. Two of them, a man and a woman, had died in the ICU a few hours after the revolutionary surgery. Both were younger than Córdoba. Of their deaths, at least to Luis and me, no one said anything. They only told us that they had operated on several patients and that they'd all come out of the surgery alive and were in recovery.

Batista's plan was to operate on two patients that Thursday. They had told us the procedure would be a long one, five or six hours, so when they took Luis away, I went to celebrate Mass at the convent of the Precious Blood and to pray for my friend's health during the Eucharist. All the nuns, on their knees, joined in my supplication. Priests don't know how to give up prayer because without prayers we feel naked and voiceless. We've been convinced that we are privileged intermediaries with the great beyond and that we have contact with the Holy Trinity, even if we sometimes feel that no one is listening to us or that in the heavens others are heard more.

What happened in those hours we can reconstruct from the clinical history and from what Joaquín heard from a surgeon who watched the Batista procedure on that day. Joaquín gave me the notes from his conversation with him, a young man at the time, taking his first steps in cardiac surgery and eager to learn something new. It's incredible that this surgeon, a quarter of a century later, still remembers in such detail what happened during the operation. For him it had been a dramatic, unforgettable day.

All the surgeons were eager to learn from the eminent Brazilian physician. Dr. Villegas, the founder and chief of the clinic, was the most enthusiastic about the visitor. Dr. Villegas liked to be in the vanguard of everything to do with heart disease. His motto that "nobody should be denied an operation," which might seem a bit rash, was also optimistic and generous, a product of his confidence and love for his service. Without that faith in the scalpel, he would never have managed to get his clinic as far as it had got. Even if the survival rate of a surgery was only 10 percent, he did not hesitate. If someone died on the operating table or a short time later in recovery, it saddened him, but it did not discourage him. It was the curve that mattered, the curve that improved with the learning of new procedures, which gradually could be perfected. Martyrs who fall on the altar of science. It was the same with Batista.

Batista was a casual type. He worked quickly and without superstitions. He scolded those who were operating with him; he called them "brutes," "beasts," because according to his judgment, there were things they shouldn't do the way they'd always done them. Every hospital and every surgeon has their customs, their habits, and even their whims. But Batista voiced his criticisms with a tone of superiority; he also treated the perfusionist (the person in charge of the extracorporeal circulation) thoughtlessly. He told her that his perfusionist in Curitiba was not a professional nurse but a ranch hand, an intuitive campesino who did a much better job than she did because he did it fearlessly, as decisively as he would prod his mule with a single spur to get him moving, to keep him from standing still. "We have to spur the left ventricle, gentlemen."

Just before the surgeon spurred Luis's ventricle, there was a brief encounter between Córdoba, stretched out on the operating table with his cap and green hospital gown open across his chest, the beams of cold light directed at his sternum, and the Brazillian dressed with his cap and his plague mask, his wet hands half open at the level of his face, seeming to pray between drops of water. A nurse told me, that same evening, that the father had smiled at the surgeon staring at him from above, that the father had bid farewell to consciousness with a smile. I still remember what I thought when the nurse described Luis's last smile to me: that it was like giving a tip to the executioner who's going to cut your throat.

Córdoba, then, smiled at Batista and asked for a moment longer to pray out loud. What he said, one of the doctors told me, he had said several times, still smiling, and it sounded like Latin or Italian. It ended, he said, with something like "anima fa" (the soul makes?). And I knew what he had said: *Oraña figata fa, marina gamina fa.* Then the surgery began. After the sure steps of the anesthesia, Dr. Villegas had the honor of making the first incision with the scalpel, marking the path the saw would take as it sectioned the sternum longitudinally. In Luis's first wound, the blood found its exit. Then one of the assistants began placing the sensors for vital signs, which read blood pressure, heart rate, and oxygenation. They hooked up cannulas to replace the veins and arteries of the body, connecting him to a machine that would take the place of his lungs and heart while the latter was touched, cut, altered, sewn up again. For now it beats with a rhythm that seems correct, there it is, in full view of all those present, big and shiny in the middle of the chest, the Sun, the Sun that lit the life of Córdoba, and our own, for a luminous half century.

In the cardiovascular clinic, the delicate moment when they stop the heart had always been done very carefully, slowly, with an almost ceremonial respect for well-established protocols. They used an expensive but well-proven mixture, frozen, that they introduced little by little through a cannula into the aorta. For the cardioplegia (the solution administered to stop the heart), Batista had his own formula, quite different from the clinic's. The prepared solutions seemed to him a method for ladies-in-waiting or little girls, and he told them so with his air of superiority. His way was to take an enormous syringe and shoot a stream of potassium directly into the ticker, flat out. Something so brutal, according to the clinic's protocol, could make some of the heart's cells that were in systole – that is, contracted – stay frozen like that, like stone, without the possibility of restarting with fluidity when the moment came to start the heart up again. But no one dared question Batista, that prodigy from Curitiba, not even Dr. Villegas. At that moment, Batista was the master from whom they must learn, and they had to respect even his harmful stunts, his recklessness.

There he was, then, my friend Córdoba, anesthetized, his arms stretched out, chest wide open, sawed in half, from top to bottom. That was, and in part continues to be, the canonical procedure for open heart surgery. The interior becomes exterior, as in a confessed man. The clinical history said it in a more technical and exact way.

"A median sternotomy is performed and the patient is cannulized in this order: arterial cannula in the ascendant aorta, cannula for the superior cava vein, and another for the inferior cava vein. Initiate extracorporeal circulation and proceed to perform in the first term a ventriculoplasty of the right ventricle, placing a suture on the front face in order to diminish its size . . . Then the wall of the left ventricle is resectioned sufficiently to reduce its size and surgically remove all the abnormal or extra tissue. Approximately two hundred grams of myocardium tissue is extracted."

From this I understand that after stopping his heart brusquely with a syringe (the clinical history does not describe the type of cardioplegia he preferred), after collapsing the lungs and connecting his circulation to the machine, the Brazilian took the scalpel, sliced off his wedge, his shield-shaped piece of myocardium, the extra part of the left ventricle, and then sewed it up with an enormous needle he'd designed himself, curved and long so it could pass through the thick, hard dilated walls typical of the enlarged heart. Then comes the most important moment: They begin to moderate the extracorporeal circulation and observe how the heart that has been opened and closed starts up again.

"There is nothing that closer resembles death, Lelo," Joaquín told me. "The heart is quiet, cold, extremely cold, so its cells won't degrade. What most damages an organ is heat. The man cannot breathe either, for his lungs are collapsed. In those days, they lowered the patient's temperature to just above eighty-six degrees, with the intention of protecting the rest of the body's cells. The blood in the brain, oxygenated mechanically, does not circulate in pulsations, as our body has been accustomed to for its whole life, but in a continuous flow, because the machine does not beat, it just pumps. The anesthetic produces a much more profound sleep than our deepest sleep; for those who wake up, no perception of the time passed nor any memory remains at all. It is a total void, the nothingness of death. Unless there is a hidden spirit, Lelo, a soul that has not yet left the body, but I don't see how. Maybe you can."

I prefer not to speak of this mystery. My heart, no, my being believes the soul exists; Joaquín's heart and mind do not feel or see it. I'm here and he's there.

When Luis had entered the clinic the previous day, his vital signs were not bad. Cardioplasty was scheduled for the next day, Thursday; the priest was conscious, afebrile, breathing without difficulty, blood pressure: 114/70, with a rhythmic pulse of 70, without murmurs, with well-ventilated lungs, with no swelling of the extremities, asymptomatic in spite of "hypertensive myocardiopathy in dilated phase." His weight surprised them: in the months spent in the Laureles house Luis lost more than 40 pounds and now weighed 203. The problem was his ejection fraction, which had gone down to 15 percent.

Those who asked how he was, almost always received the same reply: "Aside from my heart, all is well."

Y

When I come out from Mass, I see a line of priests, nuns, and novices winding around outside the clinic. They have all come to donate blood for Luis. I greet them as I pass. Among them are friends, journalists, actresses, movie directors, lovers of classical music, opera fans who have not missed his radio program in years. All dream that their blood could circulate through the body of that good priest who has just entered surgery. A radio journalist is broadcasting news of the operation live, raising his voice as if he were commentating on a soccer match and the local team had been reinforced by a striker from Brazil.

I look through the clinical history for the last time. Señor Luis Córdoba, fifty years of age, priest, entered the operating room May 23. Surgical team: Arturo González (assistant), Randas Batista and Alberto Villegas as chief surgeons. The file mentions, without giving names, that the operation would be attended by a group of surgeons. Surgery start time: 8:00 a.m. Finish time: 7:30 p.m. El Gordo, who was not so gordo anymore, was in surgery for eleven and a half hours. At the bottom of the page there are two squares in front of the words "State of patient." One says ALIVE, the other DEAD. The doctor must put an *x* in one of the two boxes. In the space that says "Complications during the procedure," the assistant (Dr. González) writes: "It was not possible to remove him from the pump. A counterpulsation balloon was also inserted."

The history relates the crisis that occurred when they attempted to disconnect him from the extracorporeal circulation (they remove the cannulas and make a "careful hemostasia," that is, they stop any hemorrhage): "When it was thought the patient was in stable condition, about to begin to close him up, an increase in the pulmonary artery pressure began to present. This being palpated, the left auricle presented very low pressure; important pulmonary hypertension is suspected. Then proceeded to severe pharmacological management of pulmonary hypertension."

The observing surgeon explained to Joaquín: "We fought it all day. Pulmonary hypertension is a serious complication after cardiac surgery because it doesn't allow the blood to pass through the lungs. The right ventricle pumps up, as if inflating, and thus compresses the left, not letting it work the way it needs to. It's a storm of events triggered in a cascade which will most likely end in failure."

The clinical history describes: "After the pharmaceutical treatment there is a certain improvement in the patient's state. After a few minutes, he deteriorates again, so the cannulas are replaced, and Dr. Randas Batista resolves to perform further ventricular resection to try in this way to improve still further the function of the left ventricle and thus lower the pulmonary hypertension slightly. To proceed to dry out the left ventricle, it's necessary to surgically remove the papillary muscles and, therefore, the mitral valve; it is then decided to replace the mitral valve with a St. Jude 31-millimeter mechanical prosthesis, which is inserted ventricularly with separate

Ethibond 2-0 stitches. Then a wider resection of the left ventricular wall is completed, and the ventricle is closed up again."

The afternoon wears on, the light fades, the heat as well. Every hour one of the doctors comes out, or a nurse, and with dismay etched on their faces they tell us more or less the same thing. That they are fighting, but his heart seems not to be responding as it should. Their sweaty, reddened faces, with the consternation of exhaustion and failure, gradually sap our hope and then our faith.

I read in the file what was going on behind those hermetic walls: "After the ventricle is sewn up, the patient does not show a great improvement, and we then initiate high pharmaceutical support: adrenaline, amrinone, Isuprel, nitroprusside, etc., without adequate response. Multiple attempts to remove the patient from the pump are made. At one stage he is successfully off it for half an hour, and protamine is administered, but the patient again deteriorates, and it is necessary to administer heparin again and reconnect him to the pump. Both left and right ventricles are in disfunction. He is well supported by extracorporeal circulation and was helped a bit more with an aortic counterpulsation balloon, which was placed in the right femoral artery. There is a significant improvement in the patient's hemodynamic state, but there is difficulty registering the cardiac rhythm because with the balloon he presents multiple arrhythmias. The patient's pacemaker is interfering substantially with the formulation of the balloon. Eight, nine, ten hours of surgery have gone by, and the patient has not been stabilized. His condition is deteriorating."

The surgeon who Joaquín interviewed assured him that they spared no efforts to resuscitate Father Córdoba. We must admit the cardiovascular clinic was, and still is, the best place for heart surgery in Medellín and one of the best in South America. The method was not their own but imported from Curitiba with certain rashness. Desire to always be in the forefront. They also knew there was a lot of press outside, awaiting the results of the operation on a priest beloved by the city's cultural crowd. "I knew the father and held him in high esteem. He ran the film forum at my school, San Ignacio, and his talks were unforgettable. He's one of those patients that hurts for the rest of one's life; I had seen him the previous day, and he was jovial, very optimistic, convinced he would be saved. Batista could not operate any longer that day. Father Córdoba was the only one who didn't come out of the operating room alive. Of the seven Batista operated on, two survived for some months, until they could have a transplant, and then they lived for longer. The Batista procedure, in their cases, was just a bridge to a transplant. Although we learned how to do it, we did not put it into practice even once. If you mentioned the matter to Dr. Villegas, he would maintain a discreet silence or change the subject."

Dr. Jaramillo and Dr. Isaza come out, heads hanging. They have been chosen as the messengers. What kind of time is this to announce your death? I think to myself. I hear, almost without paying attention, what I already know because their faces have told me. A few words mumbled in something that sounds not like Spanish, but like something that would be understood in any other language. A silent horror film, with gestures that would be understood by a Japanese person, a Mongolian, a Malaysian, someone like me who no longer understood any language. It is dark now, nighttime, after seven thirty, and there is nothing to do and nothing to think and nothing to say. Angelines and I hug without crying. At least I don't cry. It is a quiet, dry embrace, an embrace of bones between two skeletons. I don't remember much else. Or I do, something strange: that I felt more fear than sadness. We go to the cafeteria while they prepare the "patient." (They still call him that after death, as if he could still have patience.) Yes, infinite patience, eternal patience, I think, at the same time as they are preparing him to take him to the hospital morgue. There, if we wish, we can see him. While I force lemonade down my throat, I try futilely to remember a Vallejo poem.

    I know how it starts, and I murmur it to Angelines: *Some blows in life, they're so heavy ... I don't know. / Blows as if dealt by God's own wrath, as if, ahead, / the rip of every single thing we'd ever suffered / had pooled inside our souls ... I don't know.* It goes on to talk about something like trenches carved open in our souls or our faces or bodies? I don't know where these trenches are carved, maybe because in me I feel them opening everywhere. I tell Angelines I feel a trench in my chest, finally I feel something, as if they had sawed apart my sternum as well, as if they had forgotten, what would it matter, to close it up. Angelines just says: *the black heralds that Death has sent us.*

Then I remember how it goes, of course, and it gushes back into my memory: *They're the steep fall of some Christ from the soul, / of the laudable faith that fate can make foul of. / Those bloodied blows are the sounds of bread / cracking*... I no longer remember how it goes, and nor does Angelines, so we sit in silence, enduring the blow in each of the seconds and the minutes that begin to run into hours, into the days and the years in which we can never again have a conversation with Córdoba, with Luis, with el Gordo.

⁓

There is something in clinical histories that does not manage to capture what death is. Perhaps this needs to be told *transcending all science* and of course from the place of the living, from their beating and beaten hearts, not from the place of the dead, who, especially if they are anesthetized, without sensations or thought, are the ones who least experience their death. Death is a matter for the living and not the dead because only the living feel and suffer it. But how to express what we feel? The technical prose has the chill of the operating room, the operating table, white, hard, marmoreal, perhaps with the odd spatter of blood on the disinfected sheets, but nothing that generates the illusion of life, which is what terrifies us about death. It all happens in a territory out of our domain, outside of the natural world, and turns every human being into a machine that does or does not respond to physical and chemical efforts to repair it. Luis, in that moment, inert, cold, without pulse or breath, seems like an automobile in a garage where they've opened the hood to adjust part of the engine. His blood could be gasoline or oil, the valves could be spark plugs or coils; the arteries, wires; the ribcage, a chassis, a fender, or a radiator. The heart doesn't even reach the status of carburetor (that seems more like the lungs). A distribution pump without which the car, although intact, perfect in all the rest of its components, does not work, is stranded, useless. But it does not rot no matter how still it is. At least not for a few hours or days.

Yes, what is described in the clinical history is, without doubt, death. We can talk about death that way. But when it's the death of a daughter or a friend or the brother you've lived with for half your life, the words we read there are not satisfactory. Living was his pulse? What's extinguished with death is not just an engine. Living was his music, his voice, and his films. Living was the love (laughter, joy, sadness) with which he lived, listened, and spoke. The pulmonary hypertension can explain many things (like an oil leak in an airplane), but the words *pulmonary hypertension* mean nothing to our primitive brains. It's like knowing a car's radiator overheated and seeing the steam. With pulmonary hypertension we don't even see the steam.

What we're missing is not limited to the mind or to the air (some of us would say spirit) that is exhaled and vibrates in the throat to form words that transmit ideas composed in the neurons. There's something more: the gesture, the smile, the gaze, the caress, the shared memory, but life is more than these things too.

Death is all that is cut short and cannot be. Death is not being able to imagine a future of love or of pain. What dies is not the lived life, which is now unerasable, but the new life that Luis longed to begin if the clumsy mechanic, Batista, had been able to repair his heart. Death is the films he won't see, the music that will no longer stir his emotions or give him shivers of happiness or sadness. It is losing the gaze of understanding that requires nothing more than an instant and shared comprehension of the human, the inhuman, of the sad or joyful or ridiculous or despicable. Luis's way of reprimanding, forgiving, allowing, or forbidding (he actually never forbade anything; he advised against things), of improving or approving, is gone. His way of loving and savoring will die with him. I wish I had the consolation of believing in the resurrection, but, here between us, I do not always believe. There are days when I do and nights when I do not.

The clinical history speaks only of the body, and those of us left alive do not know what to do with that cut-open and hastily sewn back together body, with that quiet heart and airless lungs, that pale and uncomplaining face and those cold feet, with those dull eyes, with that bulky lump. That's why Angelines and I sent him to be burnt. Cremation they call it, but it's the same thing. And they cremated him not on a pyre of sandalwood beside the sacred Ganges River, but in a methane gas oven, or an electric oven, I don't know. And after a few hours of high combustion, they handed us our gigantic friend converted into a bag of gray ashes, with blackish fragments, weighing less than the heart that Batista mutilated to finish him off. Perhaps Batista would go down in history as Bach's doctor, who operated on his eyes and caused an infection that killed him, did. Or like Mozart's doctor, who bled him.

Z

"I wanted to leave, and he wanted to stay," Joaquín said to me after the funeral, "but both of us, deep down, wanted the same thing: to begin a new life. Me, away from a traditional marriage, and him, away from the priesthood and within a normal family, with a wife and kids. I felt guilty, then, for not occupying the position he wanted for himself, because if he wanted it so badly and with so many hopes, obviously it wasn't a bad position. Maybe too much is demanded of you priests, Lelo, and you make so many sacrifices that even the chains of matrimony seem like cushions to you. I don't know."

I had seen him from the altar while co-officiating the funeral Mass for Luis. I saw Teresa too, in the distance, sitting in the back row with their daughter, Julia, and also with Darlis and Rosina. They were crying like twin widows, two Magdalenes united in sorrow. Well, there were a lot of widows at that Mass crying disconsolately: Martha Ligia, Luis's editor at *Kinetoscopio*; our friend Sara Cohen, more an orphan than a widow; Angelines, who didn't cry because she had run out of tears between the hospital morgue and the house at Villa and San Juan.

Víctor Gaviria, his eyes red, seeing so many beautiful and downcast women, smiled, saying that the funeral reminded him of the one in *The Man Who Loved Women* by Truffault, a film el Gordo loved. I had never seen most of the women who approached and left him a flower, a note, trailed a hand over the box or along the portrait we had placed beside it, leaning on the wood that enclosed his ashes.

Success has a thousand fathers but failure is an orphan. The only doctor of Luis's who was there was Fernando Isaza, the first to diagnose him and the most candid about the prognosis of the operation. He was in one of the front rows, openly holding hands with his new boyfriend, Eduardo. He had introduced me on their way in. During the homily I watched them, envying their courage. I looked at them when, in the sermon, I began to talk about the new types of families my friend Luis had helped us to glimpse with his life: a family of two men, which is what he and I had formed in the house at Villa and San Juan; the family with two women, which had taken him in at the end of his life. I raised my voice to say that all these families that seem strange but are united by love were blessed by Jesus exactly with the same love he always showed. He even blessed broken families, which were not without love, which stayed alive despite ruptures, and here I looked at Joaquín, but Joaquín was not paying attention. Then I added the most heretical phrases I've ever said in a Mass, but that almost no one, luckily, seemed to notice: "Remember that everything, even the death of a beloved friend, can be the beginning of a new religion. A much kinder religion, a reformed religion that does not judge others by the type of family they choose to create."

I don't think Joaquín heard that heresy, but Fernando Isaza, the doctor, did hear, and smiled at me from one of the front rows, a sad and sympathetic smile. I think Víctor Gaviria heard it too, because he nodded visibly, through his sniffles. I'm sure the

Calderón brothers heard me, and they didn't judge me harshly, because at the end of Mass they told me that their brother who died in Africa might have said the very same words if he were alive.

Joaquín was distracted. He was not beside Teresa and Darlis, but in one of the aisles, behind his son, watching him. Jandrito had not stopped playing with a little car during the whole service. It was he, perhaps, who best perceived the dimensions of what was happening, and he preferred to convert them into a game. His father let him play but kept an eye on him to make sure he wasn't noisy or bothering anyone. I think Luis would have loved seeing a boy playing with a little car at his funeral, calm and concentrated on the comings and goings of the four wheels under a red body. He didn't make any noise, just pushed it back and forth on the floor, as if his game were his sermon. Alejandro had painted and brought to the church the portrait of Córdoba that we had placed beside the box of ashes, a small oil painting, at once beautiful and childish, which the boy, at the end of the Mass, gave to me, and which I still have. He had signed it with the name of his imaginary friend, Simón:

My homily, sometimes interrupted by silence because the emotion forced me to stop every once in a while, continued to be a defense of people who get together to live lovingly under the same roof. "Our houses, the houses where Luis lived, were never tombs or prisons for us, just as the body is not the prison of the soul or even the prison of the heart. The purpose of these unions is to diminish solitude and pain, to help with grief or illness, the challenges all human beings are exposed to. When needs and abilities, joy and scarcity, are shared among a small group, which we generally call family, the undeniable fragility of all of us is made lighter. That's why we gather; we are social beings. Anyone who has lived with Luis knows that at his side, with his joy in living, the inevitable suffering is less noticeable.

"Suffering is lessened and each of us can live with the amount of solitude we tolerate or desire. For this family union between men, between women, between men and women, between young and old to work well, the only thing needed is love. Remember the words of Paul: 'Love is patient, love is kind; love does not envy or boast, does not dishonor others, is not self-seeking, is not easily angered, keeps no record of wrongs. Love does not delight in evil but rejoices with the truth. Love bears all things, believes all things, hopes all things, endures all things. Love never ends. As for prophecies, they will cease, tongues will be stilled, knowledge will pass away. For our knowledge is imperfect and our prophecies are limited. If I do not have love, I am nothing.' Judging the bonds of that love according to old habits and prejudices, or according to what happens beneath a roof or even between the sheets, makes no sense if all that happens is decided by free and responsible adults. Let us stop being judges of others; let us stop judging what is moral and immoral. Moral is that which includes love for others, generosity, mutual respect, reciprocal liberty, and nothing more.

"This is what Luis taught us through the most sophisticated and valid tools that exist: though music and film; that is, through beauty and art. His was a constant message celebrating open minds, joy, tolerance, and love in all its manifestations, all the human sentiments that exist and cannot be denied. Luis told us once, at another funeral, that since life was a gift, the only sin we can commit is not to receive and honor that gift, that is, to not be happy with life. Luis's large and ailing heart thought that was enough, or at least that was what was most important. I, for my part, will try to live according to the teachings of Father Luis Córdoba, and I invite all of you to also live in accordance with what he has taught us."

I could have finished there, but I went on: "Following his example is, however, only a partial consolation. Partial because I would not be sincere if I denied the seriousness of his death, the pain of his death, that is, what death has taken from us. When Luis died, my friends, what died for us was his exquisite way of existing. What we don't hear now and will never hear again is his wise voice, which consoled, advised, and illuminated. What has stopped, more than his heart, is his way of being a dear friend, a beloved colleague, and also an exceptional priest, capable of curing the incurable without boasting of any miracle. His heart beat in everything that was life and joy. His enthusiasm and spirit was infectious for the downcast, lifted those wounded by the defeats of love and life. Without knowing how to cook, he had a recipe for transmitting serenity and calm, acceptance of all. Luis, through his attitude and his words, gave us hope, trust that in the end, the forces of life would prevail, the forces of love would eventually prevail.

"Luis inspired us with his mere existence. We breathed easy just knowing he was breathing. That's why I ask you, I beg, that we don't let oblivion rob us of Luis, that we keep him alive in our thoughts and in our joy, as a child protects a candle flame threatened by wind. Remember that through Luis we learned what we did not know, understood clearly what was just a confused idea, managed to hear beyond our deafness, began to understand what our pusillanimity denied to us and, most of all, Cordaliano brothers, to forgive and let be what our dogmatism led us to judge and condemn."

Almost without my noticing, the ceremony finally ended, and I went to take off my vestments. When I came out into the atrium, almost no one had left, and a lot of people came over to hug me and offer me condolences. I remember, most of all, Luis's female friends who came over, my companions in grief, as weepy, sad, and widowed as me. There were Sara, Darlis, Teresa, Laura, Angelines, Marito, Bárbara, Mónica, and many others. I thought that Córdoba had loved a lot, and that was why now so many people were showing how much they loved him. Men, women, young and old, artists, actresses, filmmakers, cinephiles, photographers, directors, nuns, prostitutes... We were all suddenly equals in sadness, but also in the joy of having known him. That was what most united us: the beauty of having known him. Now that I think of it, and now that I'm at the end of these notes, I realize this is what keeps us united after all these years: the presence of el Gordo, his permanent memory alive in those of us who knew him and upon whom he poured his insight, his teachings, his tenderness, his sincere and wise and sensitive way of being.

When Luis and I happened to say a word at the same time, whatever it was, *lemon* or *Easter* or *miracle*, he wouldn't say, as everyone said, "Jinx, we killed a devil," but rather, "An angel flew past: make a wish." I remember once, when he already lived in the house in Laureles and I was feeling quite lonely in the house at Villa and San Juan, we killed a devil with the most obvious word, the one that was ever-present in our conversations in those days: *heart*. And he said what he always said, "An angel: make a wish." I, without closing my eyes and looking up at the blue sky through the window, wished. I wished with the same fervor we pray with as children, convinced that one day the wish would be fulfilled. I can't say what it was, because for wishes to come true, they can never be said out loud. What I can write here is that the wish I made, even though I never uttered it, was not fulfilled. Well, since I haven't yet died, there are days when I wake up with the vague dreamy sensation that it could still come true and that we're on the brink of fulfilling it. Being a priest, I still have faith.

CODA

The papers you have just read were handed to me, Joaquín Restrepo, in a sealed manila envelope, directly from the hands of Father Aurelio Sánchez, shortly before he resolved to cloister himself forever in the Yermo Camaldulense de la Santa Cruz in the Llanos of Cuivá. In a brief note that came in the same envelope, Lelo begged me not to ask him anything else about Father Luis Córdoba, not to ask for any clarifications, that he had completed what I'd asked for, that he was sick and tired of the whole subject, wrung out to the last drop, and was unable to add or remove anything, not even a comma. His life, from then on, would be silence, rest, penitence, and nothing else. Now, rather than a priest, he wanted to become a monk.

The originals are written by hand in the neat and even writing of a well-educated priest, although they are on loose sheets of different-sized paper. The story is less careful than the handwriting. You can see that on some days Lelo was more concentrated on and committed to the writing than on others. The papers are not published in exactly the same order as they were given to me, mainly because the pages were not numbered and once, when I had barely started transcribing them, I dropped the pile on the floor and they got out of order. Since they didn't always follow a chronological or clear sequence, and since they sometimes strayed from one theme to another according to Father Sánchez's memory or a whim, I tried to arrange them as best I could.

My laziness, or my incompetence, prevented me from treating them simply as raw material for the book I once wanted to write, a novel or biography, or something else. I confined myself to putting the bewildered Aurelio's papers into some sort of order, resembling a cinematographic montage. I can assure readers that, save for a few grammatical corrections, I did not intervene in the text. I think I can say that I simply typed out a clean copy.

Nota bene: If anyone suspects that this story is based freely on the life of Luis Alberto Álvarez, an extraordinary priest who was a friend of mine, they would be right.

ACKNOWLEDGMENTS

While writing this book I have had swirling around in my head, as well as my few memories and many obsessions, the voices and words of innumerable people. My method was not to repeat faithfully what I heard or was told, but to let things filter through my elusive memory, which is the only fantasy I know. I would like to mention all these people, but I will certainly forget some.

I cannot forget Aurelio Sánchez, who gave me the gift of aspects of his private life and his life in common with the protagonist of this novel, which, without Aurelio, could not have happened or been written. The Casa Estudio Cien Años de Soledad, in Mexico City, and the Fundación para las Letras Mexicanas gave me a fantastic place to advance the writing of this book under the shelter of the ghost who gave us Colombians the greatest example of a life dedicated to telling tales and writing: Gabriel García Márquez. I owe this generous grant to two friends: Juan Villoro and Miguel Limón.

Ángela María Chica opened the museum of her memories, films, and documents to me. Julio Jaime and Luis Fernando Calderón helped me to reconstruct the story of their brother, Carlos Alberto, and his relationship with el Gordo. Fernando, Cristina, and David Trueba encouraged me not to abandon this story when I was on the brink of accepting defeat. Víctor Gaviria, Sergio Cabrera, and Martha Ligia Parra shared with me their sentimental and professional memories of el Gordo. Lía Master gave me the material of several anecdotes and conversations she had during her long friendship with Luis. Sergio Estrada told me in detail a whole chapter of this novel. Another chapter, no less clerical, was told to me by a philosopher, mayordomo, and barber in the Madrid neighborhood of Chueca, Guillermo Zapata. Fernando Isaza gave me, generously, medical and cinematographic memories, first in the presence of Eduardo and later in his definitive absence due to the plague of these years. This absence also broke Fernando's heart, almost the same day I wrote the last lines of this book. Andrea Karich, Carlos Mario Aguirre, José Adrián Zuluaga, and Santiago Andrés Gómez shared interesting documents and thoughts with me. I owe Jorge Volpi, great expert on the subject, valuable operatic advice. Ana Bernal for invaluable family documents, among them photos, stories, and private letters. Juan Gabriel Vásquez helped me greatly with what he least imagined: his questions. Reading notes from my dear literary agent, Nicole Witt, were also very important. Bárbara Lombana shared images of the house in Laureles where a good priest spent the last weeks of his life. Darlys (with a *y*) Blandón lent me her name, and I invented past and future adventures for her. Daniela and Simón Abad gave me memories and a portrait.

While I was writing this novel, I also suffered from heart disease, like the protagonist priest of this fictional story, and was therefore in the hands of a cardiologist and a heart surgeon: Luz Adriana Ocampo and Juan Camilo Rendón. Before them I was also seen by an electrophysiologist, Eduardo Medina. These three doctors, as well as my anesthesiologist, Juan Espinal, taught me the little I know about the heart. My own heart served as my master of this story, and I am grateful to it for still beating even though it has been opened, touched, and mended. Someone who witnessed Batista's surgery several times described it to me in detail: the heart surgeon Juan Camillo Jaramillo. In this task of understanding our viscera full of metaphors, the work of the following writers was vital to me: Haider Warraich, Gail Godwin, Sherwin B. Nuland, Maylis de Kerangal, and Sandeep Jauhar. The letters of the word *corazón* are borrowed from Juan Vicente Piqueras. From other poets, Eduardo Carranza, León de Greiff, Carlos Marzal, Jaime Gil de Biedma, Yehuda Amijai, César Vallejo, Fernando Pessoa, and perhaps others I don't remember, I borrowed poems, lines, and words.

Once the novel was finished, five editors helped me to repair and mend it: Alexandra; Mario and Pilar; Carolina of the north and Carolina of the south.

A dear friend, Albert Bensoussan, paid me the greatest homage a reader could offer: as soon he finished reading a draft of this novel, he translated it into French.

And finally, I thank Sebastián Estrada on my knees for the three monumental blunders he saved me from. How many more might there be? I ask your forgiveness for all the rest.

archipelago books
is a non-profit publisher devoted to
promoting cross-cultural exchange through innovative
classic and contemporary international literature
archipelagobooks.org

elsewhere editions
translates luminous picture books from around the world
elsewhereeditions.org